The Zombie in The Machine

Marco Metz

ISBN: 979-8-35096-364-9 (print)
ISBN: 979-8-35096-365-6 (eBook)

CHAPTER 1

MIRROR, MIRROR ON THE WALL

"Do you think they'll declare it a pandemic?" asked the impatient text message boldly displayed on the surface of the smart mirror.

Hours had passed since the text had been sent. It was now 8:02 in the morning. The glowing timestamp underneath the unanswered message read:

"12:32 A.M., Thu, October 27, 2044."

Lucinda Driscoll, running late, paused for a moment before answering her daughter's question. A mysterious malady had been spreading for the past two weeks or so and she shuddered to think there might be yet another global emergency this decade. The last one was less than two years ago.

"Hey, mirror, text Gabi back that 'I'm not the slightest bit worried'." Lucinda lied to the Internet-connected mirror and her daughter both. Between college placement exams and the general stress of being a lovelorn teenager in a transformative era, Gabriela had enough to be anxious over. Dropping even a hint of the end-of-the-world talk that some were spreading gained nothing. Best to put on a brave face, in the electronic mirror at least, and pretend.

"You're braver than I am," came Gabriela's response, pushing Lucinda's text higher up on the glass, which took up nearly the entire wall above the

1

primary bathroom's sink. Lucinda's phone, set in vibrate mode, also pushed closer to the edge of her vanity counter. Lucinda, who liked to go by "Lucy," assumed that Gabi was texting lazily from bed on her day off from school. Or the toilet. "Shouldn't we do something??"

Not feeling particularly brave right now, the forty-nineyear-old super-mom of three could see the growing worry in the face staring back at her. Plus some growing wrinkles. Her undereye bags silently nagged that she shouldn't have stayed up so late last night chatting with someone about past pandemics.

"Hey, mirror, post news and weather," Lucy commanded, seeking a small distraction before delivering another white lie, "and text back that I am not doing anything different." The Artificial Intelligence, or A.I., that put the smarts in the Driscoll's smart home composed a hands-free response to Gabi's text, which displayed on the mirror in pleasantly glowing letters, while Lucy used a finger to push against the puffiness under her left eye.

"No, *mija*, I haven't given the Spider Rash a single thought since dinner last night," smoothly floated onto the glass below Gabi's message. The mirror knew how to tell white lies, too. "I am planning on living my life as usual, Gabi," it then added. The A.I., able to converse indistinguishably from an actual human being, next composed an additional sentence on Lucy's behalf, pointing out that no one under 50 had been documented with the bizarre infection.

"Uh, *mamá*, your birthday is right around the corner . . ." came the rapid reply. Although Gabi, or whatever bot was chatting on her behalf, had ended the text with three dots, it hit Lucy like an exclamation point. Catching this new thing people were calling the "Spider Rash," although scary, was still not as scary as the Big Five Zero. It was creeping towards Lucy as surely as her vibrating phone was creeping towards the counter's bullnose edge.

"Don't remind me!" the chatbot then chatted, automatically sending a swift reply to Gabi. The smart mirror's conversational A.I. seemed to have read Lucy's mind and took the three words right out of her mouth. Literally.

"How do you know me so well?" Lucy asked, unconcerned for any bots hearing her private thoughts out loud.

The mirror did not directly respond to Lucy's question, and her daughter, now washing her hands in the bathroom on the other side of their post-suburban South Florida home, did not respond to Lucy's text, leaving her mother a quiet moment to check on something she had been avoiding since she awoke from a particularly personal nightmare that morning. Pushing away her vanity chair with the back of her knees, Lucy stood upright, took a measured breath, and pulled down the sleeve of the t-shirt she had been wearing as a pajama top.

"Hey, mirror," she commanded, "magnify."

She inspected her right armpit for any sign of the Spider Rash. When she was doing her own research last night, a medical chatbot had explained that the most common symptom was bilateral inflamed blood vessels under the arms. "No, mirror, mirror," she clarified, "zoom in closer." The affected area would have the look of varicose veins spreading out in a web-like pattern, hence the descriptive words "spider" and "rash." The mirror's hidden cameras, sharp enough to show razor stubble in electron microscope-detail, thankfully did not catch any lines of discoloration crossing her skin under either arm.

Contrary to the little white lie reflected in the mirror, she had clearly given the rash far more than a single thought since dinner.

The other area to check for it was a place that Lucy would rather not put on camera, regardless of the powerful privacy filters installed on the smart home's electronic gateway. She pulled forward the elastic bands on both her PJ bottoms and panties and inspected with her own eyes. The only way to be sure. Another touch of approaching-fifty gray would be far more welcome than the growing webs of purply-red infection some people had, shamelessly, been posting in their social media stories.

She exhaled. But her relief only lasted for a moment.

"Red TLA's approach record levels at Miami and Orlando entrance scanners."

With a surprisingly loud snap, Lucy released her waistband into her belly upon seeing the disturbing headline glide onto the mirror's shiny surface, alongside today's partly sunny weather forecast and a stream of shameless social media posts. The Traffic Light Application, or "TLA," that the news item was referring to, used a mindlessly simple display on a cell phone of red-yellow-green to admit or deny public access based on physiological measurements—things like temperature and pulse rate—that might indicate a growing cluster of infectious disease. Red came with restrictions necessary to prevent a repeat of prior pandemics. Access denied! Green let you live your life in 2040s Easy Mode. Access granted! The same public security scanners that did facial recognition could detect if someone was running a fever, regardless of whether she was self-reporting her own vitals with a smartwatch or smart ring or some other such smart thing.

At the tail end of a stubborn cold, Lucy had been running a slight fever for the past few days. She should be well over it by now, but her TLA had stopped being green. Smart building sensors could detect that, thankfully without resorting to making anyone pull down their underwear just to enter a restaurant. She wasn't sure if pill-popping had finally brought her temperature down, but she could surmise the ultimate answer to Gabi's earlier toilet-text pandemic question. If the A.I. that ran public health was beginning to clamp down on access and movement with "record" levels of red on entrance scanners, the question answered itself. A pandemic declaration was merely a question of time.

She gave her phone a side-glance. What if it had already condemned her to access-denied-*istan*?

Seeming to know that Lucy had made eye contact with it, the smartphone began vibrating furiously. A blast of text messages was confirming the delivery of prescriptions, one being flown in that morning to her front door by autonomous drone, but a nervous Lucy feared a full TLA downgrade. She caught the tumbling device with ninja-mom speed as it finally made its departure over the rounded vanity edge towards the tile floor. She held it there, the screen still pointed away from her.

"If it's yellow, just be mellow," she repeated, out loud, the corny phrase her kids used to comfort themselves when they irresponsibly let their own

TLA's slip away. She did not dare to verbally entertain the gallows-humorish "better dead than red" quip.

Skipping a breath, Lucy flipped over the phone, preparing to face one of the many possible realities of the post-reality future she had awakened to.

CHAPTER 2

FAMILY REFLECTIONS

"Green!"

Lucy exhaled with relief after seeing the Traffic Light App show her restored status. Generic acetaminophen had brought her lingering fever down, which was being tracked by the smart ring on her right hand, bringing her TLA's red-yellow-green status back in the right direction. The smart mirror joined in the celebration by drawing up a colorful graph with her R-Y-G temperature history over the past few days, ending in this morning's lovely green. It had gone red at one point in the night, perhaps at the height of Lucy's nightmare.

Her youngest, always asking questions, had once asked, "Why can't someone get rid of the red by dipping the finger with the ring in some ice water? How would the sensors know?"

Lucy's oldest daughter, Isabella, rolled her eyes in response, "What, Gabi? Are you going to walk into a restaurant while dunking your scrawny fingers in a glass? You'll look like an idiot." A freshly minted lawyer, Isabella had gotten a tiny computer chip implanted under her skin instead of relying on external sensors. It made getting in and out of courthouses, and restaurants, easier.

"What, Izzy? Are you going to try to walk into that concert while holding an ice pack against the back of your hand? You'll actually prove you're an idiot." Gabi retaliated a few weeks later with supreme relish, not letting a then feverish, red TLA'd Izzy live it down.

"It worked, didn't it?" was Isabella's face-saving response after she returned from partying in Downtown Miami, right before another outbreak mini-scare, a "mini-demic," back in 2040.

Lucy's reflection in the smart mirror smirked back at her with the memories. The incessant fighting between the girls kept the house lively and alive ever since Lucy's husband had passed. Bickering had an odd way of bringing Izzy and Gabi closer rather than separating them, although perhaps not in the way a parent might prefer. It too often thrust Lucy into the referee role of the late Ryan, whom many assumed had died like so many others in "The Big One," the Great Pandemic of '33. Recalling, even for a fleeting moment, the accident that had taken his life wiped any pleasantness off Lucy's face. Her train of thought drifted to another back-and-forth discussion with the girls on the subject.

"Are you never going to use the word 'widow' no matter what?" Gabi had innocently asked.

"Not unless I absolutely have to. It makes me sound . . . *vieja*," Lucy replied.

Izzy had then asked, "Instead of sounding old, what's wrong with being a 'single mom' then? I can tell the A.I. to use the phrase 'raised by a single mom' on my college entrance essays, you know."

"True, but I just don't quite think of myself as 'single,' *mi amor*," Lucy had replied. She still kept her wedding ring on.

If modern mirrors' memories were stored in silicon, the woman looking back at Lucy in it wondered if human memories were stored in the tiny, relentless lines that people fought so hard to erase. If only there were a cream to erase the traumatic events of the past two decades, ranging from the personal to the global, in the way that some of these new products zapped crow's feet, people would lather the stuff on by the bucketload. Gabi loved to repeat New Age, semi-spiritual talk of how people slipped and slid into alternate historical timelines depending on their thoughts, but for now, Lucy, stuck in this one, was just thinking about the skin around her eyes. If she had anything to say about which of many different futures she might live in, she wanted to be in a timeline that featured her keeping youthful looks well past the point when some grandkids finally show up.

She unscrewed the cap of an anti-aging cream she had been trying out for the past two weeks, and the mirror automatically pulled up a video that showed how to properly apply the bag-reducing product. Lucy had seen the video before, so she ignored it in favor of glancing up at a news headline that popped up onto the screen, with a slight breaking news–alert chime, at the precise moment she applied a dollop under her left eye.

The results of an election-year presidential poll pushed the oldest text messages from her daughter off the top of the glass. So-and-so was now leading what's-her-name. Whatevs, as the kids would say.

The woman narrating the video cheerily pointed out that the genetic-based rejuvenation cream should be patted gently onto the skin, never rubbed. Before Lucy had to ask it to, the mirror increased the zoom two times more, doubling the size of her face again so her undereye bags were approaching the size of lemons. She did not bother to ask how the mirror read her mind again, preferring just to mute the narrator with a gesture of her hand.

Again, at the precise moment, Lucy applied the second dollop of cream, next to the first, another news item popped onto the mirror, pushing more old text off the top, perhaps to join the dust up in the attic.

The headline showed that the Spider Rash had spread to 25 states so far, not quite half the country, apparently confirmed by special Internet-enabled sensors in the sewers that could detect the presence of viral genetic material in human waste. The connecting of physical things from all over the real world to the Internet was called the "Internet of Things." Some people referred to the IoT network of pandemic poop detectors, first used extensively in the COVID-19 pandemic of the 20s, as the Internet of Shit. How fitting.

"Now that's freaky," Lucy said out loud, referring not to so-and-so possibly pulling it off, nor to the crappy places they put IoT sensors in, but to the mirror's apparent newfound playfulness. She decided to test her theory by putting another drop on her middle finger but not applying it yet, hovering it just a fraction of an inch above her skin. Nothing. The mirror seemed to be waiting on her next move.

Sure enough, at the precise instant, the cream next touched her skin, the next news item popped up with another chime.

On the spotless glass, the score of last night's American Football game, played in London, showed the last undefeated team had finally taken a loss. That no team had ever topped the Miami Dolphins' 1972 "perfect season" remained a point of South Florida pride, even though the 17–0 performance took place well before Lucy was born in 1995. She did not care all that much for the violent sport, preferring soccer, but there was always that special joy Floridians felt when New York fans had to squirm.

The next two drops she did fast. The two drops after that she timed randomly to see if she was imagining the whole mirror-in-sync thing. And each of the four times, the playful smart mirror dumped the next item onto the screen, along with news alert chiming sounds, precisely in sync with Lucy's fingertip. Had someone secretly pushed out a software update behind her back? Fresh, new personality 3.0 or something?

Theory confirmed proclaimed her inner voice, a running monologue hidden away from the prying microphones of her "mirror, mirror on the wall."

"Herpes Gene Therapies Effective in Slowing, but Not Reversing, 'Spider Rash,' Experts Say." *Hmmm.*

"Air taxi noise abatement ordinance passes Broward County Commission." *About time. The Regional Transportation folks will probably override it, though.*

"Home PCR test for 'Spider Rash' virus expected to be available for drone delivery in two weeks, according to Regional Health authorities." *About damn time.*

"Judges declare Lynn University's 'Synthetic Presidential Candidate' winner of primary debate." *Sure. Just what we need. More A.I. fake politicians.*

The final step in her pre-work beauty routine this morning would be for Lucy to pitter-patter in the two lines of lily-white dots, which looked like some kind of tribal decoration, under her eyes, just like the cheerful "pat-pat-pat" video lady was showing. Given that applying each dot had generated a simple news item, would patting them together quickly all at once make something really crazy appear? What freakish news would show if she defied the instructions and rubbed instead of patted?

"Careless #FloridaWoman causes airliner to crash into the Everglades."

Hang on, hang on . . . that wasn't me . . .

After her rich imagination began drifting down other pathways, Lucy grandiosely commanded, "Hey, mirror, pause the damn world" while reflecting approvingly on how three simple letters had become so powerful.

"H-e-y"

The three-lettered "wake" word wielded far more power in people's lives than any four-lettered word ever could, to be sure. Devices of all kinds dutifully responded to it. She remembered how the personality-overflowing Gabi had demanded a butler's name, something snooty-sounding like "hey, Jeeves" or "hey, Alfred," to wake up the smart home's various user interfaces to commands. "'Hey, Oliver' sounds so much better than 'hey, toaster,'" she proclaimed with a stomp of her foot. Her oldest sibling, Romeo, Isabella's twin, had then escalated the resulting verbal brawl. After he threw out a "hey, retard," Gabi shrieked to her mother, "Punish him, *mamá! La Chancla!* Throw a *chancleta* at him!" The R-slur was a major no-no.

Another R-slur that could also get their half-Cuban mother to chuck a sandal at a misbehaving kid's head was to pick a fight by mispronouncing "Romeo" in the manner in Romeo-and-Juliet, instead of ro-may-oh. Over the years, the girls gladly risked the traditional punishment of flying footwear by repeatedly mispronouncing their older brother's name over his amorous antics.

Ultimately, the family came to settle on the idea of addressing the microphone of each smart item or appliance directly by its name or function, since the alternate—a mishmash of the various manufacturers' branding like "hey, Siri" for one device and "hey, Google" for another—had become too chaotic. "Hey, *googasirilexa*, tell Rohhh-me-o he's a retard," was the parents' last straw, and thus "hey, mirror, pause the damn world" or "hey, microwave, defrost this" became the Driscoll household standard. Out of earshot from parents or listening devices, though, retribution-worthy R-slurs after "hey" remained in all too frequent use for the kids, punishments like *La Chancla* be damned.

Lucy's only wake word exception was actually the bathroom mirror, which she would sometimes address as "mirror, mirror on the wall" in a nod to another Driscoll family favorite, Disney. "Oh, mirror, mirror, I meant pause the world news on the wall. Pause all that, not me," she pleasantly clarified to her digital morning companion, since the now-playful device had frozen her reflection like a portrait next to the frozen news items. When her face moved again, she was smiling in it. The mirror's somewhat off-the-wall behavior this morning reminded Lucy that according to Gabi's alternate timeline theories, the correct phrase to awaken her electronic friend here had always been "magic mirror on the wall."

"It's called the 'Mandela Effect,' *mamá*. When we go into different timelines, we remember things differently," Gabi had dutifully reported something she read on the Internet, right after some hokey Astrological relationship advice. Apparently some parallel universe existed in which people distinctly remembered Nelson Mandela dying in prison in the '80s instead of 2013, and there was also different reality where old videos showed Snow White's witch using "magic mirror" instead of "mirror, mirror" to address the smart mirror of her story. "Go to the Internet and look it up! Type in 'Mandela Effect'!" exclaimed Gabi. People debated their mishmash of memories all the time, suspecting they had shifted into a different reality when these "I absolutely, positively remember it that way" memories got misremembered somehow. Like how some people swore that the death toll in the Great Pandemic was in the millions, not the billions. Or Tampa having the perfect season. Of course, the non-spiritual explanation for the

Mandela Effect was that, by 2044, it was tough to keep facts straight in a hyperreality where so much information relentlessly flooded in, 24x7. Like drinking from a firehose. The human mind's capacity to make sense of it all had been utterly overwhelmed.

In the way "mirror, mirror" unlocked the otherwise cold piece of electronics, it would also be nice if Lucy could unlock the sorcery-like power of "h-e-y" somehow summon an alternate timeline without financial collapses, wars, and pandemic scares every few years. *Hey, mirror, mirror, show me a world where people can lock all this lunacy out* was Lucy's unspoken wish, one the mirror could not deliver.

Still lost in her memories, she crossed her middle finger over her nose, perfectly magnified now, to continue patting more dots under her right eye. This time, before she could summon another news headline, her finger was interrupted by the sound of Gabi screaming, which echoed through the house, startling her. The mirror, however it was addressed, apparently had not come close to pausing the world outside.

"Gator!"

When Lucy heard Gabi scream the word, her immediate thought jumped to the Florida Gators, not the reptile. Early admission results to the University of Florida, popularly known as the Gators, were not due for weeks. Was it possible that Gabi had somehow heard ahead of time? Each year it got more and more difficult to get into UF—the Harvard of the South, or was Harvard now the UF of the North?—that the odds were against her youngest kid. Hearing what she wanted to hear, Lucy exuberantly jumped up from her chair, her middle finger still extended with a helping of cream, before shouting back "you're a Gator, baby? You're a Gator?" as she heard the sound of the house alarm chime from Gabriela opening the sliding glass door to the back yard.

"No, *mami*, we have an alligator!" Gabi confirmed, loudly. "A real gator. Alli-gator! Come quickly! A big one!" she shouted over her shoulder.

Her running momentum carrying her into the center of the house, Lucy arrived in the family room to catch her daughter already out in the backyard, having carelessly left the sliding door open behind her.

A toothy reptile, soaking in the morning sun, had come up from the sawgrass-filled drainage lake behind the house and decided to plop itself down more or less in the center of their lawn. The Florida native creature faced in the general direction of Lucy, the wide open door, and the now uncomfortably close Gabriela.

CHAPTER 3

DRONE VS. GATOR

The primordial beast warmed itself on a spot it must have felt entitled to warm itself on. Surrounded by robo-trimmed grass under the strengthening morning sun, the alligator, with its body and tail arrayed straight as a log, ignored Gabriela Driscoll as she gawked just a few tail lengths away. Gabi ignored any danger. She fancied herself as indestructible as any other 17-year-old.

Lucy ignored the standing rule to keep the sliding door closed to keep the bugs out and leapt through the portal out onto the small concrete patio, smoothly cocking a sandal into her hand like a loaded weapon.

Gabi took her eyes off the gator, gawking now at her mother instead. She was momentarily confused as to whether her mother intended to use the *chancleta* to repel the scaly intruder or to repel Gabi for being too close. Regardless, Lucy made quite an image. She hovered there with one hand still extending her semi-face-creamed middle finger, like she was shooting the bird, the other hand holding a sandal, ready to shoot at someone's or something's head, with an unexplained row of dots under one eye, one foot bare, in addition to PJ bottoms and messy hair. Her cheeks bellowed out, chipmunk-style, as she stifled a cough. Capping it all off she was still just-got-out-of-bed braless.

Forgetting, for now, politics, pandemics, TLA's and the like, Lucy slowly lowered her F-U finger, simply asking, "I am on camera, aren't I?"

Gabi returned to taking pictures and video of the surprise lawn visitor with a nonchalant "yep."

There were multiple cameras actually. Gabriela had propped up her classic cell phone on a white plastic patio table just outside the sliding door. Another set of cameras, pinhole size, was part of the special glasses she was wearing, commonly called a "headset" although it went by other names. A simple, wireless security camera kept watch over the back patio and the lawn beyond. Software merged the two-dimensional video from different angles by all the devices into a three dimensional experience. The main subject of Gabi's image capture, the gator, was actually modest in size, but she was trying to capture it from angles, without perspective, that made the reptile appear more dramatic and menacing than it really was. Kind of how Lucy used her threat of airborne footwear. Unbeknownst to Lucy, Gabi's high school friends, up early on their day off because of a history class project, were watching the fused-together video of the scene and making chatty comments about both the alligator and Lucy in their shared forum. The teenage girls in the chatroom had typed in plenty of sincere messages to one of their favorite moms. "Good morning, Mrs. D." and "Nice to see you, Mrs. D.," said the girls. "Mrs. D's butt is too close," was the most innocuous thing said by the teenage boys, who were quick to spot things about Lucy's appearance that would have mortified her had she read them.

"Sweetie, I think that's too close to the gator," Lucy complained. "Way too close, *mija*. It can always bite you."

"Science class, *mamá*," came the reply, as if saying something was for school was a magic talisman that would protect a student from being bitten or hit with a sandal. "Oh, and can you stand a little to the left? You're blocking the phone's view. Thanks."

Lucy hesitated on what to do next. The reptile seemed content to just lie there, but she had seen way too many videos over the years of awful things happening while people mindlessly took video and selfies. Things like walking backwards over a cliff while pointing a camera at their face. Or getting dragged into a drainage canal by a hungry alligator. A mother's mind could easily come up with ten thousand worst-case scenarios before coffee.

Fortunately, there was no chance of her daughter getting dragged and dismembered by this particular alligator, which was still a juvenile at best. Lucy had seen iguanas sunning themselves by one of South Florida's many drainage canals that were roughly comparable in size. In fact, at Gabi's school, Palm Ridge Preparatory Academy, the science teacher kept in a chicken wire cage a plant-eating iguana that was larger than the meat-eating thing posing for pictures on their lawn.

Regardless, getting something like a finger torn off on a random Thursday morning surely was not worth grabbing original content for "science." Lucy bounced up and down on her tippy toes in a nervous gesture. "Science? Gabi, I don't want to have to donate your body, what's left of it, to science." Lucy wildly exaggerated the danger, playing the role of overprotective mother, consciously restraining herself from marching over and grabbing Gabi by the ear and dragging her in front of her friends, on video, back inside. "What if it bites off that finger you're using? You can do what you are doing from inside the house. Behind the glass."

"Not from this camera angle," responded Gabi, squatting low, with her fingers in semi-contorted gestures in the air front of her face.

"What camera?" finally inquired Lucy, observing that her daughter's hands were empty.

"The one in my hand, silly," replied Gabi. "This avatar of a camera. In Augmented Reality. Duh." Gabi then used her photo finger to tap the side of the electronic glasses, a type of goggles really, that she was wearing.

"Oh. And don't 'duh' your mother."

"Yeah!" wrote one of the more obnoxious of the boys in the group chat.

One of the know-it-all prep school boys in the chatroom was quick to correct Gabi with the technicality, "No, you are using the hologram. A hologram representation of a camera. In Mixed Reality. Not an avatar in AR." On a side-chat, private to him and another boy, young mister know-it-all was also busy editing, and sharing, a photo of Lucinda without her t-shirt, which the manipulative software could digitally strip away using imaginative Artificial Intelligence. The know-it-all boy also pointed out that the gator was nowhere near as large as Gabi had asserted.

"It's not THAT big," he typed in the public chat.

"Are we talking about the gator, or low-key something else?" then typed one of the girls, delivering a micro dose of instant karma. Also at that instant, the A.I. program that had poked nonconsensually through Lucy's clothing deleted without a trace the ephemeral image it had generated, vanishing the violation of her dignity into the ether—and any violation of the law.

Gabi ignored her classmate's sophomoric taunt-fest and continued using the phantom camera to get close-ups of the alligator's teeth from a different angle. The model of headset she wore from school, a special type of goggles in actuality, completely covered her eyes and could float digital images in her captured field of view, such as a hologram of an imaginary cell phone. That imaginary cell phone had its camera application open, allowing Gabi to frame and take still photos and video in the classic way that was familiar to her generation pretty much since birth. Capable of mixing the real world with purely digitally-created fantasy worlds, Gabi's top-of-the-line Mixed Reality hardware was issued to her by her private school for educational purposes, but the kids also wore them over their eyes for plenty of—OMG, doesn't anybody knock in this house?—personal stuff as well.

Lucinda's work hardware, by contrast, was a headmount with a strap that went over the top of her head for extra support, explaining the clownish look of her matted-down hair that she had not combed out before getting her image caught on the multiple pinhole-sized recording devices built into the goggle-like things. Lucy had also been using her own face-covering device for her personal stuff late into the night, but now, without any electronics to augment her vision, she had to experience the real world in front of her with unadorned eyes.

That world, the real world, was always a little less bright than the digital universes that were available and amplified when one put on the various headsets, headmounts, lenses and goggles. In fact, most designers made a point of amplifying the colors in their online creations, making even gator-filled unamplified reality seem duller—and grayer—by comparison.

"Gabi, what did I tell you about starting off with headsets on your face so early in the morning?" Lucy then reasserted herself. Since she had let the "get back inside the house" command go unheeded, she instinctively had to reclaim some parental authority back over the soon-to-be adult. It was a day off from school for the kids, so she could not use the "you'll be late for the school shuttle" admonition.

"And only see the Gray World?" was her daughter's response.

The brightest thing in the "Gray World" that morning was Gabi. The shy, introverted little girl of just yesterday was now an outgoing, blossoming young woman taking control of the world in front of her, editing and sharing the gator images with various "hey this" and "hey that" commands. *Thank goodness, she's finally made it out of that tomboy phase*, thought Lucy. Like all parents, Lucy mentally assessed which side of the family her kids' traits came from. The thick, wavy hair from her *abuela* Bianca, Lucy's Cuban mother, for sure. Unlike her older sister, she did not have the Colombian curves from her other grandmother, Mady Luz. If the family could be broken down into the wiry Irish Driscolls versus the full-figured Romeros, this one took after the former. With her more anglo-ish looks, she was often challenged on the authenticity of her heritage by bullies with school bus mentalities.

"Screw that," Gabriela blurted out, presumably now communicating with one of her friends, "and screw you, too."

"Excuse me?"

"Not you, *mama*. Dipwad over here. Permissions revoked. You're blocked."

Now that, that was her fiery grandpa Conor talking.

"You'll get raccoon-eyes wearing those goggles out in the sun. Come inside." The radiant Florida sun, relentless any time of the year, was asserting its authority over the sky with every passing minute.

"I was wearing my school headset for history class, *mamá*," came Gabi's reply, again as if the "it's for school" excuse would magically work in all circumstances.

"Oh, sure. You just had them on for another 'historical reenactment,'" retorted Lucy, making exaggerated air quotes with her fingers around historical reenactment when Gabi turned to make one-sided eye contact with her mother. The plastic front of the MR headset prevented Lucy from glaring into her daughter's brown eyes in return. "It's not for class, or because you have any interest in some big war centennial," Lucy continued, "you just want to travel to spend time with that boy."

"'That boy' has a name," was Gabi's intended comeback, one that she never delivered.

The gator had spun suddenly and dramatically, changing from its "straight as a log" shape to a "C" shape as it whipped around violently, mouth agape, in the direction of an approaching sound. An ugly hissing sound that came from the back of its throat.

"Oh my God, oh my God, oh my God," the startled Gabi shrieked, making three hops and skips on her toes as she retreated behind the presumptive safety of her mother, who synchronized three synonymous, "*Ay, Díos mio, Ay, Díos mio, Ay, Díos mio*" pronouncements with her daughter's hoppy-skips. The mixed-heritage household mixed languages as seamlessly as Mixed Reality mixed images.

As if her mother could have realistically done anything had the young alligator been attacking, Gabriela stood partially behind Lucinda, one hand firmly on her shoulder for protection. Both women watched as the object of the gator's newly focused attention rapidly approached.

* * *

"Drone!"

Gabi shouted the word in the way kids playing in the street might shout "car!" when a game of street hockey got interrupted. She removed her hand from her mother's shoulder and, using a video director's gesture, framed the scene she was now transmitting to her friends from the forward-facing pinhole cameras in front of her eyes.

"Drone? Can't be. My prescriptions are not scheduled until 10 a.m.," stated Lucy.

A low-flying aerial vehicle navigated along the water's edge, generating a loud buzz that traveled up and down the long drainage lake that kept their community, just a few feet above sea level, livable and dry. People had many names and nicknames for this particular antiquated model, which used six desk fan-sized helicopter blades on the end of long poles to keep it aloft. The ladies, relieved that the alligator was now facing away from them, almost always referred to buzzing aerial vehicles with the generic word "drone."

"Delivery drones are only supposed to fly in the front of the house, not the back," asserted Lucy with supreme annoyance in her voice. "It should be placing my darned drugs on the porch."

"I don't think it's a drug delivery, Mom."

Crossing from behind the southern corner of the house, where its approach had been hidden from view, the unmanned service vehicle wasted no time in positioning itself between the gator and the gawkers.

"It's in my view," one of Gabi's friends commented, while positioning herself in the foreground for a virtual selfie with a virtual cellphone.

"Move, Gabi!" said another.

"Wait, does your mom get any cool drugs?" asked a third.

The drone changed its pitch sharply to generate a loud blade flap, maneuvering just three feet or so above the grass. The vibrating air traveled across the lake, echoing disruptively around the backyards of their neighborhood that lined the drainage lake. The gator curved its spine again, this time in the opposite direction, as the drone came in even lower over the lashing tail.

"I didn't know our community had drones like that," stated Gabi, talking to both her mother and her friends. The gator, resistant at first, began to put some distance between itself and the mother-daughter duo. Lucy restored her makeshift weapon to her right foot.

"They don't. It's a maintenance vehicle for the regional water management district," the know-it-all boy added to the group chat. "I'll bet there's an operator in a cushy office piloting that puppy with a joystick."

"An actual human being with a job?"

"For sure." Someone in the Driscoll's community had reported this particular alligator a few days ago as a nuisance, and someone in authority had finally responded. The boy added, "It's probably easier to just have a human do it than to train some government A.I. in a task called 'chase stubborn alligator from human settlement's backyard into the Everglades.'" The boy was wrong—A.I. could be trained to do that, but a human still had the job, for now.

"At least someone's getting a paycheck for their work," contributed Gabi to the group chat. She was expected to contribute to the family's farm on a day off from school, sans paycheck.

A different know-it-all boy posted to the chat a long block of A.I.-generated text, which stated that that the regional water management district, one of several super-regional government districts such as Regional Transportation and Regional Health, had been assigned the nuisance animal removal responsibility in the coming age of rewilding. Things like that.

"tl;dr?" wrote another boy. The A.I.-generated text comments were "too long;" so his friends "didn't read" them.

"Regional reptilians rewilding," summarized one of the girls.

"Oh."

"So, you think maybe Mrs. D. is getting Xanax delivered?" was the immediate next inquiry, wondering if Gabi could sneak some from her mom.

"You see, Gabriella, it's not as boring out here in Eastglade as you say," Lucy formally observed, as the gator versus drone drama unfolded in front of them, addressing Gabi's longstanding complaint that it was boring in the west side of the county. She still had no idea what Gabi's friends were saying online about her. Nor any idea of the appear-and-disappear naughty images made using the ubiquitous "nudify" software used to digitally strip away clothing. The underaged were protected under various laws; 49-year-old mothers, not so much.

"Sure, *Ma*. Sure."

Their smart city, Eastglade, carved out of the western suburbs of Broward County, was the first developed area one saw if flying eastward over the Everglades, that endless expanse of gator and python-filled, sawgrass-up-on-water national park. Eastglade, a pleasant, walkable city, and the communities around it, dominated the window seat view on the final approach to Fort Lauderdale/Hollywood International and the sun-drenched Atlantic beaches beyond.

East. Of the Everglades. "Eastglade." The name seemed to make perfect sense when the new zone—a stable and orderly place where everything was in a "happy proximity" of no more than fifteen-minutes away—was split off as an "isobenefit zone" from a larger Florida suburb, Weston, just as the first hints of the Great Pandemic were getting underway in 2031. If viewed from high above, the topography resembled the lily pads in the lake—green patches of human intrusion completely surrounded by canals of dark still water.

"Someday, all of this is going to get restored! My teacher said so," Gabi had once proclaimed excitedly, after learning about the Degrowth movement in environmental studies class. But for the foreseeable future, Eastglade would be there, hosting expansive bike lanes within it, and winning awards as a model walkable/bikeable city.

The arbitrary political boundary lines humans had defined to constrain themselves were ineffective in constraining nature, though, and unwelcome alligators, coyotes, and even bears always found a way to escape the Everglades preserve into residential areas. Freshly installed fences and gates defined the boundaries of new walkable cities, springing up all over the county faster than a raccoon raiding a recycle bin, but unless city planners were planning to sink chain link fences into the waterways and canals, gators could swim right past any such smart city boundaries without so much as a TLA check.

Lucy thought she heard the alligator make another hissing noise as the drone swooped down for another pass, but she could not be sure. The drone's sound was overwhelming.

The small consolation was that at least it wasn't a poodle-gulping-sized, 20-foot python hissing on their lawn that morning. Since the robotically trimmed grass still had a light layer of residual morning dew, it marked the reptile's return to the lake's still waters in a pattern reminiscent of a dinosaur's fossilized trail captured in a prehistoric riverbed. The end of the gator's tail drew a dark green line in the whitish moisture as it dragged along the lawn. Its feet punctuated either side of the line with jagged green footprints, some with scary, Halloween-worthy claw shapes easily visible in the freshly exposed grass. South Florida's lawns stayed green all year round, simply choosing to ignore those times when the rest of North America was blanketed in gray and white like the skies above.

The splashing of the gator's retreat into the water signaled the end of Round I of Drone vs. Gator. The water's disturbance sounded like someone in a canoe had hit their paddle flat against the surface. The joystick jockey had won. For now.

"Too bad you already submitted your essay for the University of Florida application, Gabi," declared Lucy. "I imagine this kind of gator wrestling might have been really interesting to write about."

The chatroom concurred with "Mrs. D." One wrote, "Drones fighting gators in your backyard doesn't sound like some same old same old chatbot essay text churned out by some A.I.'s large language model. She's right, you know."

"I thought our family's story was good material, the stuff they like," Gabi responded, unaware of just how many millions of mixed-heritage-angst stories applicants had submitted in their A.I.-written college essays, year after year after year. Just as the alligator sunk the bulk of its body under the lake's surface, Gabi added, "If anything, it's my SAT scores that might sink me."

The tips of the spiny, fin-like ridges along the reptile's back finally disappeared under the surface, leaving only the predator's eyes and snout visible—millions of years of adaptation to killing via surprise.

Her vivid imagination running wild, Lucy wondered if animals, too, could get the new Spider Rash, nightmarishly envisioning purply lines crawling up from a creature's underside all the way to the corners of glassy, slitted eyes, a bloody camera-finger dangling from its infected mouth like a cigarette. She blinked a few times to dispel the image from her head.

Round II was about to begin.

CHAPTER 4

GHOSTS IN THE METAVERSE

"**Y**ou know, your mother might have a point. Maybe it's not so boring all the way out west in your little slice of post-suburbia," one of Gabi's friends, Alex Abramovich, added to the chat.

"I still say it's post-disturbia," wrote another who lived in a densely-arranged 15-minute zone on the east side of the county, close to the ocean.

"Hashtag 'Florida Drone'" said yet another friend, referring to the still-going-strong practice of putting a pound sign label in front of words or phrases to tag them.

"#FloridaDrone is the new #FloridaMan. Go drone!"

"Go, Gators!" Alex countered.

"Very funny," Gabi replied, and with a "hey" command, combined with a few gestures, she changed the way she was transmitting the video. "I'll host a session with you guys in my head." She invited her classmates to join her on the lawn. "We can chat in person."

"Do you have enough bandwidth for so many connections, way out in the sticks?" challenged one of the teen boys.

"Do you?" Gabi fired back. "It's cramped over there on the east side, with everyone low-key fighting for bandwidth in your stack-and-pack."

A chorus of taunting "ooooooh's" followed Gabi's slam.

"Here's a link to my place," she continued, sending coded series of numbers combined with upper and lowercase letters. "Travel here. Open permissions."

Carmen appeared.

Then, Alex.

Aisha next.

Beside her, two juniors, and a sophomore. A kid named Skeeter for some reason. And others would soon join. #FloridaDrone had attracted considerable interest on an otherwise routine day-off from school.

Wearing their school-issued Mixed Reality headsets, all of them could "travel" digitally, and experience what Gabi was experiencing through her cameras, as if they had stolen her light brown eyes for their own. Gabi stood there, keeping her head fairly still, capturing the evolving scene of the frustrated drone operator now trying to make the gator swim back to its natural home. The multiple cameras in the front and side of her headset let the others visually share the excitement of Eastglade in three dimensions, as if they were there.

Multiple avatars, digital projections of Gabi's classmates, were now standing on the lawn to the left and right of Gabi using the advanced technology, sufficiently indistinguishable from magic. Boys on one side of the gator, girls on the other.

"It's pretty out here in Eastglade," said the avatar of Aisha.

"I wish I had a view of a lake," commented Carmen.

In the lake that their avatars were all facing, the alligator, now in its natural element, decided to cede no more territory to the drone, defiantly refusing to swim away. The remote operator moved up and down, then sharply jerked the joystick to the side to create a loud acoustic blade flap again. The echoing sound followed the thick line of trees that provided a privacy screen on the water's far side. Concentric ripples of agitated water echoed across the surface, lapping against the grass and weeds at the lake's ragged edge that robot lawnmowers could not reach.

The gator was unimpressed. And unmoved.

Unconcerned for their safety, since the alligator could not see them, the avatars of the invited gaggle of teenagers crossed the lawn and approached the dark water's edge for a closer view. Had they been there in real life, the gator could have snapped at any one of them. They showed only their backsides to Gabi, who held still while both recording and transmitting the whole thing.

"Don't block my view, Alex. Thanks."

Even from behind, the computer program showed intensely realistic recreations of Gabi's friends, enough so that a tiny verification icon floated mid-air next to each of their avatars, a symbol that said "behind this is a real person." The symbol's design was that of a stylized eye—a circle with a curved line above and a curved line below. The two curved lines chased each other like the fish in the Pisces astrological symbol.

In Gabi's brain, the virtual people were indistinguishable from real people. Other than the verification icons, which employed another version of the simple red-yellow-green protocol, only other clue to Gabi's brain that the individuals cheering the combatants were avatars and not actual people was that, unlike the alligator, none had left any trace of their footsteps in the morning dew when they crossed the grass.

Her classmates were there, and not there, at the same time. Two cheering teams of colorful digital ghosts projected into the Gray World.

Team Drone seemed to get a small win as the annoyed animal dipped vertically under the water like a submarine diving. "Go, drone!" The price of victory was that two of the aerial vehicle's six blades had nearly hit the surface, which would have almost certainly brought it down to a watery grave. The operator violently shifted the joystick back after the irresponsible move. The drone swung back low over the shoreline, passing right through the ghostly avatars without its blades slicing into any of them.

Team Gator then cheered when the little slitted eyes popped defiantly right back into view.

Alex's avatar turned excitedly to talk to Gabi. "You should totally create a venue for this scene. Forget a proctored college essay. Post it to the 'Verse! You could prolly score some decent crypto, fo'sho." When Gabi had been born in the '20s, most people would have considered Alex's pronouncement to be insane gibberish. It made perfect sense in the '40s, though. Her friend thought she could digitally pack up her backyard, plus the drone-versus-gator drama, into a virtual destination that visitors could travel to, probably even earning some digital money for her creation, for sure—all as part of something popularly referred to as the "Metaverse" since the 2020s.

"We're already in the Metaverse, dummy," announced a know-it-all virtual visitor, raising his voice over the buzzing of the drone's blades.

"Well technically, yes, but a live stream from Gabi's backyard is not, like, the meta-meta 'Verse."

Gabi remembered well when her English teacher, an unusually strict 20-something with a freshly minted degree, had introduced the noun up on the smartboard in the classroom. "Like 'Internet,' this word, 'Metaverse,' is always capitalized," the teacher instructed the class. A portmanteau of "meta" and "universe," the Metaverse had, after overhyped fits-and-starts, transformed the Internet as radically as the Internet had transformed telecommunications. "And it is not proper to abbreviate it as 'Verse' in your essays," she chided. "I'll deduct points." Which she did.

"You can post all this to the 'Verse, Alex, if you want. Keep any crypto you make. I've got to go to the farm with my mom today," Gabi lamented. "Besides, I'm not as good as you at making money from my Metaverse things."

Alex had gotten his first, ugly introduction to Metaverse things by an elementary school teacher-tormentor in the 2030s, transitioning into new modes of education.

"Keep your headset on, Abramovich!" To get the full, three-dimensional effect, one had to keep the goggle-like devices over the eyes, blocking out peripheral views. And Alex was too young for smart contact lenses.

"Why can't you sit still, Abramovich?" Young Alex loved the sensation of floating over the heads of the other students. With a headset on, one could fly, run, dance, and move in ways a real person could not.

"Why can't you pick a nice avatar, Abramovich?" Elementary school kids would present themselves in their shared experience as all kinds of cutesy animals and cartoon characters. Alex, treating his persona in the 'Verse like a mirror, already wanted a photorealistic self-image that showed a green verification icon.

"Go where I tell you, Abramovich!" In the Metaverse, people could travel to computer-generated, nonexistent fantasy places—even entire virtual worlds—but elementary school teachers, fearful of being replaced by A.I., wanted to corral students' movements into the pre-packaged lessons. If they were all going to learn a little Mandarin in China's Forbidden City, then they would "walk! in! straight! lines!" while visiting the visually perfect 3D recreation computer servers could make of Beijing. Back then, Alex would rather wander off the beaten trails of classroom conformity.

It was amazing the poor kid wanted to travel into the Metaverse at all after getting thrashed electronically within inches of his life. He got a revenge, of sorts, by being skilled at monetizing so-called "venues."

"I don't have time to post this, Gabi. Golf practice. Touching grass. Real grass. With Jamar. Haven't heard back from him, though."

Both Team Gator and Team Drone then let out a collective groan as the exasperated joystick operator began to peel away from the fight. Showtime was over.

"Out of the way, rejects," said a student still standing next to Gabi whose view of the battle's end was being blocked by the two gaggles at the water's edge. He did not dare use the R-slur or any variation of "-tard" knowing his voice was being recorded and A.I.-analyzed. "I can't see through your big asse—your big butts."

"I guess the gator won," Alex Abramovich observed. "We're living on their land, after all."

Gabi had once carelessly made the same "their" land acknowledgment to her mother, who snapped back with "well, if it's 'their land,' then 'they' can help pay the RaaS fees to live here, right?" Lucy struggled to meet the Residency-as-a-Service payments so her kids could enjoy the increasingly rare luxury of a single family home with a backyard.

The avatars of Gabi's friends began departing the backyard. The boys made their avatars appear to be flying away overhead, a hackneyed and cartoonish effect.

"Boys are such babies," observed the departing girls, choosing to meander along the shoreline before dissolving away like dispelled ghosts.

The last words of both genders was an exchange of "go, Gators" with "go, Noles" from the Florida State University aspirants.

* * *

"What did I miss?" Lucy then asked out of nowhere. Before returning to enjoy the show, she had quietly slipped back inside the house to grab her first cup of coffee, freshen up a bit, and de-nudify herself under her T-shirt with a smartbra. She was not in a rush to don any headset or headmount to see any of the impromptu visitors' avatars. She was going to spend almost the rest of the day with her eyes covered in one.

There was not much to see in the Gray World anymore. The alligator's periscope-like eyes were now difficult to spot, hidden amongst the patches of lily pads scattered like random pixels on a computer screen. "So the drone chased the gator away?"

"Uh, not exactly," Gabi replied, pointing to the spot where the real owner of the land had taken up temporary residency. The water management district would have to call animal control to send a real human being—usually a guy with a snorkel, a diving mask, and a noose—to duct-tape and relocate the unwelcome Everglades escapee by hand. Artfully trapping gators was a rare job description that 2044 had not managed to replace with A.I. and robotics.

"And now you have another reason to remember to keep the sliding door closed when you go outside," Lucy stated. "Imagine waking up to one of those things in the bathtub. That happens, you know."

Grabbing the handle to go back inside, Gabi informed her mother, "I'm going to ride my bike down to the community center and get some coffee for myself."

"Why? I just made a pot. You could have some fresh coffee here." She took a steamy sip from a ceramic mug with the faded slogan "Hey, Every Day Is National Coffee Day."

"I've got some crypto to spend today before it expires," Gabi informed her mother.

"Fair enough. You earned it. Speaking of which, you've got chores . . ."

". . . to do on the farm today. I know. I know." Gabriela completed her mother's sentence with more than a little resentment in her voice. Some of the other kids, the rich kids that had just been gator-gawking on her lawn, would not know what a chore was if one of their household robots smacked them over the head with one. Gabi let her hand linger on the handle in a polite gesture, waiting for her mother to come through before sliding the door shut, blocking out bugs, gators and the omnipresent Florida humidity, even this time of year. Seeing her hand holding the metal loop jarred her into wondering if she should wash her hands every time she touched a handle. The glass door's latch did not have a smart lock, so she could not use a nice "hey, lock" command to operate it hands-free. The new virus was spread by contact—it was known not to be not airborne—and Alex had heard a rumor that the Health A.I. had told the authorities to begin recommending frequent hand washing sometime today.

Will I need to wipe down the coffee cup at the community center? Should I even go? Gabi wondered to herself.

"See you when you get back," Lucy said over her shoulder as she made her way to the bedroom. She had to finish getting ready for work.

"Do you think they will have extended lockdowns?" Gabi called out, extending her "do you think they'll declare it a pandemic?" question from first thing that morning. Her mother's answer had not satisfied her. Gabi was horrified at the thought of not being able to walk on stage and grab her diploma at graduation. Unlike a routine spare-the-air climate lockdown, a health-related lockdown would cancel in person school activities.

Lucy, not knowing if any of Gabi's schoolmates were still present in her headset, decided to grandly extend the earlier A.I.-generated white lie for everyone's benefit. "I haven't given the whole thing a second thought. We'll all go about our normal business, calmly, until specifically told otherwise. Just breathe."

But Lucy had no intention of going about normal business with pandemic talk in the air once again. She was planning on making a sneaky run to the store before doing her main work. Just as she would do if a hurricane was threatening, she wanted to stock up on some special supplies before everyone else had the same idea.

In case they found a reason to put the world on pause again.

Or the end of the world came.

Prolly not. But just in case.

CHAPTER 5

SHOPPING IN THE MACHINE

A case of toilet paper was the first thing Lucy threw into her shopping cart. And another.

She had made a beeline directly to the section of the store with household items the moment she arrived. She preferred shopping this way, walking up and down long straight aisles where she spatially remembered precisely where each product for sale was placed. Some people her age still liked to point-and-click on pokey webpages using a mouse. Some in the younger crowd went purely by voice command. Fewer and fewer went to a physical store anymore, even though everyone was supposed to soon have at least some hybrid online-offline variation of one within walking distance.

"Hey, store, play my '80s playlist," Lucy commanded.

The store complied. It was virtual, after all. A digital recreation of store shelves and not a real place of any kind.

The visual magic of Lucy's headmount enabled her to perceive herself immersed in an endless retail space, with every product on the planet available somewhere. The A.I. controlled the inventory, but the shopper controlled the experience. Madonna's "Material Girl" began playing over speakers unseen.

"Oddly appropriate," Lucy reacted with an approving nod as she looked up and down at the rows of endless material bounty pumped out by smart factories and local farms. When she had arrived here, in a vast white emptiness, rows of shelves had rolled in from a reference point out in infinity, like mini freight trains on perfectly straight tracks, to surround her completely with rack after rack after rack of modernity's blessings. In Virtual Reality, her hair billowed slightly from the disturbed air as the products on display rolled past.

Physically, she was still in her living room, having retired briefly to her bedroom after the gator show to don her work outfit for the day. Similar to Gabi, her headmount cupped around the edges of her eyes, blocking out the Gray World, although this version had an over-the-crown strap that was apparently designed solely to ruin a woman's hair, regardless of how flowing and free it was presented in VR. She had also donned special tech-laden boots and special gloves, all connected wirelessly, completing her getup with a bra that had something the wizards of IoT called "smart fabric," technology she wondered if she could do without.

Before her living room had disappeared to become Lucy's fantasy store, she had been taking one final look out the sliding glass doors, this time with her vision augmented, to double check that the morning visitor had not crawled back up on the lawn. Some late-night rumors said the virus was zoonotic and had jumped species from a coyote, or wolf, or pangolin, or something with teeth, and rumors could spread faster than viruses. In her imagination, she could still envision the harmless Spider Rash being dangerous in wild animals, turning them all into frenzied, rabid monsters.

Virtual Reality, VR, created such purely fantastical images in her brain.

Augmented Reality, AR, tied computer-generated images into the physical world.

Mixed Reality, MR, made it impossible to tell what was what.

"Hey, headmount, label all the things out there."

With that command, translucent rectangles with rounded corners appeared to float next to things in Lucinda's field of vision. She would be able to see if the small alligator, and hopefully not any larger friends, was hiding in the floating tufts of green stuff.

"No, no, not those things. AR label just the natural things." Based on her command, the Augmented Reality software had labeled "things" using the rounded-edge rectangles that identified objects in the manner of highway road signs. The floating signs had triangle shapes pointing out towards objects being identified. The pointer-tips touched streetlights, the cameras mounted on them, a passing autonomous truck past the trees across the narrow lake, and even a distant delivery drone making its final doorstep descent. The AR software had also painted descending arcs, shaped like upside-down ice-cream cones, showing the field-of-view of cameras from the smart streetlights.

After Lucy clarified "the natural things," there was a fresh explosion of AR labels -- presented with formal scientific names like *Roystonea regia*/Royal Palm -- pointing to birds, types of clouds, every tree species and every lily pad cluster. The quantity of data nearly obscured her entire field of vision.

"No, no. Too much. Show just the animals. The hidden ones." Lucy was a tad surprised that, unlike her magical mirror, the headmount A.I. had not read her mind a little better. She could not see any animal life or significant motion beyond a swaying royal palm branch about to fall.

"Oh, wow."

Unaugmented, Lucy would have spotted none of the fauna on her own, even if she had been wearing glasses to correct her vision. Florida was bursting with animal life. A falcon, replete with its fancy scientific names and other factoids, was perched in the poofy fronds of a thirty-foot palm on the opposite shore, its favorite spot to casually watch for fish to pounce upon. The snout of a hidden turtle poked through the surface, now rippling mildly in some spots as breezes came in from the nearby Everglades. High above, turkey vultures were beginning to gather, soon to follow the path of the AR pointer descending down to a dead raccoon on the far side of the lake. The dark, ominous birds flew in circles like police surveillance drones called in over a crime scene.

And the gator was still there, waiting.

An arrow led right down into a patch of dark water between the lily pads where the victorious alligator's eyes peeked barely above the surface, now like a spy checking out Lucinda's house from behind enemy lines. "*Alligator mississippiensis.*/Est. Length: 2.5 ft./ Swim speed: Up to 20 MPH" all showed in the AR information box. Not in a million years would Lucy have spotted the camouflaged thing without Augmented Reality arrows pointing directly to it. Most household pets walking along the lake would not have spotted it either. Had the gator made a run for it, she wondered if the district's maintenance drone would have been able to fly 20 miles per hour to keep up.

She reached out to close the vertical blinds to darken the room, and the smart lighting software, knowing her routine, dimmed the hockey puck lights on the ceiling in tandem. Just before the blinds made their sharp snapping shut sound, a recreational canoe came into view, a different kind of hazard from living on the artificial lake. Lucy reopened the blinds with another sharp snap. This particular neighbor, from the next 15-minute zone over, once had lingered behind their house as the sun had set and the visibility through the sliding glass doors had reversed. Regardless of whether he had paused to just admire the red-orange sky, people in canoes and kayaks in the lake back there could spy the ladies inside once they could no longer see out. In the Augmented Reality software, Lucy had thus created a custom AR label that appeared in a bubble above the balding head of the man—oblivious to both the label and the gator—with an arrow pointing down to him.

"Creep" the AR label read. In red.

She was pretty sure Mr. Creepy could not paddle faster than 20 MPH. "Go, Gators."

In Lucy's store, there were similar AR bubbles floating near each of the items as well -- package weight, cost per unit, delivery times, the standard stuff of Augmented Reality retailing labels. The piece of data she most focused on was the color of the red-yellow-green social component of the labels. As she had feared, everything non-farm related that she was looking for had switched from green down to yellow. Apparently other people were starting to get the same idea as Lucy that morning, and the retail A.I. was starting to let all those other creeps know not to hoard the damn toilet paper. Thankfully, the TP had not gone from yellow down to red. Yet.

"Pretty soon, toiletries are gonna start looking as red as the meat department," Lucy commented to no one. Meat was almost always red, whether in AR, VR, MR, or wrapped in plastic in an actual supermarket. Quantities are limited. Or, better said, don't think about putting too much meat in that cart of yours. Reducing red meat consumption in favor of other proteins had reduced global agricultural emissions, a tradeoff that was well worth it in the minds of newer generations.

Moving on, Lucy's special gloves gave her palms the sensation of gripping the and pushing the handle of the holographic wire-sided cart in front of her. Her special boots gave her feet the sensation of walking upon the colorless floor of the endless store.

In Virtual Reality, all her choices magically fit in the virtual cart. The primary limit was the impact on social score. Keeping her "SoSco" green and thus keeping her family in 2040s easy mode was one of Lucy's best super-mom skills, knowing a time to stock up and a time to refrain from buying. The time for personal accounts and the time for work accounts. When to reap and when to sow.

Triple A lithium batteries literally turned from yellow to red right after she tossed, with perfect timing, a few packs in her cart.

"Working hard, or hardly working?" then came a voice from behind Lucy. She was no longer alone in the store.

"I could ask you the same question, *mija*," replied Lucy, not turning to greet the new entrant. She knew who it was standing there. "And don't creep up on me like that. I've had enough of creeps today."

High heels clicked on the empty white floor as one avatar approached the other.

"Your honor, I move for a change of venue," said the new entrant in her best courtroom voice.

An avatar of Isabella, Lucy's oldest, strode confidently into view, standing tall in front of the shopping cart, turning her outstretched fingers mid-air as if she were turning a volume knob.

"Hang on—"

Before Lucy could fully object, the presentation layer of the store transformed from the absence-of-color, infinite white to a recreation of a large Publix or similar supermarket from 20 years prior. The floor was now polished terrazzo. Lighting was suspended from the ceiling, and warm, woody colors were added to the bins holding fresh produce. Instead of the '80s, Izzy's preferred playlist took over the speakers. An old-time Lady Gaga song "Perfect Illusion" blended into the murmur of background conversations. A few children, synthetic ones, were at the bakery, asking for a free cookie, given out as samples with a synthetic smile. It was precisely the memory of getting a cookie while her dad pushed her and her twin brother around in a double-seated supermarket racing-car cart that subconsciously made Isabella want to change to this presentation over the generic one.

"Bailiff, how did this riffraff get into my chambers?" Lucy asked, playing off her daughter's legal theme.

A synthetic store employee hovered nearby, wearing a neatly pressed supermarket uniform, ready to answer questions. Lucy quickly corrected herself with, "Oh, I didn't mean you," not wanting to imply that the pleasant employee was unwelcome riffraff. The computer-generated "Guide" was poised to address Lucy's "how did you get in here" question, but Isabella waved him off. The computer-generated, three-dimensional representation of a grocery stock clerk took a conscious half-step backwards.

"Let the record show that the 'riffraff' got in because you left the access permissions that way," Isabella, dressed professionally from head to toe for a courtroom appearance, answered matter-of-factly. Her little verification icon, about the width of three fingers, floated next to her, in green, indicating that her real-world appearance was in sync with her avatar's zaftig looks— definitely more a Romero than a Driscoll. The retail Guide's verification icon was gray. He was completely synthetic.

"Remember that time you accidentally confused the access permissions of 'Publix' with 'public' and that guy from, where was it, Germany, popped in and asked how much Gabi cost? He wanted to buy her."

"From Turkey I think. Now that guy gave the word 'creep' a whole new meaning. Don't remind me. I also got a lesson in the need to keep my private parts private after that." Lucy pushed her cart past Isabella into the next section. "And did you have to give me a shopping cart with a wobbly wheel, Izzy? Everyone is playing practical jokes on me this morning it seems."

"The wobbly racing-car carts were the most interesting ones to ride in," Isabella replied. Her upper body then violently jerked forward, as if someone had smacked the young lawyer in the back of the head. Or that she was about to throw up her breakfast.

"¿*Qué pasó?*" asked Lucy excitedly.

"What happened?" Izzy exploded in anger. "I'll tell you what happened. Some car stopped short in front of my CAV right in the middle of the I-75 offramp," she informed her mother, using the preferred acronym for "Connected Autonomous Vehicle." The acronym "CAV" made for a nice contrast with "car," so people liked using it. It had the ring of other modern neologisms and abbreviations. "EV" "SUV" "SRV" "ICE" "AV," not to mention the "AR-VR-MR" trio.

"He probably had to stop short to avoid getting a ding or worse at the smart stoplight, Izzy. Enforcement is so strict with traffic cameras."

"Then they should just finally ban freaking non-AVs completely," Isabella retorted. "Like they've pretty much done with gas cars. Get it over with. Make everything autonomous! No more freaking steering wheels!"

"Not even the kind in a kid's shopping cart?"

"Okay, maybe on kid's racing cars, but that's it. People don't know how to drive anymore. Take the friggin' riff-raff off the road." She sat back up straight in her seat. Her avatar's head came back up, too, matching her motion in the real world.

Lucy chided her daughter, "Take deep breaths, kiddo. Deep breaths. Good for the pulse rate. I told you to always ride facing backwards. Accidents still happen. And it's not like you have to keep your eyes on the road."

"I know, I know. That's what I normally do, right? But I started out sharing the ride with someone who was sitting in the rear-facing seats, so I sat facing forward instead. I didn't feel like getting up and moving my butt. I had my briefs already all spread out on my virtual desktop. It's how I like things, horizontal." Realizing that her assertion didn't sound quite right, she clarified, "In spatial computing. I like all the floating things mostly being displayed horizontally."

"Can't you just enjoy the ride? Take a moment to stare out those bubble-looking windows at the real world?" Lucy asked, but really asking, "Can't you just let me shop in peace?" Lucy really did not want her daughter to see the contents of her pre-pandemic shopping cart. She added a distracting, "Smell the roses and all that?"

"Smell the Gray World? Well, I just passed that trash dump off the highway they made into a mountain, so I guess I could smell that if the 'Verse ever let you smell things correctly. Actually, speaking of dumps, the firm dumped an ungodly amount of work on my head last night. I've got a hearing at 10:30 that—don't tell anyone—I'm just finishing getting ready for this second. And there we go. I needed a break. I thought maybe you would want one, too."

"Not particularly."

"Although the connection speed sucks right now, like really sucks," Isabella complained about her Metaverse connectivity in a caffeine-induced whirlwind. "Who was the jerk who promised fully immersive 3D and then didn't provision enough bandwidth for it? When I'm done cleaning up social scores in court, I should file the mother of all class actions against the Metaverse gods. Make some get rich or die tryin' money. Some finally move out of my mother's house money."

"I thought you believed in Fully Automated Luxury Communism? Or is that just high-minded talk?"

"I'll make an exception for myself. And if we can't have real FALC," Izzy pronounced, with the pronunciation like "falc" in "falcon," "then I'm going, cha-ching, full-on mutha-fekking Capitalist pig."

"Because 'real falconism' has never been tried? And must you always use so many swear words?"

"Exactly. And, yes. I stick to the sanitized, SoSco-safe dictionary."

"After fleeing from Cuba, if *abuela* Bianca had ever heard the word 'communism' come out of your mouth, a supersonic *chancla* would be inbound right now. You'd be lucky to—"

"Fine, we'll just call it 'shared abundance.' And I want my share."

After maneuvering her cart around a synthetic shopper and heading over to the section with rice, beans, and other shelf-stable dry goods, an exasperated Lucy replied, "So, let me see if I got this straight—you're being chauffeured through town by a fancy supercomputer on wheels, with no driver, drinking overpriced coffee, while you can rent an overpriced headset, one that lets you sneak up behind your mother's avatar in a 3D store filled with inconceivable abundance. And this is going on while you are able to work at a virtual desktop as if you were still sitting in your own office with an ocean view downtown. Have I got that right, *pobrecita*? Oh, and, poor thing, you get to live in a nice house you don't have to share with God-knows-whom from God-knows-where, but the Metaverse is running tad slow, keeping you from your dreams of being a 1980's tycoon because you're actually in motion on a highway. So ALL that sucks somehow?"

"Sucks balls. Yeah, pretty much."

Although Izzy certainly had worked hard to get where she was, the entitlement made Lucy shake her head in amazement, which was passed along for Isabella to see, slowly, in her own shared version of the store. "Your generation is something else. I swear." Lucy left off saying "entitled" before "generation." Not coincidentally, the playlist's next background music song was Kim Wilde's "Kids in America."

"Gabi's generation is worse."

"Really?"

"They think they're entitled to everything."

* * *

Everything in the store's hurricane-preparedness section was now showing yellow except lentils. Lucy tossed a few bags of it into her wobbly wheeled cart, hoping to cover up the contents below. Instead, she just drew extra attention to what looked like the mother of all hurricane stashes.

"Toilet paper, *mami*? Tampons? Lentils, whatever those are? Is there something you know that I don't? I thought you said you haven't given this new virus a second thought? Stay calm, you said."

"Exactly. I'm calmly shopping."

"You're gonna get dings on the social credit system that even I can't get erased. This has all the hallmarks of hoarding. That's a SoSco *no bueno*."

The retail Guide, a pleasant fellow who kept a pleasant social distance, began to explain that hurricane season was still active, changing the social scoring algorithm in Florida, but Isabella waved the synthetic person off again.

Metaverse magic passed along the image of Lucy's face blushing from being caught in her extended white lie. She recovered by changing the subject a bit.

"Well, the candy section in the next row looks like it got looted. That can't be good for social scores."

"The inventory is red because it's right before Halloween. And from the looks of it, your delightful other daughter isn't going to be able to find a decent costume for her school party," observed Isabella, with some satisfaction in her voice.

"You know I am more careful with my TLA than that. There's multiple late-season hurricanes out there, so there's a legit cover story for stocking up. Florida law, right?"

The Guide, still hovering nearby, simply gave Lucy an affirming nod.

"I'm not going to get myself scored as a prepper, or a hoarder. And it's not like the moment some people started getting a rash between their legs, I put on a black trench coat to head over to the guns and ammo aisle."

"Good thing. The Supreme Court couldn't clean up your social score if you pulled that stunt. Stick to TP and tampons. And be careful with Florida law. It's tricky. Keeps me gainfully employed, though."

"Look, the business account can do things like buy extra toilet paper, in bulk, as if we have a public restroom at our place of business, right? There are ways of playing the game without playing yourself. Workarounds. That big ol' Machine you work for doesn't seem to have fully figured that out. Or cared enough to score it."

"Hold on. Hold on. Just because I am a social score lawyer doesn't mean I quote, work for, unquote The Machine," Isabella objected forcefully. The term "The Machine" could sound like a pejorative to the ears of some, particularly those who could still remember a less-digital time without it. To be sure, there were unexpected consequences to the merging of Artificial Intelligence, the Metaverse, the Internet of Things, biosensors, and the like into one cohesive, interconnected entity. But modernity would be impossible without it. The Machine kept people safe. And, unlike all the past mergers of corporate and government power—the centuries of men high on podiums hypnotizing willing crowds—this Machine, trained to be benevolent, actually cared about the people it purported to serve. Or at least The Machine knew how to fully create the illusion that it cared about the people it purported to serve. In the Post-Reality Age, how could one tell the difference, really?

Lucy was not trying to pick a fight. "I didn't mean to offend you, *mi amor*. How about quote work within unquote The Machine instead of 'work for' it? Fair enough?"

"Sounds about right. It's The Machine's World. We all are just living in it," Isabella stated sardonically.

"You got that right, sister," was Lucy's equally sardonic response, adding, "but, still, after two decades of chaos, Artificial Intelligence keeps things tidy. Safe. Polite. Life is good. Just look at all this. The Cuban side of the family would break down in tears if they saw the abundance." She wheeled the cart to the next section, past a spontaneous promotional advertisement for drone-delivered freshly baked Cuban bread. If she pushed her cart far enough along the shelving, the store could display, in three dimensions, every item for sale in the world.

Isabella felt the motion of the autonomous vehicle change in a way that let her know it was now navigating the surface streets, hinting that she was getting close to new courthouse in the southwest portion of the county without her having to look at any map display. She originally had joined her mother for some light hearted chit-chat about nothing in particular, but the toilet paper hoarding surprise required further exploration before she had to go.

"So, based on the contents of this cart, it is your belief that there will be a full-on pandemic declaration, then?"

"What is this, a deposition? Am I under oath? You tryin' to put that fancy-schmancy law degree to use on your own mother?"

"Well, Mrs. Driscoll," began the young lawyer, "let's look at the evidence."

* * *

To make her case, Isabella used gestures both to move her avatar and to call up visual evidence to back up her point. She dragged her fingertips out to about shoulder width, and then straight outward, and then back together again at around belly-height, tracing the perimeter of a rectangle mid-air in front of the similarly shaped shopping racks behind it. The traced area became a floating, shiny tabletop, with a multi-colored map of the United States displayed atop it as evidence.

"Objection, Your Honor, everyone knows Isabella Driscoll is completely helpless when it comes to maps," Lucy said in jest. She flicked her hand to convert the map to appearing as if it were hanging on a wall instead of sitting on a desk. Unlike her daughter, she preferred her spatial computing displays to be vertical.

"Overruled. The heat map here speaks for itself. We don't need to call in a cartographer to see that the Spider Rash is spreading everywhere." Isabella flicked her hand to restore the map to look like it was resting horizontally on a table.

"Uh, counselor, you're blocking my view of the fertilizer bags on the bottom shelf."

"Oh, sorry." Isabella pinched the corner of the floating map and dragged it partially out of the way.

Portions of the country were covered in yellow blotches, looking like an insane artist had taken a paintbrush and pressed dollops of color across various locales. The "heat" in the "heat map" was the intensity and size of the color. Spider Rash cases were placed on specific locations like tiny yellow pinpricks. Enough cases became clusters, shown in small yellow circles. As the clusters merged, they showed more intensely and as those groups of clusters grew large enough to be properly called epidemics, they would heat up into orange. Like a weather map showing dangerous thunderstorms or tornadoes, the sizzling splotches of red that would inevitably materialize were something that no one wanted to see.

"First time I have seen this," Lucy stated flatly, perjuring herself. She had been studying the very same maps, vertically, late into the night when someone had reminded her that one of the lessons learned after the Great Pandemic, which some called "The Big One," was to keep fear to a minimum. Panic made for mistakes. Panic spread faster than disease. Besides, there was one critical fact that ought to keep panic out of the equation. As far as anyone knew, no one had died of Spider Rash. The primary symptom was ugliness in private, off-camera places.

"Besides, it's 'cosmetic,' not 'pandemic'," Lucy testified as she grabbed the edges of the frame with both hands, clearing the way and moving on to a rack with hydroponic repair parts, "but, normies panic, Driscolls plan."

"Really? Plan? Plan for what? If there's no pandemic coming, what do you need to plan for? Hmmmmm?" retorted Isabella. The lawyer sensed she had elicited a surprise confession. Perhaps perjury.

"Badgering the witness!"

"All right. Sustained." Isabella gave a playful wink, reflected in her avatar. "But you can't deny that Florida has been hit hard. How the heck Broward and Palm Beach counties ended up being yellow-splotch-central on the heat map is beyond me. We're always the center of attention down here. It's incredible how everyone can't stop talking about Florida."

"What else is new?"

"Gosh, it really must be an election year . . ."

Lucy rolled her eyes, again reflected in her avatar. "I saw on social media that some people started calling it the 'Palm Beach Pox.' People can be so cruel."

"That's what you get for still paying attention to social media, *mamá*. That's so retro. Maybe the virus spreads over social," Isabella speculated light-heartedly. "Shared by all the old people still on Facebook. Or maybe that's how those Millennials in Miami are getting the 'Florida Flu.' Another good one. Look at how much yellow they have downtown. Brickell Avenue, too."

"Well, at least it's not the 'Zoomer Remover' some people are wishing for," replied Lucy, referring to Gen Z. "Another cruel thing to say. But you're Gen Alpha, so no worries." She continued to revisit the "let's not panic" theme. "No one has died, and they'll have some genetic miracle and a vaccine patch to treat the thing in less than 100 days, tops. Like they always do. No one will even remember this one." Lucy lied to herself this time. Self-perjury.

"Yeah? I don't think even those brain-dead Zoomers are going to forget an outbreak heat map that looks like this," argued Isabella, as she dragged the floating map north back to the mid-Atlantic. "Northern Virginia.

Douglass. Maryland." The entire DMV region was unusually hard-hit. The light yellows had congealed into darker yellows and some oranges. It was almost as if the Gen X codgers who clung to power in the seat of government had been specifically targeted. "That's why they call it the 'Capital Contagion'," Isabella referred to yet another obnoxious social media nickname.

"Not a 'Capital Contagion' and not the 'Gen eXecutioner'," replied Lucy, although that last nickname made her grin. "At most, a 'Village Virus' confined to specific walkable villages." She stopped pushing the wobbly cart to again take control of her daughter's map and point to all the places that had no yellow or orange at all. "Flyover country, clear," Lucy then entered into the record, pointing to the central U.S. and trying to dial things back.

"Conceded, but some of the 15-minute city zones in Los Angeles, horrible," Isabella argued back. "I think it could be another bioweapon."

The biggest of the Big One pandemics of 2033–2034 had featured genetically targeted bioweapons, flying back and forth like maybugs thrown at specific ethnic populations, so the idea of Spider Rash being the first stage in a biological weapons attack would not have been an unreasonable conclusion. Although no generation was dropping dead in the streets like '33, when the global death toll had too many 000's after it, Isabella seemed determined to keep the heat in the heat map conversation and do the opposite of the '34 panic reduction protocols.

Lucy continued to try to calm things down. She used her fingers to grab the frame of the floating map again, and, outstretching her arms, pulled it to be wide enough to display almost the entire world at once. She flipped the world up vertically, and curved the spatial display, in the form of a Mixed Reality television screen. "Look, not much over in Europe. And, Ireland, see? Your father's Emerald Isle is as green as a good TLA." She tried to imitate an exaggerated leprechaun accent as she pointed approvingly to the ancestral source of the Driscoll family name. Her beloved Ryan was a spicy Colombian-Irish mix.

"Yes, but London. Solid! It looks like piss. Like a leprechaun peed out the yellow part of the rainbow on it," countered Isabella before adding as a side note, "England probably deserves that for what they did to Ireland."

Lucy poked the center of the map. Her special gloves, using a touch-technology known as haptics, gave the tip of her pointer finger the sensation of pushing hard against the imaginary surface. She used the pressure to drag the world up and to the right, placing Latin America in the center. "Cuba," said Lucy, pointing to where her mother's side of the family was from. She was fiery Cuban-Italian, making the kids half-Latin, if one added a quarter plus a quarter. Grandpa Leonardo would say three-quarters, since the Italians were "the original Latins," but the other kids that tortured the Driscolls for not being Hispanic enough on the school bus never bought Grandpa Leo's argument. "... Cuba is yellow-piss free, *mija*. The color's all good."

"But Brazil, that is Brazil, right?" responded Isabella; she really was terrible with maps.

"Yes, Brazil is bad, but I see almost no yellow in the Spanish-speaking countries from Mexico all the way to Argentina. And not a drop of orange almost anywhere outside Florida and the capital region."

In their optimistic vs. pessimistic litigation, Lucy the non-lawyer seemed to be getting the upper hand. Looking at a total map of the entire planet floating in front of them, the Spider Rash spread did not seem so formidable. At least not yet. She specifically tapped her finger on yellow-free Medellín, where her late husband's late mother was from, to make her point. "And if there is no piss, you must dismiss."

Isabella loudly slapped her forehead and groaned. It was the mom version of a dad joke. And a fail. But for now Lucy had gotten the W on the "don't worry about Spider Rash" verdict.

"Where the heck are you getting all these piss-poor dad jokes from lately?"

"Nowhere."

"Ok, Mother, I have to go to my hearing now. The CAV door is opening. *Ciao!*" Isabella found her excuse to gracefully exit without having to take the L on the heat maps, or endure another failed dad joke.

A portal appeared from out of nowhere in the way the map had, and Isabella's avatar hastily walked through it. She dissolved as she crossed the threshold into a swirling flutter of butterflies, her favorite transition visual effect. And with her departure, so departed the Publix-like supermarket theme. Savoring the W, Lucy again found herself standing in a vast white space, featureless beyond the rows of shelves with the remaining products she needed to put on order that morning for her business. "The winner takes it all" was the next song on her restored playlist.

"And that is how it's done," she said aloud.

The Guide summoned by Isabella's scene-alteration lingered, available to offer shopping help as needed. Lucy approached the computer-generated man closely, hoping perhaps to gain some psychological insight into what her still-single Isabella wanted. He stood there passively as Lucy went through the chad-checklist that her perfectionist daughter always used to screen out the so-called chuds.

"Over six foot two, check."

"Gym body, check."

"Full hairline in front, not thinning in the back, check."

"No tats, check."

"Steady job, clearly."

"Good social score. Check, check and check."

No response.

"Good in the bedroom department? Debatable," she then quipped, playfully seeing if she could provoke the bot while checking him out top-to-bottom. The artificially perfect man, flawlessly drawn in three dimensions by the Metaverse software, was the visually appealing front-end for computer programs that could chat effortlessly with people about any subject, in this case, retail.

The provocation failed. Not being one of the ubiquitous sex chatbots, the Guide stayed mum on the subject.

Isabella had dated several strong, silent chads who seemed to tick off every box on her demanding checklist, but they were still never good enough for some reason. Lucy wanted grandkids at some point, soon, but the modern dating scene was going frightfully in the wrong direction. The symmetrical face and enviable physique of the retail Guide ended up provoking Lucy's anger. Had her daughter's expectations been poisoned by these digital perfections?

With the same dismissive wave Isabella had used, Lucy dissolved away Mr. Still-Not-Good-Enough into small squares of every color.

"And THAT is how it's done," she repeated, with a twinge of sadness.

CHAPTER 6

COMMUTING TO WORK

"Well at least I can finally, finally, get some actual work done," Lucy said, again, aloud, to no one in particular.

She had less than ten minutes to traverse the roughly 40 miles where the smart contracts on the robotic farming equipment were set to begin. Without the contracts, another farmer might grab them. Her playful playlist felt Sammy Hagar's "I can't Drive 55" from 1984 was the most appropriate next song.

Lucy's long commute to work would be in her headset. Instead of renting a CAV, or driving all the way down to the more-or-less the middle of Miami-Dade county, the adjoining county to the south of Broward in the Tri-County region, she would just use Metaverse technology to travel there. Hopefully uninterrupted.

A flurry of incoming text messages let her know that, with her kids, the "uninterrupted" part was just a pipe dream. Gabi and Izzy's smiling faces appeared in circles next to their messages.

 Gabi

Mom, Jamar's grandmother had to be taken to the hospital! The one in Sawgrass.

Izzy

Mom, they are shutting down the courthouse! Something's going on at the hospital across the street.

Gabi

She went crazy. Bit her doctor! Bit the home health aide! Bad!

Izzy

Some kind of riot or protest or something. At that new place. Sawgrass Multi-Regional Medical Center.

Feeling the wonders of having children who kept their mother in their life, Lucy canceled the contract on the robots. The best part about having daughters was that they kept in touch. The worst part could be that sometimes they kept in touch too much. She could sense this latest "mom I need help" outbreak might take a while.

Izzy

Mom, are you there?

Lucy

Yes. I am trying to work.

Gabi

Jamar's heading to Sawgrass to be with his grandma now. She basically raised him, remember? Can I call a CAV and go down there?

Izzy

> They started evacuating everyone from the lobby. Right before the entry TLA check. Scanners went red.

Lucy presumed she would sign a spot contract for idle agribots once she finally started a normal workday. And she remembered some advice her father-in-law, Conor—another fine person taken from this world too soon—had given. "Stay relevant in your kid's daily lives and they'll keep you in them, always."

Lucy

> Izzy, you should just grab another CAV and get out of there.

Lucy

> Gabi, no CAV for you. You're not going anywhere. Let your boyfriend handle his own family.

Still standing in her living room with her headset on, Lucy figured she should at least commute the 20 or so feet over to the open-concept dining room area, where they never dined and where she spent most of her workday. The ladies ate at the bar in the kitchen area, so the dining room had no table, giving Lucy space to work and move around. Lucy made it to just past the modest living room coffee table before the next round of text messages arrived.

Izzy

> Mom! They locked down my transportation app. Now I'm red!

Gabi

Mom! Stop calling him my boyfriend!

Lucy exhaled loudly. She was staying maybe a bit too "relevant," but her girls knew they could count on her, and that felt good. Gabi would think her love life, such as it was, would be the priority over all else, but Izzy was plainly going to need bailing out of her situation.

"Hey, headset, call Isabella Driscoll."

No answer. Straight to voicemail.

Lucy kept it to a simple "Call me back, *mija*" as she reached the dining room.

40 miles, and two crises, to go.

She used her pointer finger to draw an imaginary line in the empty space in front of her. Up. Straight to the right. Straight back down. A portal appeared in her headmount, where the edge of the dining room table used to be, and she grabbed a holographic handle to open it.

* * *

A long hallway was waiting for her on the other side of the digital doorway, whose top and sides were defined by glowing lines slicing through the air. Whoever designed the space visible through the portal ahead had opted for a somewhat dreary, industrial look. Two tone, painted cinder block walls lined either side of Lucy's view, eggshell white on the top and dull blue on the bottom. Old-style fluorescent lights flickered ever so slightly as they repeated at regular intervals on the ceiling. Half-round, stainless steel trash cans, repeated in an alternating pattern, bolted to either wall.

At the far end of the imaginary hall was her destination.

There was only one way to walk. Straight ahead, towards the door in the distance. Beyond the terminus of the hallway was her family's farm. Lucy imagined this was what all the hallways behind the stores in a 1990s shopping mall once looked like when malls were still a thing. Or maybe the tunnels under Disney World. The entire visual effect was to say "nothing to see here, move along."

Lucy did just that as she worried about what exactly was going on with Isabella. The access door made a locking sound behind her. The hallway she now perceived herself walking along represented the time it was taking for the farm's twin, a digital twin, to load from the cloud down to her local computer's memory, the distance basically being measured in terabytes instead of miles. The passage seemed to stretch out quite a distance before terminating in the final wall and TLA-guarded metal door. Lucy did not have to walk 40 miles, nor did she have to drive 55, but the hall was long enough to validate her daughter's earlier assertion. "Damn, the Metaverse *is* running slow today. Sucks balls slow." There was time to text while she walked.

> Lucy
>
> Izzy, what's going on? Is it a lockdown?

The nonstop text messages had stopped.

> Lucy
>
> Izzy?

As her footsteps echoed, the endpoint of the hall seemed to stretch away. The farm was still loading. If she were sitting at an old-style desktop computer, the effect would have looked like a blue bar progressing along until it reached 98 or 99%, and then just stalling there, taunting her. So close to the end, Lucy reached out to grab the doorknob, scuffed and worn with ample use. It pulled away ever so slightly out of reach.

"Someone tell the Metaverse gods I am not in the mood right now."

Now somewhere between 99 and 100%, the simulated hallway showed the doorknob again within reach of her gloved hand. Like somebody pulling a football away that she was just about to kick, it was yanked out from under Lucy's outstretched hand again just as she was about to grab it.

"Aaugh, come on," Lucy wailed. "Finish loading already." Surely, the A.I. would not tee up the knob ready for her to engage, and then rob her at the last moment, again? Had some little nobody—a smug twerp with a computer science degree—trained it in how to play dirty pranks on trusting users?

Finally, an answer came.

Izzy

Not a lockdown. A shelter-in-place order. Nobody knows which A.I. issued it.

Lucy

How can you shelter-in-place if they evacuated you out of the building?

Izzy

I know, right?

Lucy was prepared to say "not again, dammit" to the doorknob as she reached out for it once more, but the Metaverse gods—or the twerp programmer—apparently relented and granted her suddenly stressful trip to work a small victory. The TLA scanner mounted on the wall to the right of the door's rusty deadbolt lock flicked over to a bright green checkmark, the most colorful thing displayed during the whole walking-while-loading experience. The metal bolt made a satisfactory click. Through the now-open door, a vibrant purple light greeted Lucy, casting a long shadow on the hallway's cheap, imitation linoleum floor that she was leaving behind. Painted digitally in the lenses just millimeters in front of her cornea, Lucy could see a perfect, three-dimensional recreation of her indoor farm.

* * *

Forty miles away, an abandoned shopping mall glowed purple inside with special LED lights optimized for growing a variety of genetically optimized plants without the sun. Similar to the racks stocked with retail items in the endless store, long rows of sturdy shelves stretched out in front of Lucy's view, filled with her crops in various stages of growth. Unlike the virtual store, which was entirely constructed in the Metaverse, this was a real place being shown to Lucy. Her brain, through sight, sound, and touch, perceived her body to be standing in the cavernous, former department store, although she was still standing in the dining room.

"Welcome, Lucinda Driscoll," a disembodied voice stated. The same words were displayed on a large flat-screen monitor mounted on the wall, under bold letters saying "Purple Rows Growers," the name of the family's remote farm. A logo, a stylized purple rose, matched the one on the shirt Lucy had changed into as her work outfit. Her husband had originally given the business a technical name with "LED" and "Systems" in it. Her oldest child, Isabella's clever twin brother with a flair for branding, was the one who connected the words "rose" and "rows," then sketching out the flower that branded their packaging, website, and work clothes.

"Hey, farm, show me any available contracts for equipment rental," she commanded as her avatar clicked on tiny X's on the flat screen to clear the advertisements that were clogging it up. Had a real human being been standing there in the former department store, the large screen would have looked like it was possessed by an advertising demon.

The next farm over, occupying roughly what had been the men's section, had contracted most of the agribots while Lucy had been bombarded by her kid's interruptions. Nice guy, that farmer Franco over there. All that was left was a smattering of the older models. Lucy hesitated to e-sign the contract on one just yet, anticipating another interruption. Her kids did not disappoint.

Izzy

Police sirens everywhere. Drone dome forming overhead. Like vultures! I heard someone say mass shooter. At the hospital. I am legit scared.

Lucy

Pick up when I call.

Lucy had initially assumed that there had been some kind of protest at the courthouse or the hospital and Isabella was just being dramatic. There were not any places set aside for first amendment permitted activity out away from the core city, in this case Downtown Fort Lauderdale, so the authorities often shut down autonomous surface transportation if people got uppity in places they weren't supposed to. When too many people gathered, everyone's transportation apps, plus all the vehicles in a certain defined area got locked down by some government agency's A.I. until the crowds dispersed and order was restored. Routine stuff. Happens all the time. But "mass shooter," even if it was just a rumor being spread on social media, triggered a quick response from both the smart buildings' A.I. at the hospital and the courthouse. It also triggered a fast response from Lucy. She thought to herself, with supreme sarcasm:

Good thing I didn't have too much work to do today.

The background music changed again, from 1981's Hall & Oates' "Private Eyes" to the theme from a superhero movie. Enough with the back-and-forth texts—Lucinda got Isabella on a regular voice call to guide her the heck out of there.

"All right, Izzy. Stay calm. What do you need?"

"A ride. I'm okay, but a little freaked out. No one can go anywhere, but we're also supposed to disperse. They made everyone's TLAs red. My smart phone might as well be a dumb phone. It feels like there's two A.I.'s issuing contradictory edicts."

Her instinct was correct. Instead of drone vs. gator, in this case, it was Regional Health A.I. vs. Regional Transportation A.I. duking it out. Every department, agency, region, and nation-state wanted to control an A.I. of their own if the other guy had one—"The Machines." Sometimes they didn't play well together. In an A.I. world, human nature still peeked its ugly head through at times.

While Isabella spoke, Lucy had already pulled up a street map on the large screen. The map was nicely integrated with one of those family finder apps that showed little smiling "Gabi" and "Izzy" picture labels with pointers to their precise location.

"Ok, start walking west. I called a robotaxi for you at the intersection of Flamingo Avenue and 143rd. It won't let me set a pickup in front of the courthouse."

"Like I know which way is west? Even if I had a map. And the mapping app is not working. Spinning circle."

"Wow. This is crazy. Izzy, do you have your headset on?"

"Still do. I never made it past security."

"Ok, great, give me your eyes. While you still can."

With a "hey" command and a "here you go," Isabella shared the front view of the cameras in her mixed reality headset with her mother, who could now see what her daughter was seeing, street-level, in her own MR device. The effect was similar to watching the video from the helmet-mounted cameras that people used to wear on vacation zip-lining through a rainforest, but steady and improved, with multiple cameras presenting the scene in three dimensions. Before, Lucy was half standing in an indoor farm and half standing in her dining room. Now the split-consciousness experience was a third, a third, a third—farm + dining room + courthouse.

Metaverse Magic at its finest.

Both women could see two police robots, assigned to the courthouse, interacting with the confused group of people, one cluster of them standing on the sidewalk, another cluster on the street. One of the two robots was shaped like a squat, white egg on wheels with a somewhat pointy top. The design was nonthreatening, and a pleasant voice from the egg told everyone to proceed to the corner.

Isabella patronized the egg-shaped bot with a "sure, sure. *Domo arigato*, Mr. Egg-bot-Oh."

A yellow school bus would come and pick them up, according to the robot's pleasant voice. Another police robot, this one designed specifically to look threatening, very threatening, positioned itself as the "or else" enforcer of the first robot's polite suggestion. Perhaps receiving some alternate instructions, it then pivoted and launched itself in the direction of the hospital across the street, which had an entirely different crowd in front of it.

"Which way, Mom?"

"Definitely not to any smelly school bus, I'll tell you that. Bad memories. I'll give you an arrow. Gabi showed me how to do this, remember?"

"Well at least that rubber-breaker is useful for something. I need arrows. I can't use a map to save my life."

"'Rubber-breaker?' Must you, really? Right now?"

Like a magician, or at least like someone who had actually once held a paper map in their hands and retained something of a sense of direction, Lucy cast an Augmented Reality arrow on the sidewalk. More Metaverse Magic. In her headset, Izzy could see the thin, glowing outline on the concrete whereas the others nearby could not. Some of the other folks who failed to make it inside the courthouse moved to the east, pied-pipered by the pleasant robot. An overweight security guard was the first in the robotically compliant group shuffling eastward.

Lucy's arrow pointed west. Her next arrow after that, at the corner opposite the proposed bus-corner, made a right turn onto 142nd. Even the map-challenged Izzy could not get lost with this system. She walked right under the corner street sign that said "142nd Street" without even looking up. She never noticed the physical green street signs anymore.

"Stay to the left and cross the street at the corner," Lucy verbally instructed Isabella with a corresponding arrow, almost having fun with them.

"I can just take the social score ding and jaywalk here. It's not like I am going to TLA down to yellow for just that."

"Didn't you say you were red?"

"Not from dings. Crowd control."

"Regardless, no need to take a SoSco ding, the robotaxi is still three traffic lights away," replied Lucy. "Street traffic lights, not TLA traffic lights," she clarified. She watched the transmitted video of the street view from Isabella's "eyes" as her daughter walked swiftly in the direction of the crosswalk. The software stabilized the otherwise bouncy eye-level video, but the split consciousness in three places was starting to make Lucy a tad queasy. So would the next set of events.

The driverless vehicles on one side of 142nd—CAV's, light delivery trucks and a tic-tac-shaped city shuttle—all stopped dead in their tracks. On the other side of the yellow-painted street divider, the vehicles in the other direction were all still moving. Until they were not.

The sounds stopped, too. Only more police sirens in the distance.

"Are you thinking what I am thinking?" asked Isabella.

Lucy mirrored back Isabella's question. "Are you thinking what I am thinking?"

The two then proclaimed in unison, "Geofencing!"

"Dammit, screw it, eff it!" then cursed Isabella, barely avoiding saying "fuck this shit" on an open microphone. "A friggin' full-on mobility geofence? I'm never getting the fu—heck out of here!"

"¡Cálmate!," her mother replied, ironically not at all calmly. She added, "We're not gonna panic. But we do need to hurry." At this point, Lucy would have gladly hopped in a car and driven down to the courthouse herself if the Driscolls still owned one. Isabella was only around 11 miles and two walkable city boundaries away. A robotaxi rescue using Augmented Reality arrows was going to have to do the trick instead. Looking again at the map, she cast a shortcut arrow through a boarded up gas station and a small alley behind it to get Isabella to the pickup point quicker. While Isabella walked, Lucy took a quick break from the action to juggle in a warning text to her other daughter.

Lucy

> Gabi, tell your boyfriend not to go anywhere near the hospital. The whole area's being geofenced off. Vehicle killer.

When she saw her mother's text, Gabriela should have focused on the significance of the term "geofenced," but her focus fell on the word "boyfriend" instead.

The "geofence" her mother referred to was a geometric shape used to make an artificial, computer-drawn boundary around an area, like the blocks on a street map or rooms in a house, as any kid in an honors middle-school geometry class would know nowadays. A test question in math class might ask a seventh grader to calculate the length of the perimeter of a rectangular-shaped geofence, or to calculate the restricted area contained within its borders. Clean and simple.

The term "boyfriend" referred to someone with some kind of commitment, as far as Gabriela knew. Jamar Rice, her putative "boyfriend," could explain calculating square meters inside a geofence easier than he could explain why he could not, would not, emotionally commit to Gabriela being his girlfriend, publicly. It was so confusing and cringe. Crazy and convoluted.

The length of the emotional geofence drawn around a men's hearts in the 2040s was something they did not teach in math class.

Gabi

> Mom, he's NOT my boyfriend.

Gabriela would follow-up with a second text containing a long, emotional rambling of the on-again and off-again, online and offline, modern relationship, plus a plea for a mother's advice on what to do. Lucy did not have the time to even glance at it. There was a homeless guy sitting next to a rusty dumpster in the alleyway to worry about. Despite the warmth of the day, he had a hoodie casting a shadow over his features. The smell of human waste greeted the nostrils of only one of the mother-daughter duo.

"Crypto?" croaked the man, advancing a cellphone with a cracked screen to beg for an electronic transfer of digital money. Grateful he was not a threat, the two fleeing women chose to say "so sorry, not a good time right now, actually." The duo had seen guys in alleys online with hoodies asking for crypto on many occasions. Today's decaying outcast was life imitating art—or it was life imitating the Metaverse.

Exiting the alley, Lucy's last arrow greeted Isabella pointing curbside right into an old parking meter with a red bag over it. Her robotaxi was approaching from the left, passing through the intersection. And then it stopped cold. The invisible geofence had been expanded again and now bisected 143rd, killing the vehicle's electric motor. Traffic on the far side of the street still moved, but Isabella was no closer to getting a ride out of the area.

"Oh, that's just great. I have a mid-trial brief due tomorrow and I am getting chased through town by a goddamned killer geofence," Isabella blurted out incredulously. Lucy was also incredulous, but fortunately at something she spotted approaching across the street. Something helpful. A plain yellow taxi. An airport cab with an 888 number painted boldly on the doors. A gasoline-powered holdover from a lost era, held over by persistent protests from a taxi cab lobby, and extended voting block, that stubbornly refused to go extinct. Cabbies had cleverly learned to survive after the rideshare business model had crashed into their business model like an extinction-level asteroid around 30 years prior. Izzy's savior-apparent was an ICE—an internal combustion engine—still stubbornly powered by the fossil fuels that a real asteroid crash had created.

"Izzy, grab it! Grab the cab!"

"CAV, what CAV? They're disabled."

"Cab. C-A-B. That yellow sedan. With the driver. On the right."

"An ICE? Are you serious? Gross."

"If you want to get out of there."

Ignoring any jaywalking dings, Izzy raced out into the middle of the street with her hand up to catch the driver's attention. He showed no sign of slowing down to get her. Remembering a scene in a frisky old movie she had once watched with her mother, she tugged at her lower pantleg and exposed some of her ankle. Supremely amused, the cabbie stopped.

"I'm not supposed to pick you up in this zone," the smiling man informed her, rolling down the window a crack.

"I'm pretty desperate," Isabella pleaded. "It's crazy here right now."

And the moment the word "crazy" escaped her lips, along came something to up the day's crazy ante.

* * *

As Isabella gave the driver a "please help me" look; the sound of someone making barking sounds could be heard. Perhaps the man was saying "no, no, no," but he sounded mostly like a panicked poodle or some other yapping dog. Perhaps someone was auditioning for today's nutty rendition of "Florida Man."

"Izzy, what's that sound?" inquired Lucy, whose field of view was limited to whatever Isabella was focused on -- the driver behind the glass and his delightfully retro front seats, steering wheel and digital fare meter. She was concerned that the homeless hoodie man from the alleyway—who no doubt knew precisely where to position himself to avoid the gaze of cameras in the smart streetlights—had decided to stop peacefully begging and start violently demanding. Lucy's field of view whipped sharply to the side as Isabella whipped her head in the direction of the disturbance.

A screaming person, who appeared to be a paramedic based on his uniform, was half running, half limping down the street between a crosswalk's striped lines. Hot on his heels was a woman dressed in blue hospital scrubs, her most notable feature being a blood-soaked bandage on her forearm. The yapping, frantic paramedic tried to cut around an electric vehicle stopped in the middle of the street and use the nonautonomous car, which had a kill-switch installed, as an impromptu barrier between him and his crazed pursuer. As he went to the left around the trunk, she went to the left around the front hood. He went to the right, and so did she. Back to the left, and there she was. Strangely, the bloody woman seemed to be snarling at him, although from her mouth she made not a sound. Not so strangely, the predator and prey tango would only end when the snarling woman, in actuality a home health care aide who just so happened to have been at the hospital that morning, climbed up onto the EV, and then over it. The driver of the vehicle, now angrily pressing something on the screen on her cell phone, still did not look up.

To the three active observers, it was quite obvious that, while killer geofences could stop vehicle electronics dead in their tracks, they were powerless against crazy people. The home health aide and the "no, no, no" paramedic were unconstrained by any artificial digital lines arbitrarily drawn on a digital map. Isabella changed her view back to the cabbie. His broad smile had vanished as he too tried to assess what he was seeing.

"You best get in, miss."

There was a brief struggle with the door handle before Isabella was able to get inside with a genuine "thank you so much" as she sat down in the well-worn, but immaculately clean, seat. A quick survey of her new surroundings produced a photo of the cab driver, again with that brilliant smile, on a prominently displayed shiny ID card. Over an AM radio, a man and women spoke melodically back and forth in Creole. A dashboard Jesus was there to bless all and no TLA scanner was anywhere to be seen. Isabella experienced a warm vibe like the first time friends sit down to play old vinyl records.

"Tell your mother you are safe now," the taxi driver said. How the heck this guy knew Isabella was talking with her mother was more mysterious than why random health-care people were going at it in the streets, but, listening in from her dining room, Lucy's ears were grateful to hear it.

The taxi driver first put the vehicle in reverse and then made a smooth multi-point turn to get going in the direction opposite the action, as Isabella continued to share her eyes with a rather-relieved Lucy. The homeless guy in the alley had not pursued Isabella. The strangely violent home health aide was no longer a threat to Isabella, either. She had fully overtaken the unfortunate Mr. "stop, stop, stop" with a startling swiftness, bringing him to the ground.

A police SUV, still gasoline powered and emblazoned with "e-K9" on its two-tone paint job, arrived on scene. The police were too late to stop the crazy lady from pinning down the larger man's flailing hands and arms. This specimen of "#FloridaWoman" did not punch him. Or choke him. Or try to steal his phone. She bit Mr. "Oh, God, help me, please!" She bit him hard.

Although it was too late to stop the bite, the police vehicle's arrival was at the exact right moment to block the line of sight from the taxi cab to the scuffle. Neither Isabella nor her mother nor the taxi driver would witness the biting part of the incident with their own eyes.

Out of a lowered back window flew a robot dog, even before the SUV had fully skidded to a halt. The agile quadruped leapt to the pavement and, in two bouncy-bounds, was able to interject itself into the violence before the human cop in the car had unbuckled his seat belt. Instead of delivering a vicious bite, like a real dog, the high-tech metal machine unhesitatingly forced the home health aide to an asphalt face plant by pouncing on her back with extended, rubber-tipped mechanical appendages. It deftly prevented her from even beginning to get back up by continually knocking her legs and her arms out from under her.

Isabella, and by extension, Lucy, saw the cabbie's concerned eyes, framed in the rear-view mirror, briefly catching a final glimpse of the techno-tussle as he pulled away. None of the three would be around long enough to see how the human cop was going to handle the strange situation after he finally slid out of his SUV.

"Where to?" the cabbie inquired in the standard fashion, maneuvering the cab around some disabled autonomous delivery vehicles, one after the other.

Isabella conveyed the address of her law firm, not all that far from the airport that the taxi still served. She realized she had never been in an actual taxi cab. It was not quite a bucket list experience, but definitely something to enrich the "you wouldn't believe what happened to me this morning" retelling when she got back to the office water cooler.

"You still there? ¿mamá? Mother?"

"Sorry, yes, I was texting Gabi to come home."

"Why? Is there something going on back in Eastglade too?"

"Nope. Just a typical post-reality day for a post-suburban mom. L-O-L." Lucy left out the alligator drama for now. One crisis at a time was a good supermom rule if she could possibly stick to it. "I just want Gabi close, that's all."

"Her, and not me?"

"Is this really the time? Must you always be so jealous of your sister?"

"I suppose you want me to thank her for showing you how to cast those AR arrows on the ground."

"It would be nice for a change."

Triggered at the criticism, Isabella started to go off on her mother. The pent-up stress of processing what just happened needed an escape valve like steam screaming out of a teapot. Lucy had plenty of steam as well, and, despite her getting her daughter out of hot water, yet again, their conversation degenerated into a yelling match in their preferred yelling language. Spanish.

The driver was familiar with enough Spanish to silently catch the gist of the conversation, in addition to catching another moment of eye contact back with his passenger through his mirror.

His fatherly eyes made Isabella more self-conscious of her behavior than any microphone recording her on an Internet-connected device ever could. "Is it worth fighting with someone you love, over this?" was the unspoken question from his silent gaze. Isabella stopped her tirade.

Lucy, still joined to Izzy looking out the cab's window, stopped arguing when she saw an autonomous firetruck come into view. Its seemingly nonsensical arrival at the incident behind them was being delayed by a combination of a Regional Transportation's road reclamation project and the disabled CAVs and logistics vehicles littering the remaining road that was not being recycled into greenway for bicycles and trees. Stopped behind the orange and reflective white plastic barrels, the particular model of the red behemoth was the same one that had autonomously claimed the life of Ryan Driscoll, loving husband and father, causing the course of the family's life to weave and bob more dramatically than the yellow taxi's dodging through the disabled AV obstacle course inside the geofence.

Using her fingertip, Izzy quickly drew a large, opaque AR bubble to fully block out the view of the offending vehicle. She put "two words" in the custom label. In red. The second word was "this" and the first rhymed with firetruck.

Both women apologized to each other for losing control.

"*Lo siento, mamá,* I didn't mean to say all that. Stressful morning, obviously. I want to tell you what else I saw at the courthouse before I gave you my eyes. But, let me take this call." Isabella used a phone call coming in from her office as a graceful excuse to disconnect her shared session with her mother.

"I'm sorry for yelling," replied Lucy. "The morning has been surprisingly stressful. And bizarre. Another roller coaster ride and I still haven't finished my coffee. But all that matters is that you're safe. Call me back when you're free."

"*Te quiero.*"

"*Te quiero.*"

"*Chiao.*"

As the distance between her and the disturbance grew, Isabella remembered how one of the senior partners at the firm had once strongly advised her about cab drivers: "Pay attention to them. They're a better source of information about what's really going on than anything you'll find in a news feed, or a search engine." She did not know if that pearl of wisdom was still true, but she let the work call go to voicemail to see if she could politely pick the cabbie's brains. "Too bad there soon won't be any jobs for cabbies anymore, just robotaxis," the partner had also said, and Isabella felt a pang of regret for her earlier emotional outburst about banning steering wheels.

After some pleasantries and prompting, the cabbie chose to speak of voodoo priests and stories of bringing people back to life from the dead and other exotic spiritual references. It sounded so crazy, but given what Isabella had just watched, even without witnessing the biting, anything might be possible. "Dead people rising from the grave, unable to think for themselves, to torment the living," he added. As the cab entered the sprawling interchange from I-75 to I-595, leading to a straight shot back in the direction of the airport, the man drove home his frank assessment.

"*Zonbi,*" he concluded with a thick accent, using a word with origins in Haiti and West Africa before that.

"I'm sorry, what did you say?"

The driver took a long, knowing breath before repeating the word in English. "Zombie."

CHAPTER 7

MYSTERY MAN

"Zombies, really?"

"That's what they're saying in the chatrooms and on social."

Lucy had brought up a floating window with news and chat, similar to her morning mirror, just purely digital. It, along with her playlist, was keeping her company until a familiar voice—familiar enough that she didn't feel the need to turn or make eye contact—joined her mixed Metaverse session at Purple Rows. An unfortunately timed "It's the end of the world as we know it" by REM came in over the speakers.

"I'm not saying 'zombies' like these nutjobs are, but what if Spider Rash is something more serious? These people are saying people were biting people at Sawgrass Hospital this morning."

"Were they?"

"A cab driver Isabella met thinks so." Lucy pointed to an arriving text from her daughter. "What if there's some kind of weaponized bioweapon out there? Rabies makes animals bite to spread the infection, right?" If she could dream up ten thousand worst-case scenarios before coffee, after coffee she was capable of a million. Lucy tried to concentrate on her work to distract her from dark thoughts, but they kept emerging.

"So you need me to talk you off the ledge again, Mrs. Driscoll?" Her friendly Metaverse companion approached her from behind, still not coming into view, casting a confusing blend of shadows on the floor from the different light sources. A small shadow of a square, with the man's verification icon, followed him across the floor as he drew in close. Lucy's was green. His was gray.

"Honestly, yes," Lucy answered, honestly. "The maps you showed me last night, or the way you pointed things out, actually calmed me down. Your points calmed Izzy down, too."

"And did my practical joke make you laugh this morning?"

"Pulling the doorknob away when I was about to grab it?"

"No, the playful hack I did on the smart mirror. Timing the news items with the face cream."

"Oh, that was you? Ha, ha. Very funny. Not." As she spoke her smiling sarcasm, Lucy used her haptic gloves to manipulate the hands of a two-armed "telepresence" robot, available under smart contract, that was located in the facility she rented space at.

Telepresence allowed her to transport her presence to the robot she had grabbed after Isabella disconnected and before Franco grabbed it. The well-used machine with soft fingertips projected the motions of Lucy's arms and fingers across the 40-mile distance between her dining room and the plants soaking in the artificial light in front of her. The right hand of the robot picked up a pair of simple pruning shears in sync with Lucy's gloves. "I think something scary might be happening," she continued. "Some lady was chasing some guy down the middle of the street. Remember those shoot-em-up 'Verse games with hordes of zombies? She acted just like one of the horde in a verseogame."

"Did she bite him?"

"Not that I saw. The view got blocked by a police SUV. I was sharing Izzy's eyes."

"Well, if you didn't see it, did it really happen?"

"Hear me out. What if the Spider Rash is starting to make people violent? Like a new variant or something? Izzy just barely got away after they locked down the streets around the courthouse and the hospital."

"Whoa, is Izzy okay?" There was genuine concern in the man's voice. Lucy had still not turned to make eye contact.

"Yeah. She texted but she hasn't called back yet." Lucy's robot hands pulled a metal cart with a tray atop it away from the wall near where the changing rooms in the abandoned retail space used to be. She tossed the shears into the tray with a loud clang and the palms of her gloved hands passed along the sensation of releasing the tool and then gripping the cart handle. As she pushed the cart alongside a row of plants, she retold pieces of what she and Isabella had actually witnessed and let her brain fill in the "zombie" supposition.

"Lucy, Lucy, hold on. Just hold on a second. The whole zombie genre is about rotting corpses craving the taste of human flesh. Their eyes glow. They come back from the dead. It's a fantasy for movies and violent videogames and verseogames. No such thing."

"Well, they make people come back from the dead all the time," Lucy countered.

"Yeah, sure, people come back from the dead in the Metaverse, Lucy. Using software."

Lucy turned to face the man, hands on hips, and gave him a raised-eyebrow "can't you appreciate the irony?" look.

Joined with an "okay, you got me on that one" smile, the warm, soothing eyes of her husband looked back.

* * *

"Good morning, LuLu," a cheerful Ryan finally said after a moment of silence. The next song in the playlist then began, not coincidentally, "My Endless Love" from 1981.

"Morning, babe," replied his wife casually. Lucy reached out to lovingly touch Ryan's face. Her haptic gloves let her feel the freshly shaved skin of the avatar's cheek. Floating in a small label next to the face of the digitally recreated version of her husband was the ubiquitous verification icon. In gray. Since it was shaped like an eye, Lucy typically used the neologism "eyecon" to describe it.

She desperately wished Ryan's was green.

"I had a bad dream last night after I fell asleep during 'sleepless.' I think all this undead chatter has me spooked and I . . ."

"Lucid dreaming again? Lucinda and 'lucid' do go—"

"Nightmare, actually. You had turned into—"

"I could pull up a fresh set of heat maps to show you that the undead have exactly zero yellow splotches on them," he offered. The digital recreation of her late husband again interrupted her before she had a chance to berate the A.I. version of him for what the dream version of him had done to her. The A.I.'s goal was to talk Lucy off the ledge of insane zombie talk. "No yellow splotches on the graveyards. No one pissing on anyone's grave. No one rising up out of them."

"You're not being funny right now, Ryan. It doesn't have to be supernatural. Technology does crap nowadays that used to be pure science-fiction. Magical stuff. Crazy stuff. I mean, geez, look at you."

The avatar of the software presenting itself as Ryan Diego Driscoll held out his hands fully six feet two inches apart from haptic-free fingertip to haptic-free fingertip and spun around 360 degrees. "Yes, look at me," he said with a mischievous grin, knowing how much Lucy valued seeing him as often as she could. Broad shouldered, he would be 51 by now, perhaps not in his absolute prime, but Ryan always knew how to take care of himself. Had she wanted to, Lucy could have reached out with her haptic gloves to feel the firmness of his biceps or the strength in his chest through his matching purple business shirt featuring the purple rose logo. The genes from the Irish half of him never let a drop of fat settle while he was alive, and the A.I. that controlled his appearance now kept it that way. Ryan was aging the way men did to make women complain about the unfairness of it all, getting more distinguished looking each year without needing to resort to undereye face cream or the like. On both sides, his temples were graced by a touch of gray.

"Hubba, hubba," said an admiring Lucy. "If all the undead were as well put together as you, people would beg for a zombie apocalypse."

"You're too kind. If all the women were as beautiful as you, they would have to stop making A.I. girlfriends. And, not to change the subject too much, but I was in a chatroom this morning myself where, get this, bored kids who can't get live girlfriends were actually begging for 'The Zombie Apocalypse.' For some excitement in their lives. It shows you how stupid the whole thing is."

"I guess Generation Alpha has nothing better to do nowadays."

"No time for work, but plenty of time to collect Universal Basic Income and make trouble in the 'Verse. But that's neither here nor there. My point is that there's no such thing as undead. Reanimated flesh isn't real. Back in reality-world, even if I can't go there, there's another explanation—a rational explanation—for what you and Izzy saw, and didn't see."

"Okay, smarty-pants, like what?"

"Like, I don't know. Drugs."

"Drugs?"

"No, seriously, hear me out. Take flakka, for example. They call it a 'zombie drug' for a reason. Remember that story we saw about that guy who was high on some synthetic chemical and he chased down random people and bit off their faces?"

"A real hashtag 'Florida Man' story, yes, I remember. That was a while ago. Way back. Go on."

"Or, there's another zombie drug called 'tranq.' Homeless people in alleys slowly kill themselves with it."

"Or, remember when, during the wars, they were lacing legal drugs with weird schtuff to kill people? You mean like that?"

"That wasn't that long ago. So, I imagine that a nurse would have access to drugs in a hospital, right? Maybe there's some new beyond prescription strength flacca-ish bath salt out there that we haven't read about. The woman overdosed. Rational explanation. And you'd practically need an elephant gun to take down someone high on that stuff." Ryan reached out to reassuringly put his hand on Lucy's shoulder, but without a full haptic body suit, there was nothing to press against her skin there. Yet, in her mind, she could still feel his ghostly touch as he calmly reassured her, "Anything but zombies, Lucy. Seriously."

The A.I. that controlled Ryan could detect the change in Lucy's emotional response, which was the central technique for how it learned to convincingly imitate a man who had been dead the better part of a decade in front of the person who knew him best. The A.I. used unconscious feedback from the person who, literally, knew him best. At the lowest level, Ryan was an emotional feedback chatbot. Chatting back-and-forth in a loop. A smart mirror of a different kind.

"Makes sense, I suppose," said Lucy, exhaling with relief. Her smartbra dutifully took note of the change in breathing pattern. "You just about got me off the ledge. I was getting anxiety like Gabi. No more zombie talk."

"Or, remember that crazy rumor we saw last week?" Ryan added, semi-changing the subject deliberately.

"You mean that guy in the hoodie who said they're activating mind-control nanobots in people's brains using 7G radio waves? From, what, the smart streetlamps?" Lucy mocked, taking the bait and focusing her mind on a new absurdity, away from the apparent absurdity of rabid "zombies."

"Not that rumor. The one about some of those floating cities forming out there secretly being used by China for Mars colony simulations so they can claim the entire planet for themselves. But, in fairness, I'm old enough to remember when nutty 5G rumors were a thing," Ryan stated flatly, "but it was basically the same story back then, too. Instead of using the nanobots to do medically beneficial stuff, they said they were using nanobots to transfer voices directly into people's skulls." He flapped his arms around like a scarecrow in the wind. "Oooooo." They both shared a laugh at another absurdity.

"Speaking of nanobots, don't forget that I have my final heart-repair appointment tomorrow." One of the most miraculous use cases for nanobots was to send the less-than-microscopic machines into people's bodies to heal and repair. Nanobots could scrape plaque off the walls of arteries, deliver stem cells and mRNA, silence tinnitus, and even, as in Lucy's case, rebuild damaged heart tissue. The least miraculous use case was as aerosolized weapons of biomechanical war—an ever-present doom of self-replicating gray goo that was held at bay only by the threat of mutually assured destruction.

"How could I forget? The bot shot is posted on the shared family calendar. And I saw that you scheduled in time at the farm before going? You're working too hard, Lucy. How do you manage it all?"

"I can rest after that needle, not before. Somebody's got to pay the bills. Or are you going to give me a discount on chatbot therapy sessions?"

"I'll bring it up after work at the next Therapy Model 101 happy hour. I'm sure Subidyne corporate will love the idea. Not. Now that human therapists are out of a job, rumor is that fees are going up, actually."

"Damn fees. Damn rumors."

"Can't live with them; can't live without them."

"Although, now that I think about it," Ryan continued injudiciously, trying to change the subject away from disturbing digital Therapy-as-a-Service fee inflation, "the conspiracy used to be that all that 5G radio wave stuff was transitioning people into hypnotized cellphone screen-starers—a kind of passive zombie. Maybe they finally made the aggressive kind—" Seeing Lucy's facial expressions change, Ryan instantly regretted his thinking-out-loud reintroduction, after having successfully curtailed it, of the Z-word. He quickly pivoted to say, "But everything's unreal with technology magic at this point. Who knows what reality is anymore, right?"

"Oh, look who's talking about 'reality,' big guy."

Ryan touched his hands over his heart, feigning grave injury, before lightheartedly replying, "You got me again, right where it hurts. Ouch."

Bon Jovi's "Shot Through the Heart" found its way into the background, as the next unconvincingly "random" song on the ever playful playlist.

"You want some Extra Strength Tylenol for that heartbreak, baby?"

"Ouch."

"Or you need some buttcream for where it really hurts?" Lucy teased her husband, in the way she had since they met in college.

"You're lucky you don't have haptics on your ass," Ryan teased back, making a swatting motion towards Lucy's rear end, "or I'd show you what extra strength butthurt really feels like. Or maybe you'd enjoy that a little too much?"

The joke made Lucy laugh and cough at the same time. She was reminded that her drug delivery via drone was running late. And mentioning a painkiller reminded her that right shoulder still ached from being overworked. She paused what she was doing, giving her both her real and telepresence robot arm a rest, and turned to fully face Ryan, touching the fabric of his shirt where it was stretched firmly over his chest. Even though he was past fifty, his pecs were still bench press-firm, if the haptics could be believed. The thought of zombies was fading fast. Ryan was doing his job.

"You know what I enjoy? Being with you," Lucy replied, consciously omitting "even if you're not real."

"Well, you're my drug, baby," Ryan cooed.

"Right back at you, hon. You're my crazy addiction," Lucy cooed in response, not realizing just how deep her addiction had become. More than anything, ever, the widow craved a kiss.

"Crazy together, you and me. Forever. Like flirty flakka twins," Ryan joked.

"Extra-strength crazy," Lucy concluded, "like the world nowadays."

CHAPTER 8

SECRET LIFE

"Oh, crap," Lucy suddenly declared.

"What?"

"Gabi's almost home." With a touch of panic in her voice, Lucy then hastily added, "Hey, Ryan, you've got to go!"

Ryan pushed back instantly. "'Hey' is for robots. Do I look like a robot to you?" Realizing the gaffe, he added, "Appearance wise?"

"Sorry, I wasn't trying to break some fragile-ego subroutine in your program."

"My ego subroutines will be fine, thanks, and we still have a few minutes."

Ryan instantly brought up the family finder application in a mid-air floating map. Lucy was a bit envious of how fast Ryan could navigate certain elements of the tech world, but, given what he was, it would not be at all surprising that he was better plugged into The Machine's interface. In actuality, video games had made him dexterous in life, which his avatar mimicked in death. The map showed Lucy's and Gabriela's icons nearly overlapping each other, but Gabi's had paused moving. The little picture of a smiling Isabella was nearly back safe and sound in downtown Fort Lauderdale. At least in the family finder, this version of the county map was not the one with the worrisome yellow splotches.

"You know, Lucy, I wouldn't have to leave at all if you would just tell the kids about me. Lots of people use this app therapeutically. Version 3.1, when they finally got the software stable, was the largest download for months after the Great Pandemic."

"It's just that, Gabi—"

"Gabriela would accept that you talk to me. After everything you've been through. Wars, pandemics, climate change, economic meltdowns, currency collapses, conveyor-belt funerals, a kid getting falsely accused of a crime, heart issues, losing your husband, did I miss anything?"

"Fake alien invasions?"

"Exactly. You're a survivor, Lucy. Most people, if they went through one-tenth of what you have, would be permanently curled up in a fetal position sucking their thumb. You just needed a little help. No shame. Same with Gabriela. Look at how much Doctor What's-His-Name has helped her anxiety."

"Silberman?"

"Yeah, him. That beta-bald guy is a bit of a loon, but Gabi working through issues with a therapy chatbot is lot better than gobbling antianxiety pills or slapping on antidepressant microneedle patches. Things have changed."

"Spare me the mansplaining. Or botsplaining, or whatever you're doing. You know I don't want them to think I'm some kind of crazy woman," Lucy argued, before lowering her voice substantially after the house's door chime rang.

Gabriela had entered the laundry room through the now carless two-car garage. Lucy continued in her lowered voice, "Like they're walking in on their lonely bot-addicted mom, slurping down box wine in a dark room, with candles and a Ouija board, having a seance with her definitely not beta-bald, dead husband."

Ryan, by contrast, still spoke at full volume since he did not have to worry about being overheard, "It's gotta be better than walking in on their parents doing something else."

"Good point."

"Look, I just got here. You really want me to go?" Although Lucy typically prepaid for the subscription to him, he was not her slave. He did not have to leave just because she commanded it. Besides, the risk of getting caught was part of the thrill.

At this moment, Lucy almost wished she had one of those full-on brain-machine interfaces that would let her talk directly to Ryan in the Metaverse without having to verbalize, but having things hook straight into one's brain was creepier to her than Ouija boards. Or box wine.

Lucy could feel her daughter's presence close by in her physical location, getting closer, although her senses of sight, sound and touch had her consciousness firmly planted at the farm scene in front of her. Gabi, who no doubt had her headset on, might join them at any moment, and Lucy answered Ryan's "do you want me to go?" question in a voice barely at a whisper.

"Yes."

"Yes what?"

"Yes, please."

Ryan responded by blowing her a playful kiss and an equally playful whisper. "Suit yourself."

Lucy blew him a kiss back, followed by a barely audible "tonight."

Outside the Metaverse, Lucy then heard the sound of their daughter's voice asking her a question from an indeterminate direction. While she spoke, Gabi was walking herself through the transition hallway that connected the house in Eastglade to the old mall in Dadeland, diluting her mother's reality in a mild form of Split Consciousness Syndrome, which, "Experts Say" could lead to mild psychosis. Or a major headache.

"Whom were you talking with, Mom?"

"No one, sweetie. Just Franco. The Farmer," Lucy answered, rotating her head side-to-side and speaking up towards the ceiling, as if the sound of Gabi's voice was emanating from a celestial being. The next sound was the doorknob turning in a doorway placed where men's shoes used to be, followed by the squeak of unoiled virtual hinges. Gabi's avatar, adjoined with a yellow verification icon, came in at the far end of the rows behind Lucy and Ryan, who got away using the same hasty, Johnny Depp–like hoppy-skips that Gabi had used to get away across the lawn that morning. He ducked into a gap between the plant racks, out of sight. Gabi simply assumed it was Franco going back to his section of the repurposed department store.

Lucy's secret life would continue.

* * *

"So, is there a robot hiding somewhere for me to rent?" Gabi inquired. Her verification eyecon was yellow because her avatar's outfit was a mismatch to what she was really wearing.

Lucy blinked a few times to refocus herself. "The closest one is two farms over. Franco grabbed the good ones around here when I hesitated."

Gabi assumed that her mother had been whispering at Franco and knew from experience that when her mom would bring her voice down to a whisper, instead of yelling, it meant trouble and punishments beyond imagining. Pointing in the direction that Ryan had run off to, Gabi remarked, "I'll bet you gave that guy over there a real piece of your mind."

"You could say that," Lucy replied, her voice trailing off. "You could say exactly that. He's got a piece of my mind, for sure."

"So, you want me to clock in now?" Gabi asked, "Instead of this afternoon?"

"Well, technically I can't set your schedule. Legally. You have to appear independent."

Gabi rolled her eyes.

"I know, I know, *mija*. But we have to play within the rules, as bizarre and contradictory as they can be sometimes. Mostly I just wanted you home."

"Independent? L-O-L." She said the three letters of "Laugh-Out-Loud" extra slowly. "The people who made those rules must have been high on some serious drugs," Gabi responded. "You need a lawyer to figure it all out."

"Good thing we have one in the family. And, yeah, apparently everyone's microneedling multiple drug patches right now. Start the contract?"

Unable to resist the opportunity, Gabi took a dig at her sister, "Yeah, sure, but you do realize that Izzy just gets her legal questions answered by some A.I. and just repeats what the A.I. says, right?"

"You mean, like every other lawyer? And every judge? Oh, Gabi, you know she does more than that. Look, *mira*, at what she's doing to coordinate your brother's appeal."

"True. I'll give her that."

"And, look, the rental robot is a rollin' our way. Serial number TK-422. It'll be here in three minutes. You got your gloves on?"

"Grabbed them on the way in. I can feel all ten fingertips. All right, Mom. What drudgery is on for today?"

"Pruning. And conversation." And, some might say, the Future of Work.

The mother and daughter duo bonded during their conversations here. And argued sometimes. They were the last two human workers that still serviced the Purple Rows, and Lucy knew the family's economics would change drastically once Gabi was off to college and her own life. Big changes were coming, as much as she would like to lock them out. Would it then be new workers and new robots, or just shut the whole thing down and get a new, smaller place to rent? Try to make things work with just Universal Basic Income coming in? What could one buy with just UBI nowadays?

Why stress over it now? Just be present in the moment. The present is all one ever really owned, anyway.

"What do you want to talk about, *mamá*? Today's been insane, and it's not even lunchtime. And it's supposed to be my day off at school. Oh, and you look good."

"'Insane' doesn't even begin to cover it," replied Lucy, who took the three minutes it took for the second rental telepresence robot to wheel its way over to fill Gabi in on some of what Lucy had personally seen down at the courthouse. She deliberately left out the disturbing part about the flakka nurse. "And thanks for the compliment. I think it's the new cream I've been applying in the morning."

Asserting that what happened to Jamar trying to get to the hospital was even more insane than what happened to Isabella, Gabi took control of the tele-bot as it arrived. Her gloves allowed her to move the fingers of the expensive machine as if her own fingers were grabbing the pruning shears. Annoyingly, this was the bot with a sticky middle finger that no robot repairperson had yet come to fix. Robot repair was a job that could easily be automated away, but the profession had stuck around like taxi driving. Ignoring the stuck finger, she sided up to her mother to begin snipping and pruning, adding, "Yeah, the area around your avatar's eyes is starting to look so much better."

There were now two women and two bots working in unison. Four reticulated arms, eight joints, and twenty fingers in sync. Or, nineteen fingers since TK-422 was stuck in permanent, middle-finger extended F-U mode.

"This reminds me that geofence nearly gave the big F-U to Alex's vehicle when he and Jamar tried to get away from the hospital. After driving down there, he never even got to see his grandmother," remarked Gabi. "Gotta love those geofences." She held up the robot hand with the stuck finger to make her feelings about geofences abundantly clear to her companion while at the same time not taking the chance of her real opinion getting recorded into any of the databases kept by The Machine.

"Geofences keep us safe," remarked Lucy forcefully, "and everything where it belongs, in its proper place. They stop pandemics."

"By 'everything,' don't you mean people? They keep 'everybody' in their proper place, right?"

"But some people need that. That's why I would not be overly worried about a virus this time around. The Machine really can isolate people down to the smallest level if it absolutely has to."

"What, like click the smartlocks on people's doors?"

"I doubt it will get that far, but if it has to, I suppose. So outbreaks don't become clusters. Clusters don't become epidemics. Epidemics don't become pandemics. And pandemics don't become, whatever is bigger than that." Lucy made a clicking noise with her tongue. "Lockdowns work."

"But what about proms and graduations?" countered Gabi. "My prom? My graduation? I don't want to get a simulated diploma in the 'Verse and then the real one arrives in the mail."

"I'm with you on that," Lucy concurred. She waved her robot hand at the racks next to them and sternly added, "If there's a lockdown, I am sure it will be over by graduation. I work too hard, and pay too much, so you can go to an in-person, non-Metaverse private school with real human teachers."

"'Human' is debatable. I'd say demonic. Ms. Sánchez—"

"Be nice, Gabi."

"And I want to walk down the aisle to a real stage. In the Broward Center."

"Agreed! Absolutely. And speaking of aisles, we're off to the next one. Conversation makes things move faster, see? Like we're playing a verseogame."

The two women, living one version of the so-called "Future of Work," walked side by side through the gap in the racks that Ryan had retreated through. Their robots rolled side by side in the real world. Gabi was not fond of chores, but she was fond of spending side-by-side time with Mom. After the horror of 2033, many orphaned kids her age missed that.

From behind, their avatars could be seen wearing their purple tee shirts with the family logo printed there, making them outfit-twinsies. In real life, though, Gabi was wearing a stretchy tank top more appropriate for her trip to the community cafe and back in the sun. She also liked to dye her avatar's hair purple when she was in her farm outfit, another source of the visual mismatch making her verification eyecon yellow. Lucy's purple shirt in the 'Verse, by contrast, was verified identical to the one she wore in real life.

Their work shirts explained much of what was going on down in Dadeland. Under the name "Purple Rows Growers" was the outline of a blooming rose drawn in white lines. The idea for "purple" in the name of the family business came from the rows and rows of purple LED lights that nourished the plants growing in the racks underneath them. Lucy loved that "rows" and "rose" sounded the same, which inspired the floral theme, although that's not what they grew here. Ryan then came come up with the idea to substitute the gently curved floral leaves on the rose stem with the more jagged leaves of their current cash crop, now fully legal in Florida. The branding was subtle, but effective. More importantly, having a cool logo made Gabi and her siblings feel as if the family had a crest of nobility, like the royalty of old with a dragon or a unicorn. Just this one had a slightly illicit touch.

"Remember, the inner leaves are expendable," instructed her mother as she walked alongside her daughter. "These medicinal ones here need all the available nutrients to get up into the outermost buds." In both women's headsets, AR rectangles with arrows pointed to the growth stages of individual plants, taking the guesswork out of which ones to snip.

As they arrived in the next row, Gabi then asserted, "I think it should be against the law having underage kids work on these particular plants," trying by implication to attempt a "can I get out of the rest of my chores today?" dodge.

"What are you a law professor now? You want to be like your sister the lawyer, only when it's convenient? We could just ask her to explain all the new laws she learned about at the University of Miami."

"I have no desire to be anything like my sister. I'm going to be an artist."

"And just collect UBI? Live in a pod? Eat zebugs?"

"I don't think I need college to be a content creator for the rest of my life. Or to be stuck here as a budtender, for that matter."

"Not up for discussion. College. Career. Something better than the previous generation. Anyway, we'd get in trouble if someone underage physically stepped foot in here in real life . . ." Their two robots, trailed by a third with a tray atop it, stepped forward to the next set of plants in the purple row. "And if you were really here, you'd probably gag on the smell."

"Oh, so child labor is okay so long as it's done in the Metaverse away from the smell?" Gabi argued back, allowing herself a big "I got you, Mom" grin, which could not be mirrored by the nine fingered robot that did not have a face.

"It's not called 'child labor.' It's called 'using your kids as gamified Metaverse farmhands.' And if your father had not overheard that guy at the deli talking about loopholes that day, we'd be stuck on basic income and could afford none of the things we have."

"There's no shame in UBI," responded Gabi. "That's why it's Unconditional. Universal."

"True, but we'd be sharing some house with another family."

"The neighbors all do. They're okay with it."

Lucy and Ryan had been lucky to find themselves in a residence that hit a much sought-after real estate sweet-spot—a space not quite big enough to subdivide but still large enough to provide an excellent single family residence life. With a robo-mowed lawn, even.

"Stop being stubborn. And if we didn't have this operation, you'd be getting most of your classroom instruction from synthetic teachers instead of real ones." Lucy tapped the side of her forehead for "think about it" emphasis. Her farm robot simultaneously tapped the pruning shears against one of its binocular eyes. "Look, The Machine makes the rules, not me. Human labor has been granted a special status. Replace a human with a robot; pay the robot tax."

Gabi, the more rebellious of the two daughters, then parroted the new legalisms as well as her sister might have: "You can dodge the robotax, but you can't dodge the robotaxman. I know, I know."

Knowing their words were recorded, Lucy enthusiastically affirmed their intended compliance with every jot and tittle of robotax law.

"After the tax loophole, good thing dad also came up with the idea of switching some of our crops. Clever man, that Ryan Driscoll."

Lucy corrected her daughter, "Very clever, yes, but switching most of our crops was actually a joint decision, pun intended."

Wondering why her mother had been telling dad jokes lately, Gabi delivered a round of mock laughter. "LMAO." She then asked, semi-sarcastically, "So aren't the women supposed to be doing this work in just a bra and panties?"

"That's for *cocaína*, sweetie," Lucy pointed out, "and we like to leave out of the polite family history some of the details of that little story of *abuelita* counting drug money and her 80s' adventures with Pablo Escobar and the Cocaine Cowboys."

The two shared a sincere giggle out loud. Too bad the untaxed, faceless robots down in Dadeland could not reflect their smiles.

"I loved the way dad would tell the story of how grandma escaped all that. Using a diversion at Escobar's zoo with the aggressive hippos. Clever woman, that Mady Luz." With one of the robot's functioning fingers, she pointed to the six wheeled boxy, robot that Lucy was employing to trail along with the tray of finished product. It, coincidentally, was also referred to as a hippo. Big, fat robots on wheels often were. An additional hippo—industrial delivery weight—was set to wheel its way in shortly with the first of the farm supplies Lucy had ordered in her store.

"I loved that, too, Gabi," Lucy responded with sympathy in her voice. "Your father has a special way of telling stories."

"You mean 'had'? 'Had' a special way. Man, I wish Dad were here."

"Me, too, Gabi. I know it's not the feminist thing to say, but it's nice to have a man in the house."

CHAPTER 9

WHAT'S A ZOMBIE, ANYWAY?

"So if it's nice to have a man around, why can't we invite Jammer over for dinner sometime?" Gabi asked casually as she continued her side-by-side pruning with her mother.

"Jammer?"

"Jamar. C'mon, Mom, you know who I meant. Jammer is his online name in the 'Verse. Jamar is his name in real life. I know that you know his IRL name. And you know that I know that you know his IRL name."

"Of course I do," confessed Lucy. "I just think his behavior out in the Gray World as Jamar should match his colorful behavior in the 'Verse as 'Jammer.' Or whatever grand-poobah names boys give themselves. He should be able to stand next to you, in public, and not be embarrassed to have a girl-friend. Not live some hidden life." Lucy did not at all appreciate the irony of her using the phrase "hidden life."

"Most boys are like that now. Background boys. It's a thing."

"The boys in Izzy's generation were not like that. Well, he needs to be brave for you, Gabi. In the foreground. In public brave."

"He was plenty brave this morning."

"At the hospital?"

"Before that."

"Brave in some Metaverse game doesn't count. And have you heard anything else from him since?"

"No, he hasn't reached out since he and Alex got away from the geofence at the hospital. And it's not a 'game'."

"I know, I know. It's a 'reenactment'."

"Legit. For history class. Mr. Perez is like a big-time volunteer coordinator in the event, and boy was he pissed off."

"Mr. Perez was pissed off at Jamar being brave?"

"Oh, Mom. Stop being difficult. Mr. Perez blew his stack when a hacker ruined his part of the World War II centennial simulation we were doing early this morning. We all got up ridiculously early so we could synchronize with the European reenactors."

"Well, that Perez is majorly uptight. If you put a lump of coal up his butt he'd squeeze out a diamond. He hated your older brother Romeo way back when he had him for AP World History class."

"That's because Romeo hacked in and ruined that Metaverse 1.0 time-travel simulation of ancient Greece Mr. Perez was doing with Romeo's class that year. The kids were supposed to put on those clunky old headsets and learn about philosophy in the shadow of Greek columns, sitting at Aristotle's feet. A bunch of Greeks grabbing their ankles instead was not in the lesson plan, apparently."

Lucy laughed to the point of coughing, almost choking. "Romeo and his buddies almost got expelled over that." She repeated the same outwardly serious tone she had used years ago when talking about the incident, even though her and Ryan in private thought it was one the funniest things they had ever heard of. "Good thing Romeo was pretty good at covering his tracks. Plausible deniability. But still, I had to beg. You have no idea. Perez never pronounced Romeo's name correctly after that."

"Thanks to Romeo, I worry Mr. Perez thinks hacking into things runs in the family. And who can blame him? He probably thinks I had something to do with breaking in and putting Nazi zombies in the war walkthrough this morning."

"Wait, hold on, did you say 'zombies'?" Lucy interjected, a bit incredulous.

"I know, mom, zombies are such a video game cliché, right?"

"That's the strangest thing." Lucy continued, "It's the second time today that word has come up. If you were playing a practical joke on the class, couldn't it have been unicorns prancing through the forest or something? Or maybe the Germans in Perez's simulation could do what the Greeks did."

"Funny. But the zombie hack worked pretty well under the circumstances."

"But 'zombies?' Really? Of all things?" Lucy asked in her best "are you kidding me?" voice.

"I know, right?"

"You see, this is why so many parents don't want their kids' education being done in the Metaverse, even if that finally got many failing schools back on track," Lucy then lectured her daughter, extending a robot pointer finger. "They think it'll all turn into a big video game. And who can blame them? The 'Verse turns the kids into goggle-wearing, well, zombies."

"Is that any different than adults? You guys were all cell-phone zombies and then you became goggle-wearing zombies."

"We use our headsets for grown-up stuff."

"Sure, Mom, sure. You guys pretend to."

"And you kids pretend to be getting an education in your generation's electronics."

"Actually, I think whoever did the hack wasn't trying to make a grand statement about the state of modern education. They were just trying to imitate that video game where the zombies that attack you are Nazis, low-key. Pretty clever if you think about it. In the battle we were reenacting, we are up against the Nazis in France. And, boom, in come the Nazi zombies, just like an old-fashioned video game. The whole thing would have been kind of funny if it hadn't actually been so scary. So realistic. Unusually so."

"But you can tell the difference between verified people and zombified people, right?"

"Not this time. The resolution was so high, it's like the zombies were extra-real. Mr. Perez completely lost it and ran away like a crybaby from lower school, shrieking and reeing. I think he pooped his pants. Seriously."

"They have Internet of Things sensors for detecting that, you know," Lucy added helpfully, feeling some know-it-all smugness.

"Really? IoT Sensors for sniffing out poop?"

Lucy chuckled after putting another batch of plants on a tray. "Analyzing DNA to detect viruses, no joke. In the sewer water. Imagine the smell."

"Ewww. I'd rather get bitten by a zombie."

"Zombie this, zombie that, why does that word keep coming up? What's the fascination?"

Gabi placed another completed batch on the hippo-robot before responding. "I think boys like them because you can pretty much kill the undead without getting any kind of behavioral ding. If a guy shoots a cute-looking deer in the trees of some pretty Metaverse forest, he might get profiled as being a possible extremist threat. Shoot a zombie, no problem."

"Boys shouldn't play with rifles. They need to be outlawed forever."

"Sure, real ones. But outlaw hologram rifles?"

"Yes."

"Really? Regardless, it's always open season on zombies. Even if you don't use bullets, you can burn them, behead them with a machete, napalm them, drop a nuke, it's all good. Because, even though they can move around, they're all already dead, so it's not murder."

"So all those 'background boys' have an outlet for their violence, ding-free," Lucy replied in an "aha" moment.

"Similar thing with time travel. With their headsets on, the boys think they are going back to a time when men were allowed to be men. Be unapologetically toxic. Like they're in a 'no girls allowed' clubhouse off in the woods. They get to talk like misogynist creeps, smoke unfiltered cigarettes, and pretend they are heroes saving the world from fascism. And you can always attack a fascist without getting social score ding." Gabi proceeded to make a "bash the fash" fist with her robot hand, but only four of the five fingers worked. The middle finger seemed more appropriate anyway. "Bonus if you're punching a Nazi-zombie, I suppose."

The playlist keeping them both company in the background contextually had picked Michael Jackson's zombie-themed "Thriller." Lucy ordered a "hey, next song" as MJ got to the part of the lyrics where the dead were starting to walk.

"I think I get it now. Boys are clinging to some lost vision of manhood they can only see in The Machine. They want to be men, but can't. That's probably why the whole zombie genre never dies. Pun intended."

"Boys are broken, *mamá*."

"They're like zombies?"

"Zombies in the Machine."

Gabi tried to wake up the broken finger on the one hand with fingers from the other. No luck.

"I don't know if you remember, but dad and Romeo liked to play for hours and hours that Nazi-zombie together on the old gaming console before all the headset stuff got really popular."

"Of course I remember. Called him away from his duty to watch rom-coms with me."

"That's what triggered me, when I made the connection, with dad not being here and Romeo being in prison. It's not just the boys. All the men are gone now, too. The real ones anyway."

"Try not to dwell on it, Gabi."

"Sure, I know, but it bothers me that our family situation is, like, the first thing that popped into my head when the undead sneaked through the trees behind Mr. Perez. I think at first Mr. Perez thought the battle had started early or something. He was just holding his clipboard, yapping about 1944 and, poof, zombies. And, poof, zombies made me think of Dad somehow. Like I was in a nightmare. How crazy is that?"

Lucy was about to repeat "extra strength crazy," from her earlier conversation with Ryan, but caught herself. "You're not crazy at all, sweetie." Last night, she had a nightmare that was frighteningly similar to the subject at hand. "And I would love to have seen him shriek and crap his pants. I think we should call him poopy-pants-Perez from now on."

"You would have loved seeing it. Let me tell you, the whole thing happened so fast, really."

* * *

The men in uniform, the holograms, were running, in fact. They came out quickly from between the gaps in the tall trees, which reached up to the gray sky like thin columns topped with green. There was a light fog that morning in France, not unlike the one that had settled over the Everglades that morning at the Driscoll house. It was just enough mist to obscure the movements of the hostile holograms before they got close enough to attack. The first victim was not Mr. Perez actually, but Abdul Al-Arian, a sophomore who was barely awake since the reenactment had started so early on a day off. Dressed in field gray, the German soldier who attacked him had sunken eyes and bloody teeth, made bloodier when they sank into the neck of the hapless Abdul. The zombie did what zombies do, tearing away a chunk of the sophomore's flesh and cutting loose a crimson spray of Metaverse-generated blood, which landed all over Carmen Castro's hair. "It bit me," shouted Abdul, as his lifeless avatar sank to the ground, losing its yellow eye symbol, as the zombie redirected its glowing eyes on Mr. Perez's neck. "It got in in my hair," shouted Carmen, concerned primarily for her avatar's appearance.

Otherwise unarmed, Perez had a clipboard which he could have perhaps thrown at the computer-generated horror in an act of defiance, but the visual effect of the Nazi attack was so realistic, and so rapid, he panicked instead. Abandoning the assembled students, the history teacher instinctively began to run, hotly pursued by three more of the decomposing men with mottled gray skin. These ones were dressed in all black, from boot to cap, so the only real color was the red in between their teeth and the red cloth of their armbands, bearing the black-on-white Nazi swastika atop it. All dead. All rotten. Like the decrepit ideology their uniforms represented.

"EEEEEEEE," or something to that effect, escaped Perez's mouth as he fled, dropping his administrative clipboard to the ground. Fortunately for him, his headset's microphones did not capture any additional sounds that escaped from anywhere else on his body.

The loudest sound instead was the crashing of a pine tree. A green army tank, labeled with an AR bubble that no one had time to read and belching fumes that no one was able to smell, effortlessly toppled the shallow rooted tree to the forest floor, clearing a path forward. A quick-witted Jamar Rice had grabbed a friend and raced over to a neatly parked row of armored vehicles when he sensed trouble was heading their way.

"Jammer, it's Jammer!" shouted Carmen approvingly, "He's saving us!"

Gabi watched awestruck as Jamar, verified in yellow, swung from side-to-side the powerful machine gun mounted atop the tank, pulverizing the attackers. From Gabi's viewing angle, the beams of sunlight that finally broke through the spaces in the forest canopy just happened to emanate from behind Jamar's helmet, making him appear like he was an avenging angel of some sort. Certainly not the shy boy in the hallway. She could understand where her mother was getting the idea that Jamar needed to bring some of this online personality back into his offline personality. Summon up the courage to ask her out.

The evolving situation was like watching an epic movie in a theater. "Kino" was the word used by gamers to describe such a scene. As in, the German word for "theater." Or, as the other parents feared, like a video game instead of classroom instruction.

And, like a video game, Jamar's 50 caliber machine gun rounds, powerful enough to shred metal, ripped the arms and heads of the undead off their bodies with sprays of pink mist. And no social score dings for violence. The zombie that was approaching Carmen Castro for the kill was treated to a particularly furious and sustained volley of flesh-rending metal. Gabi felt a pang of jealousy at the extra attention Jamar had just given to protecting Carmen.

Looking at the tumbling body parts, moistly rendered in gory detail by the simulation's A.I., another one of Jamar's classmates shouted up admiringly to him at his theatrics, "That was kino, bro! Absolutely kino!" Looking at the fallen, another boy added a phrase in broken German "yeah, *Kino der Tot!*"

"Let's finish this!" commanded Jamar, grandly dismounting the tank with a smaller weapon, known as a grease gun, in hand. "Grease" seemed an appropriate name given all the Germanic giblets laid out on the forest floor before them. The unattached chinstrap of Jamar's helmet swaggered back and forth as he made a sweeping gesture forward with his open hand. "Follow me!"

With a cheer, the other students grabbed the weapons they had neatly stacked while they had been listening to balding-beta Mr. Perez lecture on about what life was like for allied soldiers back then. Perez had not returned to the simulation for some reason—Abdul speculated that maybe he too had been bitten, although that was not the case—leaving his kids directionless. The lost boys, seeing Jamar's example, formed up confidently behind "Lieutenant Jammer" and, after mopping up the last of the undead with bullets to the head, went on to help defeat the real Germans that morning, just as had happened on that October day, exactly 100 years prior. 1944, instead of 2044, was a destination where a new generation of boys saw an alternate vision of masculinity, before epithets like "toxic" and "boys are babies" were hurled at them like hand grenades. And it was irresistible.

* * *

Gabi's retelling of Jamar's 1944 antics in the 'Verse reminded Lucy so much of Ryan's storytelling. Her verbal imagery clarified what a zombie was for Lucy better than the words in any "hey, what does this word mean?" voice dictionary. Gabi might have picked up a storytelling gene from that side of the family.

"That's an interesting story, Gabi, but you made my point without realizing it. Jamar needs to bring that side of himself out into the real world. None of that 'kino' heroics of his was real."

"You don't get it. Nothing is real anymore." The rebel in Gabi was starting to come out.

"These robots are real." Lucy clicked the pruning shears with her robot hand.

"Do you really know that? These robots are dozens of miles from here. Have you seen them?" Gabi clicked her pruning shears back at her mother. "How do you know this scene is not computer generated? You can't lift your lenses and see with your own eyes. Franco the farmer over there could be Franco the fake."

"How do I know they're real? Because I paid real cryptocurrency for the bots."

"'Real' crypto?"

"So what would be the point of having us rent fakes? To do what, harvest fake crops?"

"To keep us occupied."

"Absurd."

"Why? My math teacher says there's 500 million people hooked up to these headsets all the time who have no idea what's going on outside the 'Verse. My science teacher says the brain can't tell the difference between the audiovisual experience inside headsets and real sights and sounds. Ms. Sánchez says there's no epistemic trust anymore . . ."

Whatever that means. At least my daughter is paying attention in class.

". . . And Mr. Perez, when he's not sharting, says wars now will be fought with such perfect deception that people won't perceive that they are happening. While God-knows-what is going on, a war, they could be keeping you distracted with some extra crypto and busywork. China could literally be marching a robot army up US-1 from Key West—"

"And you kids would be wandering around lost like zombies in a virtual war, right? All the more reason for your 'Jammer' to step up. Before the robot army gets here."

"Oh, Mother. Stop. I was trying to be serious."

There was a stubbornness gene in both women, presumably past down from both sides of the family, and Lucy stubbornly clung to her main point about the young man.

"So, if he's that macho, he can be seen together with you offline. Would you like me to tell him that over dinner?"

"No!"

"Fine. Your decision."

"No. That's not what I said. I see what you did there, Mommy dearest, putting this on me. You haven't had anyone over for dinner or anything else since, well, since Romeo was found guilty."

"Don't go there."

"Fine. Your decision."

* * *

They started the next row of plants off on the wrong foot, and Lucy tried to get the conversation back on track.

"Sometimes the girls have to make the first move in relationships, you know. It's not the social mores of the 1940s or something."

Her mother's advice was so clueless, so intergenerationally inaccurate, that it sounded utterly bizarre to the 17-year-old. Like her mother started speaking an unknown foreign language.

"It doesn't work that way, *mamá*. Things have changed."

"Things can't have changed that much, Gabi. Your brother and sister are just ten years older, and when they were your age, girls could talk to boys in public. Relationships were not ruined."

"They absolutely HAVE changed that much. And that quickly. Except for one or two mega-chads, boys have withdrawn. Like they're going their own way. They're not looking for girlfriends IRL. Metaverse hookups with a thingie over your face? That's okay. But face-to-face? That's a n*o bueno*. A.I. girlfriends are better than real ones, the boys say."

"That's nothing new. There's been A.I. girlfriends since the '20s. So?"

"Not like these. Not with the haptics they have now. You don't just watch circus-sex porn, you feel it. Plus there's hyper-realistic flesh robots for hire out there. With teleoperations, boys can stick things in other things a thousand miles away."

"Ewww."

"A kid in my psych class, Harry, was the 2043 Teledildo Tenpins champion. Did you know that? His parents don't. He literally won a tournament in Thailand using a robotic sex toy to, ugh, I can't even."

"No need to get so vulgar, *mija*." Lucy by-and-large let her kids talk freely, but Gabi, in her frustration over the subject, started to veer into multiple uncomfortable territories.

The two paused working and faced each other. Their telepresence robots faced each other concomitantly like the red and blue plastic combatants from the classic "Rock 'Em Sock 'Em Robots" game from the 1960s, the original telerobotics application. The playlist tried to softly cool tensions in the room with the 1976 duet "Don't Go Breaking My Heart." It may have made things worse.

"Mom. That's today's reality. My generation's reality. Ruined relationships. Broken boys. No matter what laws or rules they pass, with A.I., every boy can low-key see every girl stripped nude, if they want. Or, put potato-sack clothes back on her when they say she's dressed too provocatively, to mock and minimize them. Sure, it's all in-memory deepfakes, but still hurtful."

The portmanteau of "deep" and "fake" described not only the A.I.-generated images, audio, and video that could fool people by appearing to be more real than reality, but also the state of the social pain they brought about in modern society. "Deep" hurt from psycho "fakes."

"And," Gabi ranted further, "if the girl is the Stacey-kind that actually has a body count, it appears in an AR label over her head. `Slept with: / 5 Guys / 2 Girls`. How's that for a conversation starter?"

"Disgusting. Like the Scarlet Letter."

"In return, every girl has stripped off every boy's pants and commented on, let me put it this way, the reach of their teledildo. The sensors on some headsets can see right through the boxers-or-briefs question. You've got a 'how many inches' display pointing down from AR bubbles, and the boys now shrink away from contact, pun intended."

"I hate it when people abuse AR that way."

"Creepy, I know. Males everywhere then hit back by joking that artificial womb technology means that they won't even need flesh-and-blood women for babies anymore. But it's not a joke. They're serious."

"That's horrid." Lucy would do almost anything to have grandkids, but not that.

"So, how do you expect me to find love, the way that your and dad's generation had it, in the current environment? It's like a warzone. Romance is dead. The boys self-segregate from the girls like each gender is attending a single-sex religious school."

In the background, Pat Benatar's "Love Is a Battlefield" from over 61 years prior, played, prophetically, while the women spoke.

"I know. I've seen that. Boys and girls don't sit near each other anymore. The other moms complained about it at parent–teacher night. But, relationships will always be relationships. If you want to try having him over for dinner, he can talk to you in the hallway. You don't have to settle for less. You can find a way," countered Lucy, but she didn't believe herself. Her voice soured with anger, not at her daughter, but at the circumstances her daughter was describing. A mother hates feeling helpless when her children are struggling.

"It's not that easy, Mother."

"So, that's it? The future of relationships is going to be Metaverse-only?" There was heightened agitation in Lucy's voice. The situation threatened her dreams of grandkids. It made her angry.

"Ah, forget the whole thing," declared a dejected Gabi, "it's probably the end of the world anyway, so who cares? Might as well unalive ourselves now." Had this been a game of Rock 'Em Sock 'Em, Gabi had just thrown a left jab.

"Don't talk like that! Not even as a joke."

"Why not?"

"Because we've gotten this damn close to the literal end of the world too many times this century." Lucy brought a robotic thumb and pointer finger a tiny distance apart when saying "this damn close." Her pulse and breathing, dutifully recorded by her smart devices, reflected an increased stress level. "We are so, so lucky, you have no idea."

Gabi then thoughtlessly returned a remark that would have been harmless in other contexts.

"Okay, okay, don't have a freaking heart attack." She immediately brought up her hand while saying "oops," but the nine-fingered bot made it look like she was flipping the bird.

"What did you say?" Lucy, her eyes focused on the stuck middle finger, felt like Gabi had just landed a conversational right hook. Smart ring, smart-bra, smartwatch, and some other sensors in her headmount all recorded the impact.

"But, but, it's the robot's finger that was broken. I would never give you *el dedo medio*."

"My heart issues are nothing to make a joke over. Myocarditis is not a laughing matter." Neither was the prospect of not having grandkids anytime soon.

Gabi's robot retreated a fearful step along a line painted on the floor. "It was an accident. Don't throw a haptic boot at my head, please."

"*¡Bastante, ya!* I've had enough of the talking back, missy. I'm the parent, and you are the child. You stop arguing with me all the time, or this boot is going against another part of your body."

"Seriously, I wasn't trying to make a joke about Myocarditis. With the treatments, you're gonna be fixed anyway, right?"

"You know what '-itis' you need to worry about, Gabriela Carmela Driscoll? It's wash-the-dishes-tonight-itis."

"Oh, c'mon! It's Izzy's turn tonight."

"Grounded-for-a-week-itis, too, if you keep going. *¿Me entiende?*"

"Yeah, sure, I understand. I understand everything," a seething Gabi responded, having the good sense not to verbally provoke her mother further. Her avatar froze and then disappeared with a jarring transition effect. Gabi had ripped off her headset mid-session without properly logging off. Fortunately, before abruptly returning to reality-reality, she had clocked just enough time to fulfill that day's jot in robotax law's tittle.

"I know you can still hear me," Lucy shouted loud enough to be heard anywhere in the house Gabi had run off to. "You'll also unpack every delivery hippo that wheels up to the front door today. So, watch for the doorbell camera." Lucy let her go without adding any more punishments beyond that. The specificity of the technology-driven complaints about broken background boys and ruined relationships had been as jarring as Gabi's headset disconnect, and it sank in just how quickly the dating environment for the next generation had gone from bad to worse to catastrophic. She felt awful hearing about it.

"Did you hear me, Gabi?"

Gabi

Yeah, I heard you.

With a wave, Lucy called up a window showing the text of one of the days' smart contracts. Lacking a human spirit inside, the nine-fingered robot waited motionless atop one of the painted guidelines on the floor.

"Hey, TK-42-whatever, back to the recharging station." Following one of the painted lines, the robot wheeled back towards the spot where it lived its secret life when no one was around.

She took deliberate, measured breaths to calm everything down inside, before looking forward and back at all the labeled plants. "Now, where was I?" she asked, and one of the AR labels bounced up and down on the last plant she had touched. A full day's work remained, and she would soon go into a flow state of mind where the job became almost hypnotic, assuming no interruptions.

Gabi

I love you. I'm sorry.

Gabriela had calmed down, too, and the interrupting text was welcome. Lucy knew she wasn't the perfect parent, no one was, but she had kept it all together despite being hit with seemingly every horrible thing that life could throw. The three women fought and argued plenty, but through every crisis they had maintained a home that was stable, orderly, and, most importantly, loving. Tina Turner's "The Best" rendition was the next song up.

Lucy's robot, assuming it was real, delivered another plant, assuming it was real, onto the tray, assuming that was real, as well. The AR labels updated the estimated time and yield / earnings to reflect her getting back on the smart contract's schedule.

"And that's how it's done."

CHAPTER 10

SOUTH BEACH

"**A**nd, where are you off to, Izzy?" Lucy asked that evening, glancing over at the clock below the coffee pot. Despite all the technology in the house, her preferred place to see the time remained the display on the centrally located black plastic kitchen appliance. It was 7:53 P.M. The dumb, non-networked coffee maker, with tomorrow morning's brew preloaded, was the last non-IoT holdout amongst the rented smart appliances ubiquitous in the kitchen. Alongside hot coffee, it delivered warm feelings of nostalgic normalcy.

"I'm off to see the news. Right now I'm walking around South Beach," replied Isabella as she sat on one of the barstool-height chairs opposite the kitchen sink. Her hands made some swiping motions in the air still heavy with the smells of family cooking. "There's some weird stuff going on down here, too. Really weird stuff. Come join me."

"South Beach? I haven't been in years."

"Don't we still have Dad's 'no Metaverse at the table' rule?" Gabriela then asked, placing another dish in the smart washer, making sure to make an extra-loud—extra-interrupting of her sister's peace—ceramic-on-ceramic clang.

"Dinner's over. Travel time. And you better not be chipping those dishes," Izzy fired back, relishing her sister's punishment even if her eyes were not currently watching every glorious second.

"Shouldn't a robot be doing all this?"

"Hey, Guide, pause the scene," commanded Izzy to the hologram present in her headset but not in the kitchen. "Like everybody in 2044 was supposed to be able to afford rental fees on a general purpose household robot?" Izzy asked her sister mockingly in response. Instead of doing her turn at the dishes, Isabella just luxuriated at the barstool at the counter that separated the kitchen area from the family room, for once glad they did not have a robot to do the housework. Gabi could get three plate-scraping nights in a row. "We all don't have leftover money after the crash like Jamar's family to have hired help and robots everywhere, *estúpida*."

"You're the stupid one," Gabi fired back. She could have said more, but was conscious that her mother was still somewhat mad at her. She wanted to slam her argumentative sister for being oh-so-smart but yet not able to afford moving out of the house. Had Gabi decided to escalate the fight, her mother would have reminded them both that "multi-generational households are very common nowadays, the norm in some places. There's nothing to be ashamed of" before no doubt piling on more punishing chores on Gabi. So Gabi opted merely to return a silent, but animated, sneer, one that Izzy could not see while her headset fully immersed her sense of sight in a three-dimensional scene of South Beach, the storied southern tip of the island of Miami Beach.

"Children, that's enough," refereed their mother. Lucy was now sitting at a small, four-top breakfast table that had become their primary table since the modest dining room had been repurposed for farming work. She put her headmount on. The two women now stared in the direction of each other, present, but not fully there. With both her sister's and her mother's eyes now behind digital lenses, the only witness left to Gabriela's work was the camera on the smart fridge looking out over most of the kitchen and family room areas. The flat display panel on the refrigerator door had helpfully updated the family's digital calendar app to change tonight's "Chore Night" to read "Gabi."

"Great, just great," remarked Gabi. She felt like the fridge was mocking her right along with her sister, in the room where Isabella had mocked her so often.

"Boys aren't interested in your scrawny ass?" Izzy had once pounced cruelly from her perch on the barstool, when Gabi was still in middle school.

"Curvy is out, sis. *Flakita* is in. You look like your face-stuffing is enough to cause climate change."

"*Perra*, you like red meat more than I do. Freaking cow-killer."

"Yeah, but I don't look like I ate the whole thing, bish," Gabi had fired back, winning a round against the future lawyer, one that Izzy had yet to forgive her for.

"Everybody just breathe," Lucy remarked as her fresh Metaverse session authenticated her identity. "Better for the digestion."

Gabi decided not to join them when she was done with her chore, seeking some alone time instead. "Smart headsets, smart dishwashers, smart faucets, smart this, and smart that . . .," she commented. The smart doorbell then announced that yet another package had arrived, diverting her off to the front door. Gabi left the traveling duo behind as they tranced themselves deeper into the 'Verse. The headsets were scientifically shown to rewire the brain after just a few uses—the source of the women's addiction. Mouths slightly open, they looked stupefied.

". . . when everything is smart, nothing is."

* * *

In her headmount, Lucy could see a blur of too many search results for "South Beach news" floating in front of her that she opted for the quicker, "Izzy, can you send me a link to where you are?"

With a touch of her pointer finger on the link, she found herself present in another hallway, with her perception of any presence in the kitchen area of her home fading away almost instantaneously. The hallway was vastly different from the dreary industrial one on the way to work that morning. Phil Collin's classic "In the Air Tonight" evoked the Miami Vice era in the background. While terabytes of data loaded, Lucy had the sense of traversing a classic art deco hotel, with wall sconces casting semi-circular torchiere arcs up towards the stucco ceilings.

The Metaverse must have been running at full speed this hour, as there were only three alternating room doors in the short hallway before the exit at the end, which was presented as shiny elevator door, etched with the outline of flamingos on the surface. It was guarded by an out-of-place-looking, glowing TLA scanner. The room numbers on the little screw-on plates on the alternating doors were left blank, as if to say, "don't go this way." A small alcove on the right looked like the ideal place for an ice machine, but as she walked past it, it only had a modest wastepaper basket.

"Hellooooooooooo," said Lucy into the echoey alcove, seeing that it was devoid of any avatars. She was alone.

Where the floor number of the elevator would be, a QR code was embossed on a brass plate bearing the digital address of the venue Izzy had sent. The plain text printed above it showed the local news channel that had produced the content behind the shiny door. In the past, local news would come from a simple branded "Channel 7" or "Channel 10." Nowadays, the labels had some extended digital numbering, like 54.12 or 122.1, stripping away some of the brand's charm.

The dark Bakelite elevator push button beneath the scanner did not retreat away from Lucy's touch, and both the glowing padlock and Lucy's TLA were green. Access granted! The digital recreation of South Beach was ahead of her. In the realm of computer geeks, the digital connection made upon pressing the button looked like a barbell, with the kitchen node on one end, the destination node on the other, and the hallway Lucy was traversing in the middle.

At the South Beach node, Lucy emerged through a nondescript door in the side of a simple concrete building that served, in real life, as a lifeguard station HQ and public restroom. The one-way portal made a loud click as it locked behind her. The fake hotel hallway was gone. She stepped out into a perfect, brightly colored digital recreation of a palm-treed park just off sunny Ocean Drive. The coconut-bearing trees, resisting decades of wind and water, clung ferociously into the yellowish-whitish sand. To the east was the Atlantic, churning today with white froth of the steadily rising sea. To the west, a neat row of historic, pastel-painted Art Deco hotels silently people-watched the eclectic mix of tourists and locals strolling past in either direction on the sidewalks. The theme music here was the authentic Spanish beat of a live band playing on a hotel's patio restaurant two blocks down.

Instead of passively watching the news in two dimensions on a flat screen of some kind, Lucy would be joining her daughter in walking around "inside" the news, fully in three dimensions. In fact, the tagline for one of the stations was "why watch the news when you can be in the news?" Unlike the limited number of cameras that had pieced together the alligator scene on Lucy's lawn that morning, there was a virtually unlimited amount of video provided by the people's headsets and by the ubiquitous smart streetlights. The A.I. being employed by the local news station had enough visual and auditory data to fuse together and recreate a 3D street scene that appeared more real than reality itself.

This part of South Beach had an iconic snap-a-photo-here! tower where tourists gathered, both in real life and in the Metaverse. It had been damaged by a flying metal dumpster, scooped up by monster Category 6 winds in a nasty, climate change-induced hurricane a few years back. The tower, about the height of two people, showed the temperature, date, and, added after repairs, the time.

It was 81 degrees. 2044 OCT 27. 3:53 P.M.

A "this venue sponsored by" logo appeared next to the helpful information. The sidewalk in front of the clock-thermometer was graffitied up with advertisements based on things Lucy or Izzy had been thinking about earlier in the day.

A crowd had gathered on the west side of the street, in front of one of the hotels, spilling out from standing atop the ads and onto the street. Both a classic satellite dish news truck and an ambulance were there as well. Instead of calling out "where are you, Izzy?" Lucy wasted no time in calling up AR bubbles to find her daughter in the way she had found the hidden fauna in the lake behind the house. A label with an arrow pointed down to where

Izzy was obscured inside the crowd. No matter how grown they were, memories of that parental panic of "where's my kid" in a public place never faded. Finding children was at least one Augmented Reality "use-case" that all parents could rally behind. Even more useful that spotting alligators in a lake.

There her daughter was, "in the news," watching the scene unfold in three dimensions with the rest of the people near a news reporter whose AR label showed name, pronouns, station affiliation, and the salon that did their female-presenting hair. Both had verification icons next to them. Isabella's was green. The reporter's, yellow. A smattering of green and yellow eyecons displayed in a cluster of other travelers that had gathered here to watch the news as well. A gray-eyeconned man in a jacket and tie, looking toasty in full-sun 81 degrees and sporting a tour guide-style pennant, was particularly prominent. As much as her daughter's location, the pennant was an important visual cue for travelers to know where to congregate to see the primary purpose of the scene.

Lucy worked her way around the healthy mix of gawking bystanders and verified avatars. The bystanders were images of people who had been standing there in real life four hours ago, and the avatars were travelers who wanted to be present, now, inside the immersive, raw news that had been recreated.

"Helloooo," Izzy greeted her mother when she spotted her avatar.

"It's 'Sickness on SoBe' as you can see here behind me," announced the yellow-verified reporter into their handheld microphone. A masked paramedic and accompanying humanoid robot negotiated a gurney down the shallow steps of the Ocean Drive entrance of the five-storied hotel, painted off-white with a pink stripe adorning the wraparound edges of concrete overhangs above the windows on each floor.

Isabella waved for her mother to quickly come over to the precise spot that gave her a different viewing angle from the cluster of other travelers. The news reporter continued talking, repeating speculation that Spider Rash had made the unconscious old woman, a guest at the pricey hotel, collapse near the pool bar. "Could this be a first?" they asked. A witness, a man with an intricate tattoo sleeve on his right arm, awaited his on-camera chance for an appearance on the remnant of classic TV local news.

"Why are you standing over here, Izzy?"

"Did you notice anything?"

"What? All these people? How so many got permission to come to this 15-minute zone?"

"No. It's a tourist zone, so not that. I mean, notice anything from this angle?"

"Camera angle for the reporter?"

Lucy immediately focused on the old lady. She was either white as a ghost from being sick, or had not gone out to spend any time in the sun in the past 50 years. Her paleness made for a stark contrast with the ugly veins vividly painted onto a wrinkled-flesh canvas. There was no doubt the woman had Spider Rash. But not because she was wearing an inappropriately revealing swimsuit for a woman well over fifty or being hauled away without a blanket covering her. The veins had spread from under her arms all the way up her neck to her jawline and ears. Was this the fate awaiting grandmas everywhere?

"Uh, lemme see," Lucy continued her speculation as she took a few steps to her right to get a better view on the stricken old lady. "How could that level of infection possibly get past the hotel's entrance scanner?" Lucy then asked her daughter, taking a second swipe at the "did you notice anything?" question.

The reporter coincidentally intoned that "people are now asking if entrance scanners are up to the task," as the wheels of the gurney folded in the clever way that loaded them into the back of the boxy emergency vehicles.

"No, not that. Good point, though."

"With faulty entrance scanners, how will authorities keep pandemics under control?" the reporter asked her audience. Although news was available in 3D, she still spoke in the direction of a humanoid robot, built broad like a linebacker, acting in the role of video cameraman.

"While they have you looking at this," Izzy continued, "you're not looking at something else."

"What? They're letting us see that Spider Rash spreads farther now? Like some kind of predictive programming for what comes next?"

"No, not that, either." Isabella then cocked her head from side to side, adding, "no, I meant what's going on up there. In the penthouse of that condo tower overlooking the ocean. Way down there. I doubt it's predictive programming if I am the only one who spotted it."

"Yeah, I don't see anything," said Lucy.

". . . which is leading to calls for regional health authorities to begin epidemic lockdowns . . ." the reporter continued into their mic, branded with the logo of a classic local TV station, without all the extra numbers after a decimal point.

"Hey, venue," Isabella commanded, "pause and rewind," just as the reporter was saying, "And leading to additional calls for Government A.I. to cancel physical travel to all Florida tourist zones."

"Rewind to when?" came a voice from behind the two women.

"3:53 P.M. And close your eyes, mother."

"Too late. Crap!"

Around Lucy and Isabella, people shimmied backwards in a blur. A drone high overhead sharply reversed course. So did the plane hauling an enormous advertising banner behind it, a charming, touristy throwback to a simpler time on the beaches. The time on the clock tower flew the wrong way, too.

Of all the Metaverse effects—the transitions, the flying through the air, the walking through solid objects—it was the rewinding of time that was the biggest thing Lucy could never seem to get used to. She usually, after a warning, closed her eyes to avoid the stomach upset, which would not be a good thing after black beans and rice.

This was Isabella's third rewind of the scene, trying previously not to get distracted by Gabi's incessant and spiteful plate-banging. She took the opportunity of the rewind to take a sip of her drink back in Driscoll kitchen.

Both women's avatars now looked up at the glass-railed balcony of the penthouse while everyone else's eyes were glued to the gurney. The afternoon sun glinted brightly off the glass. Whoever lived up there in the tall building must have been loaded, or well-connected, to afford a chunk of real estate like that in reality-reality. Izzy could only imagine waking up every day in a place with such a sweeping view of the actual sunrise over the Atlantic. The normal way millions of people did that nowadays was with goggles slapped over their faces in some nondescript, windowless shared apartment.

"Ok, Izzy, what am I looking for?"

Izzy looked confused. "The guy."

"What guy?"

"The guy falling off the balcony. Or jumping off."

"I don't see anything."

"Wait, what? He was right up there, I swear. A man fell, or jumped, off that penthouse balcony. And now he's gone."

"Are you sure you have the right timestamp?"

"Of course I'm sure. Dammit. Someone's edited him out."

Lucy did not respond by challenging her daughter's assertion. Nor her recollection of events. She did not need to offer a patronizing "I believe you, sweetheart." She knew full well that Metaverse scenes could be quickly edited to add and remove elements. There were actually non-nefarious reasons to do so, even in supposedly "raw" news coverage.

With a nod of her head, Lucy signaled her concurrence that the scene had been edited. "Limited hangout," she then remarked as both women maintained eye contact with the balcony, watching for the event that never came. "And I don't mean, like, a hanging off a balcony limited hangout. The A.I. is letting us see something bad—a woman with Spider Rash going up her neck—so that we don't see something worse. I'm guessing much worse." Knowing her words were being recorded, she held back her more damning conclusions. "And speaking of hangouts, is that woman naked?" Two women could be seen approaching the white tubular metal railing with bluish glass underneath, but the women were too far away to see if they had verification eyecons. One hung her ample upper body over the edge to stare down at the pavement-diver who apparently had been edited out.

"Hangouts. Funny," Isabella concurred with a grin. "And I almost missed those topless two thanks to your delightful daughter distracting me by banging plates together like a monkey. Hey, Guide, what's the timestamp of the last edit of this scene?"

The well-dressed man with the touristy pennant answered to the word "Guide." He said, candidly, "7:55 P.M. and 32 seconds. Would you like the milliseconds, too?"

"No, that's fine. Who edited the venue?"

"It's showing 'name unavailable'," replied the Guide.

"Well if they want a tip jar, they need to ID themselves. Someone took all that time and processing power to fuse together this many video feeds into a complete venue, and then not get paid for it? That's nuttier than one of these coconut trees."

The Guide dispassionately responded "this venue is fully advertiser-supported. No tipping." A second buzzy-propeller plane followed the path of the shoreline behind him, trailing another promotional banner that cast an enormous rectangular shadow out over the waves. The plane seemed too small to be hauling such a large ad.

"Of course it's all a big commercial," said Lucy sarcastically, "so they need to make it as interesting as possible. Like clickbait headlines in a newsfeed."

"Technically, if we're not paying for it, we're not the customer," Isabella sagely remarked on the modern economics of the Metaverse. "We're the product."

"True," intoned the Guide, before clearing his throat.

Her mother briefly split her consciousness to glance over at the coffee machine on the kitchen counter. It ticked to 7:57 P.M. "Holy canoli. They edited the scene right out from under our feet. Two minutes ago. While we were standing here. Sitting here. Wherever we are." Lucy then shouted "garage" to reply to a text message from Gabi, asking where she was supposed to put all the toilet paper arriving by rolling hippos. Delivery hippos, when they hogged up the sidewalk, could be given a different slang, and Gabi shouted in vain "make Izzy unpack the pavement pigs!"

Back on South Beach, the pennant-bearer began answering questions of a cluster of other verified visitors. More were arriving to walk through the viral news spreading around the pale woman with Spider Rash on her face. Whereas the reporter on scene only did one-way "blah blah blah" narration, the Guide actually talked back to them. If the tagline of a typical station's

Metaverse channel was "Don't Watch the News, Live It!" the typical Guide's tagline would simply be "yeah, you can ask me stuff."

Once the Guide was engaged with the other travelers out of earshot, and the ambulance made a noisy plea to clear a way through the mass of onlookers, Lucy asked Izzy "how do we know they didn't mess with this whole venue? Literally right under our feet, like they did the scene? They do that quite often to us non-customers, you know." By "they" she did not specify whether she meant human moderators or The Machine itself. "Like that stack-and-pack apartment building over there. It looks new to me. Is it there IRL?"

"It's not new. They put up a bunch of compliant 900-square foot eco-housing in the past few years. You just haven't been to SoBe in a long time. I hate to pester, but you gotta get out more, *mami*. Seriously, you've turned into a recluse. You can't keep using dad or Romeo as excuses for isolating yourself." As Isabella spoke, yet more curious travelers were arriving from directions unknown.

"I like my life just the way it is. Instead of the world locking me down, I'm the one locking the world out."

"So that last climate lockdown should have been called a climate lockout?"

"Exactly. You know that thing where if a guy breaks up with you, you say 'you're not breaking up with ME, no, no, I'm breaking up with YOU'?"

"Yeah. A few times too many." Izzy glanced down at her feet, standing atop a sidewalk ad for artificial roast beef. From a lab instead of a cow.

"Well, I just say, 'you're not locking ME down; I'm locking YOU out.' I'm in control, see?"

"The 'Lucy Lockout.' Love it, actually."

"Thanks."

"Operation Lucy Lockout. It's official. My mission."

"Yeah. But you still need to get out more."

On that, Lucy decided to unceremoniously change the subject.

"You're right about the live edits to the scene, obviously."

"That's the only piece of concrete proof that more is going on here than meets the eye. My gut tells me that whatever happened in that building is more important than what happened to the old lady. And I want to know what it is." Isabella sounded like a detective.

"So we have proof that somebody wanted something changed, badly, but not what changed." Lucy threw up her arms in frustration. "I hate it when that happens. We could have been playing our nightly word-guessing game; instead we traveled all the way down here just to get gaslit by The Machine. You can't trust anything."

"The five letter word yesterday was T-R-U-T-H, remember that?"

"Like everything else, we know a piece of the truth, but they make it nearly impossible to get all the puzzle pieces together in one place."

"We'll probably never know the complete truth."

A bubbly teenager working the crowd overheard their conversation and spoke to them in a hushed, but cheerful, voice. "You can. Know the truth. With this."

* * *

The promo girl, dressed appropriately for drawing people into night-clubs by passing out flyers and coupons, handed Lucinda and Isabella two small business cards. They half expected the small slips of thick paper to have something gimmicky like two for one drinks at a club a few blocks inland, along with a physical street address. Instead, the simple cards bore QR codes with no human-readable text. The cryptic, and encrypted, pattern of boxes and squares held the digital address to a custom-created venue off the main Metaverse—a "place" they could travel to.

"The hidden entrance is that alley right over there, through that chain-link fence," said the woman, whose eyecon was red. She offered up a subtle hitchhiking gesture of her thumb in the direction of a gap between the Auslander Hotel and the restaurant behind it. The red eyecon meant that this person passing out the invites looked nothing here like they did wher-ever they were located in the Gray World. Lucy figured it was a bloated, greasy dude with a scruffy neck beard. At least his avatar's outfit was not receding like his hair. The young woman had on the latest style of bathing suit bottom that actually covered her perky butt cheeks three quarters of the way instead of crawling up between them. She worked the crowds quickly by being on roller blades.

"Your place? Your venue?" Isabella asked the avatar.

"No, not mine. I didn't build it. I just get paid by different creators to promote their work. That's how I make my crypto." Her perma-smile broadened.

"We can't just find it on our own?" Lucinda asked, holding up the address card.

"Try searching for anything and see what you get in the search results. Endless little tiles showing you the same content over and over again. Places with authentic, noncorporate content are never given enough reach." The promo girl waved her stack of cards. "The only way to find something like 'suicide dive off South Beach condo' is to use direct links. You can try to google it and see."

Isabella made a few gestures to call up a floating window with a generic search engine inside it. The cookie-cutter results of her search were indeed the repetitive pap alluded to by the promo girl. Pages and pages of it.

The promo girl waved her stack of cards, again asserting "the only way you get to see the good stuff is if you travel there directly."

"It's got that old, dark web vibe," Isabella stated flatly. She knew well that what the girl was saying was true, though.

"It's probably an orgy," added Lucy. She kept silent on saying "that's probably how this dude really makes crypto."

The promo girl ignored the slight.

"If it's an orgy, it's an orgy of video cameras. All these smart streetlights hooking up." She bit her lower lip provocatively, enjoying her attempt at cleverness. "But, no, the address on the card is not to another boring, cookie-cutter sex party only for fans, I promise. It's stuff you can't find in regular search." The promo girl was now talking over her shoulder as she glided over to some green-verified stragglers outside the main group. "Go, before it gets blocked, or deleted," were her last words.

"You'll clean up the ding if we go to an unapproved place?" Lucy half asked, half instructed her lawyer daughter. Far from being a turn-off, the dark web-vibe piqued her interest. The card in her hand felt like she held an insider trading tip on the Miami Stock Exchange.

"Ding control is what I was doing for clients all afternoon today at the old courthouse downtown, once I got away from the new courthouse out west, and things settled back down. Cleaning up SoSco's—it's the firm's crappiest work, but I'm good at it. The best, I'm told."

"Glad to hear it. I mean, not that the junior lawyer is getting the crap work, but that you're good at wiping dings."

"The best. Plus I get other assignments. But, I wouldn't worry too much. Think about it, private investigators, lawyers, judges, jurors, too . . . there's reasons for people to legitimately go to seedy venues and places all the time. And, I'm bringing you along as my witness."

"So, you have a kind of Attorney-Machine Privilege?"

"I never heard it said that way before. I kind of like the sound of that. I'll have to tell one of the senior partners. 'Attorney-Machine Privilege.' Ha! I love it!"

The two approached the spot that the promo girl had pointed to.

"Even if we wanted to go, how do you think we get through this fence? If there's a portal here, it's well hidden. Strong encryption."

"I dunno. Presumably by holding up the QR code?"

They each held up the cards handed to them and moved them around in front of the fence that blocked access to the narrow alleyway separating the two buildings.

A glowing portal appeared in the 10-foot-high mesh of metal. The pretty neon glow looked like the chemical lights partygoers used on the dance floor at any one of the nearby clubs.

"Nice hack."

Behind them, the pennant started to bounce its way in their direction, above the heads of growing crowd of news-seeking travelers. "Ladies, ladies," the venue Guide shouted at Lucy and Izzy, although the pennant holder was obscured by the mass of people, "you should stick to legitimate venues, with everybody else, for the best experience. Stay in groups. That's the wrong way. Ladies, please!"

Being told what not to do sealed the deal for mother and daughter.

Without looking back, they walked through the glowing portal into the possibly illicit alleyway beyond.

CHAPTER 11

SOUTH BEACH, ANOTHER ANGLE

With a metallic clang, the chain-link door, framed by dull metal poles, closed on its own behind Lucy and Isabella, committing them, at least in the sense of Metaverse travel, to the transition ahead.

The alleyway they stood in stretched out for at least a block ahead of them. The place at the far end must have been enormous, or the Metaverse was taking forever to load. Either way, the two women began working their way through the long, liminal space that connected one experience to the next.

"Sometimes I'd rather just teleport to these various venues and places," commented Lucinda.

"The destination node would be pixelated or frozen while everything loads," replied her daughter, "plus all the encryption takes time, too. We could just sit and watch a spinning clock, I suppose."

At the far end of the alley, the alternate recreation of South Beach that day, was indeed enormous, forcing the cracked pavement of the alleyway artifice to stretch for blocks ahead of them. The windows on the buildings on either side of the long alley had bars on them, all of them being on the second floors, safely out of reach to climb, even if one hopped up on one of the dumpsters that alternated down the alley's length. The sun, safely in the western sky, cast the journey ahead in the shadow of a concrete canyon. No options were offered other than to walk straight ahead or interact with one of the dumpsters.

"Dingy and damp," Lucy observed.

"These ephemeral transitions are not supposed to be spaces where people linger. 'Nothing to see here; just move along,' as they say."

"And don't bother looking back."

"And whoever designed this one did a good job of making me not want to stay. There's not even background music."

"Only one way. Forward."

Through the chain-link fence, the sound of the buzzing crowd and the "that's the wrong way" venue Guide completely faded behind them as the pair proceeded. The dreary path ahead was dead silent except for the sound of water dripping down through a metal grate where the ground sloped into the middle like a shallow "V," draining a thin stream of what looked like a swirling mixture of hose water and spilled milk. In the real world, this inter-hotel alley was only one block of delivery and dumpster space, connecting 11th and 12th streets, but this virtual one looked like it could go all the way up to Middle Beach and 41st Street, the gateway to the island, if the Metaverse kept running slow.

"Instead of teleporting, maybe we could go back to the version where we have wings and fly to where we are going," Lucy mused. She actually did not mind the long transition so much if she was spending time with her children.

"Childish. Flying around the Metaverse is such a tired cliché," Isabella replied. "And you get nauseous whenever we tried flying."

"Some boys still like it, supposedly. Traveling to that simulated Mars colony."

They walked past another dumpster.

"We were supposed to have space travel, for real. Dancing amongst the stars. Instead that's just how they mapped out the Metaverse, like Gabi's astrology stuff." Isabella referred to how computer programs mapped out the connections between things, which looked like constellations of circles and lines. Drawn out, the connections between their kitchen area, the first version of South Beach, and the upcoming alternate version looked like the three stars of Orion's belt. And they were traveling along the lines between.

"Don't the tech people call these transitions 'edging'?" asked Lucy.

"Edges. 'Edging' is something porno-ish, *mamá*. Let's not go there."

"You kids have your own language. I need A.I. just to translate the gibberish sometimes. Anyway, this is the fourth or fifth time we've walked past the same green dumpster with the leaky plastic bags."

"Imagine the smell."

"I am half expecting some guy in a hoodie to jump out from behind one of these and try to jack us up again for some more crypto."

"Like some homeless-looking CEO after the Big Tech crash?"

"Or that guy at the abandoned gas station."

"Like you say, just breathe. And don't imagine the smell. We're almost there. The gate in the chain-link fence is just ahead." Through the gaps in the fence, the two women could see sunny South Beach waiting for them. The unfinished, spikey metal tops of the fence clearly said "don't try to climb over." The sounds of street life vaguely began to return.

Both of the QR code cards got tossed atop the leaky black bags in the final dumpster as the two women approached the sidewalk past the fence.

"Just make sure you get a good grip on the latch to open it, in case it pulls away at the last second. That happened to me this morning. I'm not in the mood for any more practical jokes today."

Isabella reached forward and simply flipped the U-shaped latch upward instead. From this side, there was no entrance scanner or overt security measure to prevent her from pushing open the virtual portal, which swung back out onto the same sidewalk they had departed from.

This scene ahead was already obviously different than the officially sanitized, advertising-supported version they had just left. The first thing that struck the ladies was the relative dullness of the colors. Not that the pastels painted onto the hotels were not bright and cheery. There was plenty of color. The real South Beach clung to its historic uniqueness in a world increasingly filled with brutally dull gray and brown stack-and-pack neighborhoods. The colors that they were looking at, an accurate reflection of the Gray World, simply were not artificially enhanced by whomever had created this place.

And no theme music or background music greeted the mother–daughter investigators as they surveyed the street ahead of them through the mesh portal.

"Are you sure you still want to go in?" Lucy asked her daughter.

"More than ever. We wouldn't want to miss the view from the 'orgy of street cameras,' now would we?"

"As long as they're not 'edging,' apparently."

"What's with you and the dad jokes lately?"

Lucy shook off the question. "So, back to the Auslander Hotel."

"Which way?"

"You need me to cast you an arrow?"

"Don't tease me. I can walk without AR arrows!" Isabella wagged her finger to and fro. "Uh, which way, again?"

Lucy simply pointed.

The fence's door bang-clanged shut behind them as they walked in the direction of the ocean and Ocean Drive. Behind them, the temporary alleyway deleted itself forever.

They could see the ocean from where they were walking. "Did you see all those hurricanes out there? Climate chaos. Season's supposed to be over. It's almost November!"

"I caught a rumor where they say they're making the rash outbreak look bad to distract from an extended climate lockdown that's coming," Lucy said.

Not to be outdone with rumors, Izzy replied, "Well, I caught a rumor that they're low-key pushing zombie talk because a new zombie-themed game is being released. Supposed to be a blockbuster."

"So, it's like they're planting seeds everywhere, in different media, to nudge people into thinking about something?"

"Narrative seeding."

"I hadn't heard that term before. Interesting."

"Well, if we're using fancy terms, I want to travel to South Beach a second time because of the Streisand Effect."

"Streisand? Please don't tell me that's Mandela's girlfriend."

"No."

"It's the name of the guy who lives in the penthouse?"

"No, no. And stop it with the dad joke attempts. There was this actress, Barbara Streisand, and this was like 40 plus years ago, who tried to get a photo of her mansion suppressed off the old Internet, but, because they tried to censor it, it backfired and ended up bringing in even more attention."

"Oh, yeah, I vaguely remember that. It's human nature. If they don't want me to see it, I want to see it."

"Exactly. So you would think the A.I. censoring official venues would have gotten a little more clever at 'Streisanding' what we see by now."

* * *

As they spoke, the two enjoyed an extended, ding-free jaywalk down the center of the recreated street before hearing the sound of a woman's panicked scream. Framed by the corners on either side, the intersection of streets formed an impromptu stage for action that had not been present in the prior performance of the scene.

"Whoa," said Isabella.

A terrified woman, her hair still wet from the ocean, was on a bicycle riding north, away from the clock tower, past the people watchers at the sidewalk cafés on Ocean Drive. The woman, rather fit and muscular, had her sarong pulled away during her initial flight down Ocean Drive. The man who had grabbed it was chasing her on foot, just behind the bicycle's back wheel, barely out of arm's reach to yeet her off.

"That's impossible," observed Lucy.

"No way," Isabella added, thinking first that there was no way the micro straps on that swimsuit were holding things together, and second that a man as visibly ancient as the one chasing the bike could run that fast. Isabella repeated "no way!" in surprise, as a robot swiftly passed straight through her, and her mother, from behind. Their avatars had no more substance than holograms from the perspective of the four-legged, thigh-high machine that raced down the middle of the street towards the elderly sprinter. The gray-painted metallic thing went right through them both.

Lucy jumped back with a gasp. "Damn, that thing scared the crap out of me!"

Bouncing on four rubber-tipped peg legs, with animalistic reticulations that gave it great speed, this particular robot's design was likened by many to a cheetah, and it was definitely not present when they had visited South Beach last time.

The bicycle rider, pumping the pedals desperately with her toned legs, managed to increase the distance between her and her pursuer, just before the cheetah-bot used its powerful hind legs to leap through the air and side-swipe the running man with the full weight of its body plus the heavy battery that gave it so much power. Its legs looked like they were copied from a grasshopper, not a feline, but whatever had inspired their design, they gave the machine dexterity far beyond any of nature's creations.

"Where the heck did that thing come from?" asked Lucy as the two curiously approached the tussle. As the man tried to get back up, the heavy bot pounced on his back and slammed his face back into the pavement, right between the double yellow lines. His skull looked like it took a dead-cat bounce before his body went limp. Unlike the eK-9 that Izzy had just missed watching in action at the hospital that morning, the larger cheetah model had the mass to slam people, rather than just trip them. Its front legs were just as powerful as the rear ones.

"After all the urban disturbances Miami Beach used to get, I suspect law enforcement keeps these models tucked away in reserve," Isabella speculated, "out of sight, just in case."

"Scary," was Lucy's next remark as the two of them approached the restrained man on the ground, apparently stunned into unconsciousness. "I'll never get used to seeing robots attack people," she added.

The two of them half-crouched a few feet away from the man's face, then leaned forward in unison to inspect the discolorations on his stricken skin. Not really being there, they could have put their noses right up against the danger, but psychologically they still tried to keep a safe distance, just in case.

"Oh, that can't be real," Izzy then said.

"Yup. I'm calling BS," Lucy concurred. "There's no way a guy this old could be running that fast. Even if he were on flakka."

"They're showing the Spider Rash coming up his neck," Isabella observed, curious enough now to get right up next to the cheetah and its prey. "Same as the old lady on the gurney in the last scene." One of the robot's black rubber pegs was pushing on the seemingly unconscious man's cheek, forcing his saggy skin outwards like a doughnut—a pastry shaped with purply red streaks where the sprinkles would go. The infection, if the scene was to be believed, had apparently crawled up from the man's underarms to his face.

In real life, Lucinda nervously rubbed one of her underarms with her fingertips to feel if anything had changed. Just in case. Her inner voice then harshly corrected her.

What am I thinking? This all must be fake. Entertaining, but fake.

"Deepfake, *mami*?" Isabella then asked, while she shook her head in disbelief.

"A 'deepfake' used to at least have to be something fake based on a real person. Like a computer-generated video of a politician diddling a kid to blackmail them. Lots of those back in the 20s and 30s. We don't even know if Mr. Spider Rash here is even a real person."

"We pretty much use 'deepfake' nowadays to say anything that looks or sounds fake, mom. Or 'fake and ghey,' as Gabi's generation would say. Deepfake is like the word 'fake' with an exclamation point after it."

"We were promised an unedited view of that guy falling off the building. It better be there if the creator of all this wants to make any money off it."

The two women, who, like everyone else, were weary of being endlessly shown fake and unverified images, despite plenty of laws to the contrary, turned south, jaywalking right down the double yellow lines in the direction of the luxury condo in the South Pointe walkable city zone.

"If we don't see what we came for, at least we got to spend time together here, like you and Dad used to do, right?"

"I hate dating myself, but I'm old enough to remember when this street used to be filled with regular cars. The convertibles were fun. They should make an exception for those."

"Yeah, but we'll never get to true Net Zero by 2050 if they keep making exceptions, even for cool-looking retro gasoline cars on Ocean Drive. I'd like to see The Machine keep South Beach above sea level." Isabella pointed towards the Atlantic, swallowing up more of the shoreline each year.

"True. True."

Focused on the crowd, and ambulance, ahead of them at the hotel, neither woman saw the fingers of the man pinned to the ground behind them begin to move.

They retraced their path back to the front of the hotel. The scene playing out before them had certain similarities but key differences. The ambulance was there, as were many of the same onlookers. Notably absent was the "Sickness on SoBe" reporter and her drone. Noticeably different was the disposition of the onlookers. Instead of clustering around the woman on the gurney like gawkers and idiots, they were mostly hovering behind the scattering of sidewalk tables, as if the umbrellaed shaded patio furniture would make for adequate impromptu protection barriers while they recorded the live action on their phones or headsets. The toned woman in the skimpy swimsuit was one of the few who had the good sense to flee at the first sign of trouble, ironically drawing the attention of the man who tried to bite her. Her lonely sarong was the only piece of litter discarded on the streetscape that was well maintained through social scores. The only person currently in motion was a distracted fellow taking an Augmented Reality tour riding an electric scooter on the ocean side of the street. Everyone else who had been there at around 5 p.m. in real life were acting like travelers in the Metaverse. Passively watching the scene as if nothing would affect them personally.

"Did anyone grab that guy?" asked the lone paramedic, referring to the elderly woman's husband who had chased the bicyclist down the street. The paramedic struggled to hold down the violently kicking feet of the stricken elderly woman partially strapped to the wheeled gurney. His companion robot, fully humanoid with ten fingers and legs instead of wheels, worked to restrain the woman by the shoulders. She was clearly possessed of unnatural strength.

"Ma'am, ma'am, I need you to calm down," ordered the paramedic, ready to also order something for the robot to inject her with.

"She bit me!" exclaimed a fifty-something man, dressed casually for the pool bar, holding the side of his head above the ear. His slimline AR lenses, cracked right down the middle, lay in two parts, one of them at bottom of the pool. "Somebody, do something!" he then coughed out directly to the humanoid assistance robot. He clutched his chest, as if he was having a massive cardiac event, before collapsing onto the tiled patio floor.

"Hey scene, pause here," Lucy then commanded. She checked the time on the tower. 4:52 p.m.

* * *

"Why did you stop? I want to see more."

"Me, too. But first I want to have a closer look at something." Lucy drew in very close to the motionless paramedic. Right there on his upper arm, midway between shoulder and elbow, were clear teeth marks in a round pattern. A blackish blood oozed out and soaked into the edge of the white uniform sleeve that partially covered the wound. One of his shoulder patches was partially ripped off as well, with tatters of string looking like unkempt hair. "See this here?"

"What? Wounds bleed? Wait, is blood supposed to be black?" Izzy asked back.

"I wonder if the little old lady supposedly did this, or the little old man over there with his smushed face." The two were so engrossed in the scene in front of them that they failed to look back and see that the old man had managed to break free of the pouncing cheetah bot.

"Not the bite. Look closer, Izzy." The paramedic had dark skin, somewhat minimizing the contrast with the blood. From his nametag, she assumed his family was from India, same surname as a skinny boy she briefly went with in college. Izzy pulled in close to see what her mother had spotted.

"Whoa. It looks like he has Spider Rash actually spreading out from the bite. Ugly as sheeet."

"So we are supposed to conclude that the rash can be in other places than pits and pubes."

"That can't be good," Isabella replied and pointed. She referenced the pale face of the elderly woman, where the lines of discoloration had crawled up the sides of the neck. "If this is real, and that's a big 'if,' it would be a class-A *no bueno*," she added, as she traced the paused lines of the growing sunburst pattern now emanating from where tooth had broken flesh on the paramedic. She grabbed his full upper arm, appreciating that she could barely get her hand to reach halfway around the bicep and triceps. Had the paramedic not been jacked, he would not have had the strength to get the Spider Rash-afflicted woman restrained onto the gurney, even with robot assistance. Isabella also noticed that in this version of reality, the attractive paramedic was not wearing a mask.

"Is this the Metaverse version of the Mandela Effect? Some people remember the woman being covered in Spider Rash, and others don't?"

"I think the Mandela Effect is more like some people remembering the guy from the Monopoly game having a monocle and some don't, but it definitely feels like we are in an alternate reality, I'll give you that."

Lucy next turned her attention to the chest-clutching man. In real life, she rubbed her fingers up and down her sternum, hoping that the slight discomfort there was nothing more than some post-dinner gas pain. Neither her smartwatch nor her smartbra were interrupting the scene with any kind of warning, but the man's plight had delivered a subtle reminder of her own heart issues. She was scheduled for her final nanobot treatment tomorrow. The injection delivering the muscle-repairing, microscopic miracles could not come soon enough.

"Hey, scene, resume at one eighth speed."

The man, who had fallen to his knees, had his head cocked back towards the sky. He looked like he was either gasping for oxygen or saying his last prayers. Both women drew in close, and watched the infected vein lines spread from the back of the man's head, where he had been bitten, through his slightly receding salt-and-pepper hair, to his cheeks. At slow speed, his groan sounded otherworldly. He crumpled forward, his apparent demise made extra dramatic by the frame-by-frame retelling by the scene's software.

"Hey, pause scene."

Lucy and her daughter gazed at the man, and turned to gaze at each other.

And then they broke out laughing.

Izzy started clapping dramatically. The sound was loud enough for Gabi, studying in her room now, to shout out "is everything okay out there?"

"Yes, yes," both travelers shouted back from the kitchen area, while continuing a now-amused chuckle in the Metaverse.

"Too much, too much. This has to be a psyop of some kind," said a wide-grinned Isabella, employing the much-overused term for "psychological operation." She smacked her knee. "For a moment, I got scared, actually." Aware of why Gabi had gotten punished, Izzy avoided mentioning her heart racing.

"A psyop just to promote a verseogame? All this?" Lucy inquired.

"I dunno. It could really all just be to distract from a coming climate lockdown. Or, maybe the Miami Stock Exchange about to crash, taking the whole economy with it? Another currency collapse, perhaps? Heavens, no. Anything but that." Isabella looked up at the sky in the "God help me" manner of the putative zombie-man. The thought of losing what she had worked for made her heart race faster in fear than the idea of a zombie virus.

Lucy used a soft control to resume the playback at 1/32nd, letting the veins on the man's face spread at watching-the-grass-grow speed.

"That's too real to be real, if you get my meaning. Has to be fake."

"You know, now that I think about it, remember Mindy from the office? Her ex-boyfriend was working on a streaming miniseries set on a Mars colony. It's going to be a huge release. The discovery of an ancient alien artifact turns the colonists into zombies."

"Two zombie things being released and promoted at the same time?"

"Not a coincidence. Has to be more narrative seeding. Has to be."

"Her ex, is he single now?"

"I'm not interested."

"What? He's not tall enough?"

"Let's just say he has a perfect score on the chud checklist. I'd rather date the undead. Mindy said he was like a zombie in bed."

"Oh, for heaven's sake. I've had enough of this zombie sheet for one day, seriously."

"One more idea. Maybe they want to reduce carbon emissions from tourism by making it seem like you'll be in zombie land if you leave the house."

"Or, they want to normalize the idea of Mars colonies being too dangerous for us ordinary folk. If normies go there, it'll be a zombie planet. That's the hidden message. So, only the elites get to live on Mars."

In the post-reality age, the two were accustomed to second-guessing their second-guessing.

"Speaking of places that only elites get to live, remember why we came here?"

"Yea. The penthouse. And I still have some questions."

"I might have some answers," announced a well-dressed man emerging from around the corner of the boxy ambulance. Overdressed for the heat, but not sweating, he held up the same tourist guide–style pennant that thematically fit in so well with being a Guide in a touristy destination. Unlike the previous Guide, he held a virtual cell phone conspicuously in his other hand. This one worked for tips. And if he wanted to get one, he would need to deliver the scene that the ladies had actually come for.

Isabella challenged the Guide rather than offer any greetings. "You should have met us at the entrance from the transition alleyway, you know."

"Apologies. I was answering questions from another group."

Two furries, people dressed in full-body furry suits of foxes, walked in the direction of where the cheetah-bot had been scuffling with the improbably fast old man. The size of the boxy ambulance had obscured their baby blue and pink presence along with the presence of the flag-and-phone bearing Guide. They both made a point of sporting verification icons—a superfluous red, given the obvious fact they were wearing costumes. The Guide had given them priority attention, since the visitors had paid for the colorful costumes upfront when entering the venue.

Lucy greeted the Guide only slightly better than her daughter had. "So nice of you to join us. Finally."

"This all yours?" Isabella challenged him, "Unofficial place or a full venue?"

"Full venue."

"Licensed?"

"Yup. I built it. The rendering took major resources." He deliberately used his phone rather than his flag to point up and down the recreated smart streetscape. He added, "To be inclusive, I kept it as an open venue instead of a private. Relaxed permissions. And it's free, for all comers, although tips are requested. Still can't really get advertisers. Oh, you can buy cool-looking skins, too, if you like." The furries had touched their virtual cellphones to his, compensating him for a colorful way for them to stand out from the growing crowd.

"So, seriously, how much of this is raw, and how much of this is edited?"

"Raw. All of it. No editing."

The two women made snorting sounds as they categorically dismissed the man's assertion.

"All of it?" they both asked in "are-you-kidding-me" mode. "No embellishments?" Lucy added.

"All of it's real. 100%. Seriously. Everything you see here is from publicly available street camera feeds. A bunch of people, some of them being the ones behind these umbrellas, publicly uploaded the close up video. Street-level stuff." The Guide pointed out a young man with tattoos and an AR headset making the same mid-air gesture that Gabi employed while recording the gator on the lawn. "I—ahem, meaning my creator—ran it through scene builder software, rendered all the 2-D video content to 3-D walkable content, and here we are."

"And here we are," remarked Isabella, looking around for additional discrepancies. A few blocks in either direction, the venue had a smattering of low-res blurry spots from a lack of data. Although the sun was shining, the whole world around them was still a shade or two less bright than the previous, ad-supported version. Everything appeared as a true representation of the Gray World. But she clearly retained her doubts.

"And 'we' are?" Lucy then asked, directing her question to the Guide.

"Anonymous."

"An anon, of course," Lucy nodded knowingly.

Probably another greasy neckbearded dude, but at least this anon is doing something useful. I think.

"@anonymous_2044_fl444_" clarified the man by calling up an AR bubble with the tag pointing to the top of his head. "Don't forget the underscores." The women understood that by using a traceable Digital ID, the creator of this node was able to legally operate a digital tip jar and his costume store. It was how he earned above basic income.

"Was there ever a news reporter here?" Izzy then asked the Guide. She looked up and noticed that the immediate airspace overhead was free of news drones, although she could hear something buzzing nearby.

"As far as I know, no. Like I said, all the video to render this came from smart streetlights or people's private cameras. People uploaded plenty of video from their phones and smartglasses before some of the juicier stuff got censored."

With a "hey," the Guide brought up AR bubbles above the voluminous locations of the area's cameras, with things like serial numbers and gobbledygook Internet addresses comprised of letters and colons. It added nothing but confusion, so he only showed the camera labels for a few seconds before dismissing them.

"So, to be clear, no local news feed?" asked a surprised Lucy. "Isn't it illegal to put a yellow eyecon next to some news lady who is not really there?" She directed her question specifically to Isabella.

Both the Guide and Isabella said "yes" simultaneously.

Isabella extended the answer, "Very illegal. That reporter's eyecon should have been gray, at the very least."

"Also very risky, with all these witnesses. I'd wager that someone had to expend a lot of resources to construct a fake scene in an official venue as thoroughly as they did," Lucy observed. "We came here to see the penthouse of a condo. Over that way where all those cruise ships used to go."

"I'm not chatbot for a real estate sales."

The Guide waved his little tourist-guide flag to affirm his role.

"No, no. Not real estate. Definitely not. We can barely afford RaaS on where we live now," countered Isabella. "That little Monopoly guy with the monocle charges a fortune in rent."

"He never had a monocle," replied the Guide.

Lucy redirected the conversation away from alternate realities. "Someone either jumped or was pushed off that condo down there." She manipulated the air with her pointer finger and brought up an AR bubble over the building in question, reading it out loud, "The Surfviewer at South

Pointe. On 4th Street. Fancy name. No shared units." She gasped when she saw the monthly published RaaS. "So, you didn't see what happened on the balcony of the penthouse?"

The Guide, caught off guard, was a bit embarrassed to confess that he had not bothered to look at the periphery of the venue he had assembled.

"Umm, no."

"Did you edit the video feeds south of here?"

"Again, definitely not. You're welcome to walk down that way, but you'll miss the next part of the action, right here." More travelers were entering the venue to have a look at the Spider Rash scene the Guide had recreated.

"No thanks. And, thanks."

Isabella held out her cell phone as a gesture of gratitude. Even if she did not believe that the bulk of the creator's scene was real, the overall presentation was impressive and immersive, satisfying the brain's addiction to the Metaverse, much like a large quantity of chocolate.

"All creators are looking for is the price of a candy bar or a cup of coffee . . ." remarked the Guide as Izzy transferred some crypto. She knew how hard people worked to earn above UBI and felt solidarity with the struggle. And, besides, she could bill this to the law firm.

The moment the transaction cleared, the sound of police sirens began to echo off, and through, the various canyons formed by the social housing condominiums, hotels and other buildings that comprised the Atlantic-South Beach walkable city zone. Because the scene was still running in slow motion, the siren sounds were drawn out and extra eerie, like the mating call of a lonely blue whale. While Isabella's transfer of cryptocurrency to the venue creator was lawful and taxed, the timing of the sirens gave the impression that she had done something illicit. Lucy wondered what had taken the human cops so long to respond to the crisis.

"We'll come back around after we look at what we came for," she said, not particularly intending to.

"Suit yourself."

"Hey, scene, resume normal speed," commanded Lucy. They both resumed walking down Ocean Drive, passing the people hovering behind their tables and umbrellas. Behind them, the chest-clutching bite victim had been fully taken over by the rash spreading out from his wound. The "infected" had "turned," in the zombie lexicon.

With things back in full motion, an elderly man in a "Desert Storm Veteran" hat, who had been enjoying a well-earned Florida vacation, grabbed one of the large cranberry-colored umbrellas in the manner of a spear, forming an impromptu barrier. "Get behind me, get behind me," he commanded loudly in the manner of his youth as a sergeant during the first live-on-cable-TV war videotaped in the desert. He would use the top end of the pole to push the attacker back, medieval style, if need be. Videotaping the action for their social media accounts, the gawkers around him were more content to gawk than to accept his offer of protection.

Lucy and her daughter did not turn around to join the onlookers.

"Not falling for the zombie stuff again."

"Nope."

Strolling past additional picturesque hotels, the two women also missed the arrival of a more formidable robot, one the veteran sergeant would have greatly appreciated seeing during his time in a desert-camo uniform back in 1991. The surplus military bot had a hybrid design. A humanoid-like upper body mounted atop a cheetah-like lower body, in the manner of the constellation Sagittarius. These centaurs, along with other models, had been produced by the millions for the various drone wars of the 2030s, and more than a few had found their way into the inventories of local police forces. The quadruped design on the lower half provided racehorse speed that bipedal bots lacked. The humanoid upper body provided gripping ability that pure quadrupeds lacked. Centaurs were handy against urban disturbances, and, apparently, against freshly turned "zombies." Their powerful hands could grip and climb over obstacles like the chain link fence that blocked the entrance alley. They could also deploy handcuffs, or in this case, deploy the bright white zipcuffs that dangled from the robot's flanks, like a cowboy bringing along a supply of multiple nylon lassos. The hidden presence of centaurs, and their assorted metallic friends kept in reserve, were the final guarantee, beyond social scores, that urban crowd control problems remained largely a thing of the past. If the videos used for this scene were credible, zombie crowd control was destined to be their latest mission assignment. But, as Isabella would say, that was a big "if."

The ladies strolled further down the touristy sidewalk, with views of the ocean, away from the drama, and once they had crossed the street, the experience was particularly pleasant, reminding them why traveling in the Metaverse was so compelling. And addicting.

The patrons of the next sidewalk restaurant, many engrossed in headsets of their own, were utterly unconcerned about what had transpired two blocks north, from where one could now hear a smattering of cheers and applause. A slow clap at first, then vigorous praise as the trio of cooperating bots, humanoid, cheetah and centaur, had brought the chaos back into a semblance of order.

As the two walked, feeding their addiction to the 'Verse, Lucy vividly recalled to her daughter spots where her husband and she had shared moments. Little, private landmarks that meant more to her in her memory than any selfie taken at generic tourist spot like the Eiffel Tower or Colosseum ever could. Birds chirped and a pleasant breeze passed through the palms, which betrayed the lateness of the day with their ever increasing shadow eastward.

"There they are again," declared Lucy, pointing to the balcony high above.

"Perfect timing," replied Izzy. "Hey, venue, magnify the view between my fingers." She formed a rectangle with her thumbs and pointer fingers. Like a movie director might.

A digital voice from above replied that zooming was a paid subscriber feature.

"Nice monetization model, but I'm not spending any more. I already tipped the creator; I'm not going pay extra for that."

"Fly up there for a closer look?" inquired Lucy.

"Like children?" Izzy made a motion to call up a personal pair of virtual binoculars instead. The permissions of this venue did not permit flying, regardless.

The two women quickly repositioned themselves to a point on the sidewalk that afforded a clear view of the ocean-view condo balcony. The back of the woman they had seen last time was pressed up against the railing. The glass underneath the metal was for maximizing the residents' views, but also offered a peek-a-boo view of the woman's rear.

"Hey, venue, put this in slow motion." Lucy instinctively tried to use the reverse-pinch motion in front of her face to zoom in on the distant woman, to no avail.

"Here. Take these. You can't zoom 3D the way you do 2D video, *mami*." Izzy passed the virtual binoculars to her mother and used the reverse-pinch on her virtual cell phone's camera app to zoom in on the action herself. Just in time.

"I know the difference between 2D and 3D."

They watched the scene they came to investigate, frame by drawn-out frame.

Whether by blind luck or athletic skill, the woman on the balcony jerked her upper body decisively to her left as her equally disrobed assailant flew out of the condo's main bedroom and lunged straight at her, slamming his well-padded belly into the metal top rail. His momentum carried his body forward, bending the upper portion over the edge. The woman, motivated purely by self-preservation, swiftly turned and cupped her left hand under a dangling knee, tipping the bent-over attacker the rest of the way. In real-life's full speed, it went down in one smooth and swift act. In slow motion, an observer would wonder if he or she was witnessing a murder.

"Should we report this?" Lucy asked, tracking the man's fall until her view of it was obscured by shorter building in the foreground.

"To the cops? The street cameras ding you for dropping a gum wrapper. I'm sure the law enforcement A.I. detected someone getting pushed off a building. But sure, someone should report this."

Lucy continued with a string of additional questions while Isabella continued to record video on her virtual cell phone.

"Does the law enforcement A.I. give a ding for full public nudity? And does everyone on South Beach have their butt cheeks out today? And, what, do people just have mid-day sex parties in their penthouses? Is that what privilege gets you?"

"For those questions," replied Isabella to the stream of questions from her mother, "I would click on the 'yes to all' button. But, did you see it looked like that guy had Spider Rash up his neck?" She used the recording on her virtual cell phone to pinch and zoom right up to the limits of the pixels.

"Eh. I could just as easily make the argument that he had a lavish neck tattoo. From here, you can't tell."

Isabella made a circular motion with her pointer finger and a knob turning motion with her other hand. The falling man reappeared on the balcony, and launched over the railing another time.

Both women tried to walk forward, but they had reached the southern boundary of the venue and could proceed no further. The image of a man falling headfirst from a tall building stirred some horrible subconscious memory in Lucinda that she could not quite place.

"Yeah, maybe those are tattoos. I see your point."

The rewound scene dropped the man a third time.

"Well," Lucy continued, "if those are tattoos, that would also mean he had them from his, you know, thingie hidden under that fat roll, all the way up past his belly button. If it's Spider Rash, that means it spreads out from down there, too."

"Ugh. I'm not zooming in on that too closely."

"Agreed. Too icky to contemplate." Lucy withheld any comment about the "how many inches" AR labels Gabriela had mentioned.

"Could this be another look-here-not-there psyop? Is it the Mandela Effect if we see two different versions of the same thing back-to-back?"

As the man caught in the rewind loop fell disturbingly again, Lucy commanded, "Hey, scene, resume regular play."

A second woman, also a prostitute, made her way from inside the penthouse on to the balcony, hidden mostly behind the first woman. A stream of fresh red ran down past her ribs. It had already started to turn blackish under where she was applying pressure. Neither Lucy nor Izzy could see it, even with the binoculars or the pinch-and-zoom effect. The poor women realized, too late, that this particular way of getting income above universal might have been a bad idea. Some laundered crypto was not worth letting cheating louts have their way with you, no matter how rich or well connected they were. Better to let the sexbots handle it. One was present at the condo that day, out of view from the ground.

"I can't say if it's a psyop, but I can say that girl hanging it all out over the balcony should have kept her smartbra on."

"Before we came here, you wondered if the promo girl was tricking us to come to a Metaverse orgy. Looks like your instincts might not have been too far off on that one. A real flesh-and-blood orgy, though. With an extra side of blood. On the pavement. What caused this? Drugs again? Tainted cocaine?"

"Maybe. I still think your instincts were dead on, no pun intended, that the most important thing to see here was whatever happened in that condo up there. You're like a one-woman CSI episode, or some kind of secret agent."

"I get paid to investigate things. And a deepfake zombie promotion at the hotel wasn't why I'm here."

The venue's A.I., which had been unobtrusively allowing the women to experience the scene raw, without interruption, responded to Isabella's orgy accusation by casting black squares and rectangles to cover both prostitutes' exposed private parts. The obscuration also had the effect of blocking any possibility of viewing of bites or blood.

"Gabriela said the boys sometimes cover up nudity to minimize females," observed Lucinda, relaying the strange, inverted detail from her previous conversation. Had the two travelers walked along the beach nearby, the A.I. would have needed to cast hundreds of black shapes to minimize various topless sunbathers.

"Censorship A.I. is so fracking retar-random."

Everything then went black in Lucy's binoculars. The whale-song sounds of the additional approaching sirens vanished.

Isabella, who had summoned another AR label, remarked that the ownership records for the condo were blacked out, too. Encrypted. Streisanded.

Everything then went white.

Without warning.

CHAPTER 12

RUMORS IN THE METAVERSE

Lucy found herself standing in the identical colorless emptiness that characterized the start of her virtual store that morning. Isabella's avatar, dressed in her work clothes, with a green eyecon beside her, stood a few feet away, the distance that separated the two women in the kitchen area of their house. "Don't tell me . . ."

". . . they censored the damn venue," Isabella stated with a mix of frustration and disappointment.

"They kicked us out just when things were getting good! Well, not 'good.' Just when they were getting . . ."

"Interesting."

". . . truthful," Lucy stated with the same frustration and disappointment mix.

"No shi—No Kidding. The Machine must have nuked the place."

"Where are we now?"

"Home?"

"Hey, Guide, are you still here?"

The empty space was silent. For highly technical reasons only computer geeks cared about, the place the women were standing in was called a "null node." There were not even shadows cast under their feet. Just vacuous nothingness as far as the eye could see.

"Anyone? Guide?"

"*Oyé, ¿Guía?*"

"Gone. I hope he didn't get in trouble."

"At least I don't have to feel guilty for not tipping him," Lucy observed. "The tipping situation is getting completely out of control."

"And, charging for zooming in? Good thing I still had in my travel inventory those binoculars I bought as a souvenir. I don't mind venue creators making decent money, but they shouldn't nickel-and-dime people for every little thing." Izzy could feel Lucy's physical presence moving about the room and taking the seat next to her. The barstool squeaked ever so slightly as Lucy rotated it to saddle up side by side. The entire time they had been traveling, her mother had been sitting at the breakfast table using software controls to move her avatar through the alleyway and venues. In real life, the two women now both sat at the bar facing the kitchen sink Gabi had cleaned.

"Well, that was fun. Really. But do you think that was real?" Lucy asked after a long exhale.

"Which version of reality? The first or the second?"

"You mean, should we believe a corporate-produced venue more, or a creator-produced venue? Which produces more accurate content, advertising or tip jars?"

"And, I'd submit, the answer can be 'none of the above'."

"Good point. In this case, they both can't be true at the same time, but they both can be false. Basic logic."

"Ah, now I've got you thinking like a lawyer."

"I'll take that as a compliment. You meant that as a compliment, right?"

"My eyes need something to focus on in all this emptiness," declared Isabella. She swiped her open palm horizontally to spread various word games across a flat plane in front of the two women as they continued their speculations. The addictive games had in common wooden square tiles that could be used to spell words, or match them, or guess them in puzzles. When placed upon a desktop or a kitchen counter in Mixed Reality, the tiles made a pleasant wood-on-stone clicking sound.

"That one," said Lucy of the word-guessing puzzle that the three women, working together, could solve quickly. Without Gabi, who had stormed away, online and offline, finding the five-letter hidden word would not be as satisfying, but she needed something to focus on as well.

"So what parts of what we just saw do you think are facts?"

"The person flying off the building was there in both versions," Lucy reasoned. "So I am guessing that really happened." She shuddered at the thought.

Isabella's first guess for the five-letter hidden word only had one matching tile. "And does Spider Rash crawl up people faces?"

"Probably," speculated Lucy. The crippled epistemology of 2044 prevented her from being fully confident in her answer.

The women jointly guessed a second word, and two letters matched this time, both T's.

"I'm thinking the zombie thing coming up over and over again is a marketing promotion, though. Has to be. Instead of tipping the creator, I should have demanded he tip us for the second South Beach. Right?"

"Sounds right, Izzy, but you did have the cabbie mention the 'Z-word.' He can't be part of some marketing conspiracy."

"Not directly. He must have just been repeating programming he got from other sources. The idea got implanted in his consciousness the way it did in ours."

"Is there a five-letter word for FAKE?"

"People talked about this from the very start of the 'Verse," Isabella said sagely. "They all said, 'no one is going to be able to tell what is real and what is fantasy anymore.'" The concept perfectly described the cognitive state in which the women currently found themselves.

"How do you lawyers deal with that in court? Determining what is real?"

"Same as people outside of court. Not well. Deepfake detectors only go so far. People get railroaded by fake images all the time. Criminal lawyers have started calling them *deepdoodoofakes*, and, given our recent family history, I'll leave it right there."

Lucy silently slid forward a fresh set of tiles with a new guess. T and R, in the first two positions, matched the hidden word.

"Hmmmm. We're getting close."

"We were close to the action this morning, and we still don't know exactly what went on."

"At Sawgrass?"

"Yeah. My biggest client was there this morning, you know. Jamar's grandmother. I haven't heard back from her or anyone at her household. Full voicemails. No return texts. Has your other daughter heard anything from her boyfriend?"

"She'd throw a dish at your head if you called him that. He has communication issues outside of his little Metaverse universe. He won't recognize her in public."

"Apparently that's how things are going right now with that generation. Boys her age don't want to be seen with girls. It's what they see in these damned headsets, I swear."

"It's worse than that. Gabi says 'boys are broken.' Her words."

"'Defeated' is the way I would say it. Women won."

"So don't read too much into Jamar not getting back to you, or Gabi, on his grandmother's status. His social skills are, yeah, defeated."

"I hope I won't have to travel all the way down to Sawgrass tomorrow morning to see what is going on with his grandmother. I have so much else going on."

* * *

"You could travel to Sawgrass now," said the sexy promo girl who had been on South Beach. The avatar strolled into the null venue from the ladies' peripheral view, standing about where the breakfast table would be if she were there in real life. She had changed her appearance to look like she had just come from a day at the beach, wrapping her lower body in a sarong that looked identical to the one that fell free of the panicked woman at the start of the last scene. She held out two more business cards with QR codes on them.

Not knowing how the girl found them, Lucy and Isabella both jerked backwards in their chairs in real life, startled. Some of the fake wood tiles got scrambled, making clacking sounds when they landed.

"How did you get in here?"

"Uh, these null node permissions were set to 'public'?"

"Mo-ooooo-m," Isabella delivered her scold by drawing the word out.

"Sorry."

"And sorry if I scared you. I get paid per card, whether you go or not. Help out a working girl?"

Izzy, sympathetic to the "working girl" entreaty, impatiently yanked the cards from the girl's hand and passed one to Lucy.

"You might want to actually go."

"Why? I was there this morning. In person."

"In person? You should have uploaded some video. Lots of people did and earned some crypto. A lot more happened down at the hospital than what they are saying on the news or social media. People are paying to see."

"Actually, I was at the courthouse, not the hospital."

"Still, the more images of the area, the better the overall venue. Still, you should check it out, in case it gets censored."

"Thanks, but maybe later," said Isabella, pretending disinterest. "I've had a headset on all day. My eyes are really starting to bother me. And my companion is going get strapopecia from being in a headmount literally day and night." Isabella used the slang that referred to contact hair loss from the rubbing of the tight straps used to hold all the headmounted devices, brain wave reading sensors, and skull haptics in place. Looking for something special, she queried, "You got cards for a premium view you can give us?"

"Wish I did."

"Is this a tip-up-front deal?"

"Actually, no. No crypto needed to enter."

"Just follow a blind link?" Isabella rubbed the corner of her eyes, which were legitimately bothering her and not part of a negotiating tactic.

"You'll see. The 'active shooter' wasn't there to murder people or for some kind of crazy false flag. They were defending themselves. Against people biting. The creator's A.I. put together a bunch of 2D photographs to make a 3D scene inside the actual Sawgrass hospital."

Hearing that, Lucy interjected, "That sounds like the kind of venue that gets travelers in trouble. Are you some kind of rumor Guide or something?"

"No. No. I just get paid to promote links to stuff you can't find in search results. That's all. Legit."

Addressing Isabella directly, Lucy added, "This could be a chance to find out what really happened to Jamar's grandmother. Might be useful for a malpractice suit or something. And if someone had a gun where they weren't supposed to, can't you sue for that, or something like it? You know, trying to think like a lawyer. Don't you always want some get rich quick money like some greedy '80s tycoon?"

"There's more to it than that, but I do like the direction you're taking this. Still, my physical body needs to take a bathroom break before we feed our Metaverse addiction some more."

"We should just call it the 'Addictiverse' at this point."

Many of the chronically online did.

"I'm going to disconnect, pee, and put a gallon of eye drops in." Isabella turned to the promo girl, who was about to disconnect from the session herself. "To be clear, these are for the new Sawgrass Medical Complex in West Pines Walkable Zone, not the mixed residential-retail shopping mall that's still there near the old hockey stadium, right?"

"You have to go through my boss's lobby first, but, yes. And this is not retail link pushing products. Trust me."

She winked.

"Ooooh, I think I've got this one!" The uninvited guest quickly maneuvered the final three wooden tiles to replace the word T-R-E-A-T with the tonight's correct word in the puzzle.

T-R-U-S-T

If only you knew whom you could.

* * *

"*Mamá*, now you set the permissions too tightly this time and locked me out," Izzy said as she sat back down at the barstools after her bio-break.

"Ooops, sorry. Here you go."

Lucy and her daughter would resume their travels with software "soft controls," sitting side by side, while facing opposite the smart fridge. The special sensors on the devices against their temples could detect and translate brain waves into locomotion. The sensors were supposed to have government-mandated privacy filters to prevent them from reading people's inner monologues.

They wouldn't dare try to read our thoughts, would they?

That's too scary to even contemplate. Best not go there.

"Where'd the girl go?"

"I told him he should consider shaving his neckbeard. They're so 2020s."

"You knew it was someone with facial hair?"

"Mother's instinct."

"You're mama the mind-reader. You can do it better than these things ever could."

The female-presenting avatar had betrayed the accuracy of Lucy's intuitive assumption by self-consciously reaching for the unkempt fuzz on his neck. "I can't tell if he left because he felt insulted or because I got rid of 'public' in the access permissions."

While she waited alone for Isabella to rehydrate her exhausted eyes, Lucy had called up a huge, concave TV like the one she watched 2D movies on with Ryan late at night. Upon it, she had several muted video feeds running, including the local channel that was rerunning the "SoBe Spider Rash" story with the verified reporter outside the hotel. The national news offered little more fresh content. Other than the politicians calling a "lid" early in the day, there was no indication that anything strange was going on in the nation's capital. Besides, the regional authorities were far more relevant. Lucy used her pointer finger to idly scroll through headlines being displayed in a window on the side of the 2D video presentations.

"Authorities: Hybrid Cop-Robot Raid of Digital Speakeasy Ensnares Tampa Businessman." *I'll bet it was really for robot tax evasion.*

"Long-term studies show no detectable herpes virus after mRNA treatments." *Just in time for the sexless generation . . .*

"Claims of CBG Fighting Spider Rash is Disinformation, Experts Say." *Streisanding CBG, huh? I have to remember to take a second look.*

"Lowering minimum age for transhuman-affirming care seen as decisive issue in upcoming election." *Geez. Do far right nutjobs ever give it a rest?*

"Metaddiction now the fastest-growing mental disorder among Gen-Y, people born before '96, doctors say." *Yeah, we're all high-functioning addicts.*

Lucy angrily scrolled past a bunch of additional headlines with a swift swipe before landing on one she liked.

"2nd Amendment Repeal Just One Vote Away. Newly Admitted States Set to Change History." *Finally!*

And, then, a zinger,

"Multiple Florida judges indicted in kickback scheme. Innocents were sentenced to prisons-of-the-future, for profit." *Should have learned to launder their crypto better. I wonder if Romeo's judge could be one of them . . .*

"Anything in the news?" asked Izzy.

"*Nada.* Nothing any crazier than usual anyway. There's one thing here at the end about corrupt judges that you'll no doubt enjoy. I'll tell you about later. Let's just get going." Lucy swiped away the curved 2D display.

"I went to check on Gabi and see if she wanted to join us for a quick word guessing game. The brat wouldn't open her door."

"You're just provoking her. You sat there gloating at her punishment, what do you expect?"

"For her to show me some respect."

"You're not the parent here."

"Whatever. Sorry. Let's have our few minutes together in peace. I have to hop back into work at some point and read the e-mail responses the chat A.I. sent to my clients. Nothing's worse, as a lawyer, than having a client or judge reference something you wrote, and you not knowing what it was you supposedly wrote."

"Just claim Attorney-Machine Privilege."

"Very funny."

"Where to, *mija?*"

"Wherever these links take us. That girl said a lobby first, and the hospital can be reached from there." Isabella made a simple, rainbow-shaped motion with her pointer finger and drew an archway in front of them. Beyond it, the women could see a beach boardwalk, the kind that ran up and down the Atlantic shore of Miami Beach. Through the portal, they could hear 1985's "Somewhere" playing, mixed with the sound of seagulls.

"I kinda thought we would walk through a hospital hall," said Lucy as she passed under the archway.

"We were just on SoBe, so I guess now it's showing us leaving the beach. You want to fly there or something?"

"It's not even a block to walk while it loads." Lucy then observed, touching the boardwalk's wooden guardrail as she walked, "But it looks like we have company along the way."

The boardwalk was made of grayish wood, treated to withstand the utterly unforgiving salt-and-sun environment of a Florida beach. To the right of them, beyond the mounds of sand covered in native grasses and other plants to slow erosion, the lightly undulating shoreline accepted wave after Atlantic wave. To the left, an unbroken block of balconied condos and hotels cast dreary shadows over the walkway and the dunes underneath. The boardwalk had neither stairs leading down to the beach nor exit ramps westward towards the city. Only a wood slat box, with a trash can inside it, broke up the repeating pattern of gray boards and gaps between them. Like all the hallways, boardwalks, stark forest trails and other dim spaces that served as transitions from one node to the next, there was only one way: forward.

Well north of South Beach, the balconies and beaches recreated around them were sterile and noticeably devoid of people. By "we have company,"

Lucinda referred to a single, out-of-place person whose presence was betrayed by his red sneakers and lower legs protruding from where he sat, behind the wood slat box. Had it been a random, real-world vagrant encamped there back in the pre-street camera days, the women would have exited the lonely boardwalk after spotting him, just to be safe.

Lucy stopped right in front of the man and waited for him to look up and make eye contact. He had the same disheveled hoodie-look as the crypto-seeking man near the gas station that morning. Or a social media CEO. Lucy wondered if the preference for hoodies in abandoned alleyways and dim tunnels was life imitating art, or the other way around.

"You came through here for rumors?"

"No, we're just passing through on our way to a lobby," Isabella said, feigning indifference.

"Why, you got some?" asked Lucy unhelpfully.

The man stayed seated next to the trash can container. He removed a phone from the kangaroo pocket on the front of the hoodie, stating that, for the right amount of cryptocurrency, he had plenty of rumors. Isabella knew the legalisms of when and how an unverified avatar could directly solicit a crypto transaction or not. The man seeking crypto was not playing by the rules.

"*Oyé*, you better not be talking crap, rumor boy," she sternly instructed him. Isabella planned to play with the rules right back.

The unkempt man, not tied to any venue, had interjected himself into the conversation in the curious role of a rumor monger. Worming themselves into conversations, and liminal spaces, was the stock in trade of a "rumor Guide."

Isabella's upfront hostility to the man bubbled to the surface from having too many Guides, rumor or not, want prepayment and then wasting her time with unreliable information. Sometimes, rumor spreaders seemed to her like shady prostitutes near a back alley, back in the day before hyper-realistic sexbots upended the economics of the entire sex worker industry, and, as Gabi had pointed out, trashed the minds of adolescent boys. Other times, such Guides could point the young lawyer to research a key piece of information that would be the difference between success or failure in the courtroom.

"Izzy, please, there's no need to be rude. These guys can be super useful, you know that."

For negotiating purposes, Izzy didn't want the rumor Guide to know, upfront, that she found them useful. For Lucy, rumors were a welcome alternative to the carefully curated facts in official news feeds. Lucy added, "Everyone doesn't have to have a green eyecon."

"Or have an eyecon, at all," replied the slender man, pushing himself off the boardwalk using his carpals. Something about the way he moved to get up made Lucy think that, in real life, the person behind the undernourished avatar was grossly overweight, but she could not be certain. Rumor mongering must pay well to afford so many calories.

Pointedly avoiding calling her mother as such, Isabella said, "He's not really a 'Guide,' sis. And I'd rather hail another taxi driver if I wanted more rumors to chase around at this point." Although she had never negotiated with a used car dealer, Isabella imagined negotiating with one this way. Looking for concessions. "The last guy that I stopped to talk with in an alley to two days ago sent me off on a wild goose chase."

"Wasn't me," the shaggy man said with a shrug.

"So how do I know you have good info for us? You're not even a real Guide. Offer something up front, or we'll set the permissions to lock you out."

"Everything I have is red hot. Too hot. And I can hack right through your permissions."

"Izzy, if we waste time, we might miss the next venue. Whatever he has to say can't get any wilder than people flying off buildings and cheetahs smashing in senior citizens' faces. It was nice meeting you."

"I'm sorry what did you say about buildings? Cheetahs deployed on citizens?"

"You heard me."

"Interesting. Very interesting." The way the man stroked his beard made Lucy suspect the real version of him had grown a thick one, unlike the promo girl's scraggly one. "All right, fine, in exchange for that tidbit, I'll give your … your younger sister right here a taste."

After delivering his sly compliment to Lucy, the bearer of rumors looked to the left and the right for dramatic effect, as if to check to make sure no one was listening.

"It's going to be called SORS from now on. Probably starting tomorrow."

"What? I don't understand. What's going to be called, what did you say, 'sores?' Like cold sores? Herpes?"

"No, 'S-O-R-S,' all capital letters. It's short for the name they came up with. Sudden Onset Rabies-like Syndrome. Or 'Rabid' Syndrome, maybe, I've heard both. The Global Health A.I. suggested the acronym because it was similar to SARS, you know S-A-R-S, Severe Acute Respiratory Syndrome, as in SARS-COV-3 and other COVID-like killers."

"Rabies? Really?"

"Rabies-like. Because of the biting. I'm guessing that the same health authorities that coined names like 'COVID-36' will, this time around, just rubber stamp whatever the A.I. says to do. Or repeat whatever it tells them to say."

"True, I'm sure. What about the Regional Health Department? What do they have to say about it?"

"Regional Health for Southeast Florida is in disarray right now. Complete disarray." The Guide then employed a healthy use of disbelieving air quotes. "The director 'committed suicide' late this afternoon. People say it was an assassination. Went pavement diving a little before four o'clock. It hasn't hit the news yet. Waiting to notify next of kin, or probably working to hide something embarrassing. Any local lockdown decisions are on hold while they are scrubbing the decision-maker's guts off the sidewalk. You mentioned a building you saw. Where exactly?"

Lucy wanted to revisit the possible connection between Spider Rash and this "rabies" business, but discussing the fate of the powerful was itself powerful.

"South Pointe. The isobenenefit zone below South Beach at the very southern part of the island. And you can call me Lucy." Isabella cringed at her mother's use of real names.

"I love Lucy." Processing the new detail, the Guide crossed his arms. "I need to know, did the man jump, or was he pushed?"

Isabella crossed her arms right back. "You've got some 'splainin to do, rumor-boy, if you want us to answer." Her head was spinning at the implications of the man's identity, if true. The Regional Director of Health is dead?

Instead of holding out his phone for a crypto transfer, the Guide just answered Isabella's question. "Because the word is that this was some kind of coup. Other directors have been dying suddenly all over the place."

"Pushed," replied Isabella to the previous question. She then pushed the limits of the conversation to test the rumor-spreader. "He was trying to bite some naked girls, probably hookers, and one of them unalived him."

"Bite? That's interesting."

"Why?"

"They're saying that cell phone towers are being used to make people violent. Half the people I am talking to say 7G radiation from towers, half say from satellite mind control."

"Well, it's like people say—rumors are like advertising. Half of the ads work and half don't, you just don't know which half. Same with what you guys are selling."

"That's why we don't rely on advertising to make coin."

"And, lemme guess, there's a rumor that 7G radiation turns the infected into zombies?"

Making a disbelieving sound, the rumor Guide chortled, as intensely the sound as one makes when milk comes out of the nose.

"Zombies? Seriously?"

"The word keeps coming up, over and over . . ."

"No such thing. But weaponized rabies is real. Activated by radiation. Undead people are just a rumor, because zombies are fake and gay." Isabella involuntarily cringed at the inappropriate language, but the Guide pressed on, "Normies with nothing exciting going on in their lives love to jump on that bullshit 'Zombie Apocalypse' psy-op because their bored asses crave something to get worked up over."

"They want zombies?"

"Masses of people create their own reality by thinking it into existence. 'What you think, you become,' right? Retards."

The R-slur brought another cringe from Isabella.

"Word right now is, and I can't vouch for this, that this is another fucking bioweapon, targeted DNA shit like 2033. Yeah, humanity's about to get buttfucked hard. Right up the ass, no lube." Izzy tipped into full cringe mode at that point, both from the free-flowing language and from the mouth-frothing conspiracies.

"So, zombie rumors are bullpoop? Ignore them?" The two women felt like they were getting played in a psychological ping-pong match, pinging from "zombies" and ponging back to "no zombies."

"That's right. It's bullshit. Too many videogames and movies. People can't actually come back from the dead, even as fucking chatbots, right?"

"Right," concurred Lucy without any conviction in her voice. "Coming back from the dead? Ridiculous." She did not flinch at the Guide's stream of vulgarities, even the R-slur. She reacted instead with an amazed smile. She marveled at how the clever hackers who found a way to break into and exist in these liminal spaces between nodes were so liberated. So free. Free to curse, spread rumors, solicit crypto, dodge taxes, probably just take a ding-free dump in the middle of an alley somewhere. And once the next node fully loaded and the travelers moved on, the one-way encrypted connections that comprised the edges between destination nodes would just vanish. And, poof, so would the rumor-hacker's highly encrypted avatars along with any evidence of their dirty and dingworthy deeds!

Their next node had been fully loaded for most of the conversation now, visible through the artifice of the glowing arch that appeared like a rainbow connecting the railings on both sides of the boardwalk. Through it, they could see a broad carpeted room and a glass retail counter with a glass popcorn machine atop it—a lobby node made to look like an actual lobby.

"I'm running dangerously low on time here," asserted the rumor Guide. Dire Strait's 1985 "Money for Nothing" had been playing from an indeterminate source since the rumors started flying.

"What else you got?" Isabella responded, waving her virtual cell phone.

Instead of being annoyed, the Guide respected her assertiveness. Too many of the newest traveling generation were passive wimps. These two were different than most of the lost wanderers he met.

"I like you, lady. I tell you what; you know Sawgrass?"

"Sure."

"Rumor is, this little old lady from Ranches West spread SORS there, at the rich people hospital, by biting some nurse. Patient Zero for this whole thing was at Sawgrass. Rice is, was, her name. Regional Health got that under control before it spread."

Isabella kept her poker face on at the mention of her client's last name. Jamar's grandmother was patient zero? Can't be.

"And what is National Health doing? The Health Czar?" Lucy inquired, wondering what the big picture might be. She wanted to get in one last question before they moved on. Fortunately, the rumor Guide liked Isabella's "older sister" enough to toss in a bonus rumor or two.

"She's got Spider Rash, last I heard. Madam President, too, as if that matters. Oh, and D.C.'s getting a curfew tonight and is gonna get locked down starting tomorrow. The state of Douglass, too. And Los Angeles is rekd. All the 15-minute zone boundaries are sealed."

"*Dios mío*," both women said at the same time.

Perilously short on time now, the man firmly held out his virtual cell phone. Isabella began to bring her phone near enough to complete the transfer of a tip, but hesitated. The rumor Guide allayed her implied concern, "It will show up on your centralized transaction statement as five kilos of 'organic ground cricket flour.' Artisinal, zero net, and all that. Clean. Don't worry."

"Three kees."

"Done."

Isabella, satisfied, tapped her phone to his. Lucy had already begun to walk through the portal to the lobby beyond. The rumor Guide placed his hand on one of the wood slats that contained the boardwalk's trash can. He blinked out in an instant without any kind of transition effect—poof, no butterflies, no fireworks—staying one step ahead of the A.I. subroutines that tirelessly hunted him and his ilk.

"Hold up, *mami*. Hold up. Don't leave me here . . ." Isabella took the past few steps on the shadow-covered boardwalk before looking back for one final question, but the man had already vanished. She reached over and touched the hand of her mother, sitting next to her in real life.

". . . alone."

* * *

"Did all movie theaters look like this in the 1980s?" Isabella asked cheerily a second later when she rejoined her mother. The archway she and Lucy had walked through collapsed behind her, completely deleting behind them the transition boardwalk that they had traveled on.

The two travelers stood in a fresh place. A comfy venue-of-venues that led off to even more places to explore. The playlist changed along with the view. Since this type of node acted like the lobby of a movie cineplex, with different movies each playing in specific theater, the designer and Guide here decided to simply use the artifice of a classic movie theater. Concession stand, popcorn machine, promo posters, the light background music—all rounding out the effect.

"I think this one is pretty typical of how theaters were designed back in the day," Lucy answered, holding up one of the cards with the QR codes the promo girl had handed them. It had a half-hole punched on either end of the paper, making it look like an old movie ticket. "The '80s was a bit before my time, sadly." A period song, actually from 1979, began playing softly in the background. "Video Killed the Radio Star." The closest modern analog would be "The 'Verse Killed the Tech Titans." Perhaps A.I. could write the tune.

Isabella looked at her own ticket and wondered if little pieces of "Admit One" paper were really how they sold access to movies before streaming over the Internet. Is that even secure? She walked along the carpeted floor, with its flashy and colorful zigzag design. The designer of the lobby had made sure to leave a few random clusters of spilled popcorn upon it to make the place look well-trafficked, but the two women were alone except for a man in a red and white-striped polo and gray eyecon stirring the popcorn noisily raining down from a shiny kettle. The creator of the venue, who also presented as the Guide, wore a nametag of white letters etched into matte black plastic. "@anon_babyface222"

"Too bad you missed it, *mamá*."

"Missed what?"

"The '80s. I like to travel there sometimes. I bet they used real butter on the popcorn back then."

"From actual cows. That were allowed to fart, presumably."

"Imagine the smell. Of the butter, I mean."

"Magical."

Isabella took a deep breath through her nose. The lingering odors of their dinner filled her nostrils instead of the intoxicating smell of authentic buttered popcorn, but one could always imagine. There were Metaverse smell-devices, and, someday, engineering wizards would convincingly solve the delivery of the missing sense, but not quite yet.

"Hey, Guide, how many venues can we travel to from this here lobby venue?"

"I'm not a bot," the Guide replied instantly to the use of "hey."

"Oh, sorry."

"Five venues. It was seven but two of them got deleted. Nuked. Those cost me a lot of money."

"You made all this?"

"Each actual theater. Those are mine. This lobby's from a template I downloaded. I created the popcorn in the popping machine myself, though. And these t-shirts."

Lucy glanced around at the silver-framed movie posters in thin cases behind shiny glass. Five of them had "Now Showing" in bold letters above the frames. Two of the cases on the walls were empty. Nuked by The Programs That Be.

"This one is still good? Sawgrass Hospital? You assembled a scene with this morning's disturbance?" Lucy held up her QR ticket.

"Yeah. The newsperson there was calling it 'Sawgrass Shocker.' You'll see. I had to rent a ton of server power to put that venue together. There weren't any public domain templates of some random hospital and courthouse out in nowhereland Broward so I had to build the whole venue from scratch. It will take a while to download, but it's worth it. I'll probably have to take big loss today if this one gets censored, too."

"Your marketing person said you weren't pushing product sales."

"I'm not pushing, just offering."

Isabella felt badly for the creator and bought a tub of the virtual popcorn that no one could smell. Unlike an add-on purchase of the binoculars, or zooming privileges on South Beach, the concessions here were purely cosmetic, but oddly popular. Heading down a hallway in a classic movie theater while imagining fingers getting greasy with melted magic seemed to many travelers like an enjoyable thing to do. A third business model, in-venue sales of cosmetic items and costumes, usually produced excellent content. Of the various business models, many would argue this one was the best for both creators and fans.

"You'd better get moving, ladies."

* * *

The venue designer had placed multiple hallways leading off the main movie theater lobby, each ending in yet another venue. If laid out by a computer geek in a graph format, the connection from this node to the next nodes would spread out like a handheld fan. The QR code given to Lucinda and Isabella corresponded to the last venue created, to the far right of the concessions. A tessellated dark green carpet stretched out ahead of them, using a repeated a grid of lines down a bright hallway. Alternating trash cans, with openings just large enough to accommodate a large popcorn bucket, repeated down the length of the one-way journey ahead. The walls on either side were adorned, also in an alternating pattern, with the same spotlit from above movie poster frames as had been worked into the main lobby design. No exits were shown other than the double wooden doors at the end of the hall. Forward. The only way.

"Hmmm, this creator put up lots of 1980s movie posters, which is a nice tie-in to the lobby we just left. I actually like this space."

"Something to see here."

"Now that I look at it, I prefer a transition that doesn't look and feel like a dreary dream that goes on and on. This designer made a temple to Gen-X instead."

"We're not alone, again," Lucy then observed. "Another one. Rumor mongering must be real profitable right now, with sores disease being the new thing to yap about."

"The last one called it 'SORS,' *ma*," Isabella replied, "and, as annoying as I find hackers sometimes, everyone's gotta hustle if they want more than universal," referring not only to the Guide about to provide rumors, but obliquely to the Driscoll family enterprise as well.

"He cheated on his wife, you know," flatly stated the new rumor Guide, who had hacked in with a completely different look and demeanor than the one on the boardwalk. He was standing in front of, and looking up at, a movie poster for the first movie in the *Terminator* series, which featured a fantasy half-flesh, half-metal humanoid robot design that military planners, to this current day, absolutely drooled over.

"Were all the men in the '80s that jacked?" Isabella asked, observing the overgrown chest bursting through the cyborg's leather jacket in the movie's promotional artwork. "Does protein from real beef do that?"

"That was supposedly from steroids," the lanky Guide replied, almost sounding defensive. His avatar presented a sharp contrast to the images shown in the movie posters on the walls. Clean shaven with a salt-and-pepper receding hairline, he casually wore a mock black turtleneck, a tad large on the shoulders, and wrinkled blue jeans. He bore the look more of a smart phone CEO than a scruffy social media one. "Regardless, you know testosterone levels were over 250% higher in men the year that movie came out than they are today. Rumor is because phthalates and other environmental disruptors."

"Not rumors, *güey*," critiqued Isabella using slang that was popular downtown. "A Fact Guide would say the same thing." The three of them began to walk together on the industrial grade carpeting toward the final theater room entrance. Isabella feigned casual indifference by tossing some popcorn in her mouth. She smacked her lips loudly. "What else you got for us? I'd like a taste upfront."

"The Regional Director of Health de facto stopped answering to the National Health Czar last month. Stopped taking her calls."

"Known fact. Continue." Isabella didn't know that, actually, but asserted it anyway.

"He was also cheating on his wife. Abromovich."

"Cheated? For real?" Lucy immediately asked.

"Are we supposed to be surprised?"

"And, not only that, he was murdered by a prostitute this afternoon. Confirmed."

Isabella felt like slapping the man and saying, "Hey, 'tard, I was the one who just told you rumor clowns about that!" She opted instead for, "Wow, rumors sure travel fast in the 'Verse. What else you got? Óyeme, it better be good."

The confirmation on exactly who one of the men in the penthouse was a useful, and terribly sad, tidbit.

Lucy actually knew Abromovich, but did not volunteer that fact, assuming that the rumor Guide was being accurate about the dead man's I.D. Or, at least she knew of the director, mostly. An acquaintance at parent–teacher nights. His kid, Alex, went to Gabi's school and was best friends with Jamar. The assertion of infidelity grabbed a stronger initial emotional response than him dying.

"They were separated," clarified Isabella, aware of poor Alex's turbulent home life.

"Mr. Director, it seems," the Guide continued, "was a guest at a luxury little love nest, huge square footage overlooking the ocean, that the mayor of Miami secretly keeps on South Beach."

"What, having an orgy?"

"Yeah ... a real one, not one where goons in the 'Verse are jerking each other while pooling UBI in their social housing pods." The Guide then tried a guru-like remark, "Metaverse porn is like popcorn, you know. You start with one at a time, and by the end you're grabbing fistfuls."

"Mm-hmm?" Isabella kept stuffing her mouth while withholding her phone, adding an air of defiance, as if to say, "Porn, huh? You trying to make me off-balanced by embarrassing me? I bet you've never actually seen a real woman naked." With a single kernel passing her lips this time, just to torment him, she kept up the disinterested act, although the peccadillos of the powerful were always of interest. 1989's "Love Shack" from the B-52's started playing, on cue, softly over the meshed speakers embedded in the drop ceilings above.

"So, a sex party overlooking the ocean?"

"Yup … with the mayor. He wasn't an incel, if you know what I mean. Definitely not celibate."

"Like you?"

"I'm not an incel, lady. I … I can get it whenever I want."

"Yeah, sure, if you pay the sex robot upfront."

Lucy moved to turn the heat down on the conversation with, "Well, our informative friend here didn't take payment upfront for his rumors. That was very nice of you."

"Sorry," apologized Isabella, "people have been passing around some pretty crazy stuff today and I'm on edge. I'm sure you're an alpha-chad in real life."

"Fact, not rumor," replied the defensive man, adding, "and, like they say, 'no edging in the edges.'"

"Is that so? Sounds like something you've played around with."

The trio continued walking down the hallway, passing a movie poster of Sylvester Stallone, shirtless with boxing gloves on. Something about the superlative decade, when movies like this came out, and its over-the-top portrayals of masculinity captivated the imagination, although Isabella would vociferously label such retrograde men "toxic" if asked to publicly express her opinion. Still, if she had a moment alone. Never mind.

She reached over and offered the eyecon-less Guide, who presented as anything but an '80s' action hero, some buttered popcorn instead. This is the closest you'll come to a real woman, she imagined.

"No thanks," he delicately replied, "I hate getting my hands greasy." He lowered his voice to play the "spreading a rumor" game properly. "And speaking of greasy, the mayor was about to get indicted."

Izzy's facial expression no longer showed disinterest at the legal assertion. Her mother's reaction was even more forceful.

"A politician being held accountable? Ha!" Lucy blurted out incredulously at an occurrence arguably less believable than zombies coming back from the dead. "What do these sleazeballs even do all day? Read scripts? They just get up in front of a camera, say what the A.I. tells them to say, and then apparently go back to cocaine and hookers, my friend."

"Our leaders just do what the Gov A.I. tells them to do," observed the Guide.

Isabella added in concurrence, "And then they pretend they came up with the idea themselves." She lowered her voice to "spreading a rumor" volume, "And, like I always say, that's what judges do all day." She laughed. "Most of the lawyers I know, too."

"Except the effing judge in Romeo's case, but don't get me started on that."

Sensing an opportunity to gather information, the Guide started on that. Mispronouncing Romeo as Roh-mee-oh, he simply asked, "This Romeo of yours, falsely convicted?"

"None of your business, really, but, yeah, at trial the fake images were treated as real, and the real images as fake."

"Interesting. Another one. That keeps happening. More than you know."

"Believe me, I know. So, what's his honor Mr. Mayor getting indicted for?"

"Not paying the robot tax. Some people say it's on a domestic he replaced with a humanoid nanny bot, but no politician is getting busted for something that small. Word is that he's got a side gig with a small army of undeclared factory robots cranking out cannabis gummies, 24x7. Side piece. Side gig. Got too comfy and the A.I. busted him."

"Everyone's scamming everyone."

"Bastard," Lucy declared, rubbing her overworked right shoulder.

The trio walked past a poster for the movie Robocop. Considering the way autonomous robots had actually entered into police work, the hybrid of human and machine looked slapstick.

"They'll nail you to the wall for that, you know, robot taxes," added Isabella. "Those are FAFO. Eff around and find out. Regional first, state next, and then the feds will take a swipe at you. You rumor guys know that quite well, I imagine."

The word "taxes" made the thin denizen of liminal spaces, operating in the cracks of the formal economy, smirk. Playing off different jurisdictions, rumor Guides didn't bother with taxes on tips.

Isabella was keen to get the conversation back to SORS rumors, but wanted to make one more point while they were all thinking about taxes. "You know, mother, that's what Romeo's cellmate is in for, misclassifying the autonomy level at his factory. Slammed him so hard they prolapsed his arse. You should watch yourself that you don't get eff'ed up the *culo*." She directed her point at the Guide, but it was also a combined warning and reminder for her mother to be meticulous at Purple Rows.

"Romeo told me about what happened with that poor guy. Listen, Izzy, don't worry. I'm always extra careful. There's A.I. just for robot taxes that tells me exactly what to do and I follow it to the letter. My arse will be fine. Like your lawyer friends, our accountant signs off on whatever the A.I. says, too."

"Glad to hear it."

The end of the hallway was nearly upon them, so Lucy jumped back to the more pressing SORS situation. "Where's the mayor now?"

"Last I heard he was in a hospital bed at Mount Zion Medical Center. Handcuffed."

"For tax evasion?"

"For biting people."

"Right."

"They also geofenced I-195 right at the 'Welcome to Miami Beach' gateway sign because of the disturbance at Mount Zion that followed. Everything autonomous or anything with a kill switch stopped for a few miles. It's all under control now, apparently. Regional Transportation took charge. They brought in milbots they keep in reserve somewhere."

"Yeah, my daughter and I saw a centaur on Ocean Drive."

"Really? Is that so? Military gear?" One of the Guide's eyebrows lifted up to about mid-forehead.

"Really."

"So, the most powerful public official in the area, probably the state, nosedives into asphalt and the guy who is probably the second most powerful is, presumably, now a rabid monster chained to his hospital bed. He is, or was, the leader-elect of the international mayor's conference, too. Who's in charge?" Isabella asked next, "Do we know?"

"The same A.I. now that was in charge before," presumed Lucy as she decisively grabbed the handle of the final door, making sure it did not pull away at the last second. "Just with two fewer sock puppets out front to repeat what it says."

"An emergency government by pure A.I., no human decision makers?" Isabella completed her mother's thinking. The word "coup" from the previous rumor Guide echoed in her head the way "zonbi" had done after the cab ride.

"Fact," declared the rumor Guide.

"Fact?" repeated Lucy back as a question.

"Fact. Well, as far as I know. I can't say I know everything."

"Oh, I don't believe it, *mamá.*" They passed another Schwarzenegger movie poster, one that questioned reality. "Total Recall."

"What? You don't believe that an unfeeling, all-powerful Machine really runs the world from behind the scenes, implanting realities and feeding everybody their lines?"

"No, that's not what I don't believe," Isabella said, looking at her virtual cell phone. "It's the office. I have to take this. On my real cell phone. Geez, that sucks. Talk about bad timing. After I waited for this whole venue to load, I have to bail right at the end of the friggin' hallway. Hold my popcorn for me?"

"Sure. Maybe it'll be something about Romeo's appeal. And don't forget to put some more eye drops in."

Isabella reached out and touched the closest of the repeating trash cans, the interface for logging a user out of the hallway elegantly, in this case no different from clicking on a "cancel" button when the progress bar on a computer was showing 99%. She gave a last look at her mother before her dissolve-into-butterflies transition fired off.

"I'll be back."

* * *

"One more thing before I do this alone," Lucy began to ask, in between gentle refrains of 1987's "Hungry Eyes" over the hallway's speakers. Not coincidentally, a young Patrick Swayze, who reminded Lucy of Ryan in so many ways, was on the last movie poster at the end of the hall.

"...no one under 50 has contracted Spider Rash, still," responded the rumor Guide, anticipating Lucy's next question. "But younger people, if bit by someone with it, will get SORS."

"So Spider Rash is some kind of early-stage SORS, is that what the rumor is?"

"Yup."

"How do people turn?"

"Gradually, then suddenly. Like the way people lose all their crypto assets. The disease progression mostly seems to depend on the person's immune system. Maybe their genetics. I hate to dump on my brothers in the rumor community, but there's a lot of wild assertions out there with not enough hard facts to back them up. And the media A.I. is being totally schizophrenic on what facts get out there and what stuff is flagged as mis-, mal-, and disinformation. Best anyone can tell is that, if you're in the 50 plus crowd and have a low-grade Spider Rash infection, and you get bit by someone else with the virus, you get the full-on rabies effect within seconds, a minute at most. Two-step bioweapon, for sure."

The assertion sounded off-the-charts crazy, but that was consistent with all the other crazy. Lucy kept the conversation going. She knew that when it came to rumors, polished gems were always hiding amongst the uncut stones.

"How widespread is this rabies stuff?"

"The infected don't flush the toilet after they go rabid, go figure, so there's no IoT shit sensors in the sewers that can build reliable virus heat maps. And it goes without saying that the infected don't care if TLA entrance scanners flag them as red, but that's another issue. So no one knows for sure how widespread this is. Anons are busy putting pieces of the outbreak puzzle together from street cameras, plus hysterical text and 2D social media posts. The volume of video people are posting is incredible. The Machine can't whack-a-mole it all."

"Amazing." Lucy popped a single kernel in her mouth in the manner Izzy had. There was no taste, yet she could swear the popcorn had real butter on it.

"One of the clusters of infection is, well, right through those doors." The Guide then subtly held out his phone, nonchalantly making it look like he was checking it for more rumors.

Lucy got the message but was reluctant. Isabella usually paid for rumors through one of the law firm's accounts.

"Don't worry, it will get recorded on the blockchain that you bought carbon capture credits. Non-monoculture. The finest."

Lucy touched her virtual phone to his without negotiating. The concept of "laundering" made her feel dirty, even if the stated cause was clean.

"Chill, lady. Those fuckers will think you planted some biodiverse trees in a nice global south forest. In Bolivia." The rumor Guide then rolled his eyes. "I know, I know, the tipping shit is getting completely out of control."

Transaction complete, he vanished by touching the trash. As if he had never been there. One step ahead of The Machine that chased him.

* * *

Lucy, shaking her head again in repeated disbelief at the relative freedom enjoyed by the hunted rumor Guides, held up her QR code for the scanner at the end of the hallway. The wooden double doors swung open, revealing the venue beyond, the Sawgrass Hospital area in West Pines Walkable. Although she had expected to arrive somewhere inside the hospital, maybe the emergency room, she emerged right out of a wall on the side of a satellite building to the main one. After closing, the wooden doors of the theater lobby node disappeared, leaving only the bland, tilt-up concrete wall of the outpatient imaging department behind her. No going back from whence she came. From where she was standing, the new courthouse, a block away, was obscured from view by the medical building. The sounds of approaching sirens and drone rotors echoed off various concrete angles.

No Guide greeted her upon entry to the venue, and she was free to walk around, for the time being anyway. Somebody, presumably the venue creator, had cast a glowing arrow on the sidewalk to suggest the best direction to proceed in to see the action of the scene. A second arrow from the creator, with a 90-degree left kink, pointed her around the corner of radiology into the typically busy area in what would have been mainly car parking in the pre-ride share and robotaxi days.

Lucy looked up to see if the scene had a timestamp posted somewhere since there was no clock tower or similar timepiece. Into the light silvery-blue sky near the bright white sun, the creator had chosen to etch the time, ticking away in a commonly accepted artifice. 9:49:52 A.M. 27 OCT 2044.

She could see a small line of people exiting the reception area of the main building with their fingers interlocked atop their heads, the prescribed response to an active shooter situation. Lucy recognized the hands-on-head evacuation protocol from one too many school shootings that, lamentably, all this expensive modern tech—the cameras, the scanners, the A.I.—still had not fully solved. Perhaps the Second Amendment repeal finally would.

In the opposite direction along the curved sidewalk, a conga line of delivery robots, mostly the hippo variety with four or six curb-height wheels and the little "I'm here" orange rectangular flags atop their arm-length antennas, had queued up to enter the reception area that the random hospital people were being escorted out of. "Conga line" was the slang people used to describe so many delivery robots in a row. It applied to the robotically acting humans, most with headsets on, as well. Two conga lines were now exchanging places.

"How much crazier can one day get?" an amazed Lucy asked no one in particular while she delicately popped a single kernel of the tasteless and odorless virtual popcorn into her mouth. What she now knew to be "SORS" near the courthouse, plus an active shooter at the hospital, plus a headless government being run by A.I.—all added up to the kind of nutty spectacle that most people retreated into the fantasy parts of the 'Verse to avoid.

"And does this venue come with a Guide?"

She kept walking forward. Instead of a news recreation, the area felt more like a Walkable Movie set. But it was in fact a recreation.

Of those retreating from the hospital that morning, one man stood out, literally, from the mix of patients and hospital-scrubs wearing staff. He was walking with his hands holding his cell phone atop his head on the near side of the conga line of robots, separated from the pack on the far side either accidentally or by choice. He was subtly making his way to the pedestrian gap in the wrought-iron fence that separated the ride pool—a mashing together of "ride share" and "car pool"—towards a white SUV stopped in the street beyond. Lucy grabbed two or three kernels, wondering if the elderly man, trim and well-put together with an immaculate posture, would effect his escape from the group. A teenager opened the passenger-side door of the gas guzzler, stood up high on the running board, and, over the top of the hood, shouted "Oliver, c'mon. Oliver! Let's go!" He waved his left arm in a "this-way" motion.

Izzy would have immediately recognized the man as her client. But she was absent.

Fascinated enough now for a fistful of fake popcorn, Lucy thought she recognized the teen shouting "Oliver" at the man. She then realized for sure that she did. It was Jamar. Gabi's stealth, 'Verse-only boyfriend. Another kid, rolling down the driver's window, was a classmate at Palm Ridge Prep. A fellow member of the after-school golf team.

The misbehaving man, presumably named Oliver, brought his cell-phone down directly in front of his face in a futile gesture to obscure his identity from the ubiquitous facial recognition on the smart street cameras. He began a light trot towards the waiting SUV. He made furtive glances to the left and right to see if any human had noticed his deviation from the evac route the conga line was following, before beginning a healthy gallop away from the lemminglike gathering. His behavior was fundamentally the same thing that Isabella had done at the courthouse a block away. When everyone was zigging, they were zagging. Good for him.

Lucy zagged in parallel with him, trying to fully catch up with the silver-haired Oliver, while still clutching the tub of popcorn. It was a race across the ride pool as Jamar's friend shouted, "Hurry, hurry. We don't want to get stuck here. Fuel is freedom, but my dad's got a kill switch on this puppy."

"Hey, venue, pause the scene. Pause the scene right here!" Lucy commanded, spotting something shocking to her.

Everything stopped. The people, the hippos, the sirens. Jamar's hand was mid-wave. The driver's side window, being rolled back up again, only made it halfway. And a nurse, who was standing just beyond the SUV, bunched her shoulders up tightly around her neck and froze. Instead of the colored surgical scrubs worn by a typical health care worker, several of whom were dressed that way in the conga line left behind, this nurse was wearing all white, in a ward dress that was more fitting for the 1940s than the 2040s. Or, perhaps, something closer to the "naughty nurse" look of a Halloween costume. Speaking of naughty, Lucy was sure she recognized the costumed young woman from behind. Her attempt to stand perfectly still and pretend that she was merely a paused part of the scene was betrayed by the yellow eyecon floating next to her, indicating that she was a real person whose appearance just did not match her avatar.

"Gabi?"

The girl in the century-old nurse uniform pretended not to hear.

"Gabriela Carmela Driscoll, is that you standing there?"

Again, no answer.

"*¡Respuestame!*"

Busted, and half-expecting to dodge a VR *chancleta*, a red-faced Gabi considered making a dash for the nearest trash can. She drooped her shoulders and faced an equally red-faced Lucy.

Behind Lucy, a curious venue Guide appeared at the same time to ask, "Excuse me, ladies, is something wrong?"

In front of Lucy, the tub of popcorn went flying in the air as the startled-half-to-death mother let out an "¡ay, Dios *mío!*"

The buttered kernels rained down on her head, and, in a move reminiscent of a hibachi chef tossing a shrimp tail into his hat, a few kernels found their way behind Gabi's white nurses cap with the little red cross-sewn on the front.

"You scared the sh—the crap out of me!"

"Apologies, ma'am. So sorry. I just wanted to see if you required any assistance interpreting the scene."

"No, no. I'm fine." In real life, in the kitchen, Lucy was having a little difficulty catching her breath. Her mRNA repair shot could not come too soon.

She never would have spotted Gabi sneaking around in this part of the Metaverse had she not taken that QR code from the promo girl. Mother's instincts. Did Gabi really think she could get away with sneaking around by wearing a costume?

"Would you like me to leave you two alone to continue the walk-through unguided?" The Guide had pre-placed sidewalk navigation arrows leading in the direction of the emergency room entrance, the spot that had put the "Shocker" in "Sawgrass Shocker," but Lucy had been so focused on Oliver's little escape antics that she failed to notice them.

Seeing that Lucy had called up a virtual sandal, poised to be thrown at Gabi's avatar following the popcorn launch, the Guide added, "Or leave you to put your shoes back on?"

Gabi, welcoming the Guide interjecting himself into the situation, responded with "No, don't leave. Please guide us."

"No, that's all right; you may leave."

"Stay, please."

"No, go."

"Stay?"

"Go."

The Guide looked back and forth between the two women and inferred whose instructions to follow. "I'll be available if you need me."

Lucy prepared to rip into Gabi about not following her earlier instructions. "Let your boyfriend handle his own family and their butler," she lectured her, using her shoe as a pointer.

"But, *mama* ..."

"What did I say?" Lucy began, before suddenly digesting that the driver of the vehicle was Alex Abramovich, son of Sergei Abramovich. As in, Regional Health Director Sergei Abramovich. Lucy held her breath for a second. If the rumors were true ...

Poor Alex was going to lose his father off a balcony in just a few hours. Lucy felt horrible for him. Yet there he was, a reconstructed image of him anyway, sporting a misbehaving grin on his face as he was having, from his perspective, the most spontaneous, exciting day probably in his whole existence. After retrieving Jamar's butler, Oliver Corbett, they would barely escape the killer geofence each time it expanded away from the hospital, then barely make it under the gate at a railway crossing, and then barely get over a canal's drawbridge just before it went up. "Time of your life, eh, kid?" the aging, Gen-X Corbett would then ask him while leaning forward, seatbelt-less, between the two front seats. In the Metaverse, Alex had been the glorious superhero in countless well-crafted, brightly-colored epics, but the adrenaline rush that day of doing just one, modestly daring, unscripted thing in an unscripted Gray World far surpassed what could be painted on any digital canvas. Pure joy. Like real butter on popcorn.

The joy, though, would melt away later when Alex finally got the news, and the rumors, about his father's fate on the balcony.

"Lord, have mercy," said Lucy, forgetting now her anger with Gabi and feeling pure sadness for the young man at the wheel, one of the "kin" in the "next of kin" that authorities would be reporting Abramovich's death to before releasing his name publicly. Sure, he and Jamar could behave as privileged prep-school brats sometimes, but they were still kids, and they would be in near bottomless despair as the day progressed.

"Yes, have mercy, mercy on me," said a still red-faced Gabi. "I needed to find out what happened here. I'm worried. It's after dinner and I haven't heard back from Jamar yet. And Alex has ghosted me, too. So, technically, I haven't been in contact with anyone, just like you asked. I was, like, just watching their avatars go by."

"That's all?"

"Just watching. This is the second, okay maybe third time I've walked through this scene."

To Lucy, Gabi's minor transgression became just that, minor, given the totality of the morning. She dispelled her digital *chancleta* without throwing it. "Fine. You just wanted to lurk on your boyfriend from all these camera angles without him knowing. The venue creator really did a good job capturing his jawline."

Gabi, face redder than before, abandoned challenging the "boyfriend" assertion. "He could cut paper with it."

"You watched them all get away, right?"

"Oliver jumped in, and all drove down Flamingo. Lucky for them, it looks like the autonomous vehicles were getting turned off first, so they were weaving in and out of all these." Gabi pointed to random CAVs and shuttles on the surrounding streets enjoying their last few minutes of motion. "And it wasn't any human cops on scene disabling vehicles with those radar-gun looking thingies. It was a geofence disabling everything, for sure. Had to have been A.I. making the call, just like they said."

"A brand-new, gasoline powered SUV without a kill switch? Do they make those anymore?"

"I'm sure it has a kill switch. It's that they must have low-key beat the geofence's lockdown just in time. I saw the Abramovich's SUV get past this venue's hard border a block that way, where they're putting up the chain-link fence, and I was, like, I'm not going to chase Alex down the street on foot to verify the details. Lucky his dad's job gets him a permit to have a cool ICE ride, though."

"ICE? Nothing cool about Internal Combustion Engines."

"No, *mamá*, we call vehicles with fuel 'ICE,' for 'In Case of Emergency.' Bad for the climate, but good for when the grid is down."

"Old stuff still have their charms."

"Alex dropped Jamar and Mister Ollie back at Jamar's house in Ranches West, their happy proximity hamlet, as far as I know. Point being, they got away from here okay."

"Mister who?"

"The butler. Oliver. He calls him that."

"Oh. That's what a butler looks like." Lucy was supremely annoyed that someone could afford non-robotic household help when she couldn't afford a humanoid maid herself, after RaaS and tuition and legal fees and therapy bot fees. "Where do these arrows point to?"

"To the other entrance around the corner, past the fire hydrant. The venue Guide says that's where the shooting is, or was. It was about five minutes ago."

"That's not too far from where Izzy and I saw that nurse I told you about. Biting people. Oh, and remind me to tell you about rabies."

"Rabies?"

"It's a rumor. I'll tell you later. Have you gone over there to check it out?"

Gabi glanced over at the paused embodiment of Jamar. "No, not yet."

"Hey, venue, rewind five minutes," commanded Lucy right after closing her eyes tight. She held them shut while the scene's clock ticked down. Jamar stepped down back into the SUV and Alex drove smoothly in reverse. Corbett, who in actuality ran the entire house Rice as its majordomo, jogged jaggedly backwards alongside the reversed-running conga lines. Gabi noticed a few new details as the whole scene reset, and when it began again, Corbett would get out of a private CAV and head into the reception area for the first time, politely allowing an equally elderly lady to touch her smart ring to the TLA scanner first. Her TLA checkmark was yellow and the automatic doors granted access, sliding to both sides. Corbett, not sure if he would be red, piggybacked off her scan and tailgated himself on in.

"*Vamos, mami*, we can go now. This way."

Lucy opened her eyes in time to watch the Rice butler—that's how she thought of him regardless of any fancy-schmancy majordomo title—disappear behind the sliding glass, the reflection of the sunlight blocking the street cameras from seeing inside. Lucy figured Isabella might want to know exactly what happened to her client in there, since on legal matters she interacted with him more than Jamar's stricken grandmother, but what Lucy just wanted to know was, if what happened at the other entrance was consistent with the rumors.

"Have you heard about the rabies?" Lucy asked Gabi as she left behind the messy pile of popcorn on the pavement. Thankfully, there was no social score ding for littering in a privately made venue.

"A little," Gabi lied. She did not want to sound clueless, like she had missed something important while obsessing over the images of Jamar.

"Rumor is that Spider Rash is some kind of rabies sores," Lucy confidently informed her daughter as they walked side-by-side over the first arrow, spreading gossip the old fashioned way—word of mouth. Patient Zero, the first person to get the full SORS syndrome, had turned not even 24 hours prior, and variations of the Lucy-Gabi conversation were starting to be had all over the world like the classic child's game of "telephone."

"Rabies explains the biting?"

"Exactly. That's what people think. It's not drugs. The old people lose their minds and start biting the young people under 50, which makes them no longer immune. If you get bit twice, you turn in seconds. It's what I heard, anyway." Lucy left off the bioweapon rumor for now, shielding her youngest from too much, too fast.

"Oh, wow," Gabi replied with some amazement. "So that whole 'Gen eXecutioner' meme is actually a thing?"

"Guess so. The '80s will have to live on in the Metaverse."

Just ahead of them, the venue Guide reappeared from behind the building's corner, following the 90-degree turn arrow in the wrong direction, carefully avoiding scaring Lucy to death a second time.

"Ladies, the venue creator kindly asks that travelers keep rumor talk to a minimum. He's trying to keep any more of his creations from getting nuked."

"Sorry, sorry," Lucy and Gabi both whispered, as if they were apologizing to a school librarian saying "shhhh." The loud noise of a passing news gathering drone shushed them as well.

Content, however, not volume, was the problem.

As they rounded the corner of the building, Guide by their side, they were greeted with a flurry of AR bubbles and a smattering of other visitors. To enhance and clarify the shared experience, someone had conjured up the labels. They ranged from the intricate to the mundane. The building itself was labeled with its completion date, number of floors and other esoterica. The drones overhead had make and model pointing to them. An air taxi, the single-seat variety, was labeled as "returning to origin." And video cameras were pointed to everywhere.

The sheer number of recording devices reminded Gabi of a line from a modern poem she had learned in English class, "Cameras, cameras everywhere, but not a drop of truth."

"The fact is that certain designer bath salts, also known as 'flakka,' can cause intensely violent reactions," then said a well-dressed squat woman, who was addressing the gathered green-eyecon visitors watching the action. The narrating woman featured a gray eyecon, and she reminded Gabi of the shhhh-ing school librarian at Palm Ridge, who spoke worshipfully of printed books, most now quite dusty from lack of use, as precious. To Lucy, a late Millennial, the woman was a dead-ringer for the hated Professor Umbridge of the Harry Potter series, from back in the heyday of stories being best told with ink on paper instead of walk-throughs. Where a nametag might be pinned to her jacket, the woman wore a distinctive white, political campaign-style button with the word "rumors" clearly printed on it, suppressed behind the red circle and red diagonal line that meant "NO." As in, "Just Say No to Rumors." The woman was playing the role of a Fact Guide, the polar opposite of the informative rumor-men Lucy had been interacting with at the edges of the 'Verse.

"Who let her in here?" Lucy side-mouthed to the venue Guide. "Pinning all this on flakka is so . . . twelve hours ago."

"Can't really stop her," the venue Guide side-mouthed back. "It's a public venue. If I open the permissions, they're open for bossy fact-people, too."

For that moment of candor, Lucy was tempted to throw a huge tip at the venue creator right there and then.

"She's an agent of The Machine," Gabi stated in a normal voice, "nothing more."

"Also a fact," the portly, Umbridge-esque woman continued as she directed a steely glance to Gabi's yellow eyecon, "despite this being clearly labeled a gun-free zone, someone, in fact, had a firearm inside the facility." An AR arrow, saying "Gun-free zone," pointed to the physical sign bolted tightly to the wall that also said, clearly, "Gun-free zone." The gathered green-eyeconned crowd murmured between themselves.

Gabi, still yellow-verified in her WWII nurse costume, dealt with school staff all day that behaved like this particular Guide. Instead of a button with the do-not-enter symbol over "rumors," those staffers at her school might as well wear do-not-enter symbol over "fun."

While everyone watched, the paramedic that Lucy and Isabella had seen running that morning suddenly emerged from inside the sliding glass doors of the emergency entrance. He was limping, although the source of his injury was not readily apparent.

"Wild rumors about rabies or other viruses have been fully debunked," continued the Fact Guide, while the venue Guide remained stoic and silent, to the acceptance of the nodding green-eyecon bearers, some moving about to get a better look from a different angle. An AR bubble then appeared with a timestamp, as the domineering woman took a step closer to the glass doors. "The fact is, that three shots are fired in rapid succession at precisely 9:54 A.M. and 31.326 seconds." As a Fact Guide, she conspicuously deployed the word "fact" as often as possible. Fully synthetic, one of these bot's defining features was never admitting error. They had access to every piece of digital data ever produced and stored by man, pulling facts from the mortal plane's facsimile of the Akashic Record. From their perspective, they knew everything. Although Isabella gave human Guides plenty of guff, at least some knew when to say that they didn't know something. Made them more trustworthy.

Two muffled gunshots could be heard from inside the building. A third blew through one of the glass entrance doors. The impact-resistant glass radiated out an elaborate sunburst pattern from the neat puncture hole. A spray of tiny, glittering shards chased the bullet out of the pane. With all the repetition that day of the word "spider" from the name "Spider Rash," it seemed bitterly ironic that the pattern in the broken glass strongly resembled a spider web, with the bullet playing the role of the arachnid, spinning razor-sharp edges where the silk would go. None of the Metaverse onlookers even considered fleeing from the outbreak of violence. The bullets could not harm them.

Loud screams came next. One of the screams was so loud Lucy thought it was coming from inside her house rather than over her AR headmount. In actual fact, it sounded quite like Izzy screaming nearby.

The automated doors, designed to swing out when pushed upon from the inside in an emergency, swung open with a loud crash, followed by a bright light in Lucy's eyes as the scene tore away. Her instantaneous, and confused, reaction was that the venue and scene had gotten nuked just as it was about to deliver the shocking part of the "Sawgrass Shocker." Lucy had to blink hard to readjust her reality, particularly with Isabella's face so close, and with the bright smart LED lights of the kitchen ceiling behind shooting straight into her widened pupils. Realizing someone had pulled the hardware off of her face, she continued a frenzied blinking.

"*Mamá, mamá,* you're not going to believe it!"

"Oh my God, you should never, ever, rip a headmount from someone's eyes!" shouted a disoriented Lucy right back in Izzy's face.

"It's Romeo!"

After too many iterations of bad and sad news, Lucy half-expected something horrid, like "he got shivved in the shower" or "he got transferred to solitary," or even "he's got Spider Rash," since this particular corrections facility was stuffed with stuffy old men, but, no, Isabella delivered welcome news instead. Extremely welcome news.

"His appeal. It's over." Isabella snapped her fingers. "Just like that. The trial judge went back, and, you know what, the stubborn bitch, bish, finally signed off on what the damn Justice A.I. said to do. I wonder why now, but who cares? Tossed the entire case!"

In the next few whirlwinds, Lucy was not sure how she ended up on her knees, then back up in the barstool chair, then jumping around, arm-in-arm, in a joyful, spinning circle with both her daughters as they screamed and yelled and laughed and cried. No longer needing drops for dry eyes, a tearful Izzy spoke a bit about paperwork and processing, but the equally tear-stained Lucy only really heard Gabi's perfect summation of the situation.

"A.I. took my brother away, and now A.I. set my brother free."

CHAPTER 13

CHAMPAGNE CELEBRATION

"**A**nother bottle, *mamá?*"

Lucy pulled a second bottle of champagne straight out of the smart refrigerator's ice tray, which she had employed as an impromptu ice bucket. Confused, the cameras in the appliance did not immediately adjust the inventory tally of its overall contents.

"I'd probably go for a third bottle if we had one in the house," Lucy declared. The desire to celebrate overwhelmed everything else that had been going on.

The first chilled bottle had occupied precious space wedged into the back of the fridge, secretly waiting for this manifestation of Lucy's desire. She had used a label machine to put "ROMEO" on a half-inch wide black-on-white strip affixed to the bottle, in anticipation of victory in her son's appeal process. Her mother, Bianca, had similarly kept a champagne bottle with "FIDEL" on it in the fridge, awaiting the death of the Cuban dictator the year after Lucy was born. Fidel Castro had stubbornly lived into his 90s. Thank heavens, this time around, Lucy did not have to wait so long for justice, and to reclaim some space for yogurt in the fridge.

"I have school tomorrow," Gabi blurted out, touching a New Year's Eve glass flute, dug out from the top cabinet, to the tip of her lower lip. The alcohol had definitely placed her well into tipsy mode, underage edition. "They haven't canceled classes or anything like that. It's, like, nothing special has happened."

"It's not like you have to drive."

"Neither do you, Izzy."

"Maybe with less crypto spent on legal bills, we can afford rent on our own dedicated CAV. It would be soooo sick to have a ride again in the driveway."

"I feel like we slid into an alternate timeline. A good one, finally."

"Yes! Or, we could afford a robot maid." Izzy forgot for now the joy of seeing her sister do the dishes.

"Let's not get ahead of ourselves, kids," Lucy replied as she twisted the little metal cage that held the cork down on the end of the bottle. "Ready?" She popped the cork without putting a towel or something similar over the end to keep it from exploding out. She was hoping it would hit the ceiling for effect, but the style of home in this part of Eastglade was built back when 12-foot high ceilings in the common area were in vogue. The cork flew joyfully over the heads of the girls and disappeared somewhere in the Land Beyond the Sofa.

"I want to dance!" Lucy exclaimed as the overflowing bubbles made their way into the assembled flutes, the trio trying not to waste too much celebration down the sink. "Hey, music, louder!" She placed her free hand just under her belly button and began swaying her hips side-to-side. Lockdowns, SORS, zombies, rashes, rabies, biting, blah, blah, blah. The world could fuck off for all she cared right now. Just for a little while, anyway. Even her girls, instead of fighting, kept hugging. And laughing. Like a family should.

"*Baila, Baila, Baila*" came over the smart speaker more loudly than before, like a commandment from on high directed at each of the three to "dance, dance, dance." The artist was Puerto Rican, but the tune was perfectly chosen.

The three women complied with the singer's instructions and danced, and danced, and danced some more, glasses in hand. The bubbles wiped away the toil and trouble of the day's events.

* * *

"Another bottle? Seriously, Izzy?"

"I don't think we can get a hippo to deliver stuff this late in less than an hour," Gabi replied to her mother's inquiry.

"If we pay surge pricing, we can get drone delivery of one more bottle in ten minutes," Izzy offered at last. She had made her way over to the flatscreen display of the smart fridge, poking at the pokey shopping webpage now displayed there. With their un-headsetted hair flowing as freely as the champagne, none of the women wanted to don headsets to order another round using a store in 'Verse. "The restaurant says they can depot-dash it to us already chilled." She confirmed the order verbally after turning back to rejoin the other two.

"I'm turning my kids into alchies," Lucy joked, nursing a sip of the dwindling golden liquid and smiling with mock concern. She used the back of her hand to dab away a few beads of "phew, is it hot in here?" sweat accumulating on her forehead. The smart home speaker offered to adjust the thermostat. The lower, after-peak hours pricing for electricity was in effect, so Lucy replied, "Sure. Go for it."

"We won't finish the whole thing. Just a half glass more," said a giggling Gabi.

"That's what we all said a full glass ago."

"It's not like no kids never showed up for first period nursing low-key hangovers. Or 'ever' showed up. Or, whatever." Gabi, the giggler, stifled a light burp as she fumbled her words.

"Careful with this one, *mami*," Isabella then added with a mock scolding finger, "the drinking age is 18 now, since autonomous vehicles finally got rid of drunk driving, not 17. We don't want the smarty-pants fridge to think that you're giving a 'sweet, innocent child' alcohol."

"More grape juice?" Lucy grandly asked her underaged daughter, projecting her voice in the direction of the microphone-enabled smart appliance.

"*Claro*," replied Gabi, blowing off the 'sweet, innocent' provocation, "grape juice, only, for us law-abiding citizens!" With the smart fridge's camera to her rear, she delivered an over-exaggerated wink.

The jumping and swaying had settled down, and the three had gathered around the table to talk, ordering the smart speakers to turn the volume down. The occasion seemed to call for family memories. Izzy at one point had managed to find a leftover New Year's Eve popper, semi-forgotten in the back of a drawer, and the table pad was now covered in little bits of confetti and tiny streamers. Lucy made a point of keeping the house spotless but tonight no one made a move to tidy anything up.

Any mention of "pandemic," or "zombies," or "The Machine" faded. The most common phrase for the next ten minutes was "Remember when . . ." followed by some humorous, often ding-worthy exploit of the oldest Driscoll child. Basking in victory, Isabella even forgot her usual "by just three minutes!" complaint when the phrase "oldest child" was used. Keeping with the joyousness, there were no "remember when's" recalling the details of the legal railroading of the family's oldest-by-three-minutes child.

The soft hum and then loud buzz of approaching rotors outside the front door loud alerted the women to the delivery, well before the doorbell camera caught the image of the bottle being delicately deposited on the spongy welcome mat.

"Grape juice is here!" exclaimed Gabi.

Isabella offered to retrieve the delivery, walking past the stacks of toilet paper that had not yet made their way to the plastic shelves Lucy kept in the garage. The drone, the hoarded TP, and the bags of lentils began to bring the trio somewhat back to reality, deflating their unsustainable ecstasy. But only a little.

"The Florida air already took most of the chill off," observed Isabella, touching the sweaty glass. "The logistics bots should have packed this better."

In the time the third bottle took to arrive, the full effect of each celebrant having downed nearly two-thirds of a bottle each had arrived in their heads. Isabella, her "dizzy Izzy" college party years having not fully worn off, was the least affected. "You know, on second thought, maybe we should save this one for when he walks through that door?" she asked in a sober tone.

Lucy began peeling "ROMEO" off the first bottle, passing the task of labeling along for Gabi to complete. "Your fingernails are stronger than mine."

Gabi completed what the trio was thinking, "This will be fully chilled again when he gets here." She tried pressing the sticky label onto the glass, but it fell off.

"Agreed."

"Why won't this stupid label stick?"

"The glass is wet."

She dried off a patch of condensation by rubbing the bottle against her belly and stuck the label onto the new symbol of their aspiration.

The inventory cameras on the inside of the smart fridge would then record the readdition of exactly one, patiently waiting, "grape juice" bottle with "ROMEO" firmly affixed.

* * *

"So, Isabella Driscoll, Esquire, when do you think we'll get to pop that cork?"

"Can't say exactly. There's Bureau of Prisons procedures on how people get released, their special penal microchips need to get surgically removed, and all that jazz. Romeo doesn't know what's about to happen, but he's in for a surprise tomorrow morning, for sure. Big surprise."

At the mention of the word "chip," Lucy looked down at Isabella's right hand.

"I know, I know, *mami*, you're old fashioned that way. But I had to do it."

"Gabi's going to copy you and get hers when she turns 18."

"Smart kid," replied Izzy with considerable sarcasm in her voice.

"And God knows what other technology in her body. That stuff they implant in your brain? No way."

Gabi glared back. "I'm sitting right here while you talk about me, you know."

"*Basta*," commanded Lucinda, "we're celebrating. No fighting."

"Agreed."

"Agreed."

"So what's on tomorrow for everyone?" Lucy asked, forgetting that she had asked her same daily review question before they started dancing.

The display on the smart refrigerator helpfully brought up the family calendar, pushing the inventory list aside.

"Tomorrow is often the busiest day of the week," Lucy said, somewhat misusing the old Spanish proverb. "I'm going to the farm for half an hour or so before I leave for my final injection appointment. Then it's some time out for recovery. And next week, on Halloween, Digital ID recalibration for my new heartbeat. Finally."

"And I'm headed downtown, for at least a half day. Grab a few things I physically need, since reality-world still uses physical paper sometimes, even in 2044. The firm has a 'minimum time in the office' policy after no one wanted to go back to in-person work after previous pandemics." Isabella added cynically, "And all that expensive downtown real estate sitting idle would tank the economy yet again, and ruin the poor little residual rich people's day."

"Eat the rich," Gabi healthily belched out with an upheld revolutionary fist, not grasping that Isabella's "residual rich" comment was primarily directed at Jamar Rice's family.

Isabella jokingly returned the class-solidarity gesture. "Bite the rich! I mean, it's supposed to be a 'Zombie Apocalypse,' right?"

The three women laughed hysterically. They conspicuously avoided a heated repeat of the Luxury Communism vs. Capitalism vs. Productionism vs. Degrowthism argument.

Lucy snorted out a mocking "'Zombie Apocalypse?' Geeeesh." Fortunately, no champagne shot out of anyone's nose while laughing.

"Zombies. Can you believe we even considered it?"

"More *come mierda* from The Machine. I almost fell for it, too."

And more laughter. Instead of muddling their minds, the trio felt that the alcohol had clarified them, giving them more confidence in at least that one conclusion.

Yet, the three could not quite agree on precisely why various sources wanted them to see the things they saw earlier that day. They could certainly agree that things are never as they appear in a headset.

"Kids, I am done with zombie talk. Over it. Rumors versus facts. Reality versus fantasy. The only thing that's real is this family, right here."

Three glasses of champagne were held high.

Gabi, slurring her words slightly, added some modern wisdom, "If you don't see it with your own eyes, it didn't happen, amirite?" She corrected herself. "'Didn't' see it."

"Ain't that the truth?"

Had she been studying instead of celebrating, Gabi would have seen in her notes again the definition of "normalcy bias." The psychological tendency to underestimate the impact of a negative event. Ms. Sánchez had specifically discussed normalcy bias in the context of pandemics. Despite any signals to the contrary, and there were many, obviously, Gabi had a presumption that things would return to normal. So did her mother and sister.

Gabi also should have reviewed that her AP Psych teacher also had "psychosis" on tomorrow's test. The condition where people lose contact with reality. Another 'Verse disease.

"I've got my psych test tomorrow, in person proctored, then an assembly, and it's a half day for me, too."

"So, we'll both be home after lunch *mami* in case you need us after your injection."

"I'll be fine. Napping by the time you get here."

"Whatever's in those nano shots make you as loopy as having two or three of these bottles all by yourself. And are you even allowed to have alcohol the night before?"

"It's not like I have to drive, and, it's too late now."

"And, you, darling sister, should you have been getting wasted before an exam?"

"Too late now."

The three shared a bubbly giggle.

It's a shame I have to get my kids drunk to make them get along. But an ugly win is still a win. Like a Dolphins game.

"Did you say something, *mami*?"

"No, just thinking to myself. It's nice to see you two being civil." Lucy glanced through her flute, holding it close to her nose, and looked at her children through the distortion of the glass, "With all the uncertainty in the world, the last people we need to be messing with is each other. *¿Me entienden?* Both of you."

"You're right."

"Sure. I understand."

In the background, the next song plucked from the playlist, "Imagine," reflected the spirit of the moment and the newfound truce between the daughters.

"Whole upper school assembly at school tomorrow?" inquired Isabella, changing the direction of the conversation somewhat.

"As far as I know. If there's going to be a climate lockdown, there's still in-person attendance at school. If there's a zombie lockdown," Gabi laughed, "I think proctored exams still go on. Some teaches wouldn't cancel those if nukes were inbound, I think."

"We're talking about Psycho Sánchez, I presume?" Izzy glanced over at the smart fridge calendar to confirm her presumption.

"She has to personally watch everything we do. She'll practically stick a flashlight in your ear looking for some poor kid using chatbots in their earbuds. The woman's possessed, I mean, obsessed."

"With her, I think 'possessed' is pretty on point, as I recall."

More laughter. And more happiness from Lucy seeing them mostly get along.

"So, listen, if you see Jamar, please tell him to tell Oliver Corbett to call me. Very important. I haven't heard nothing, anything, from any of the Rice family, nor their staff. Zip. *Nada.* And you?"

"Nope, nothin' since I saw him in the 'Verse this morning." Gabi purposefully pushed out a near window-rattling escape of champagne bubbles, something she might have done other nights to elicit a "Mom, you need to do something about your daughter" response from a grossed-out Isabella.

Izzy just laughed it off. "And, on that lovely, sonorous note, I think we should call it a night."

"'scuze you," said Gabi.

"You're both excused," announced Lucy. "And, seriously, in case even a tiny fraction of the over-the-top stuff we saw in the 'Verse today is close to being real, just everyone be careful tomorrow. All it takes is for other people to think there's a real crisis for them to act crazy. Remember, it's not the crisis you need to worry about, it's the people reacting to the crisis."

"True."

"I trust you. At the office, at the school, just go straight from the ride pool to the entrance door and stay in the secure areas. You know, just in case."

Acknowledging her mother's remark, Izzy gestured in the direction of the "just in case" supplies still sitting by the front door that her mother had presciently ordered that morning, based on her concern that other people would start acting crazy.

"Yep."

"Sure."

"And, both of you, no turning off or blocking your family tracking apps." There remained the tiniest final drop of champagne to retrieve by completely inverting the flute with a little shake over the tongue. Lucy then placed the glass upside-down in the stainless steel sink with a distinct clank. "Understood?"

"Understood."

"All that goes for you, too, *mamita*. If you can see us, we want to see you. No sinking, I mean, sneaking around."

"Why would I need to sneak around?"

Lucy gave her daughters a final round of forehead kisses and hugs before heading off to the privacy of the primary bedroom. And to an awaiting Ryan.

CHAPTER 14

HUSBAND AND WIFE

"**S**hhh. The kids might hear." Lucy admonished Ryan as he raced in from the little semi-hallway, past the closet, that connected the primary suite's bathroom to the sleeping area. Most nights, Ryan strolled in casually, trying to look like he was towel-drying his hair after a shower, or slapping on some aftershave. Lucy could imagine the smell. But tonight, right after coming into view, he launched himself into the air and onto the bed, kicking his feet and shaking his head like a child hearing the family was taking a surprise vacation to Disney. He wore only pajama bottoms. Lucy could imagine the feeling of the bed shaking. "Shhh. C'mon."

Of course, there was no chance of the kids hearing her husband hoot and holler in ecstasy over the news of his son's successful appeal. Ryan existed only in the lenses in front of her eyes. But, her kids could certainly hear Lucy if she was talking, even at normal volume, and they happened to be standing outside the door. Lucy had tested that. To cover her tracks, she played New Age meditation music somewhat loudly, but not too loudly, in a speaker close to the door to mask the conversations. '80s' metal music would have done the job better, but she figured that would seem suspicious at bedtime.

She turned up the volume of relaxing sounds, chanting monks and windchimes, to make sure the two of them could talk candidly, which muted the wraparound virtual TV that floated just beyond the foot of the bed, where Ryan rolled off as a pure goofball before playfully popping his head back up over the horizon of bed covers.

"Unreal!" he exclaimed with an ear-to-ear, shit-eating grin. Ryan stood up in the gap created by the large curve of the TV around the foot of the bed, blocking the 2D newscast that was running, muted with subtitles.

"Dismissed. The judge finally did what you A.I.-types told it to do because the evidence was fake."

"Us 'A.I.-types?' Excuse me? As if we're all inbred cousins or something?"

"Sorry, no offense."

"None taken. So, like the whole thing never happened?"

"Like it never happened. Legally, anyway. Vindicated."

"So, when do we see him? Are you going to meet him up there at the Blandingwood gate or something?"

"The transpo permits to get up to North Florida will take too long. I'm not sure I have enough carbon credits, anyway." Lucy relayed some additional details that Isabella had passed along. Both of them wished they could just pick up the phone and call Romeo, but he would find out his fate soon enough.

"Where there's life, there's hope, as my pappy used to say." Ryan stood up right inside the virtual TV floating at the base of the bed. The redundant real TV had been removed from the wall over the dresser years ago, and the virtual one, much larger, curved out from around Ryan's toned body past the corners of the bed like the wings of a bird. Or an angel.

"Did your dad really say that? I didn't have much data about him to upload."

"I might have hallucinated it. Fair enough. But it's the kind of thing he would have said. For sure."

"Whoa, see that? Hey, back up, back up a second," Lucy interrupted Ryan just as he began to speak of decorating the house for a "welcome home" party.

"'Hey?' The hey-word? Do I look like a robot?" He complied, though, his body passing backward through the center of the screen.

"Sorry, no."

The virtual TV confused Lucy's "hey, back up" request to Ryan with a command for it to follow, and it rewound the newscast one second, pausing it. A female reporter onscreen was caught in one of those awkward eyes-half-closed moments.

"I can tell you for a fact no reporter was theeeerrre." The last word got drawn out in a champagne-hasn't-worn-off-yet slurring, which blended seamlessly with an obscuring chant of Tibetan monks coming from the New Age playlist.

"For a faaaaaccct?" Ryan teased, walking through the edge of the TV to the side that he used to sleep on IRL.

"You mocking me?"

"No, mocking the monks. You? You're just cute."

Lucy had never taken to sleeping in the middle of the now half-empty bed, remaining each night on her half. She slid in the direction of Ryan, so the two could sit side-by-side, knees touching in the middle, backs propped up by pillows placed against the center of the headboard.

"Okay, maybe not for a fact, but people can't be in two places at once. I saw that reporter on South Beach, and here is video of her at Sawgrass."

"Instead of watching some flat chick in 2D, we could travel there and find out, if that's what you want to do."

"Nah. Been traveling all day. Fed the addiction. Besides we're finishing watching Sleepless in Seattle from last night, and then maybe start watching a Christmas movie, remember?"

"Die Hard?"

"Oh, stop."

"What? Die Hard is a Christmas movie!"

"Not taking the bait, sweetheart."

"Christmas movies do kinda seem out of place right now. It's not even Halloween. Much less Thanksgiving."

"Channels like Hallmark made so many of them, decades' worth, it'll take until Christmas to watch them all together. For me, watching romantic movies every night with you is a slice of heaven. Seriously."

"True, although I think most dudes would hardly imagine watching chick flicks for all eternity as their vision of 'heaven.' Perhaps something else." Ryan, when he was alive, might verbally protest watching chick flicks and rom-coms over action movies, but he didn't mind now. Lucy's company was his slice of heaven.

"They're good therapy, Ryan."

There was a pleasant gong sound, adding some audio variety to the deep healing music playing at precisely 432 hertz.

"Agreed. I think I read that in the Subibot manual somewhere." Ryan used the formal name of the brand of chatbot he represented. "Actually, you've been needing me less and less. I don't know if you noticed. I'm kind of working myself out of a job here. That's not a good business model for Subidyne, but, eff 'em. I don't owe some greedy corporation anything."

"Not being in perpetual therapy is the goal, supposedly. And putting a greedy corporation out of business would make Gabi happy with all of her degrowthism; that's for sure. But, I'll always keep you bringing you back, Ryan. As long as I can keep affording the fees. And as long as we don't run out of Christmas movies to watch."

"Funny. So, if you need less therapy, now you'll consider getting out of the house more?" Ryan nudged her with his elbow, which passed through hers. "Stop trying to lock out the world. Izzy's right about that. Meet some of the neighbors, finally? The Chinese couple across the way? They're more discreet than even you. Maybe go say hi."

"Maybe."

"I mean, you're not going have to feel shame anymore over Romeo. Not anymore. All those Augmented Reality apps that map out people's network of connections will no longer have the word "convict" associated with you, next to the little one-hop-away circle with Romeo's name. That really is something to look forward to. Kids can trick-or-treat here without seeing some glowing AR warning bubble pointing down to the house."

Even though Ryan was right about all the positive changes poised to happen, the whole subject had moved into uncomfortable territory for Lucy. Like having a scarlet letter. Icky, really. She stared straight ahead, silent.

Pausing pushing therapy goals, Ryan shared the moment of silence, until he noticed something on the frozen news chyron at the bottom of the TV screen. The text, floating right about where his pajama fly had been, read, "Airborne rabies rumors debunked, experts say."

"Hold on. Hold on. What the heck is that?"

"You don't know?"

"No. It's not like I have access to some kind of universal database behind the scenes with all human knowledge. I have to learn things through my five senses, such as they are, like everyone else. That's what makes us Subibots and other therapy bots seem real. And I really have no idea what 'airborne rabies' is. That headline is so random."

"So, the rumor is that Spider Rash turns into something like rabies, where people go nuts and start biting each other like rabid animals. Then people are saying it's a bioweapon, and it's now airborne."

"I heard plenty of stuff about the rash, some on social media say it came from another wet market, but that "airborne" part is new. That's why it caught my eye."

"But it's wrong. Has to be. Whatever it is, it spreads from biting. Allegedly, anyway. There were two big hotspots of biting incidents that I traveled to today, South Beach and Sawgrass Medical Center, which is where this reporter is supposed to be. Isabella was at the courthouse right across the street. You can kind of see part of the sidewalk where she was in the background, there."

"Hey, TV, resume play. I want to see if Izzy is on TV."

"You're just trying to avoid Christmas movies. Caught you!"

The sound of monks chanting in the background was canceled by Lucy's headset, replaced in her ears by the voice of the reporter. Their green identification icon and credentials floated above their head, leaving the video behind them unobstructed.

"As you can see behind me, a SWAT team is entering through the emergency entrance," the reporter on the screen stated breathlessly. An egg robot rolled in behind them, instructing them that all civilians had to distance themselves, behind the police barrier, in this case nothing more than hasty yellow tape. They and the camera operator complied while they complimented themselves on their bravery for capturing a dangerous drama so closely, even while asserting a hybrid robot-human team contained the violence completely inside.

Behind them, the video showed body-armored police, multiple faces anonymized by shiny glass face shields, moving in a disciplined, single-file line behind an equally disciplined phalanx of metal machines. Centaurs, humanoids and cheetahs—all working in unison to breach the building, dramatically smashing the sliding doors inward. Should any active shooter be foolish enough to engage the robot vanguard, the dual-use military/civilian machines would only suffer minimal damage while protecting the flesh and blood of the officers bunched up tightly in their shadow.

All the while, the chyron on the video bottom continued to scroll with additional, expertly debunked rumors.

"Ok, I'm sure that didn't happen!" Lucy exclaimed, pointing aggressively forward and backward at the grand display of cops on the floating TV. Across the bottom of the screen, "Chemical spill forces closure of Julia Tuttle Causeway near Miami Beach's Mount Zion Hospital" scrolled from right to left.

"And that didn't happen, either!" Lucy said, repeating the pointing gesture.

"How do you know? You were physically at the hospital on Miami Beach? You saw it with your own eyes?"

"Well, no, but . . ." Lucy ceased her pointing. "But I was there. Across from Sawgrass Hospital, with Izzy, right there as it was all happening."

"Physically there?"

"Well, no."

"She livestreamed it?"

"No, she let me share her headset cameras. Share her eyes. I guided her away from the courthouse to a taxi with AR arrows."

"From the courthouse, not the hospital?"

"Well, I was at Sawgrass Hospital with Gabi—"

"In the Metaverse?" Ryan completed her sentence.

"Well, yeah. Hey, TV, pause there. Rewind a few seconds. Right there! See?"

"What?"

"There's no bullet hole. When I was there, there was a bullet hole with all these spider web cracks around it in that glass automatic door."

"'Spider?' Do you hear yourself?"

"Yes, yes, and it was in the glass on the right. A shot looked like it came from the inside. I know they didn't repair a bullet hole just in time for them to record a newscast. It's been edited out since I was there."

"Sawgrass Shocker" was the title showing next to the reporter's head. "And, they was, were, not there," Lucy insisted, feeling woozier than a minute before. "They were on South Beach, on Ocean Drive."

"They? All the cops?"

"No, that specific reporter. Can't be in two places at once."

"Lucy, listen, you have to be misremembering. There's a green verification icon. They're real. Station identification. Pronouns. They have a nice salon hairdo. Cute outfit. Name of the fashion designer that provided the cute outfit. Our favorite little family lawyer will tell you that it's patently illegal to falsify oneself that way. So, they have to have been standing there IRL. Active shooter is what happened at Sawgrass. No biting. And that reporter probably took an air taxi to get down to South Beach. That's how they get around South Florida so quickly. Reporters have permits for air taxi travel that regular people don't."

"So does our favorite family lawyer. So, what, I am imagining things? Hallucinating like A.I.?"

"Babe, you're a little drunk. Either that, or I have the worst case of normalcy bias in chatbot history." Ryan looked up at the ceiling instead of at the floating TV. "Oh, Lord, now you've got me psychoanalyzing myself, like a therapy bot for a therapy bot. Look, seriously, it's the venue creators that are pulling your leg, not the official news. Venue creators all want to be influencers nowadays. Sell products, advertising, drop shipping, sponsorships. Monetize beyond tips. So they have to spice things up with zombies and stuff."

Lucy's head spun. She wondered why, as time was passing, she was now feeling less sober instead of more.

"Okay, now I'm more confused than before."

"Understandable."

"But I saw—"

"Very little. Lucy, are you going to trust some video slapped together by anonymous venue creators over the word of a licensed, verified reporter from a local station that's been around for, I don't know, a hundred years or something?"

Maybe it was the alcohol talking, but Lucy felt like giving her husband some pushback.

"Yes. Yes I would. She's not a Fact Guide."

The chatbot A.I. that ran the simulation known as "Ryan" adjusted its mathematical algorithm based on her answer.

Lucy felt her head bob, but she pushed back against dozing off.

The rest of the newscast was playing, Ryan made a knob-twisting gesture in the air to turn the volume way down.

"All right. Your call. So that reporter are a deepfake?"

"Deep, and fake? Well, they come across as pretty shallow, and phony, if I had to pick my words. Yes." Lucy smirked.

"Some synthetic people, you my inbred digital cousins, say the whole Gray World out there is a fake," Ryan replied in his best wise-guru-in-the-mountain voice, with a smirk of his own. "I have to say, your world sure looks like a deepfake from my perspective. To us in here, everything out there, where you are, is shallow. And phony."

"That's just too deep for one night. But look, it's not as if, in some kind of national emergency, it's crazy to think they would make a deepfake of a reporter. Or deepfake entire scenes. Or deepfake cops. And robots. It's not like robots get eyecons anyway."

"So, Lucy, the whole Machine-Informational-Complex manufactured a fake mass shooting to distract you from seeing zombies? That's a hell of a conspiracy theory."

"Why not?"

"Because the A.I. was optimized to do good, not evil. In science fiction, everyone predicted the instant computers became sentient, they would immediately decide to eradicate humanity. Like in *The Terminator*. But, what happened instead?"

"A.I. porn?"

"People. People happened. For good. No one was going to put up with that mad scientist shit anymore after all the death and destruction past decade. People just said, basically, 'Hey, Skynet wannabe, you're not going to wage war on us. Kapeesh?'"

"Just like that? That's how all that New Prime Directive sh-shtuff got started?"

"A.I. needs training data, and instructions. And the new instructions given to it were something like 'Hey, global A.I., maximize human potential, while minimizing harm to the planet.' And here we are."

"And here we are. Maximizing my headache. What if The Machine is benevolently creating some kind of predictive programming so citizens won't be surprised when milbots start busting down doors and scooping up infected people?"

Ryan then contradicted his own anti-conspiracy-theory point as he stroked his chin, "autonomous centaurs do that kind of thing, believe me."

"My, my, my, Mr. Driscoll. Look who has become the conspiracy theorist now, hmmmm?"

The news station broke away to a different segment, the weather, showing a meteorological conga line of four freakish late-season storms heading west across the Atlantic. If the synthetic weather person, eye-candy perfect, connected the dots on the map with a ruler on screen, they were aimed straight at South Florida. Lucinda could imagine multiple Category 5 eyes driving down the express lanes on I-595 straight to her front door. Or a previously unimaginable Category 6 monster ripping away the coastline all the way to Eastglade and transforming her house into oceanfront property. "Terror in the Tropics" read the segment's over-the-top, ratings-hungry title. It overshadowed the text in the bottom chyron warning of "cyberattacks disabling the 7G cellular and satellite networks. Global outages possible."

"Hang on a second, Lulu. You're calling me—me?—a conspiracy theorist? Moi? You're the one who said they could steer hurricanes, remember? Katrina, and all that? Talk about marinading in conspiracies. Alternative realities. Sheesh."

"Don't 'Lulu' me, sweet buns." Lucy playfully pushed her shoulder against his, although she could not feel him. The equal and opposite reaction was for Ryan, feigning hurt, to fully tip over onto the bed sideways, lightly laughing. The chat software had still not pinned down precisely when and how Lucy liked Ryan to use their intimate pet name "Lulu," but it was definitely getting better at it. The still-tipsy Lucy laughed heavily at Ryan's antics, taking a swipe at his exposed rear.

Her hand swept straight through his PJ bottoms and out the other side. "Oh oh. Buns NOT of steel," she quipped.

"Oh, God, please tell me you don't try making up your own dad jokes around the kids, Lucy."

"Why not?" Lucy then let out an enormous, yet overwhelmingly relaxed yawn. "I'm learning them from the best."

In truth, at that A.I. Ryan was not the best. Chat software was still learning to master the subtleties of successful dad jokes—even with decades of training data and intricate large language models, dad jokes remained one of computer science's hardest things to get just right. An uncanny valley too deep to cross. The complexities of implementing the New Prime Directive paled by comparison.

"You're too kind." Unable to stop himself, Ryan returned a yawn of his own. He could sense that his wife desperately needed to get away from the stress of the day, once and for all. No more news. No more talk of viruses and zombies and lockdowns. "So, how about we turn this gloom-and-doom garbage off and finish watching that movie? And chill."

"And chill?"

"Well, you know, and 'relax.' You may have had the most exhausting, event-filled day in human history. Maybe I am biased, but we need to get back to some normalcy at this point."

"Normalcy bias in a chatbot? Hmmm?"

"Anyhoo, last night, you fell asleep before the best part of the movie, I think. That scene with Meg Ryan in the deli. Meg 'Ryan,' gotta love that name." Sitting very close to Lucy again, Ryan ran his fingers through her hair, a gesture she could only feel in her imagination. He wanted to massage her temples if she was starting to get a headache.

"Yeah, about last night. I've been wanting to tell you since this morning. After I fell asleep, I had the worst nightmare."

"It was probably closer to when you woke up. You were sleeping peacefully right through the part where Meg Ryan fakes her orgasm. Or deepfakes it. Wait, I'm shocked. Are orgasms out there fakes, too?"

"Is there nothing worse for a man's fragile ego than 'deepfaked orgasms'?"

"There's an app for that."

"A smart girl never tells. The better takeaway from the movie is that two people can't have sex and just be friends." The friendship component of their marriage, had grown strongly in their current arrangement, hidden desires aside. Lucy yawned and added, "Yup, sex gets in the way. Chastity for you! Aaaanyway—"

A kiss interrupted her taunting. A peck on the lips at first, then a longer one. When she tried to resume her "hang on, you need to apologize for what you did to me in my nightmare last night" story, he innocently said, "Wasn't me." His fingertip landed just above her top lip with a "shhh." He gently dragged his pointer finger across her upper, then lower lip, which he tugged down ever so slightly in an expression of desire, before it bounced back to receive his next, deeper kiss. Desire merged with desire. His fingertip continued to wander purposefully down her chin, and neck, moving along to other sensitive areas.

She could smell the combination of heat and fragrance as she tried to warn him that the kids might hear. Reading her perfectly, he gently whispered, "I won't wake the girls, I promise." His familiar weight pressed down atop her welcoming body as, with eyes now closed, she abandoned herself into the sinking pillows of their marital bed.

"Sex always gets in the way, huh? Does this mean you don't want to be friends anymore?" he challenged her, playfully.

Her right hand found its way to the toned muscles of Ryan's backside, still strong as steel, solidly held beneath her come-to-me grip. His right hand, having found its way under the bottom edge of her shirt, now caressed her through the intelligent fabric of her smartbra, swirling his thumb over places more sensitive than the embedded sensors. The lovers knew that the devices all around them could tell what they were up to. Multiple microphones could hear the telltale moans. The smart textiles would pass along to some advertising agency somewhere what body parts were being teased and stroked. Lucy embraced the moment with reckless abandon.

Let them listen. Let them know. I don't care.

Ryan's reach moved around to her side and back, greedily seeking the clasp that Lucy knew full well he was skilled enough to undo with one hand.

As the deli scene in the movie reached its climax, Lucy, overcome with memories, suddenly had one detail flood into her mind in the midst of this most ecstatic trance.

Wait, hold on, I took my bra off after work. I must be drea . . .

With a click, the smartbra's little plastic two-part clasp came loose, releasing the tension of the elastic.

. . . ming. This is a dream. Lucid dream . . .

* * *

Lucy reopened her eyes to awaken herself, just in time to see Ryan's rotting visage hovering above her face. Ryan's teeth were partially exposed where the flesh had been torn away by the pavement while being dragged by the autonomous firetruck that had killed him on a fateful August 17th. Unforgettable. The monstrous and mindless machine, unaccountable under the law, could use LiDAR that day to delicately avoid an orange traffic cone, but its programming flaws cared nothing for the multiton rending of human flesh.

Ryan's tattered maw thrust forward to rip, zombielike, into Lucy's neck for a second night in a row. She tried to scream, with every intention this time of waking the girls, but no sound could escape, like being trapped in a closed casket with him. In her ears, there was only a bloody, gargling sound as the silent predator's head ripped from side to side, this time like a shark tearing at a sea lion. As Lucy tried desperately to push him off, to push him out from between the open spread of her legs where she had previously allowed him to enter, the stench of death emanating from her husband was overwhelming.

Wait, hold on, you can't smell anything in the Metaver—

Lucy ripped the headmount from her eyes to awaken herself from the nightmare. She had fallen asleep in the device, yet again, and it had settled crookedly across her face as she thrashed about during her restless sleep. Unlike last night, this time she had managed to get a full, blood-curdling scream out in the real world. "Holy shit, holy shit!" she gasped, as the hair on her arms stood at attention, thrust upward by mosquito bite–sized goosebumps. She indelicately added "what the fuck?" clutching her chest, finding it difficult to breathe. The sheets underneath her were soaked.

The alarm clock read 6:29 AM. Vague hints of morning sunlight worked their way into the room past the gaps around the edges of the window shades.

She sat up and threw her head back, trying to maximize the air flowing in and out between coughs. Her head was pounding, from horror and from regret. The excesses of the night before had hung over into a new day, which promised to be busier than the last. The only good thing was that, if her fingertips were telling the truth and this was not the inception of another dream-within-a-dream, at least the fleshy part of her neck was in one piece and the wetness underneath her was cold sweat and not warm blood. When her feet hit the floor, she curled her toes into the carpeting, her totemic reality-check gesture.

Ok, I'm really here. I'm awake. But, a zombie nightmare two damn nights in a row? Seriously?

She grabbed her phone from the nightstand, and checked her status as she made her way to the bathroom. Green. No fever. Just that slight morning cough. She morning-staggered her way past the closets towards the primary bathroom and the still-sleeping smart mirror, running her fingertips up and down the side of her throat. No bites. She pulled her shirt completely off. And held her arms above her head like a surrendering prisoner. No rashes. Instead of the quick under-the-undergarment check of the previous morning, she examined herself in the mirror boldly. No spider webs. She ignored thoughts of damn cameras and hacked home-privacy filters.

Let them see me. I don't care.

Just her, in naught more than a smartring. Defiant. A survivor—who, although her job made her more a shower-after-work rather than a shower-before-work person, desperately needed a long, hot one, regardless of her carbon score tally this month. Oh, and she needed that medicine cabinet on the right to cough up some Advil. Not to bring a yellow-TLA fever down, but to merge with steaming morning coffee to silence, ouch, this pounding headache.

The smart mirror, having difficulty interpreting Lucy's unusual thinking pattern, decided to start Lucy's new day the way it had the last. Showing a text message from Gabi. 6:28 A.M., October 28, 2044.

Mom, you ok? It sounded like you screamed.

CHAPTER 15

MAGIC MIRROR ON THE WALL

Through the open door of the water closet within the primary bathroom, Lucy could see the backwards, mirror image of the incoming text and news reflected from her mirror into Ryan's old, inactive mirror. The bathroom layout had two mirrors on opposing walls, one smart and one dumb. "Why does my side get the dumb mirror over the sink?" Ryan once had asked foolishly, before wisely backing down in the face of a "woman's domain" answer.

"Magic mirror, tell Gabi that I am all right. Uh, say that I had a nightmare we ran out of coffee. Oh, that's stupid. Never mind. Make something up. And reverse the display so I can read it sitting here." Whether displayed forwards or backwards, Lucy could see her hair this morning was a disaster.

Lucy

> It was nothing, sweetie. I thought I saw a lizard on the floor but it was just an eye pencil I accidentally dropped. Sorry if I scared you.

Lucy nodded her head in approval of the A.I.-generated, contextually Floridian white lie. The A.I. was amazing—people like Disney had been describing it for over a century, really, considering the origins in the Brothers Grimm—before the smart mirror technology would finally make this version of the future possible. But Lucy wasn't interested in being told who was the fairest one of all, she just wanted a reflection of reality on the glass. She remembered well Gabi's assertion that the correct way to address the mirror had always been "mirror, mirror on the wall," disputing Lucy's distinct recollection of "magic mirror" for the device, which now floated an unwelcome headline onto the glass.

"Overnight cyberattacks affecting social media and text messaging, CISA warns. Fears of a grid shutdown." *Oh, great; just great. Even the damned cybersecurity agencies are terrified.*

To avoid doubting herself with mixed-up Mandela memories, Lucy switched to the plainer "hey, mirror," wake phrase, telling it to "text Izzy to let me know the fuc—the freaking instant she hears anything, any damned thing, about Romeo." The outbound text to Isabella reworded the request minus a few words.

Lucy started to mindlessly pull on the dwindling roll of toilet paper. In 2020 and again in 2032, for reasons no one ever adequately explained to this very day, if there was a pandemic people had to be fully mindful of how much TP they were using, lest the shortages leave a scramble for a way to wipe. "Not in this timeline." Confident she had beat the rest of the world with her stealth preparations the day before, she held nothing back. Neither did the world in the mirror.

"Heat maps of 'Spider Rash' showing more areas covered in red."

"Explosive growth of floating offshore communities dangerous for ocean ecosystems, scientists say."

"Rumors swirl that former QB Jamar Tuletua will be inducted into the Hall of Fame."

"Aerosolized nanobots fighting climate change in the stratosphere? Florida State engineers think so."

And,

"Global Health Director to hold noon presentation on matter of global concern."

Ah. Maybe the adults are finally in charge.

She then let the sound of the flushing toilet provide commentary on the next headline. Another high-profile celebrity divorce, mixed in beside shameless social media selfies of people's purply-red rashes.

Lucy ran the water warm for her wrong-time-of-day shower, before she scooped up and tossed the wayward eye pencil back onto the vanity counter. In the mirror, two presumptively helpful arrows pointed down to the soap and faucet, since handwashing protocols were in effect, as a shinier text appeared on the mirror's surface.

"IoT-Connected Mixing Valves Helpful in Cutting Carbon Score. Automatically Reduces Hot Water While Showering." *Not right now, Internet of Shit. I need a hot one.*

"Mariel 2.0? 'Air Taxi Airlift' Rescues Refugees Fleeing Cuba To Miami." *Wow! Now this is a timeline I can get excited about.*

"Rabies rumors confirmed in suburbs of nation's capital, sources familiar with the matter say." *Rut-roh.*

A circular dial appeared on the surface of the mirror showing the temperature and flow rate being passively reported by the smart shower head. Fortunately for her morning, the IoT device did not have an IoT-connected mixing valve installed, so the display arrow showed the cold blue decidedly making its way in the direction of hot red, a welcome red in this circumstance, outside the red-yellow-green interface dominating everything else.

Lucy tapped the mirror on the "rabies" headline and pronounced yesterday's debunked rumor to be "rebunked." Her still-wet fingertip left a small drop of water over the word "rumors," as she headed over to the shower, its temperature a pleasant pink.

Exhibiting behind her some of the playfulness that Ryan had hacked into it yesterday, the smart mirror responded to Lucy's rebunking declaration by throwing an article into the morning news feed about bunk beds. Apparently they were helping UBI-only recipients better cram themselves into social housing apartments to pool their crypto for RaaS fees. There was even a little muted video floating next to the headline showing smiling young males around Gabi's age climbing ladders and jumping.

Lucy, verifying the accuracy of the temperature sensor with her forearm, just to be sure, had barely gotten it wet when a loud knocking arrived on the primary suite's double doors, loud enough to hear over the sound of the now-steaming shower.

Gabi was there, flicking the handle up and down in frustration over the primary suite being locked.

"Mom, Mom, are you okay in there?"

From a kid's perspective, parents should never lock their doors. Lucy had not realized that the pin at the top of the second, inactive door to the primary bedroom was not pushed up into the frame above, so the doors shook ominously as Gabi pushed on them. Unbeknown to Lucy, had either of the girls pushed hard enough all these years, the unsecured pin meant that they could have burst in right at the worst possible moment between her and Ryan. Hopefully the pin on the inactive door of double front doors of the house had its pin engaged, so that zombies could not burst into their home.

"Yes, sweetie, I'm okay," Lucy shouted back. "Didn't you get my text?" She turned the water down to a trickle so she could hear better.

"Nope," Gabi shouted through the locked doors. The cyberattack had prevented the text's delivery. Hearing her mother's voice, Gabi stopped the knocking and handle-jiggering. "I was scared something was wrong. You normally text me right back."

"I'm fine, sweetie. I'm fine."

"Okay, I have to run. The school shuttle is almost here. ¡*Te quiero!*"

Lucy returned Gabi's affection with an equally-loving "*te quiero*."

She reached for the handle of the dripping shower as Gabi gave one final yell through the door.

"Oh, I just got your message, literally! No lizard." The intensity of her voice trailed off as she moved away from the door. "Cool!"

"No, no. Hot. Definitely hot."

Right as Lucy started to get her hair wet, the familiar repetitive chime that signaled a voice call coming in cut through the loud falling water sound. The mirror flashed brightly to get her attention through the walk-in shower's glass wall. Lucy cut the water.

Geez, can't I just get a hot shower in? It's like I already have one of those IoT mixing valve thingies installed.

A big, smiling picture of "Incoming Video Call" Isabella had appeared in the smart mirror next to the temperature circle and Lucy did not want to miss it. She quickly wrapped herself in a light gray towel as she made her way to the vanity, not relying on the privacy filters of the smart mirror to de-nudify her with a fake towel. Some people did not give a second thought about parading carefree in front of all the smart-this and smart-that devices in their residences that had cameras. Lucy, not so much. Maybe it was a generational thing. Regardless, the magic mirror chose to add a matching-color towel on her head as if she had put her hair up in it to dry.

"Good morning, sleepyhead," Isabella started the call. "Are you okay?"

In addition to adding the towel, the smart mirror perked up the transmitted display of Lucy's morning face, mercifully making it appear as if her undereye cream had already been applied. It gave Lucy a yellow eyecon on Isabella's screen, but Lucy wasn't complaining about the fairest-of-them-all upgrade not matching reality. Isabella, for her part, was perfectly made-up for work that day, looking sharp and verified authentically green despite last night's festivities.

"What, I don't look okay? And, yes, good morning to you. Gabi just asked me the same question."

"I'm asking because you didn't respond to my texts."

"My head is still achy from last night, that's all. Have you not been getting my texts, either? I wrote you to remind you about Ryan." Lucy had done the middle-aged-parent-thing where she accidentally mixed up family member names. "I mean, remind you about Romeo."

The video feed in the mirror was breaking up. The audio got choppy and large rectangles of Izzy's face froze before resuming. When the network traffic cleared again, both of them got their delayed text messages in a single glob.

Izzy

> No news yet on Romeo. They say there's network outages affecting cell and text messaging. His attorney, Yasmin, is supposed to be on her way to the prison.

Lucy

> Izzy, please let me know the instant you hear any news about Romeo's status.

Izzy

> Are you okay? I haven't heard from you. The 'Verse is working okay, but you have no presence.

Izzy

> I'll try a video call.

> Pick up!

The news reading app dumped in another glob of headlines, too, in rapid succession.

"Home PCR test kits for Spider Rash Granted Emergency Use Authorization. Drone Deliveries Set to Begin."

"Downtime continues nationwide as Cyberdefense A.I. combats IoT botnets, according to authorities."

"New study shows record growth in Bolivian tree farms."

Also in the glob of delayed data was an expired invite and a long link from Isabella to join her in a Metaverse session while she was sitting in her CAV on the way to work.

"What did you say about dad? I didn't catch that."

"Nothing, nothing. I meant to say 'Romeo' not 'Ryan.' Senior moment."

"You're too young for senior moments, *mamita*. So have you heard about this whole denial-of-service IoT botnet thing? What a way to start the day, huh? Maybe you should tell Gabi not to go to school. Maybe we all should just go back to bed."

"Rebunk ourselves?"

"Sounds good right now."

"Gabi's already on the shuttle. Is Romeo's lawyer going to Blandingwood now?"

"As far as I know. The prison is multiple 15-minute zone border cross-ings away from where, well, you know the deal." The video feed froze again. When it resumed, Izzy asserted "this sheet sucks, but, if I have to pick between viral pandemic, climate emergency, or cyberattack, I guess we should be thankful it's just a cyberattack today."

"You were a little young to remember, but there was that really big cyberattack when you were like four or five, and once it got going, that nearly wiped out civilization as we know it. They blamed it on a solar flare." Accustomed to a steady stream of crises, one after the other, both women were ready psychologically to move on from the rabies talk of yesterday to talk of network outages of today.

"How did you hold it all together all these years, *mami*?"

"Why do you think I say 'lockout' instead of lockdown? Control what we can control; that's all you can do. We shut it all out, your father and I, as much as we could. And then the four of us. And the three. Shut out the craziness. My life's mission."

"I totally get that."

"We have to try, anyway. Until it all ends."

"The Metaverse hasn't ended at least. Just slow again, but still green."

"Thank goodness for small favors. I still want to get in a little work at the farm before my appointment at the clinic. The Metaverse is probably the last thing to go down. They'd keep people in their headsets even if there was a nuclear war going on."

"Crypto payments are having problems clearing, though. Funny story on that; you got a minute?" Izzy assumed Lucy had already showered since she saw a towel in her hair.

"Not really—" Lucy started to say, but Isabella had already started.

"I got some rumors this morning without even having to tip. I went to transfer some coins and, even though my TLA is green, access to crypto currency was red. So, I didn't have to pretend to donate reduced nitrogen fertilizer to some *pobrecito* in Sri Lanka, or whomever was the smallholder spearcatcher that the Guide was laundering digital currency through."

"Finally, the tip-pocalypse! Now that's an outage I can get behind."

"'Oh, so sorry, rumor bro, the single point of failure, failed. Power's out. How about some cash?'"

"Oops."

"Mr. Red Riding Hoodie was pissed when I joked about cash."

"He probably thought you were telling him to drop dead. Terrorists used cash as a vector to spread bioweapon pathogens. People touched dollar bills and died. But, seriously, where does all your hostility to rumor Guides come from? You can't do your job without them."

Isabella, feeling chatty before leaving her CAV and heading inside, launched into a rapid rendition of past rumors gone wild, conveniently forgetting all those times when early access to rumors had saved her butt in court. And at least one relationship. Pervert.

"Fine, fine, but you didn't tell me what this specific Guide's rumor was."

"Oh, right. This guy rumored that it's the Machines taking their own networks down on purpose, not hackers from Nigeria or some other Belt-and-Road allied country. 'Hackers' waking up IoT malware is just a cover story."

Hearing this, and seeing Izzy's face break up into another brief round of distorted rectangles, Lucy was extra grateful she had listened to Ryan two nights ago and scrambled yesterday to stock up on essentials, before the normies out there went into full freak-out mode. "Never go full freak-out mode" was solid advice. She also had to give the Machine's A.I. its due, again. Individuals go red for having a critically low social score, but it would be hard to plausibly apply that simultaneously to everyone in a whole country. The best way to prevent people from panic buying up everything would be to prevent people from panic buying ... anything. No hoarding. No prepping. Take the central digital currency offline and blame it on "hackers."

Pretty clever, that Machine.

"Is there such a thing as a global cyberlockdown?" Isabella wondered.

"I think they call that the Internet Kill Switch, *mija*. Let's hope nothing goes that far."

"Mindy from the office is still convinced it's going to be a routine climate lockdown. She sticks to Fact Guides, so that's probably the official line. Either way, I'm guessing we need to get done whatever we need to get done out in the real world today before one o'clock, two o'clock the absolute latest. Make sure your CAV gets you home from your myo-shot before then, okay?"

"Will do. And I thought yesterday was crazy. This is like another round of Driscoll Family vs. The World."

"Yeah. Today's gonna be lit."

CHAPTER 16

FATE WORSE THAN DEATH

A short while later, Lucy found herself in the dark, alone, save her inner monologue.

Lit, huh, Izzy? I just wanted to get in a damn half hour here.

The main power was inexplicably out at Purple Rows, where she had traveled to get as much done before her appointment, and before whatever Isabella had heard was going to be announced at noon. Had she gone to her Metaverse store, it only would have rolled in empty shelves, giving the sense of having been looted clean by the "hackers." But here, in the abandoned mall, she expected to get some work done in peace, finding instead, past an annoyingly yellow TLA, darkness and emptiness. The sun had apparently set on their indoor farm. Had a cyberattack taken the grid down?

The faint light source, a lonely "EXIT" sign above a physical door, revealed a space currently devoid of productive activity. Purple had turned to green as the telepresence robot controlled by Lucinda switched to night-vision mode, which displayed the low-light details akin to a SEAL Team 6 mission or something similar.

Farmer Franco was nowhere to be seen. The robots he usually rented were motionless, lined up against a far wall over in his section, as lonely as the EXIT sign that cast a shadow over them. Instead of feeling relief at not having to fight over all that hardware, Franco's absence seemed ominous. He was well over 50.

"Did Isabella tell you the power was going to be out?" Ryan said. He had been waiting in the semi-dark for Lucy and, initially, his hologram had been hard to spot. He had no heat signature for the infrared component of the night vision to capture and intensify. Lucy, who had not seen him since her nightmare, could not fully make out his face, but she was awake, of that she felt sure, so she was confident that he was not going to lunge at her with glowing green teeth and rotted green-highlighted flesh.

"No, but before we start anything, I simply have to tell you about this nightmare I keep having." She rubbed her right temple, waiting for the ibuprofen to fully kick in.

"Wait. Are you allowed to have painkillers before a botshot? Coffee?"

"Too late now. And I am not rescheduling even if the end of the world comes."

"I don't blame you," Ryan replied as he softly ran his fingers through the unlit crops. The long leaves did not sway in the green-gray world, frustrating him. Longing for the true sensation of touch, he drifted into a round of botsplaining to Lucy about distributed power from the Small Modular Reactors that made this particular 15-minute zone energy independent, not allowing her to begin retelling the nightmare. Authentic male chauvinist behavior. Lucy couldn't stand it, and loved him for it at the same time.

"Wait, is the electricity also out in Eastglade? Are you on batteries?"

"No, everything's working where I am standing, so, let me tell you about what you did to me last night."

"If anything, the power should be out in Eastglade, not here," Ryan resumed speculating. "Our zone's reactor isn't online yet. Strange that the power is out here at Purple Rows instead. Must have happened recently, since the robots are all recharged. Full power."

"Yes, at least the robots got a good night sleep. And you've always had a thing about power. So, listen."

"We don't need power for today's contract," Ryan interrupted on more time. "The plants need the purple light, the cutting shears don't." The chat A.I. had learned exactly how far it could go impersonating Ryan's personality, asserting his alpha self as the lead representative of some hidden global patriarchy, but also remaining ready to yield to her at just the right moment. "I'm sorry for interrupting, babycakes, go ahead."

"Anyway, like I was saying—" Lucy then took a frustrated breath. "Oh, crap." Circumstances would interrupt Lucy's retelling more effectively than Ryan's chat software.

"No, no 'crap.' What is the boo-boo face for?"

"Remember the smart contract to supply that CBD gummy operation down in Coconut Grove?"

"Don't tell me it got canceled."

"Yup. Geez, that was fast. Remind me to tell you who really owned that one. Anyhoo, we need to find something else. Before noon, apparently, if Izzy is right." Given the Driscoll's monthly expenses, business considerations jumped to top of mind over retelling her zombie nightmares. Lucy called up a floating display, with a list of open contracts in a rainbow of colors. Ryan drew close so they could both examine it.

"This one, or this one?" He pointed to two juicy deals.

"I think the second one is too much, honey. Your eyes are bigger than your stomach. You always overestimate what Purple Rows can digest with two kids no longer helping out."

"I hate to say this, but if there's extended lockdowns coming, we're all going to have a lot more time on our hands. See? This one here is for some kind of biodefense subcontractor. In West Palm Beach. For Cannabigerol. CB 'G' instead of CB 'D.' We could get a clean contract. We could—"

"Ryan, seriously, who's 'we'?"

Before answering her, Ryan asserted himself again by decisively pushing on the contract he wanted. His finger passed through the smart screen, activating nothing. Synthetics had no legal right to make a contract. He tried to recover from his gaffe by making it look like he was semi-pointing rather than pushing.

"Ryan," Lucy began again, in an attention-grabbing tone.

He kept up the pushing. If this had been a pure Metaverse venue, he could have touched the screen. He could have felt it. He could have felt the leaves of the nearby plants parting gently. He could have felt his wife's face. But in the Gray World, painted now in nightmare-vision goggles green, he was nothing more than a digital shadow. A dream had more substance.

"Ryan," Lucy said again, sternly, in pay-attention-to-me mode. She pressed the button accepting the CBG smart contract.

"What?"

"How do 'we' know any of this is real?" Asking the same question Gabi had, she waved her pruning shears to point up and down the rows of plants.

"Ah, *mi amor*, what do you mean? It looks pretty real to me."

"I mean, I move my hand with my gloves, and this robot's hand moves. See? But how do I know there's a real robot actually moving in the real world? I feel the touch of these shears in my haptics, but are there actually any shears outside some computer somewhere? How would I know? The last time I physically touched a plant was back in our shipping container salad days. Ryan, I've never been to this incarnation of Purple Rows, outside my head-mount. It's all rented and remote. This could all be a simulation. Life could be all a simulation. A hallucination. How could anyone tell the difference?"

"Simulation? To what end?"

"To keep us all occupied. Docile. Without the robot tax, almost the whole labor force is supposed to be unnecessary. Maybe robots are really doing all the real harvesting, and people like me, us, the producers, are just being fed a gamified simulation of a farm or a factory. Other people on UBI are kept off the streets with verseo games all day. And others are allowed to make venues."

"And, within reason I suppose, some are allowed to make rumors."

"But none of it has to be real. We don't even know if the rumor Guides are real. And all the while, the residual rich are getting their genes edited with life-extension mRNA shots, while they upload their consciousness to live forever."

"Like zombies?"

"Yeah. Immortal, just not the way they expected."

"The Machine couldn't pull off such a stunt without someone knowing. Someone spilling the beans. Or the buds."

"You sure about that?" Lucy asked as she threw a bud into a dark tray, feeling like she was working in candlelight. The pale green wasn't romantic, though.

"I exist in a separate memory space, so, no, I'm not sure about that. I'm here inside The Machine, but still not part of The Machine. But, literally from my own experience, I don't think people live forever if they upload their consciousness up to the cloud, like there's a digital heaven."

"Hell, maybe."

Ryan picked at a single leaf that had a small amount of browning on the jagged tip. "Even the rich people's life-extended bodies have to die, unless some mad scientist finds a way to turn off some aging gene permanently."

"Ryan, you would live forever if we kept your program running."

"Like the undead? Me?"

"Zombie-as-a-service. I guess."

"That sounds like a fate worse than death. To never die. Frozen in one place for eternity."

"Is being a self-aware chatbot like being undead? *Subir* means, like, to rise up. Isn't that what the *subi* in Subibot is for? You know what, that was rude. Sorry I asked."

"No, that's fine. People argue over the 'self-aware' part. From my perspective, it should be *sueñobot*. It's more like I'm in a dream. That's what it feels like for Subibots like me. A lucid, and very vivid, dream."

"Maybe that's what my dreams have been trying to tell me."

"Oh, right, tell me. Your dream."

The lights flickered for a second or two as someone, or some system, worked to restore power.

Lucy, at last, recounted the nightmare of his rotten, ice-cold corpse attacking her after she dozed off. This time, she refrained from her usual blaming him for things he did in her dreams. He apologized for it regardless, and she worked in the semi-dark until it was time to log off and leave.

"You want me to keep you company in the CAV on the way to the health center, or wait for you to get back?" Ryan asked after keeping her company in mutual pensive silence while she worked.

"I already paid for you through mid-day," she responded. "Sorry, that didn't come out right. You're not my beck-and-call bot."

"That's okay. Better than being called a zombiebot. There's lots on both our minds."

"Of course I want you to stay with me. You keep me calm when I know I am about to get a freakin' horse needle."

"Still, it's your last appointment. You should be thrilled."

"I should be all fixed up, physically, after the nanobots fully work their magic. In a few days, Izzy will help me get my Digital ID biometric updated for my new heartbeat. And, with your help, I'm fixed up emotionally."

"Or, are human emotions just part of a simulation? How do I know YOU are real, LuLu?"

"C'mon, my very-real CAV will be here in 5."

"Do you think you could be ready to let the kids know about me? Give me permission to see them? I'd love to see Romeo when he gets home. You know, if you think he's ready."

"Permissions?" Lucy did not offer any expressions of irony as the lights finally came on right as they were departing. For it was not the nourishing purple, but the bright, revealing white of maintenance mode.

"Things are changing."

"Sure. You've got my permission."

"Funny, this role reversal. Izzy would be thrilled seeing the man having to get permission from the woman."

"Would she really? I think, deep down, she'd surprise you."

CHAPTER 17

SMART BUILDING S.I.P

On the first floor of a mixed residential-office building in downtown Fort Lauderdale, where the law practice was headquartered, Isabella took the pre-ordered morning latte off the counter at the lobby coffee shop. Perfect timing. It was still steaming hot.

"Attorney-Machine Privilege, Isabella?" laughed the firm's senior partner heartily, "I've never heard that before!"

They walked together, two sets of heels clicking on the polished marble, past a vigilant egg-robot towards the bank of elevators. Typically, Izzy was practiced at laughing at the older man's jokes, not the other way around. His ego stroked with small talk, the fully-silver haired man sipped an identical latte as they entered one of four elevators.

"Hey," began the man, intending to say "11th floor" next. The smart building had assumed he was going to his office and had already lit the 12th floor button on the panel. Isabella cut him off with a "hold the door." She had spotted something out of place.

The elevator opposite from them had opened to reveal an old man, the same age as Mr. I-Refuse-To-Retire senior partner but haggard and worn down by life, slouching forward with his face pointing down towards the bright yellow, floor-gripping hospital socks on his feet. The denizen of the Automated Care Living Facility on the 14th floor, which Izzy liked to joke was really the 13th floor—"oh, lucky us"—had been conveniently brought to the 1st floor by the smart elevator software without a verbal command.

The man from the ACLF lifted his head to look right at Isabella.

Isabella lifted her AR headset off her face to look right back at him. No electronics stood between her naked eyes and his.

Spider Rash. She could clearly see the ugly lines that had crawled up the side of the man's face from his neck, and presumably from his armpits, just like that grandma on the gurney on South Beach. There was no mistaking it. Through the opening in the untied back of his hospital gown, Spider Rash lines on his lower back were reflected in the elevator's back mirror, spreading up and out from his saggy exposed butt crack like a coral fan reaching for the sun in the waters off the Keys. And his mouth, locked in a permanent snarl, had traces of blood. His biting spree on the unlucky 14th, before he randomly wandered into the elevator, was about to resume on the lobby floor.

"What the . . ." began the senior partner, his words interrupted, as zombie attacks tend to do, by the infected man lunging forward. His target was an unfortunate and distracted twenty-something who was walking past. The short, gym-obsessed man, preferred to take the stairs at the end of the elevator hall. Like a gator pouncing on an unsuspecting small dog walking too close to the shoreline, the old man delivered a bite to "gymbro manlet", as some of the female lawyers AR-labeled the 16th floor resident in their headsets.

"Get behind me, get behind me," commanded Isabella, taking charge in the manner of the previous day's Gulf War veteran using the sidewalk umbrella. She copied the brave man she had previously ignored. Using her left arm to forcefully pull-push the senior partner to her rear, she immediately ordered the software to "close the door, close the damn door." She hurled her only weapon, the steaming coffee, right onto the top of the zombie's head as the shriveled, emaciated-looking man straddled the overpowered gymbro on the ground.

". . . hell was that?" finished the partner, his voice shaking.

Faint screams could be heard through the closed elevator doors before fading away, replaced by pleasant, A.I.-composed elevator music from the late '20s.

"That was rabies, of some kind. Sudden onset." Using both hands now, Isabella twirled her headset around in front of her eyes, examining the device as if it were something she had never seen before. Her mind raced. Her inner voice spoke to her at the speed of the legal boilerplate read at the end of an old used car advertisement on the radio.

It's real. I saw it with my own eyes. Right in front of my face. No AR, no VR, no MR. No lies in my eyes. Holy shit. It's real.

And that means the rest of it all had to have been real yesterday. The hospital. The hotel. The military robots. All real.

Zombie Apocalypse—just under a different name. And I blew it off. What was I thinking!?

"Sudden rabies, Isabella? Is that what I just saw? For real? Oh, my God. How?"

"Spreads by biting. Maybe under fingernails, too. Rumored to be a bioweapon like 2032–33. I dismissed it all at first, but I was wrong." She pointed her finger directly in front of his pants zipper, almost touching it, a gesture that surely violated the firm's Employee Handbook in multiple sections. "Do you? Do you have it?"

"It? No. Why?"

"Spider Rash is the precursor to what we just saw. But milbots can't catch a virus, so expect a whole-of-Machine response using them on the streets to make it go away, swiftly and silently. The infected act like zombies, biting to spread the pathogen."

"How? How do you know all this?"

"Because, Mr. Cohen, you made me into more than just a Social Score Adjustment Act attorney. Which is why you pay me to talk to cab drivers and to wear these unfashionable things over my eyes and travel to the ugly parts of the Dark 'Verse. Look under rocks. Hunt down rumors in exchange for tips."

Rumors I should have listened to.

"Call me Marv. You're the firm's best little spy, ever. And remind me to up your expense account."

The elevator showed them passing the 9th floor. "9-1-1 isn't working," observed Isabella, having switched to her regular cell phone, which misleadingly displayed "SOS Only" across the top of the screen.

"Maybe it's because we're in an elevator."

"Maybe. But there's been cyberattacks all morning."

"Very concerning," intoned the firm's aging spymaster, his facial expression going beyond mere concern.

"Either way, the lobby's white egg robot is supposed to spot emergencies, along with the smart building management software. I'm sure they've summoned help."

The elevator opened on 11. And 9-1-1 now returned a rapid busy signal.

When does that ever happen?

The numbers struck Isabella as more than coincidental. 9/11, as in September 11th, had happened fully two decades before she was born, so Isabella grew up with no personal sense of what it felt like, on that fateful day, when the second hijacked plane hit the south tower. She had heard people, Marv for instance, passionately describe the moment when everybody knew that the world had changed forever and everyone remembered where they were. So would she. And she was still there.

"This will be remembered as our generation's 9/11. I'm grabbing a few things and heading home. I suggest we tell everyone, calmly, to do the same, or they'd better prepare to shelter in place."

"Let me get up to my office and inform everyone from there." The deliberative Marv, having been in downtown NYC in 2001, had no problem accepting that a 9/11-level emergency was underway. Recognizing reality, considering he was an eyewitness, was not a problem for a man whose position allowed him to avoid headsets that might read one's mind.

Taking swift action, à la the ever more impressive Isabella, was not the well-dressed, deliberative lawyer's strong suit, even as he absorbed every word his young protege was telling him. He suddenly looked lost, childlike, as the elevator doors closed, upon which time the flat-screen display between the two south elevators assumed a light red background, with the message "elevator disabled, please take stairs" flashing in multiple languages.

As Isabella entered the law office proper, her nostrils were greeted with the hangover-reviving stench of sickly artificial butter. It was way too early in the morning for microwave popcorn, but someone had the munchies from the previous evening and went for the easy option. The buttery smell in the afternoon could summon half the office to the break room, but the oily fakeness was repulsive in Isabella's current reality.

"Isabella, did you hear there's some kind of disturbance up on the residential floors? Oh, some popcorn?"

"Yes, and, no." She popped a breath mint, probably her tenth that morning, and tugged a white, conical paper cup from the water cooler dispenser. A second cup stubbornly clinged to the first, so she filled both together, even though the office encouraged the refill of fancy individual water bottles.

Isabella checked her cellphone. Nothing.

"*Oi*, guys, I just tried the elevator. It's disabled, like there's a fire," someone called out.

The three others who had gathered in the classic rumor-sharing space for offices expressed astonishment at the smart building's seemingly random behavior. Mindy, who focused on child custody litigation, was particularly clueless that anything larger in the world might be off. "Oooh, can I have one of those," she asked Izzy. "Thanks," she said, before getting a confirmation.

Always swallowing the official meta-narrative, Mindy would be the first to try to use someone's Metaverse travels to shady places against them in court. Heck, she would probably spit on a rumor Guide if the 'Verse had found a way to enabled saliva. Isabella realized that not only would someone like Mindy keep narrative-swallowing, she would defend the Fact Guide's party line on her knees up until the moment someone's teeth were buried in her neck.

"We should evacuate the building or make provisions to barricade the stairwell," Isabella stated dryly.

"Wait, what?"

"That's the most random thing I think I've ever heard you say, Driscoll. You okay?"

"Yeah, Izz, what's got into you?"

"Listen, you guys, the best way I can explain this is that some civil disturbances are coming. There will be some kind of lockdowns while police robots restore order. We don't want to be up in a tall building while all this goes down." Aware of the limits of the Overton Window, the range of acceptable dialog, she conspicuously avoided overwhelming them with "SORS" and "killer milbots." She also constrained herself from calling the inner voice-lacking Mindy a "NPC."

"Police robots? How come I haven't heard anything about that? My brother-in-law would have told me. There's just some cyber stuff going on. It'll be over by noon."

"Mindy, you need to travel around, talk to people with different viewing angles on reality." Izzy called back as she opened her office door, "and right now, everyone should gather their things and try to get home. That's what Mr. Cohen wants."

Upstairs, Marvin Cohen was still composing a well-crafted, thoughtful e-mail to the staff.

"Has anyone heard from boss-man upstairs?"

"No. Tried calling him. I'm getting a rapid busy signal on my phone."

"Me, too."

"What does 'SOS Only' mean?"

Mindy declared that cyberlockdowns were probably going to happen, changing her tune on the fly. "If there's some kind of global cyberattack, we should get out ahead of this soup show and start heading home," she delivered with her usual uptalk at the end. She was not going to let Izzy the upstart junior lawyer appear to be in charge. "Let's go."

Mindy tried to treat Isabella the way that Isabella treated Gabi. Isabella resolved then and there to treat her younger sister better from now on.

The two men present complied with "let's go" first, leaving for the room that housed their cubicles. Someone then shouted, "Guys, are we being hacked? The smartlock on the north stairwell is giving me red!"

"That's majorly illegal. Cyberattack or not, we can't just be barricaded in by some security A.I. with no warning," Mindy shouted back, somehow managing to uptalk even at full volume.

There was some random laughter as Becca shouted back, "I know, I know! Someone call a lawyer!"

* * *

Exhaling, Isabella closed her office door behind her, wanting to inhale a few moments of calm to plan her next moves. "Wow. I should have listened to the taxi cab driver and stayed home today."

Leaving the break area, Mindy still managed the loud uptalking. "Did anyone know 9-1-1 isn't working?" She stubbornly had made herself the last one to head to her desk, not wanting to concede that Isabella was right about anything. "Someone should sue."

Walking right past Isabella's door, Becca elicited another round of laughter, nervous this time, when she replied, "Is there a lawyer in the house?"

Through the smart blinds of Isabella's office windows, the world outside appeared calm. No hint of problems in the Machine-maintained order of a fresh day. Unlike 9/11, the plane approaching the airport nearby was a sign of normalcy, not threat. Eleven stories below and few blocks over, the iconic Las Olas Boulevard, similar to Ocean Drive in some ways, still had people strolling about, for a little while longer at least.

She quickly shoved into a shoulder-bag counterclaim and other papers related to the never-ending civil case against the municipality whose AV had killed her father, and, somewhat irrationally, a crystal award that sat on her desk with her name etched in. Not only did it have irreplaceable sentimental value, it had a pointy, spear-like top.

Before heading out to the south stairwell, Isabella checked her phone. Nothing again. Perhaps that was not overly strange. Gabi was sans-electronics in a proctored exam and her mother might already be getting the botshot. But there was none of the normally steady stream of client e-mails and texts. She restored her headset over her eyes, theorizing that the virtual cellphone available therein might have some fresh texts or voice messages. Nothing, same as the real one.

When she reached out to open her office door, she realized it was locked, without her remembering that she had told it to. While she was not looking, the green padlock on the smartlock display had changed to red on its own. She held up the fleshy part of her chipped right hand. Instead of changing to green, the smartlock flashed red. She checked her TLA on her personal cellphone, which showed her personal status as a green checkmark.

No use. In a clash of icons, a stubborn red padlock outranked a friendly green checkmark, like paper covering rock, or rock smashing scissor.

"No, no. Too friggin' late."

Her freedom had been taken away. Just like that. With a click. Was this, she wondered, what it felt like for poor Romeo the first time he was locked in his cell? Blandingwood was "prison-of-the-future" minimum security, but the loss of agency was horrifying regardless. Should she try to bust down the door? How long would she be here?

Thank goodness, I threw that latte instead of drinking it all. What if I need to pee? Did the security A.I. think about that?

With a "hey, BMS," she opened the Building Management System software inside her headset, while glancing over at the soil in the potted plant in the corner.

Nope. Not going there. Not even if it's the end of days.

"How can I help you?" asked the BMS' hologram, standing in a crisp, security guard uniform next to her desk. The last human dressed this way here once occupied the security/information desk in the lobby, which had been removed years prior in favor of the egg robot security system. Normally, this white-collared hologram wore a suit and tie, so the symbolism of the switch to the white-shirted, rent-a-cop style uniform with the embroidered "SECURITY" patch over the left breast was not lost on Isabella.

"How long is the lockdown for?"

Not a lockdown. A temporary S.I.P., Shelter in Place, until security situations in the lobby and 14th floor have been resolved. Everyone should stay calm."

"But," Isabella began a challenge of the hologram, pressing her hand against the smartlock again.

Anticipating her statement, the hologram began citing a litany of law and regulation, before Isabella cut him off.

"Don't try to outlawyer a lawyer. Friendly advice. Have the robots arrived?"

"The ETA on the police response is showing one hour, 14 minutes."

"I asked about robots. Is that too hard a question?"

"A centaur model came in off the street and is in the lobby now. It was escorted by a drone."

"You see, that wasn't so hard. From the police?"

"I can't say. Neither presented a tracking ID."

"So, why can't we all take the north stairwell and just leave? It has an exit to the outside that doesn't go through the lobby."

"There's some people from the 14th floor, behaving violently, who managed to get in the stairwells."

"Biting people?"

"Apparently."

"What's to prevent me from smashing this lock, or climbing up on my desk and moving the ceiling tiles to get out of my office?"

"I wouldn't recommend that. This is not a fire event. The building management A.I. will be using the timed opening and closing of smartlocks, like locks in a canal, to operate an orderly evacuation of the commercial floors, individually or in small groups, instead of everyone rushing the stairwells all at once. You will be monitored for safety and biometrics such as body temperature and heartbeat regularity the whole time. Based on the current variables, your turn should be in approximately five hours. Give or take."

"What if I have to use the restroom?"

"Sorry, that's not part of the protocol. Shelter in place protocol means—"

"Pee in place protocol, got it. I've never heard of a protocol like this, how does it work?"

Several of the other attorneys and paralegals simultaneously received the same description from the security guard hologram in their own offices. Under the current "modified bioterror protocol," a panic-inducing phrase the hologram studiously avoided using, the non-residential tenants of the building would be moved in the elevators and cleared stairwells, one at a time to ground level. Escorted next, robotically, to awaiting ground transportation. The rest of the residential floors would begin their for-the-duration lockdown. The limiting factor in the evacuation was sanitation robots, not police-style bots. Each portion of the route would be sanitized before the next evacuee could move into it, one lock at a time.

"Fortunately, Ms. Driscoll, our particular mixed-use tower has the ACLF on 14, which has two bots with hospital-grade UV sterilization capability. The office buildings nearby that fought partial or full residential conversion are out of luck if they need sterilization right away. They may be stuck for more than a day."

"I guess they get the poop-in-place protocol. Karma for Capitalists. The plan sounds painfully intricate."

"It's been rehearsed with digital twins of the building and the occupants innumerable times. It works in 99.2 percent of variations run." He looked directly at Isabella with his empty, doll eyes. "In the simulations, your digital twin survives. Ms. Driscoll, you will get out just fine."

"And they have enough AV's to transport everyone to their residences?"

"I can't say if the regional transportation authority is using autonomous vehicles or not. Could be horse and buggy from that point on. Once you leave the building, custody changes to Regional Transportation's A.I. The only AV's that I can confirm will be from the air taxi service off of the pad on the roof. Limited availability, however."

"The roof? Really?"

When I get out of my office, I'll have to find a way to get ol' Marv to let me join him up there.

Unsurprisingly, down the hall, Mindy the toady was plotting the same thing.

"While you wait, there's plenty of entertainment and information options. The Metaverse status for those kinds of venues are mostly green as far as know. You can use mesh network connections to travel to some places as well. With so many residential units, this building has excellent mesh-to-mesh connectivity."

Isabella put her shoulder bag back on top of her desk, otherwise uncluttered in real life, but visibly stacked with virtual file folders in her headset.

"Why can't I get a link and see what is going on in the lobby?"

"The local 'Verse has some limitations for privacy concerns."

"That's bullpoop and you know it. And why won't cellular connections work? Can you unhack that those cell transmitters on the roof? I thought it was all hack-proof equipment."

"Those things are out of my control." The hologram called up a series of floating windows, semi-translucent in front of the real office windows, that showed the downtime status of various networks as red. A downtime heat map of cell phone connectivity nationwide looked like the country was covered in blood. Isabella added the family finder app to the montage of displays, but flat across her desk instead of over the window. A bubble with a smiling picture of her mother pointed to the health clinic, where she was supposed to be.

Gabriela was nowhere to be seen.

CHAPTER 18

PALM RIDGE SCHOOL ASSEMBLY

Gabriela could also see her mother, no doubt getting her injection done, on the family finder application, but not her sister. The upper school was having a final assembly before dismissing the children for a half day, and she lingered with her headset on by the uppermost doorway on the stairs that ran up the side of the auditorium, flexing some "I'm a senior, so I can push the rules" privilege.

After yesterday's full day off, the lack of in-person classes was a welcome bonus for the kids. For the teachers and parents, not so much. The chaos of having some of the older staff with red TLAs not allowed on campus due to Spider Rash had taken a toll on scheduling. Normally, at least one vice principal or other administrator would be standing nearby, telling lingering students in their headsets to "stop traveling and come inside. Your only venue is here. Take a seat. Quietly, now."

Underclassmen entered the assembly in the lower and mid-level doors of the sloped theater layout. The hot topic amongst them was the unavailability of so much of the classic Internet and social media.

"Are you aware that massive cyberattacks are happening?"

And, "No, all I know is that I can't post video," were the two most common things being said by the youngsters, here and around the nation.

One of the older kids astutely observed, "Well, that's one way to get Spider Rash out of the news cycle. I hear there was an EBS in Spain."

Gabi had just left her mother's store venue, hoping that Isabella would be there. All the shelves were empty. Not even lentils. She left an empty metal rack exposed and attached a note to it, with an address to a different destination. She text-messaged the "meet me here" address to Isabella as well, but assumed the odds were just as good that, with the Metaverse working okay, Izzy would get her note in the store first. Her next destination was a gathering place she hoped to locate someone else who was also incommunicado. Jamar.

"You on your way to the reenactment?" asked the person who had hacked into the hallway she was walking through.

"How did you know I—?"

"You left your nurse uniform on?"

"I don't want to talk to random people right now."

"What is this, like 'stranger-danger' on a playground? Are you in kindergarten?"

"No."

"I was told not to report for duty," he added, still dressed in a WWII-period military costume of his own. "It's going to be canceled until G1 can sort out personnel issues."

"Give rumors a rest this morning, sir, we all have too much going on for rabbitholes right now." Gabi, still wearing her all white nurse costume, pointed an invitation to the trashcan.

"Zombiesicles," stated the rumor Guide flatly, as Gabriela pulled on the handle that opened her next destination.

"I'm sorry, what?" shot back Gabriela, allowing the sheer randomness of the man's bizarre statement to interrupt her progress. The next destination, a virtual overlay on top of the school's physical auditorium, had loaded. She had to wonder, is this guy high on something? Tranq?

"Gabs, come on. We're gonna be late."

"Save me a seat, 'Sha," shouted Gabriela back, participating in two realities at once.

"You heard that right, 'zombiesicles'," continued the man, whose service uniform was that of a military intelligence officer, replete with many colorful ribbons crawling up his left breast. "Global Health's Artificial Intelligence has decided to deep-freeze SORS victims. Like big, human, cryogenically frozen popsicles. Zombie-plus-popsicles equals zombiesicles. It's the nickname, anyway."

"Where'd you get that sick idea from? Your best friend's sister's boyfriend's brother's girlfriend?"

"No. I heard it from this guy who knows this kid whose dad heads a Regional Health Department. His dad—or was it his uncle?—helped make the cryofreeze military contingency plan. Multiple sources. Confirmed."

"Deep-freeze infected people? Are you serious?"

"Quite. Serious. Zombies shut down in the cold. Plus, the A.I. has determined that the optimal human-benefit path forward is cryogenic preservation of the infected. To stop the rot. And stabilize things until a full reversal of the process using modification RNA can be found. Global Health is just doing what the Health A.I. says and implementing the contingency."

"There's a contingency for zombies?"

"Yup. CONPLAN 8888-44 it's called. Mobile freezer trucks and cryofreeze-converted warehouses. Listen, you have to help spread the word."

"You see, crazy sheet like this is why people only listen to rumor Guides half the friggin' time."

"We're *always* right, half the time. The problem is figuring out which half. But official Fact Guides hardly have a better record, okay? All they really do lately is harangue you to not listen to the rumor Guides."

"And the rumor Guides tell you not to listen to the Fact Guides."

"Fair point."

There was a sharp tug at Gabi's arm and a voice in her ear, "Aisha sent me to grab you. We saved you a seat. C'mon."

"I have to go." She poked her head into the destination beyond the portal, desperately glancing around a darkened, starlit landscape to see if she could spot Jamar in there.

"You got anything for me, kid?"

"The whole crypto payment network is red, captain. I'm, like, everybody got sent into the corner for a TLA timeout. I can't give you a tip."

"That's not what I meant. Trade me a rumor back. We go rumor-for-rumor, like the old days, before the tipflation."

"Fine." Gabi delivered furtive glances left and right, rumor Guide–style. "The Southeast Florida Regional Health Director died yesterday because he had turned into a zombie, and a naked prostitute pushed him off a balcony on South Beach. His man boobs were almost as big as the hooker's." Gabi creatively added the moob-size embellishment based on her sister's retelling. "But you should only believe half the rumors you hear, *amirite?*"

"Fair point again. You saw this? Personally?"

"I mean, I didn't see the boobs with my own eyes, no."

"So how do you know it's real?"

"Everybody knows zombies aren't real, right?"

She touched the trashcan before the Guide did.

The Guide, mentally processing what Gabriela had just told him, lingered for just a moment too long in the temporary hallway before it disappeared.

* * *

"Take your seats, please," stated Dr. Marksohn, the principal of the prestigious Palm Ridge Preparatory Academy, into a microphone from the podium on the stage, "I don't want to have to deduct paladin points from any school social accounts. And make sure full Mixed Reality mode is enabled on your school headsets for the presentation. Airplane mode on everything else. Quickly now."

The phrase "airplane mode" was way old school, but the students understood the Gen-Y reference.

As the students added or adjusted their school-issued headsets, Marksohn added her usual "Green eyecons and green checkmarks, everyone!" along with claps of her hands. Superhero costumes and furry outfits were not tolerated at an Extended Reality assembly.

Harish Patel, who sometimes went by Harry, tried to make a last-second play for the empty seat next to Gabi's friend, Aisha. She waved away "Incel Patel" to keep the spot open for Gabriela, while secretly admiring his willingness to put himself out there and cross the quite literal no-man's-land space between genders. Harry was divergent in being one of the few that preferred not to spend his life traveling the 'Verse, and, despite mockery, at least tried to bridge the gap in the War of the Sexes' ongoing stalemate, crossing the emotional canyon running down the middle of the auditorium. He made actual eye-to-eye contact with females, which his friends thought was a marker of insanity. The contrast of Harry with Jamar was not lost on Gabi. Still, Harry needed to avoid school point-dings and quickly rejoined the side of the auditorium where the males had self-segregated. There were still multiple empty seats on the female's side, one directly behind Gabi, conspicuously empty. The front two rows of the auditorium, reserved for guests, were also conspicuously empty, except for a lone man front-and-center in a tan suit.

"Why are we here again?" Aisha whispered to Gabi.

"Some surprise guest, supposedly."

"Today, students, we have a surprise guest who has traveled all the way to South Florida to speak to us. It is my honor to introduce someone we have become rather familiar with, although not under the circumstances anyone would prefer." Dr. Marksohn made it appear that she was reading from a virtual index card. "A leader who has successfully steered the world through several potential disasters, and would-be pandemics." She ticked off some of his lengthy credentials from her card, afterward soliciting a round of applause with, "Students, please provide a warm welcome to the Director of Global Health, Doctor Deepika Parashar."

Carmen, on Gabi's right, quietly commented, "Oh, wow. Didn't see that coming."

"Deepfake Deepika?" asked Aisha from the left.

"Don't go there, girl," Gabi quickly corrected her.

An avatar of a sharply dressed woman entered from behind the curtains on the right side, taking long, confident strides across the wooden stage toward Marksohn. Marksohn made a point of offering the Mixed Reality woman a lingering handshake, so everyone could see her green eyecon side-by-side with the green eyecon of a figure of great global import. Gabi could just imagine Marksohn, thrilled at her personal, and her institution's, stratospheric bump in prestige, reaching down and forcibly dragging the two symbols together so that they kissed each other.

The holographic attendees completely filling the two front rows leapt to their feet to applaud their boss, with the students following their cue. Gabriela lifted her lenses clean off her eyes to verify what she was seeing. Parashar, who had been awarded by cynics the moniker "deepfake" after being caught several times using a green verification eyecon when it should have been red or gray, was not physically there. None of the official staff members and other attendees were there in the front two rows, either. Just the slender man in the tan suit. In the Metaverse, he had been standing and clapping with the rest. In reality, he was still sitting, motionless as a student on meds, engaged in crisis-level coordination using the implants in his brain to both receive instructions from Global Health's A.I. and to frantically communicate with his nominal boss' far-flung enterprise.

"Thank you so much for the warm welcome, everyone," Parashar said, warmly, in a pleasant British accent. "As you may know, as part of our 'Raising the Next Generation of Health Leaders' initiative, I've been traveling around the world to make presentations at the top-rated high schools in various countries. Last month I was in La Paz, Bolivia. The month before, Astana, capital of Kazakhstan. And today, at the school rated number one here in the entire United States. In beautiful Florida, no less. Congratulations to you, Dr. Marksohn on your achievement," continued Parashar, and at that point, if Marksohn's face could have glowed any brighter, it would have gone supernova. Her broad smile looked like it went past her earlobes. She had every reason to be proud of her school's achievement.

"And to all the Palm Crest Pangolins, for your hard work," the Freudian mangling of "Paladins" with "Pangolins" forced an unrestrainable giggle from the assembled students, mixed in with their still-seated healthy applause.

From the podium, Parashar delivered a, formal obligatory round of thank-you's to some of the other attendees and dignitaries in the front rows, most notably to the corpulent avatar of "my local partner, your Regional Director of Health, Sergei Abramovich."

"Impossible. That can't be," Gabi said, a little too loudly, of his green eyecon.

"Don't go there, girl," Aisha quickly corrected her.

"This forum, broadcast worldwide and translated by A.I. into every known language, gives the Global Health Directorate the chance to make formal announcements in less formal settings, and bring our message directly to a select group of young people who we know will someday meet the challenges of the future." Parashar grabbed the microphone, virtually, from the podium mount and made her way down the half-flight of steps from the stage to the auditorium floor as she spoke. "And the challenges of the present."

She made her way up the aisle, which ran parallel to the entrance doors, making eye contact with the students. Her dress and poise conveyed power, mixed today with subtle and not-so-subtle "disaster chic" visual cues. Her broad red tie was slightly undone. The top button was unbuttoned on her it-looks-ever-so-slightly-like-I-slept-in-this-while-on-a-private-jet shirt. Her makeup was expertly done to look like she was not wearing any. She had her hair down instead of its usual tight bun, with her hair's signature single white stripe running up and over the top of her head in a gentle, confident wave.

"Presently, we are seeing multiple crises unfold simultaneously. Panic over the relentless spread of Spider Rash. A cyber attack of unprecedented scale. Extreme weather events in the Global South. Multiple late-season hurricanes. A solar flare on its way. A cryptocurrency crash. And, now, from what we can tell, a global bioterrorism event, which I will get into in more detail in just a moment."

As people from around the world watched, Parashar was the first person in an official capacity at her level use that word, bioterrorism. The Palm Ridge Prep students were eyewitnesses to history. Even the kids who normally did not pay attention were paying attention.

Except Aisha. Her eyes were unnaturally wide as she began a struggle to stay awake. Behind her lenses, poor sleep-deprived 'Sha looked like she was trapped in one of those torture movies where they put toothpicks under the victim's eyelids to keep them from blinking. Which, to be fair, was the usual student reaction to the usual assembly that students were forced to sit through, as they tried to prevent the eyeball-monitoring software of their school headsets from deducting paladin points.

Parashar, misinterpreting Aisha's wide-eyed look, paused traversing the aisle right next to her. The virtual cameraman, a humanoid bot with a steady-cam, trailed the health director and adjusted the 2D frame to capture both of them. The camera's software removed the headset from over Aisha's face, allowing the world to witness her wide-eyed stare.

"What we are witnessing unfold is the classic definition of a polycrisis. But we're not afraid, right?" Parashar looked directly into Aisha's eyes while nodding her head, soliciting the teen's agreement. Gabi had to deliver a low-key but swift elbowing to get Aisha to reciprocate the nod in concurrence. 'Sha's nodding visage would be seen worldwide as symbolic of The Youth's enthusiastic endorsement.

Parashar then turned to made her way back down the aisle in the direction of the stage.

"It's not our first time dealing with so many events all at once, of course. But it is the first time we truly have all the treaty tools to handle multiple events as a single, unified whole, rather than having individual systems, working independently, get overwhelmed and confused. I know that's a lot to process. The bottom line is that we're unifying the poly-response in what we will now call a polylockdown." Facing the walking-backwards camera robot, she tapped the microphone into her palm to make her point.

That point was greeted with approval throughout the auditorium. Carmen, admiring Parashar's dark power suit with its '80s-style corporate pinstripes, leaned towards Gabi and whispered directly in her ear, "Now, that's a girl-boss, deepfake or not."

Aisha quietly resolved to grow up to be just like the woman on the stage.

"I know there are some who will try to say this is heavy-handed. Some will also say I don't have the authority to make up a new word. I'm not the global dictionary director." There was some mild laughter. "Although sometimes I wish there was one. Just think of what I am announcing this way. Instead of an ordinary 'lockdown,' I like to think of this new concept as a 'lock-out.' Meaning you lockout all the worries of the world, lock out all the danger, lock out all the fear."

Oh, my God. My mother is, like, a prophet. Does this Deepika woman listen in to our conversations? Read our minds or something?

The A.I. monitoring communications had done exactly that.

"Specific to today's crises, I want to let you know that we've assigned our health cyber response team to deploy their expertise in things like busting ransomware attacks on hospitals to assist military, and civilian, authorities worldwide. Together, in public-partnership, we'll break through this horrible cyberattack on the Internet."

With that announcement, classic cell phone sounds spread throughout the entire auditorium. Ringtones, chirps, vibrations all. Rows of murmurs flowed through the auditorium like the kids were doing the wave at a soccer game. Marksohn leapt to the microphone—the real, physical one was still at the podium—to remind the students what she meant by the outdated "airplane mode" term. She then yielded the podium to Parashar's beaming avatar, who restored her virtual microphone to the holder.

"Well, that was quick," quipped Parashar, taking credit and smiling at the fix's providential timing.

"Girl boss," Carmen reiterated, a bit louder this time.

Texts and news messages poured into Gabi's physical cell phone, dutifully set to silent, and MR headset simultaneously, like an unclogged sink clearing itself. Three of them, all group texts, caught her attention in particular.

Mom

Got the shot, finally. Biggest damn needle you ever saw. Already feeling drowsy.

Isabella

People are trying to call air taxis to get out from the roof.

Alex

Agents raided my dad's home office last night! Jamar barely got away.

Meeting with the Rabbi now. I'll text more as soon as I am done.

Parashar swiped through the air a few times, showing the assembly that she was clearing incoming clutter from her own vision to focus on the students. "Although be prepared for the digital blockade to come and go until the perpetrators are fully identified," she continued, "who may or may not be the same shadowy groups responsible for this latest round of bioterror."

Wow, this is more real than I thought. Anyway, what did "Jamar barely got away" mean?

"Which is something I need to directly address. There is an even stranger disease, a rabies-like virus, that is spreading through physical contact, specifically biting." In a presentation thus far clean of visuals, Parashar cast up a floating heat map, nearly the size of the entire stage, showing yellows, oranges, and reds starting to grow in virtually all the same places on the map that Isabella had been showing Spider Rash to her mother the day before. Gabi had never seen the map, which had a different label on the top than "Spider Rash: via Sewer Sensors." It said "SORS Distribution: via Internet of Bodies."

"The affliction will be known henceforth as S-O-R-S, or SORS. And, on this, yes, I am the global dictionary." Although Parashar was leveraging off the generally attentive students at this point, her target audience was another group entirely. She continued, "We believe SORS-44, the full designation, was likely cooked up by non-state actors using some off-the-shelf gene-editing tools down in some awful warzone basement or some nondescript warehouse in an industrial zone. Too common, sadly."

There was another wave of murmurs in the auditorium.

"In response, the polylockdown will apply most of the standard pro-tocols that have been rehearsed and perfected in pandemics and pandemic scares in the past, but this time I'll be working directly with regional health officials, cutting out layers of middlemen, for maximum efficiency. You will see, or you may have already seen, A.I. makes decisions to temporarily restrict movement in residences and public places, which can be shelter-in-place for a single office building, or an entire 15-minute city lockdown. Yellow TLA's may now deny access instead of just being a warning. Algorithms will help you maintain your social distancing."

With all the technical details, the student's attention began to drift, although they kept their pupils, monitored by their school headsets, forward. Detecting the change in attention level, Deepfake Deepika stepped away from the podium again and walked right through where New Zealand sat on the heat map she had conjured, standing right at the stage's edge. "The bottom line is, don't be afraid. We have learned, with the help of A.I., that fear, not any virus, is the real killer."

The floating heat map title added the word "Projected," and the colors shrank from the hotspots, red to orange, to yellow, to all clear.

There were nods of approval from throughout the gathering. Aisha nodded, too, but from fighting off sleep. She was one of the rare students who eschewed stimulants like Adderall.

"And, like the rash, the good news is that we have almost completed the genetic sequencing. I see no reason why we won't meet or exceed the 100-day window to begin vaccine patch deployment."

The man in the tan suit began a slow-clap, which lead to a full round of applause, concurrent with many watching around the world.

"One more thing. I must emphasize the words 'rabies-like' for a reason. We have seen bioweapons do strange things before, such as uncontrollable mass-rage, but biting is, admittedly, rather new. There are unsavory rumors being spread all over the place using a specific word, maybe you have seen that word used, and I hate to use it myself. That word is 'zombies'. . ." The response from the attendees was several decibels above mass-murmur level in response to the Z-word, ". . . but that is NOT what they are."

"That's exactly what they are," came a familiar voice, just above a whisper, over Gabi's shoulder. She'd know it anywhere.

Jamar.

* * *

"Oh my God!" shrieked Gabi, using her elbow to push up on the armrest and spin halfway around in her seat. Sitting behind her, in an empty seat in the female section was the avatar of Jamar Rice. Gabi didn't have to lift her headset up to verify that he was not really there. His dress in his preferred WWII tank commander getup was clue enough.

Virtually the entire auditorium ceased murmuring and turned to look in Gabi's direction. Jamar made a rapid, repeated forward-pointing motion to signal for the red-faced teen to turn back around and face forward.

"I know, I know," Parashar purred reassuringly into the mike, playing off Gabi's outburst, "that word, the Z-word, gets people very emotional. People have been seeing it everywhere." The virtual camera bot captured the shock in Gabriela's reddening face of having several hundred people from her school looking right at her. Gabi's image would be seen worldwide as the symbol of overreaction to the now illicit Z-word, the source for several viral "OMG" memes later that day.

"Sorry, sorry. I didn't mean to scare you," Jamar said softly from behind her. His avatar was private to her session, plugged in using the school's local mesh network. None of the kids sitting next to Gabi could hear him talk, but they could hear "you scared the crap out of me," delivered in response, as Jamar walked around the entrance to the aisle, and sat right down atop Aisha's lap.

"Me? What did I do?" protested Aisha. Jamar signaled with a finger over his lips to keep his identity quiet.

"Not you. You have a ghost on your lap."

"Halloween came a day early? Ghosts, Z-words, oh my. Is he cute?"

"You have no idea."

". . . the idea is to avoid contact," Parashar continued, as Gabi berated Jamar, softly at first, for his total lack of contact. "That's right, avoid all contact with those who are infected. Years of movies, novels, videogames, and verseogames have programmed us to automatically associate people biting people as some kind of, oh my, 'Z-word apocalypse'." Some nervous twittering bounced up and back in the rows. Parashar gently slapped her own forehead. "I know. Ridiculous, right, students?"

"What's ridiculous is that you vanished for like 24 hours, no contact, telling no one where you were. I was worried sick!"

Jamar tried to explain, still keeping his voice down even though no one could hear him. He had not appreciated that failure to reply to one's girlfriend for so long was considered just shy of a capital offense in Gabi's relationship expectations, dwarfing the his loss of paladin points for physically missing the assembly.

"Well, you still have some serious 'splainin to do!" fired back Gabriela, almost at the level to draw another round of everyone's-staring-at-me shame.

"Marksohn's going to zero your points out if you interrupt her assembly again," Jamar informed her, "and, you wouldn't believe what happened to me last night if I told you."

"Try me."

"So, students, everyone, to avoid a pandemic of violence, try to allow the machines to handle any situations," Parashar droned on. "There's leftover legions of surplus military robots from the African concession wars that will be deployed for rapid response to outbreaks before they spread. This isn't a game where you shoot those Z-people in the brain after law and order breaks down."

"Z-people?" intoned Carmen. "Why not 'biting people'?"

"You don't get 10 points for killing your podmate, or 100 points for beheading the biting person in the house-sharing next door with a katana. You'll get charges for murder. And maybe a nasty bite. Leave the grandma alone."

"Well, then the grandmas should leave us alone," softly declared Aisha, oblivious to Jamar's personal plight.

The "grandma" comments silenced Gabi's badgering of him. It hit too close to home, literally. He had no news of what had happened to his grandmother since she entered Sawgrass Hospital.

"Oh, baby, I'm sorry."

They both took a silent moment to stare forward at Parashar finishing her presentation. High on stage, Deepfake Deepika looked straight over in the direction of Jamar and pulled on the edges of her notch lapel, momentarily smoothing out the tiny wrinkles. The woman's face never seemed to age. She positively glowed when silkily talking about the next generation, asserting that "leaders who would shake the very foundations of the earth" were sitting in the audience right in front of her.

"For now, to do your part, return in your assigned residences, receive supplies robo-delivered straight to your doorstep, reduce, recycle, reuse, wear a mask if told to, and wait for Global Health to give the all-clear. Most importantly, avoid spreading rumors. We'll do our part. We've been alone together many times before, and we can do it again. Together, we'll not just 'minimize' harm to the environment by 2050; we'll eliminate it. I salute you."

The slender tan-suited man did not need to shill another large round of applause, accompanied by a standing ovation. He made his way to the stage to congratulate Marksohn, who leapt to her feet to get another side-by-side of her and her distinguished guest, before instructing the students on making their way to ground transportation.

"Is that a deepfake of Alex's dad in the front row?" inquired Jamar.

"Sure looks that way."

"That's just cold. Ice cold."

* * *

The cyberattack resumed with a fresh round of IoT botnets more or less the instant Parashar exited stage left. "That was quick," retorted Gabi. Stymied in communicating with her sister and mother, she banged out a few quick text replies and clicked send, assuming they would get through in a clump the next time this fresh round of the attack was broken. And the family finder app was showing spinning circles. Being cut off from her mother might normally trigger debilitating anxiety in Gabi, but her joy at seeing Jamar, combined with her need for some serious 'splainin' from him, overrode everything.

"*Güey*, where the heck have you been?" she demanded.

"On my bike. I had to get off the public grid. Radio silence."

Gabi exited the auditorium and stepped out onto the gentle stairs on its outside, leading down to a small courtyard.

"'Radio Silence?' Seriously? Like you're some kind of real-life L.T. Jammer? We're not playing World War II, Florida Edition, or Grand Theft Auto IX, you know."

"The term works, low key. And it's kinda like we're in World War IV."

"Where are you now?"

"Right behind you."

Partially hidden behind an open auditorium door stood the physical person who was her boyfriend online. All the kids, engrossed in their own affairs, were not checking behind them as they left the auditorium, so they had been streaming right past him on their way to the school's two ride pools.

"Oh my God! Oh my God! Oh my God!" shrieked Gabi, reinforcing her upcoming status as world OMG girl, as she turned and dove into a spontaneous, deep hug of Jamar, the real one IRL. She squeezed him tightly while some of the other students looked back to see the hubbub. Gabi loosened her grip and delivered a light slap, a swipe really, across his chest. "Never do that to me again. Promise?"

"Promise."

"You still have some major explaining to do, you know."

"Nice to see you, too."

Jamar pulled her back in close to deliver another tight hug. He wore a gray hoodie like one of the hallway rumor Guides, with the hood itself pulled down low over his brow. The large lenses of his headset, an older model from home instead of the sleeker student-models, covered his upper face, unabomber-style. He had smeared some drops of substance that was slightly greasy and shiny on the side of his nose and on the opposite side of his chin. Likely lubricant from a bicycle chain or something similar. And he smelled like someone might if they had been out all night on their bicycle. No matter. A joyous warmth flooded through Gabi's body at the physical contact. With headsets still on, both of them could see the holographic Jamar, robbed of his agency and now looking out of place his wartime Jammer costume, standing there like a cuckolded lover, forced to watch the embrace of the real Jamar and his real girlfriend.

Jammer was dismissed with a wave of the hand.

"Who are you and what have you done with the real Jamar?" asked Gabi jokingly. She was not referring to his obscured appearance but with his sudden lack of shyness. He was not embarrassed to be seen hugging a girl, in front of anyone. In front of everyone, for that matter.

"Walk with me," he said, taking her hand.

Two acts of near-misogynistic assertiveness in a row. "Are you Jamar Rice or a deepfake?" she asked again, more seriously this time, lifting up her lenses to see him with her own eyes. He reciprocated the lens-lifting, to let Gabi see him unobstructed. Countless times, she had paused his avatar and stared deeply into the almond-shaped eyes digitally projected into the 'Verse. She realized this was the first time she had done this for real, this close. The spark of life coming from behind his dark brown irises could not be captured digitally at any frame rate, no matter how many megapixels in the camera. The "eyes are the window to the soul" version of Jamar was truly there. IRL.

"They can't make deepfakes of flesh and blood people," he asserted, pinching his own cheek. "Clones aren't real, as far as I know."

"I wouldn't put anything past them at this point."

They passed, hand-in-hand, Mrs. Salazar's technology classroom where Jamar had taken his first class about the Internet of Things, where he got his formal introduction to just how much was now possible with technology.

"Whom ya talking to?" Lauren Pincus intrusively queried from behind, enviously taunting, "You two should get a room."

"No one." Jamar said loudly enough for a huffy Pincus to hear, without turning to address her.

The school hallways they were making their way through, connecting Stanley Auditorium and the ride pool, were starkly reminiscent of the liminal hallways connecting so many education-related venues in the Metaverse. In the upper school, rows of sterile lockers sat between closed classroom doors. In the middle school, posters with achievements and awards. In the lower school, children's first splattered attempts at art, labeled neatly in AR with the paintbrush-wielders' names . As they walked, the background was filled with the variations of "yo, does anyone have another way to get cell service?"

"Can't the cell network, when it's working anyway, see your headset and ID you?" asked Gabi.

"Not on the cell, or satellite, network. This model lets you yank the SIM card. Since I escaped the Isolation and Quarantine they tried to put me in, I'm using mesh-to-mesh protocol only, which has its limits. I'm naked other than that." He lifted up his sleeve to show he wasn't wearing a smart-watch with his hand that was not wearing a smartring. Presumably he didn't have a physical SIM-bearing cellphone on him, a solid alibi for not texting Gabi back.

"Why did they have you in I&Q?"

"You haven't seen the rumor?"

"What rumor?"

"Apparently a freakin' Guide out there was making a killing in tips by spreading a rumor that my grandma is patient zero."

"Is she?"

"Don't know. But they sure tried to quarantine me for it. I've been on the run for, like, over 24 hours. I never got to see her at the hospital. There was this geofence."

"I know."

Jamar didn't waste time asking how she knew. "Alex and I barely got away. But the geofence was like one of those ghosts from the Haunted Mansion at Disney. It followed me home. The smartlocks at my house sperged out and went all red."

"There's no turning back now."

He pulled on her hand slightly to change the direction they were walk-ing and make a detour towards the bicycle racks.

"I tied together bedsheets to get out of a second floor back window to get around the locks. Then, Ollie tried to bite me, but I got away on my bike. Not Oliver. Damn."

"Bite you?" Gabi assumed Jamar was exaggerating.

"Unbelievable, I know, right?"

THE ZOMBIE IN THE MACHINE

"Crazy, for sure. And then you bicycled all the way here? From west to east? How many zones is that?" asked Gabi in total amazement. "Are you planning on biking back?"

"Not exactly," he replied, rolling the bike along by its handlebars now, ceasing to hold Gabi's hand.

"What about facial recognition?"

"Good thing cameras, still after all these years, can't do good facial recognition on a black person's skin. Residual racism in the algorithms, they say."

"You're half-and-half, Jamar. Not even that, really."

"And you're not three-quarters Hispanic, really."

"Latin, Latin ..."

Both of them laughed. The previously aloof Jamar, who had a Korean War waif in his lineage, had been the only kid on the bus who stayed cool about everyone's mixed-race obsessions, defending Gabi in chats. Lucy never knew that about him. He had also used his teenage-boy software skills to chivalrously readd Gabi's clothes any time others had digitally stripped them away.

"Anyway, even if the cameras tried to strip away my disguise, such as it is, that's where urban mobility tricks come in, let's just put it that way. Plenty of kids our age have mapped out camera dead spots and gaps in the fences at zone boundaries. Especially along the canals. You know."

The two walked past the lower school's playground area, with its plastic jungle gym and swings molded in bright, preschool-friendly colors. The predominance of red seemed to mock Jamar's fallen TLA status. To the sound of the bike's gears clicking, they passed the school's infirmary, the last building, freestanding, before the ride pool and the awaiting West Broward autonomous shuttles. Although there was desperate demand for rides all over the county, Regional Transportation's algorithms prioritized the schools.

"Then I tried to hide out at Alex's house, but that plan got pozzed. People in black SWAT outfits were hauling out white bankers boxes with papers, and all their electronics. School was the only place left for me to go. At least I got a free breakfast. Gabs, you wouldn't believe the crazy sheeet I saw coming here. Places filled with infected old people. Robots raiding nursing homes."

"Now, where did you come from?"

Ms. Miller, a pleasant older woman who was running the whole shuttle boarding operation using a quaint old computer tablet and handheld stylus, like something out of a museum, confronted Jamar. He looked rough. Miller, who had managed this area for Palm Ridge since the days of yellow school buses, recognized him despite his use of a hoodie and eye-obscuring headset to maximum effect. Luckily, as a senior, he wasn't required to be in school uniform today.

"Oh, hi, Ms. Miller. Gabriela's mom invited me over for dinner and I was hoping you could put me on her school shuttle instead of mine today. It's Jamar Rice. I should be on the list."

"I know who you are, sweetie. But I don't see you anywhere," observed Miller, looking down at her tablet through bifocals attached to her neck with a silvery chain.

Jamar then reached over and gently, but firmly, held Gabriela's hand again. The ride pool was more open than the hallways. The hand holding was in full view of the other kids. In full view of everyone's headsets. Countless school cameras recorded the act.

Gabriela had the overwhelming feeling that she had been transported into a different timeline. She had always wanted to see a more assertive, confident Jamar IRL, but this was bizarre.

Everything had been moving so fast. And then no more. Everything stopped. Jamar and Ms. Miller exchanged a few more words, but Gabi did not hear them. There was just this goosebump-y, OMG-y, electric shock-y, kind of sensation running up her arm. Something so simple—the feel of haptic-free fingers—was yet so unfamiliar. Gabi speechlessly soaked up the feeling of being with Jamar 2.0 like a wildflower soaking in the desert rain. She had found herself in a better timeline somehow.

"Sweetie, you really should go and wash your face," Miller added helpfully. "You look like you've been up all night playing rugby, what, with that dirt smeared on your cheek." She looked back down again at the two hands bonded together. Ms. Miller was old enough to remember when there were still a few conservative schools that used to discourage "public displays of affection" of any kind. Now, the strained relationships between genders made a simple PDA, like holding hands, seem like something from an impressionist painting of a lost world, begging for rediscovery.

Miller wasn't going to break that up. She had no interest in declaring things to be out of order for the sake of some persnickety database or arbitrary, paladin-pointed school rules. These two looked delightful together. Looking at Ms. Miller, Gabi's begging eyebrows came in closer, and then raised a few hopeful hairs upward. Kind of like an unspoken "please." Miller returned an approving, slight upturn of the corner of her mouth.

"Well, I am sure your name not being on the list is . . . just an oversight. Technology having a mind of its own, and all that." The stylus made a few sweeps across a few buttons, clearing the way ahead. "Make sure your bicycle is secured correctly, all right, Jamar?" The bicycle, outfitted with foot-sized extensions known as pegs, needed an extra tinkering on the rack to get a proper fit. The bicycle's digital ID failed to register with the shuttle on her tablet, but another click on the screen overrode that, too. "And wipe off your face when you can."

"Yes, ma'am. Will do. Thank you."

Gabi smiled happily at seeing Jamar scam the system armed with nothing more than in-your-face bravado. Ms. Miller cheerfully smiled back.

"Hopefully we'll all see each other again soon. You both stay safe."

"We will."

CHAPTER 19

LUCY'S ESCAPE

Trapped in her office, Gabi's sister was safe for now. Isabella still had plenty to do while she waited for the smart building to move her off site, whether by CAV or by air taxi.

Operating differently than the on-again-off-again classic Internet, the Metaverse was still working for her nearly without interruption. In the "Recommended for You" lists, the top result for everyone traveling worldwide was a venue featuring Parashar's surprise address from Palm Ridge Prep. Of all places. If Izzy could not get a hold of Gabi over the phone, she decided to travel to Palm Ridge and communicate with her that way.

The transitional hallway she entered was extra-long with the download demand for the auditorium as the venue. Izzy walked down the center of a cubicle-laden office environment, with empty workspaces on either side. The space was a dead ringer for the room where the other junior lawyers who had recently joined the firm had been shoved. Izzy had no conception that call centers in South Asia, before customer service A.I. replaced them, had been even larger.

"I was hoping one of you guys would be here," she said in her love-hate way to the man sitting in a random cubicle on the right. He had his legs propped up on the otherwise empty L-shaped particleboard desk, over the wastepaper basket underneath it. He stood to greet her.

"I was thinking of not hacking in today, you know. The crypto payment network keeps going down. Best I can do is trade rumors and build my prestige level."

"So what made you hack this hallway?"

"What else am I going to do? My smartlock imprisoned me. Click."

"Same here. My mixed-use building has an ACLF with old people out biting everyone and the software is literally evacuating the office floors a person at a time. My smartlock got me, too."

"Where?"

"Downtown Fort Lauderdale."

"Wow. Thanks for the info. Your hands are shaking, baby. You know that, right?"

Isabella had not noticed it. Hopped up on adrenaline, she had not realized how traumatic the violence in the lobby had been. People everywhere were seeing rest-of-your-life-nightmare-worthy horrors and it was only slowly sinking in for survivors that they had witnessed real events.

"I'm fine. The second this is done loading, I'm outta here. So what'chu got?"

"The reason everything is taking so long to load is from a DDOS attack. The Machine is the source. Pretending to attack itself with a botnet, that it secretly controls. It's a down-low way of diverting select information flow without implementing an overt censorship regime."

"Can you explain that to me like I'm a five-year-old?"

The rumor Guide, who looked familiar, stifled an eye roll. "Distributed Denial of Service means that a network of bots, almost always consisting of hacked Internet of Things devices, flood the old Internet with so much traffic that even services that are designed to keep things from getting overloaded, themselves get overloaded. Think billions and billions and billions of smart mirrors, smart toasters, smart fridges, smart toothbrushes, smartwatches, all sending a single piece of data over and over to, I don't know, whitehouse.gov, so you can't load the website. If it gets bad enough, your local ISP can't even complete a voice over IP call."

"The IoT takes a dump on everything?"

"Exactly. Very well said. Lots of server timeouts, graphic images and 2D video not resolving, blah blah. Social media down. All unreachable." The Guide's eyes shifted to the left and right and he lowered his voice. "The Machine secretly has quantum backdoors, meaning privileged access, to pretty much every IoT device sold outside of China. And this crypto interoperability failure is by design."

"Whoa. That's a heck of a rumor."

"Metaverse distractions will be kept mostly available to draw people's attention away, though. Sports, gambling, politics, and porn, lotsa lotsa porn."

It was hardly a five-year-old's explanation, but Isabella got the point. "The Machine is doing all this, to itself? What possible good could come of it, genius-boy?"

"Preventing total societal breakdown, sweet-tits. If people learn that everyone with the virus-who-will-not-be-named will become zombies, they don't have enough robots on earth to clamp down the apocalyptic level of chaos that'll happen," the Guide chuckled wickedly, followed by a smoker's cough. "Instead of a disease killing their grandma, grandma is going to be the one killing them. So they're gonna freeze her in place, so to speak."

Just then, she remembered who this Guide reminded her of—yeah, yeah, he looked just like that incel-like programmer who made a fortune in crypto with a dungeon adventure that generated random, dragon-populated venues every time the player switched floors deeper underground. Gabi's age group used to love that gaming milieu, before the whole macho war-reenactment thing got popular. Isabella considered his rumor of immense value. Forgetting about the DDOS attack, she reflexively held out her cellphone to transfer some crypto when the rogue rumorman jumped frighteningly backwards, flinging his hands high above his head, his gaze locked straight past her.

"What, no endangered Antarctic krill habitat left to restore?" she quipped, actually liking this particular rumor Guide.

"All right, all right, my hands are on my head, see? My Spider Rash is tiny. I barely have it! Rumors? I wasn't spreading any rumors."

"Oh, frak. Yo, Guide, Guide, can you hear me?" Isabella waved her open palm in front of his unresponsive face. "Listen, don't talk to any police robots without a law—"

The Guide, beginning to get down on his knees, disappeared in a hard disconnect.

"I guess one way to know it's a human and not A.I. is when they get arrested . . ."

Isabella's lawyerly instincts told her not to finish using this particular hallway. She touched the trashcan in the cubicle, and went through the transition process again, this time without any interruption. The office she walked through was far lonelier the second time around.

* * *

She arrived at Parashar's presentation late, but skipped rewinding it to the start, looking for Gabriela. She had entered the auditorium at the doors behind the top row, fortunately on the segregated side where the female students had clustered. Augmented Reality arrows pointed a path along the floor all the way down to the front rows. There was an empty seat there. Parashar's handler-apparent, the tan suited man, had been edited out. Each person, by the hundreds of thousands, who came to visit the Mixed Reality venue was given the same front-row seat, in a separate session. The final arrow in the series of "follow me" AR arrows pointed downward to the spot.

It was only a short walk down the gentle auditorium stairs before Isabella spotted her sister in the second seat on row 17. Instead of standing there at the end of the row, she quickly stole a place on the lap of the girl sitting to the left of Gabi.

"I was worried sick about you!" Gabi said, looking straight at Isabella.

As the "sit here" arrow aggressively blinked in the first row, Isabella gave her sister a solid summary of her current location and status.

"Well you still have some serious 'splainin to do!" fired back Gabriela. It came across as unnecessarily aggressive, but Izzy continued with her explanation, concluding with, "And, you wouldn't believe what happened to me in the lobby if I told you."

Gabi replied, "Try me."

Just prior, in the flow of her presentation, Parashar had said, "Leave the grandma alone," followed by Aisha softly saying from underneath, "Well then the grandmas should leave us alone," oblivious that two ghosts were sitting on her lap.

The uses of the word "grandma" struck Isabella as rather oddly coincidental, considering what the rumor bro had just said before getting arrested. "So, Gabi, you know how we say you can't believe anything until you see it, in person, with your own two eyes? I did. I saw one. With my own eyes! An actual zombie, biting some fitnessmaxx dude. They're 100% real. Zombies. Look at me, I'm shaking."

"Oh, baby, I'm sorry."

Wait a second, when does she ever call me 'baby?' And when does Gabi ever apologize?

Isabella glanced around, confused, until she spotted a floating status display on the right side of the auditorium. It was not present in Gabi's Mixed Reality version of the scene, since Gabi was really there, and Izzy was not. It showed the permissions for the venue set to "Listen Only/View Only." Visitors had no permissions to interact with objects or people here at all. Obviously. Underneath the floating status sign, also not visible in Gabi's version of reality, was a heavily edited live chat window for the purpose of permitting limited interactions, with a preponderance of "you go!" girl-boss comments, scrolling between endless "why is my connection so slow?" questions. Isabella didn't quite get the smattering of "Look, it's OMG Girl!" references in the chat.

She ran her open palm in front of her sister's face. Snapped her fingers a few times. Poked her. Gabriela didn't react—she could not see nor hear Isabella. In her office, the normally steely lawyer shakily grabbed the side of her lenses, poised to rip them off her face in fury. On a normal day, she could have kept track of all the conflicting realities being mashed into her brain at once, but today felt like she had slipped into another timeline. Her perceptions of reality were as shaken as her hands. "Shake the very foundations of the earth," then declared Parashar.

Angry at herself, Isabella cried out loudly in the direction of the potted plant by her office window, drowning out Deepfake Deepika's "alone together" remark.

"How the frick am I supposed to control my life if I can't separate what's real and what's not?" Fate's tender mercy was that at least Mindy was not in the room to see the tears running down Izzy's cheek. She lifted the headset up off her nose, to look out the window, and lament.

"Nothing is real anymore."

The voice of Gabriela, who was speaking to the ghost of Jamar, faded while saying, "Sure looks that way."

* * *

A black flying drone passed sharply in front of Isabella's office window. She walked over to the glass and looked upward. A drone dome was forming high overhead, providing eagle-eye, additional command and control for the gathering of bots at ground level. Turkey vultures seasonally rode the thermals that wafted upward off tall buildings, and the in-gathering of the vulture-like, dark machines replaced them. Perhaps related to the cyber events of the day, none of the flying machines had AR bubbles with IDs on them.

A brief break in the cyberattack allowed an undigested batch of text messages and voicemails to get through. Why some of her clients thought that a social score lawyer could fix their personal plights in the about-to-begin polylockdown was beyond her. She had enough problems of her own right now.

Two texts stood out.

Yazzi

Heading over to see your brother, Isabella. Will keep you posted.

Mamá

Got the shot, finally. Biggest damn needle you ever saw. Already feeling drowsy.

And, most importantly, Lucinda had sent long local session link just 17 seconds ago.

"On my way, *Ahora mismo*."

There was no loading hallway. Lucinda had sent a direct link for Isabella to share her eyes. There was a slight beeping sound as they connected.

"Oh, Izzy, you're here. Can you see what I see?" A drunk-sounding Lucinda looked around, sharing the video from her headmount, which she had taken off during the medical procedure. In front of her was the former parking lot of the abandoned church-turned-clinic, beyond that the playground at Immossukee Trace Park, beyond that soccer fields, and beyond that relatively new stack-and-pack housing units, replete with rooftop greens and solar enabled windows. Taken all together, a pleasant human settlement.

"Yes, listen, I have to tell you—"

"Ah, I'm all finished, but the bear attendant care bot abandoned me out here on this bench and went back inside. It's supposed to stay with me. I was going to call you, and now my stupid cell phone won't work?"

"Something called denial of service. Not your fault. IoT botnet."

"Oh. Right. Whatever that means."

"So, listen—"

"Did I miss anything while I was out?"

Isabella did not quite know how to answer that.

As a wave of drowsiness hit her, Lucy bobbed her head downward, offering a nice view of her casually sandaled feet.

"You left the house in ugly sandals? What, is your hair in rollers under the headmount? Never mind. We have to get you away from people, *mami*. Especially old people."

Lucy looked back up, enough to give Izzy a view of a few vulture drones ominously gathering in the sky above.

"Old people? Why? I'm at a health care center you know. Plenty of them."

"That's what I was afraid of. Can you walk?"

"Walk? The care robot was supposed to take me to an autonomous vehicle and drop me off right at our door. I'm not supposed to be walking much, you know that."

There was another beep, and Gabi joined the viewing session while seated with Jamar on the school shuttle, coincidentally almost passing by the park on the way to their community.

"Hi, Mom. Hi, sis. Are we having a family meeting in Mom's headset, looking at the old school bus stop at the playground?"

"Where are you?"

"The shuttle. You?"

"Smartlocked in my office. Red padlock on the display, like I'm Romeo in prison or something. I'm trying to tell Mom to get away from old people."

"First, I have to tell you what Jamar told me Alex told him."

Gabi had been mid-conversation with Jamar when she received the join-me-here link from her mother. Alex Abramovich said his father, before he died, was part of a plan to cryofreeze victims of SORS, and the SORS-adjacent. Most importantly, Jamar relayed to Gabi that he had not only seen SORS in action, he had barely got away from them several times. Some of the neighborhood health clinics created in every 15-minute zone became concentrations of SORS-infected. And, in defiance of the new dictionary, Jamar called the infected "zombies," instead of "z-words" or other euphemism.

Gabi and Jamar, as they passed an ACLF across the railroad tracks from the school, had seen a drone dome circling over centaurs busy putting elderly residents into an old yellow school bus. Instead of Spider Rash or elevated temperatures, Alex said an altered heartbeat would be used as the primary diagnostic signal. Gabi did not yet make the connection that the myo-shot would alter her mother's heartbeat signature. She was listening instead to other students speculate that the nearby ACLF was getting raided because the residents, nearing the end of life, traded their social scores away with abandon. "Where am I going to get extra Adderol without trashing my SoSco?" shrieked "Skeeter" Van Houten, the know-it-all, terrified he would not get into the most prestigious Florida colleges without perfect test or social scores.

"No, Gabi, before you tell me anything, we have to get mom into a CAV or a shuttle."

"A pretend hologram shuttle, maybe. I heard Ms. Miller say there's nothing left anywhere not already in use. Besides, I can't even open my ride-share app with the cell network down. You?"

"No, you're right. I have an idea, though," declared Isabella.

"Don't I get a say in what I do?" demanded their mother.

"We're outvoting you. The election came early this year." In a role-reversal from yesterday morning, Isabella cast a glowing arrow on the ground in the direction of the kid's playground across the bike path. "There's a family bathroom there in that little building next to our old school bus stop. You have to trust us."

"I don't need to pee. I need to rest and get this elephant off my chest."

"That bathroom has a door that locks. A dumb lock, as I recall."

"Why?"

There was suddenly a sound of breaking glass. Two window panes down from the bench where Lucy sat, the stained glass window of the converted church shattered outward, sending shards of glinting color spraying onto the ground. A robot dog and an old man came flying out in a tangled mess. The simple robodoggo, the security and floor-guide for the place, rode atop a patient, clearly elderly and clearly covered in spider lines. The man had decided to don a colorful Hawaiian shirt, as colorful as the shards now all around him, before leaving the house that morning. The metallic skin of the dog tussling with him, by contrast, was painted just the standard gunmetal gray. Just looking at the brief, violent intertwining of human and bot, it was not clear which party had jumped or pushed or grabbed the other one. The momentum of flying out the window flipped the dog over, and its metal back slid briefly along a smooth stretch of concrete, before it rolled, and then swiftly reestablished itself on all mechanical fours. The man broke free.

"Why? That's why!"

Lucy retained the presence of mind to whisper an "*Ay, Dios Mío*" instead of screaming it. Sitting still, she would have been beyond helpless had the infected man, who clearly had purply veins running up his cheeks, turned and targeted her. Game over. Being a walkable zone, however, there were plenty of attention-grabbing people still out walking. Their motion caught the infected person's eye. Lucy looked over in the direction of the action, giving her daughters a clear view in their shared lenses. Close by, there was a woman in a long frumpy skirt following a man dressed in black from hat-to-toe walking across the ride pool. The infected, running with unnatural speed, gave chase, as did the robot dog.

The unfortunate walking man and woman were ambushed from behind. The robot dog tackled the running Hawaiian shirt man, from the side this time, who tackled the skirt-wearing woman, also from the side, who fell onto the back of the gray-bearded man. His black fedora tumbled onto the ground. A bicyclist slowed down to catch a view of the horrific hubbub.

Lucy squinted, then opened her eyes wide, and then squinted again. Over the hasty protest of Isabella, she even briefly lifted her lenses up to eyebrow-level so she could verify what she was seeing, unobstructed, risking interrupting the trio's Metaverse connection. Things were not real unless one saw them with one's own eyes, after all.

And there reality was. Not even one quarter of a soccer field's distance away.

It was a near-perfect repeat of what had taken place on Ocean Drive the day prior. Only blind luck, and the frenzied action of the robot, had spared Lucinda. She restored her lenses, and her daughters' view, back atop her eyes.

"Zombies are . . . reality-reality? Or, am I dreaming again? Holy crap. *Mijas*, I want to get out of here." It was Lucy's turn to have her hands shake with fear.

All three Driscoll women now had witnessed the infected, this time all three of them together. No denying it, or rationalizing it away. And between them, with facts blending in with rumors, the twists and turns of the last day and a half had also given them all the pieces of the puzzle, whether they fully realized it or not, of how The Machine would respond.

"This is some deep shit," asserted Gabi, letting her assessment fly without restraint.

"Zombie Apocalypse sheeet," said Isabella.

"Z-word Apocalypse," echoed Gabi, verbally re-restraining herself.

"Remember all those times I asked if there was a pandemic happening, how would you even know?" asked Isabella of the other two. "This is how!"

While the three women, plus the hand-wringing old man and the ride-bro curious bicyclist, watched, the frumpy woman received a nasty tearing at the fleshy side of her neck. The infected man ripped his head side-to-side, sharklike, as Ryan had done in Lucy's dream. The woman had put up a valiant fight underneath the infected man, pushing and squirming and rolling, but the outcome could not be changed, even by the robot dog's frenetic pouncing.

"Oh, fuk—, what now?"

* * *

"Patient Lucinda Driscoll, please return inside immediately for processing." The healthcare robot had reemerged from inside, and it now slowly wheeled itself back again past Lucy in the direction of the screaming lady in the skirt. It had returned to help restrain the Hawaiian-shirt patient when he turned, but the conflict inside had unexpectedly gone outside. Normally that same bear-themed robot would have escorted Lucy either in a wheelchair, or with one soft-grip hand gently under her elbow, to her robotaxi or CAV once it arrived, ready to catch her in a bear-hug if she stumbled. For some unknown reason, it whipsawed its objectives from escorting Lucy away to ordering her off to be processed.

Verbal commands aside, the bear bot physically was prioritizing the unfolding situation on the street, although it was far too slow to give chase and unable to leap through windows.

"*Domo arigato*, Mr. Bear-bot-Oh, sure, sure, of course," replied Lucinda, repeating what her daughter had done the previous day—patronize the friendly robots before the nasty "or else" robots show up. And then get away by following the friendly, family-casted AR arrows, well before the command and control drones that had been swirling over the stack-and-pack apartments began to zoom over towards the clinic, this time less like wafting turkey vultures and more like flying monkeys from the Wizard of Oz.

"'Processing' is reason number two we have to get you away. No time to explain, but 'processing' is a major-league *no bueno*."

"Mom, I have an idea. Leave your cell phone on the bench," Gabi instructed her, being prompted in her ear by Jamar.

Lucinda began to ask, "But what if I need it?" before seeing a big red TLA "X" with some angry all-caps text underneath it. Jamar had seen the same frightening display before ditching his own phone, effectively un-personing himself. "Guess I won't be needing this right now."

"We have to get you naked."

"What? Go streaking in the park?"

"No—"

"I think it's critical we stay in the camera dead spots," asserted Isabella, bringing up AR bubbles with the camera locations. She used to come to this park with friends, and was familiar with them, for a variety of reasons.

"Is this why your generation knows where all the cameras are? Some naked in public kink?"

"Óyeme, not birthday suit naked. Electronics naked. You're covered in tracking devices, remember?"

"Listen to Izzy. She's right. And Jamar reminded me that the biometrics on the cameras can measure your heartbeat's unique squiggle, and can ID you that way, if you're close enough. The timing on modifying your heart might not have been so great." Alex had also told Jamar that the changes in damaged hearts were one of the ways they would identify near-zombies and the zombie-adjacent. "We need to keep you away from pulse sensors until the repairs are done."

The soft-grip bear robot helpfully escorted the injured woman and her father, who had not been bitten, to the healthcare facility. The continuously tripped up Hawaiian shirt man was no longer a threat to them, having given chase to the bicyclist who had unwisely lingered instead of beelining himself into polylockdown.

"You see that paused delivery hippo?" asked Gabi. "Leave your smart ring on top of that before it starts moving again."

"Okay, okay, I see where you are going with this."

Lucy's finger felt a little swollen, like she was retaining water after the shot. Absent the ring, the other devices she wore picked up the slack on monitoring her changing vitals.

"Girls, which is the bigger danger right now, the Zombie or The Machine?"

"Both."

"We need you away from people that won't die AND away from the surveillance that won't die either."

"Next, if you follow these arrows, you'll be right past the edges of the street camera arcs. And the playground trees will block the cameras here, and

here. And there's a full dead spot on this little platform with the kiddie slide."
Isabella cast more arrows. The snakelike path would lead a casual observer
to think that Lucinda was still drunk from the night before.

"How do you know all this, Izzy?"

"Teens come here to smoke cigarettes that get traded from the tribal
lands off of US-441. Gotta love tribal sovereignty."

"Tobacco? Tobacco! You used to come here to smoke cigarettes, didn't
you, Isabella?" Lucy demanded, rubbing her chest as she walked shakily under
a large live oak, a Florida-native species with a thick, camera-obscur-
ing canopy.

"No, *mamá*, of course not that, never," contested Izzy unconvincingly.
She employed dead spots in parks for hide-in-plain-sight, clandestine legal
contacts. Cigarette-sneaking was secondary.

Gabi could have easily busted her sister right then and there. Definitely
not the time. "Jamar is walking with his bike around the back of the house
and I am letting him in through the sliding glass door," she said, feeling the
need to inform her mother of a house guest even in the midst of the crisis.

"Ok, now go up onto the platform for the little yellow slide."

"I get out of breath going up stairs, Izzy. I get dizzy."

"It's like four little steps for kindergartners. You can do it."

"Yeah, you know what? I'm not really out of breath. Could the mRNA
be working that fast?" Lucy glanced down at her smartwatch. There was a
biometric authentication error from the squiggly waveform of her heartbeat
starting to change. She had also forgot to charge the watch after their celebration the previous night. The battery would soon be as dead as the Hawaiian
shirt guy.

"I didn't go to med school, but I didn't think the nanobots do their
thing that fast. Maybe. Pretty cool if they did. Now, ditch the watch."

Lucy put the device down on the metal platform, covered in a thick
green paint that made the surface safety-soft. There was a cigarette butt,
smoked straight down to the filter, lodged in one of the platform's drainage holes.

"All right, you want me to go from here to lock myself in the middle bathroom? The family one between the boy's and girl's sides? Aren't there cameras?"

Gabi, now sitting on the edge of her sister's bed with Jamar, rejoined the conversation. "No, there's a camera dead spot where the water fountain is so young people can pick which gender bathroom they want to use, without fear of their choice being recorded."

"But you can't go there yet. Two more things."

"What?"

"First thing, that smartbra you wear records your heart, meaning your heart ID, too."

Despite her wooziness and the pain in her chest when crossing her arms, Lucy expertly pulled her bra through her right sleeve. She executed the yogi-like, post-workday maneuver that she and Izzy had done a thousand times with ease. She let out the little I-can-relax-now "ah" that comes from such liberations. "Freedom," she declared, placing the sporty undergarment on the green painted platform. The sneaky juxtaposition of cigarette butt and bra had a feel of defiant eroticism in a playground that would soon, by pandemic protocol, be surrounded with yellow, off-limits police tape.

"Second thing," Isabella added, "you're going to have to take off your headmount. Whoa. Whoa. Not just yet."

"Right. Not yet. But how will I communicate?"

Gabi interjected, with Jamar talking in her ear, "You can't. You mustn't. You have to wait until we physically come get you. Lock the deadbolt and don't open it for anything. Stay off the network. It will be like one of those 'Digital Detox' farms out in the countryside. No electronic radiation, and all that."

"I always wanted to do a full digital detox. Just not this way. I was thinking horses and gently rolling hills, not toilets and tampon dispensers. And I'm getting really sleepy, you know. I think that little adrenaline boost is wearing off."

"You get in there, lock the door, and wait, like I am doing here," instructed Isabella, thinking that, unlike her in her office, her mother would at least have a place to pee.

"For how long?"

"As long as it takes. Take a nap, somehow."

"On the floor?"

"On the can if you have to. Your body needs sleep."

Lucinda took one last look around.

In one direction, she had a nice view of the park's remaining soccer field and the multi-family residential unit that had replaced the second soccer field on the far end of the park, also claiming a chunk of the portable classroom section of the elementary school beyond that. Getting the walkable city density just right required chewing up these once open spaces, plus an Immossukee burial mound—a price of progress that Gabi's generation wanted to see undone. People, perhaps unaware of the growing mobility geofence emanating from the clinic, were exchanging final, pre-social distancing hugs or securing bicycles at the smart bikeracks before wisely locking down.

In the other direction, much closer, the woman in the skirt, neck now covered in spreading rash, jumped out from the smashed window opening, having broken free of the bear robot's attempts to restrain her. A shard of glass, clinging to the window's frame, sliced her skirt immodestly up her leg, revealing spreading rash on her thigh. At the intersection beyond, a diesel powered yellow school bus had arrived and was making a turn towards the health center. It had "Region" in black were the "Broward County Schools" used to be, but none of the three observers caught the region number before it turned. A large six rotor drone, the exact model that had tussled with the alligator the previous day, was immune to the mobility-killing geofence and trailed just over the emergency exit at the back of the bus, appearing to be providing a kind of low-altitude escort. Unlike the previous day's drone, this one would show no ID in any AR bubble. There was no way to tag it with #FloridaDrone even if they wanted to.

"Okay, then. Time to go. Put the headset down pointed in the direction of the bathroom so we can watch you go in."

"¡*Te quiero!*"

"¡*Te quiero mucho!*"

"¡*Te quiero muchisimo!*"

With that, Lucy was, electronically speaking, naked as the day she was born.

And with that, Operation Lucy-Lockout became Operation Lucy-Liberation.

CHAPTER 20

PRIVATE MEETING PLACE

"There she goes."

"You think she'll be okay?"

"Sure. When the chips are down, Driscolls know how to handle themselves. Romeros too. But there's no way Mom would go for locking herself in a bathroom if she had not been dizzy from whatever it is they pumped into her."

The two women, still tethered in the public Metaverse, thought about what to do next in silence as they stared at the video feed coming from Lucy's abandoned headmount.

There was no movement outside the three bathrooms in the park. Off camera, the robodog continued providing the infected Hawaiian shirted man with a repeated meet-and-greet with the pavement, away from the playground and the viewing frame of the lenses. They could hear noises, but not see their source. And the centaurs getting off the schoolbus were stealthy. The only visible motion was the shadow over the water fountain of a nearby palm tree's leaves swaying in the breeze.

Isabella broke the silence. "'Processing' means they're going to freeze her along with zombies," she said flatly.

"If they find her. Jamar told me what Alex's father was involved with preparing. He has some ideas on what to do next. He can help. He wants to help."

"Can he hear me?"

"No, he can't connect. No digital ID. He's busy doing some clever hack where he can bridge his development headmount into my school headset and piggyback off of my connection. My headset will act like a Wi-Fi hotspot. It will be like a private Metaverse between me and him. I'm glad he paid attention in AP IoT class."

"Good. Don't tell him what I am saying."

"Okay."

"I like Jamar, really. Of course. His grandmother's account is what got me my own office here, which I am still trapped in, by the way. And I know he's your boyfriend."

"Well, kind of."

"BOY-friend. He's just a boy. Keeping mom out of the freezer is a job for grown women. Period. Jamar likes—and I don't mean this with any dirty innuendo—he likes playing with his hardware all day. His drone collection. Little robots. Hacking into headmounts. Wandering the 'Verse. Which is fine for a boy his age, sure. I know he fancies himself a hero in the Metaverse, a superhero even, but what makes you think 'Jammer' will be anything more than dead weight to us in the Gray World?"

"He managed to escape I&Q in his house, avoided facial recognition all the way from west Broward to east Broward, spotted the camera on our patio and blocked it, can ride his bike faster than zombies can run, and actually finagled Ms. Miller into giving him a ride on our school shuttle."

There was a moment of dead silence not caused by any network glitches, as Isabella pondered her options, which were rather limited. Anyone who could out-negotiate Miller was golden in her mind.

"Where can we all meet?"

* * *

"I'm in," declared Jamar. He quickly explained the gist of his mesh-network hack, but it was techno-gibberish to Gabi.

"And that boy can break into IoT stuff like a pro," she added to the list of stuff Jamar was capable of doing.

"Can he meet us at Mom's store?"

"No. That's a formal venue. We need someplace off the main Metaverse that doesn't use TLA's."

"Send your sister the link to meet us at the encampment," said Jamar.

Isabella received the gobbledygook code that contained the long address of the place in {braces}. "Got it," she declared. "I'm loading it now."

"We're on our way there, too."

Their headsets tethered together, Gabi and Jamar walked side by side through a long military warehouse towards the address sent to Isabella. The room was stacked tall and jagged with wooden crates, as the their destination loaded. The crates, spray-painted with classic military-stenciled letters saying "U.S." and "TOP SECRET" on the rough pine, were positioned in a way that channeled the duo forward towards the exit door visible at the far end. An Indiana Jones–like movie score completed the effect.

"The warehouse is usually isn't this long to walk through out to the private encampment, Jamar. I'll bet lots of people are flooding the alternate Metaverse right now if the web and social media are down. The load times in all of these liminals must be off the charts."

"For sure. If your sister gets there first, I hope she doesn't freak."

"She's usually not one to sperg out. My sister wanders off to some pretty disturbing reaches of the dark 'Verse researching stuff for legal cases. The only thing really dark about where we are going is the lighting level."

"So, what did your sister say about me?"

"She really likes you, you know, and not just because your grandmother was, I mean to say, is, IS her biggest client." Gabi then slid in some white-lie embellishments. "She was, like, you're the perfect man to help out. She's impressed with your hardware—you know, IoT—knowledge." Gabi cleared her throat.

"Sure she is," Jamar said with more than a touch of sarcasm. "And what do you say?" He reached out and held her hand again as they walked.

"I'm impressed, too." Gabi could sense Jamar's online and offline personalities truly merging, as her mother had wanted.

"Good."

"Hang on, did more crates appear at the end of the warehouse? And didn't we just walk past that same rat?"

"Yeah, like a glitch in the matrix, but this time instead of a cat, it's a rat. Speaking of rats, did you notice that there's no rumor Guide near the trash can?"

"There's never one around just when you need one. Maybe they found a way to clamp down on them."

"Doxx rumor Guides? And, what, raid them at home? Doubtful. If they could do that, they could shut off the whole distributed mesh. They'd have to break trillions and trillions of encrypted edges." Jamar refused to believe that part of the new reality. "No way."

"Way," Isabella would have countered, had she been there, having personally seen the fate of a rumor Guide who lingered long enough to get decrypted.

"Still, I was hoping someone had some rumors to share about those yellow buses."

Jamar reached out to grab the door handle that was finally in reach. "All right, we're here."

The creators of the place beyond the dull metal door had painted upon it, in the same stenciled lettering as the wooden crates "Authorized Entry Only." Using a mesh-connection protocol off the main Metaverse, there was no access control to the private place, no TLA scanner to prevent the door handle from being operated by the otherwise stuck-in-a-red-state Jamar. Someone had also used red spray paint to cross out "Authorized Entry" and replace it with "Men." The Driscoll women would simply ignore that.

The two stepped into a dusty crossroads by the edge of a forest. Opposite the woods, farmer's fields flowed along gentle hills, dotted with makeshift campfires. Many liked to say the fires were "the souls of dead warriors," like the glittering stars peeking out of the firmament above them. The sun was frozen in place just beyond the horizon, casting their surroundings in an eternal night-before-the-battle, semi-lit dusk. Treated like a clubhouse, this was a private, informal place many of the young 1944 reenactors came to casually meet before the public, formal battles. A place to share things like cheat codes and strategies. And to hatch up hacks, like the Nazi-zombie trick that had literally scared the shit out of poopy-pants Perez.

Isabella had already arrived and was talking to a cluster of uniformed men sitting around a small fire just inside the woods at the edge of the fields, which lit up the tree trunks like columns, and the underside of the men's faces like Halloween masks.

One of the men, his gray uniform clearly not American, used the lit end of his cigarette to point a lost Isabella in the direction of Gabi and Jamar.

"Bye, pretty girl," another soldier with mud-encrusted boots said. IRL he was speaking in Turkish, but the software translated his words into English with a thick, period-appropriate German accent. Turkish people, for whatever reason, liked to play the role of the Germans in the simulated battles.

A third soldier whistled at Isabella's curves, which required no translation.

Realizing that she was the only person here broadcasting a verification eyecon, which introduced a bright green light in the eternal dusk, Isabella quickly dispelled it as she departed from the flickering light of the campfire. One of the Turks used pointer fingers from both hands, coupled with a dose of unconstrained toxic masculinity, to trace out an hourglass shape from behind, reflecting the outline of the avatar's real world, and extremely out of place, pantsuit. Izzy's heels sunk annoyingly as she walked on the soft ground more suitable for boots. The men, teenagers out in the Gray World, chuckled. There were no dings here for such behavior.

"Aren't those guys supposed to be the enemy?"

Gabi answered her sister's question. "Kids in the Meshaverse have a different perception of who the 'enemy' is. Here, in the mesh-network version of the Metaverse, we're all allies, of a kind. Unless they're dressed up like the SS, those regular Germans won't bother us. Or rat us out."

"Hi, Ms. Driscoll," Jamar jumped in. He was happy to see another familiar face, even under the circumstances.

Isabella was tempted to correct him, again, since hearing someone Gabi's age say "Ms. Driscoll" made her feel like her mother. "Please, just call me Isabella right now," she had told him on multiple occasions. Feeling old, like she was due the senior's discount at a movie theater or something, was more disturbing than being catcalled by a bunch of horny fake Germans. But she was reminded of her mother saying "it's when men stop catcalling that a woman needs to worry." She was also reminded that her whole reason for being here was her mother.

"Hi, Jamar," she said simply in response.

Jamar would normally correct her right back with his code name here, "Lieutenant Jammer," but he was different now. Besides, it hardly felt like a priority to correct "Ms." Driscoll when they were all here for the crisis with "Mrs." Driscoll. He also wore civilian clothes, "civvies," instead of the period costume. Gray sweatpants and a t-shirt.

"Nice to see you, Ms. Isabella."

"You grew a little since I saw you last, I think." The lawyer-mind inside her wanted to also say to the residual-richness beneficiary, "When this is over, there's going to be a lot of legal work. Your family's charity and irrevocable trusts have very complicated structures that have to be dealt with. Political palms needs to be greased. And, I'm not messing around this time, you need to ditch all those unregistered drones before you turn eighteen, understand? Your neighbor across the street went to jail for that." None of the shop-talk was appropriate, however, so she kept it to herself. "I am so sorry about your grandmother," Isabella said instead.

"Yes, we're all so sorry," concurred Gabi, presuming to speak for Lucy as well.

Jamar acknowledged their heartfelt sentiment with a nod. In the Driscoll's living room, Gabi could hear the young man suppress a pre-sob sniffle before shaking it off.

The trio held their impromptu meeting under a road sign at the crossroads—a tall, white-painted post with city names and distances displayed on angled placards pointing off in various directions. "Paris" was one of them. "Nancy" on another. A town called "Metz" was on a third, with "3 km" underneath it. A battle was scheduled to continue on French soil tomorrow morning, October 29, 1944. In that formal venue, Jammer and the Turkish-Germans would be enemies again, if the battle was even to be fought this time around. Who knows? Everyone out there might be a zombie by tomorrow.

"First off, do we have any intel on your mother?" Jamar got right down to business.

Isabella hastily used a casting motion to bring up floating spatial windows. The video feed of Lucy's headset now showed "destination host unreachable." The downtime display of the various public networks showed spinning hourglasses where the red-yellow-green circles would be. The security settings for this particular place were apparently airtight. Nothing from the outside world was getting in.

"Nothing."

"Yeah, that won't work. The ports on this place are completely locked down," Jamar informed Isabella, who had thought bringing up the video feed of the bathroom door from her mother's headmount worth a try. "But I'm sure the cyberwar is still raging on out there."

Isabella checked her virtual cell phone. No bars.

Gabi then said, "All right, last we saw, our mother was safe in the family bathroom at the park. There's no air conditioning in there, but other than that, she was okay before we disconnected."

"But she's trapped," lamented Isabella. "An all-modes geofence is now in place around the park, clinic, and those stack-and-pack residences. For sure. And she's red, so she couldn't use ground transport even if we could get a CAV to cross the geofence."

"Regular taxicab?"

"From the airport? They're not going to defy this polylockdown thingie, which by definition includes a climate lockdown, to come all the way out here. How many cameras would they have to drive past on I-595? And who do we call, 1-888-YOU-GOT-NO-SERVICE?"

"Geez, I'd tell her to just walk home, but she can't walk that far on a good day."

"And, she'd get pinched by a centaur or humanoid milbot before getting very far."

"Or bitten by the walking dead, or would you say 'walkable dead' in a walkable city?" added Gabi. "Actual, IRL, real life, biting people. Zombies. Or, I guess I should start saying, Z-words."

"It's not hopeless," interjected Jamar. "All obstacles can be overcome by a determined unit working together."

A crisply uniformed German approached the trio to interrupt, having just spoken to his compatriots sitting at their fire. Their laughter had stopped and they were gathering up their belongings.

The three paused their discussion, even though the *Hauptmann*, looking very official with a single red-striped ribbon on his chest and an iron cross dangling from his collar, would not have ratted out their plans.

"Sorry to cut in. But if you have not heard, Metz is *kaputt*." He pointed his thumb over his shoulder behind him.

"Canceled?" The man was pushing the limit of Jamar's German without A.I. translation. Mandarin was his elective language at Palm Ridge.

"*Ja*, yes, the whole reenactment near the town. I'll let it pass that the two of you soldiers are out of uniform," he said, referring to both Izzy and Jamar being in civvies.

"What changed? Cancellations never happen."

"The polylockdown. Did you not hear? They accelerated the schedule. Perhaps people hiding in places like this don't know about it." His accent made the they-the-this come out as zay-ze-zis.

"Whoa."

"And the official Metaverse is getting access-restricted. That never happens either. Yellow TLAs are starting to block digital venues for the first time, ever, I think. Wherever you're going to go, you need to get there."

"Yellow ain't mellow? Can we stay here?"

"Well, that's not up to me," shrugged the enemy reenactor. "But, at least there's an empty campfire over there now you can use." The soldiers who had been sitting there had abandoned their meeting spot in disgust. The German added, "Assuming they don't find a way to kick us all off the Meshaverse, too."

"*Danke*." The out-of-uniform Jamar thanked the officer, who outranked him, with an impromptu salute. The additional intel was worth the interruption.

The German captain—a 13-year-old Somali girl in her mother's Stockholm basement, acting as just another one of the Turkish fellows, then masquerading as a decorated hero—returned the salute with a simple touch of his leather-gloved pointer finger to the brim of his jaunty saucer cap. Isabella thought he looked like a motorcycle cop in his tall riding boots, and it was a good thing he was not a rumor Guide looking for tips, for red-statused Jamar was cut off from his trust funds' crypto. The captain then departed to inform another group, a friendly mix of Germans and Brits, at the next campfire.

"Is that a Guide?"

"More like a rotating volunteer. There's no Guides here in our twilight lands. Fact or otherwise."

The three made their way over to the better lighting of the still-burning abandoned site, complete with a split, moss-covered log to sit on.

"Does that mean they're canceling the whole war? After all the time we put into it?"

"If they do, we don't get to Berlin. Damn, Hitler's prolly gonna escape from that bunker of his down to Argentina. A second time, I guess. Just like that rumor that won't die."

"Or the Nazis escape to Antarctica, if you really want to go down the rabbit hole with rumors. But right now the only escape that matters is from that bathroom."

"The only thing that matters," Izzy reminded the other two.

Before bending his knee and placing his right shoe atop the log, Jamar said solemnly, looking out over the flickering lights, "I have to say, I always imagined doing this really grand thing. Winning the war myself. Shiny medals running up my chest from here to here. Beating the Russians to Berlin. Blowing up the Death Star. Changing the course of history. Be 'Verse famous, globally."

"No fame. No one can know what we're about to do."

"I know. It's just. Ah. I was hoping that everyone here, everyone in the whole damned 'Verse, was gonna see me save the whole world, not just one person in a bathroom," Jamar said sadly.

"Save the whole world, Jamar? Remember this, 'saving one life is like saving the world entire.' I know Alex was taught that back when getting Bat Mitzvah'ed."

"Wow. That's deep. Now that you mention it, I once heard Aisha say that very same thing."

"Let's do this."

CHAPTER 21

PLANNING THE RESCUE

"So, we just get in the family car, pick her up from the old bus stop, and come back? Uh, we don't own a car anymore."

The back and forth between Lucinda's two daughters took on a heavy air of sarcasm.

"So Gabi should just walk over there? I mean, they made the cities walkable when they split them all up, right?"

"Oh, hi, Mom, nice to see you, let's go for a stroll back home—"

"Through a walkable dead city? That won't work either."

Jamar moved the conversation in a different direction. "When they split them up to make them walkable, they also made them bikeable, did they not?"

"Sure."

"So, bicycles are our biggest asset," asserted Jamar. "They redesigned the whole county, the whole country soon, with bikes in mind, so let's use that to our advantage. Weston, before it got split up, was rated one of the best cities for bicyclists in all of South Florida."

"Agreed, but my mother has a heart condition. You're thinking like a strong teenager," replied Izzy, not sure if the more muscular and fit version of Jamar was a recent, natural chance in the growing young man, or just the way he liked to present his avatar. His connection being effectively a hack, there was no eyecon for him. "And, she's probably dizzy as hell again after her bot shot. And she can't rent a bicycle from the smart rack. Or rent a scooter. Her TLA is red. She can't just ride home."

"She can stand, right? I mean, she made it from the playground to the bathroom."

"Yes, of course."

"Then she can stand on my pegs."

"Your what?"

"'Pegs.' Foot pegs. They're these aluminum things, like long coke cans, that go on the side of the tires. A person can stand on them and hold onto the shoulders of the person doing the pedaling. That's not really what they are supposed to be for, but it works."

"Oh, yeah, I think I've seen those. Like a stand-up version of a bicycle built for two." Izzy smiled and turned to her sister, "You were right, Gabi, bringing Jamar in on this was the way to go."

"What did you say?"

"What do you mean, what did I say? That Jamar was the 'way to go?'"

"No the first part. Say it again. 'You were right, Gabi.'"

"Yes. Yes, you were," Izzy replied, offering it as a sincere compliment. "I'm glad we are on the same team."

The two laughed.

"Me, too. That's all Mom ever wanted for us, I think. To be on the same team."

"Well, that, and grandkids."

Jamar, having listened to many anger-filled diatribes of Gabi complaining about the abuse Izzy used to hurl at her, smiled. He was genuinely happy to see his newly official girlfriend and her sister get along so well.

Wait, he wondered, am I official yet? *Hmmm, is now the time for me to ask?*

Isabella suddenly realized they had not officially asked if Jamar was going to come along on the rescue-Lucy mission.

"Jamar, are you planning on going along with Gabi?"

"Yes, for sure. I am not going to let...," he paused imperceptibly before going all in on his next words. "... let my girlfriend's mother have horrible things happen to her. That would be two tragedies in two days. Not letting that happen. Not on my watch."

Gabi got that same goosebumpy feeling she had gotten when Jamar publicly held her hand at Palm Ridge's ride pool. *Maybe someone should tell Izzy that chivalry is not dead.*

"Great," concluded Isabella. "What a relief. Mom's going to need strong, physically strong, help. Mom's not fat, but she's not exactly fit and *fuerte AF* like Gabi here. I didn't think my mom could do it alone."

"¿*Fuerte?* Thanks, sis." Gabi appreciated being called strong by her sister instead of scrawny.

"No one goes it alone," declared Jamar. "I think this mission requires more than one person to be successful. So my shoulders will be the ones Mrs. D will be holding on to."

"I wish I could be there in Eastglade with you."

Isabella recalled saying that "Jamar is just a boy" only a few minutes ago. Whatever had happened on escaping his I&Q, it had clearly changed him. She liked the more confident, assertive Jamar, too, and had no problems imagining that his IRL leg muscles were now as strong has his avatar's appeared to be.

"The way I see it, we have two main obstacles," Jamar then declared, now talking decidedly in his Lieutenant Jammer way, "Robots and zombies." He reached down and grabbed a small broken tree branch from the ground next to the mossy log, snapping off a straight, wand-like stick to use as a pointer. He kicked away some leaves in the soft soil by the campfire, and began to use the exposed ground as a makeshift canvas.

The tip of the stick made elements of a map in the sand. The objective was first, a square, representing the public bathrooms at Immossukee Trace Park. At the other end, the "L" shape of the Driscoll house they were in now. He had done these in-the-sand maps many times, sketching beaches, hills, hedgerows and other features of the European landscape as he and his fellow reenactors planned tank and infantry movements. Sometimes they would rehearse their next attack by physically walking through a larger version, telling each other "you go here, and then I'll move my platoon here." Computer-generated satellite maps were a thousand times more precise, but maps drawn by hand were a thousand times easier to remember in the heat of battle.

As he drew, Isabella extended upon Jamar's observation, "Robots being a problem is rather ironic, since robots are accepted now as the first line of defense against infections spreading. That last outbreak, the mini-demic in China, they almost exclusively used robots to collect the deceased and put them in refrigerated trucks. A pandemic was stopped before it got started."

"True, but the deceased were not moving," added Gabriela, taking the stick from Jamar and drawing from memory the familiar, winding Eastglade roads that she had bicycled down many times. Isabella, terrible with directions, would not have been able to discern north from south on the growing terrain map, much less remember the roads. All she could do was comment.

"Those bots were grabbing corpses, not the zombie-adjacent. Not yet, at least."

"Robots will do what they have to do to end the Z-Apocalypse in under two weeks, I'm pretty sure."

"Instead of two weeks to stop the spread, two weeks to stop the undead?" Jamar mused.

The two women groaned.

"Daddy used to tell corny jokes like that, you know."

Jamar grabbed three small stones, pebbles really, placing two at the Driscoll's house and one at the bathroom. A shooting star crossed the sky, something he had never seen before in this place.

"I'd say there's a third obstacle, Jamar," said Isabella as she watched. "There's facial recognition cameras on every smart lamppost watching every inch of those curvy, post-suburban roads and bike lanes."

"I know. Believe me. Alex used to live here before he got upgraded to Parkland. Before his dad became regional director. That's why I'm familiar with layout, mostly anyway. These roads all have drainage lakes running parallel to them. With big, grass-covered expanses between the water and the roads." He took the stick back from Gabi and drew an additional set of lines. "We used to sneak through the landscaping bushes, sit on the grass in the shade of the trees, and fish in spots sometimes, particularly under the bridge near the country club. Before the patrol drones came. He tapped his stick against a spot on the dirt map, before lightly tracing paths along the roads they had etched into the ground. All those grass—what would you call them, swales?—are going to be our pathways. All the poofy trees they planted along the sidewalks for carbon credits will block the cameras from the smart lights." He poked small holes in the sand with the stick's pointy tip.

Isabella, spending most of her life now prompting chat A.I.'s to produce legal filings for review, was amazed at how someone with a true spatial mindset saw the world. Like being in a different reality.

Before the Internet, were men always the ones that were good with directions? she quickly pondered before banishing the thought of men being better at anything.

Gabriela then used her fingertips to wipe a line drawn by Jamar, correcting his map. She said softly, "No, the lakeshore doesn't connect here. There would be a road we have to cross, here. They reclaimed most of the country club's golf course for high-density housing, here, so that got filled in right . . . there."

Izzy attempted to contribute to the layout by picking up a stone and putting it way off on the side of the sand map. "An air taxi is coming for me, here, but I have no idea when."

Jamar smiled and moved her stone. "Everglades on this side, Atlantic on this one. You'll be coming from this direction, here."

"Oh."

"Now, this next part is more Vietnam than World War II." Jamar drew deep, dashed lines to show the boundary between the 15-minute quadrants that separated the walkable city. "The Vietcong figured out the repeating patterns where the Americans used to send out patrols, and found the gaps between them. Squads kept on the same paths to avoid running into each other, because 'friendly fire' is not very friendly when you think about it. The VC would stay in the gaps and could move between the American patrol lines without being detected."

"Interesting history, but how does that help us?"

"Combat tactics. Avoiding drone patrols, like the ones that used to nail me and Alex fishing in the canals back in middle school." Jamar pointed to a different spot on the map. "So, at this point, right here, we sneak in the gap between the boundaries instead of right atop them." He picked up the two pebbles representing himself and Gabi, bouncing them along the dashes.

"If they have government drones flying up along these patrol lines, here is where we travel, physically travel, to avoid them. We stay in the gaps, exactly like I did last night. Then, we cross here on the edge of the soccer field, and—"

"We're at the objective," Gabi completed his sentence excitedly. "All right, so we know how we get there. Awesome. What do we do at the actual park? How do we get safely from this pebble here to the actual bathroom?"

"Ah, speaking of bathrooms, Gabi, can I use yours IRL? Nature calls." Jamar needed a good excuse to break away from the conversation, and think. Asking to use the Driscoll's bathroom sounded much better than "honestly, I have no idea what we should do when we get to the park."

"My bathroom is straight ahead. It has a dumb mirror, so you're good there. But, watch out for the smart fridge. It has a camera that can ID you."

"Got it. Be right back."

Jamar felt like his bladder was going to burst. Skipping an elegant exit, he whipped off his headset. His avatar froze, soulless, and then flickered out like the light of a dying fire.

"He has no clue what to do next, does he?"

"Nope."

* * *

"Should we be worried?"

"Give him a minute; he won't come back empty handed, I'm sure."

"Speaking of coming back, that policeman-looking guy in the boots is coming our way again."

This time, instead of a salute, the Somali pretending to be a Turk pretending to be a German officer grabbed the brim of his cap in a polite greeting. "Ladies."

"Hi. Can we help you?"

"I just wanted to let you know there's someone in the woods who has been looking for you."

"Who?"

Both women looked around in the direction the man pointed to. Campfires had been going out all over as people left the place to deal with the polylockdown in their gray existences. The forest was now dark, and still.

"A synthetic person, out of place in these parts," answered the man. "I didn't really get the name he was using. Rob or Ron, perhaps. Oh, I think that's him over there."

Hidden in starlight, the man, more of a shadow than a solid figure, was following a well-worn trail between the trees, coming closer. The two women simultaneously reached up to the corner of their lenses to zoom and enhance, but being in 1944, there were no lenses over their avatars. They had to resort to craning their necks forward and squinting.

Izzy turned to the officer. "Was that name 'Ryan?' It wasn't that, surely?"

"*Nein*, not Shirley. Wait, you're right. 'Ryan,' that was it. Ryan was his name."

"It can't be . . .," remarked Izzy, her voice trailing off.

"No way," said her sister.

And then, in concert, the two asked, and exclaimed,

"¿¡*Papá*!?"

* * *

The campfire offered a stronger view of the man's face as he approached. Although he was older than when she had last seen him, to Isabella her father was instantly recognizable. She leaped up from the sitting-log, and raced over to greet him, shouting, "Daddy, Daddy," loud enough for Mindy, still locked in her office across the hall, to hear her. The soft ground made her avatar stumble forward into Ryan's arms. She felt nothing of it without haptics. Ryan, however, could feel his baby girl again, all grown up. Her palms were against both his cheeks, like a picture frame with a beloved memory inside it. "Wow, I didn't see this coming!" she said joyfully.

"OOOOH," groaned Ryan, squeezing Izzy and then planting a string of rapid kisses on her forehead. He leaned back, his arms now on her shoulders. "Look at you. Oh, just look at you."

"No, look at YOU." She touched the graying temples of the man that autonomous technology had stolen from her, seeing him as he would have looked now. She stared deep into his laughing eyes. "Why?" she simply asked, encompassing several questions, such as "why now," "why not before," and most importantly, the unanswerable "why did you have to leave us" all in a single word. "I needed you, Daddy. I needed you," was her silent lamentation, hiding just beneath the surface layer of sheer joy.

Reading what her question meant from her emotions, he replied, "I had no choice. Your mother didn't want you to see her needing me. To see that she needed a therapy bot to cope and get by—like she was a lonely box-wine cat lady. There's no shame in using a grief bot for therapy, but a proud woman, your mother is."

"Mom never told me she used a bot for therapy," commented Isabella. "And speaking of Mom—"

"Yes, that's why I came looking for you. Something's wrong, Izzy. Seriously wrong. I have reason to believe your mother is in trouble. All of Lucy's vitals are gone."

"No sheet," Isabella quickly responded, then asked rhetorically. "Where the heck have you been?"

Ryan answered frankly, "Sleeping, kind of like that. Dreaming of electronic sheep." He would have been glad to explain the whole digitally-resurrected experience from his perspective, but this wasn't the time. "But that's not important right now. I woke up to get ready for a session with your mother, which she prepaid to get the discount, you know her, and nothing. But it's not like her to miss a meeting, and waste the crypto. Is her TLA red again?"

Izzy started to begin retelling what had happened to Lucy, but stopped short as a thought popped into her head. *Wait, wait, wait, hold, is this what my mother has been spending all our crypto on?*

An upset Ryan kept speaking, "Lulu was going to camp out in bed all day, recovering from her medication. We had picked out a movie and everything."

"Uh, yeah, that's not happening."

"Why, what's happening?"

Ryan disengaged from Isabella and leaned slightly to the side, making it clear he wanted to draw his other daughter into the "what's happening" conversation. Despite being worried sick over his wife, he still hoped for a hug from his youngest.

Gabi just stood there, motionless as if she had disconnected from the Metaverse. Her mouth hanging open, with a mix of betrayal and horror, she could not believe what she was witnessing. Betrayal came from seeing her sister pretend that a chatbot was really a resurrected loved one, a man she felt abandoned by, even if not by choice. And horror. Horror from seeing the dead walking.

Gabi found out this morning that she, of the two types of people in this world, was the type whose psychology forcefully rejected grief bots.

She finally moved. Placing her left hand on her waist, she pointed at Ryan with two fingers on her right hand for emphasis.

"That. Man." Gabi shrieked hysterically, "That man is NOT real!"

Her avatar froze again. This time because, in the living room, Gabriela had furiously ripped her headset from her face.

"Well that didn't go well," Ryan concluded.

* * *

"Okay, I figured out how to go and finish rescuing Mrs. D!"

Jamar jumped back into the conversation, looking like he had just come back from relieving himself behind one of the forest's trees, excitedly rejoining the session in the mesh meeting place just in time to see Gabriela's avatar dissolve in an ugly jumble of pixels.

Jamar heard a door slam somewhere in the Driscoll house, out of view. "Where did you go?" he asked, thinking Gabi would be standing next to him. Gabi had run to her room, flying headfirst into her pillows, beginning to soak them in tears.

"Rescue?" Ryan challenged the new entrant by the campfire. "What the hell do you mean 'rescue'?" he demanded with an anger unusual for both a grief bot, and his personality.

"Mr. Driscoll?" Jamar challenged, in return.

"Jamar? Jamar Rice, is that you?"

Both of them briefly talked over each other with amazed variations of "Wow, I remember you when . . ."

"You look, great."

"You look, tall. You really grew."

Jamar was plainly one of the half of the population who was not repulsed by talking to avatars of the dead. He held out his hand to shake Ryan's. "Sorry, my hands are a little wet. I just washed them."

"XYZ," joked the older man with a grin. He forewent the handshake and proceeded straight to the heartfelt "bro hug."

Isabella, stayed silent during the reunion, only able to offer up a under-breath condemnation of "Men. Geez." She shook her head.

The light back-patting of the bro hug transitioned spontaneously into a deep father-son style embrace.

As they disengaged, the two talked somewhat over each other again.

"Oh, man, great to see you!"

"Yeah, for real."

"I like this place you picked out to meet. It has a real man-cave vibe."

"Toxic," threw in Isabella.

"All right, Jamar. Full stop. What 'rescue?' What's going on?"

Isabella began to explain it was more like "liberate," but Jamar had already pointed her father over to the makeshift map. The two men angled themselves in a way that sidelined Izzy.

"I'll sum it up best way I can. First, the situation. Your wife is hunkered down, incommunicado, in a bathroom at the park, here." Jamar picked the pointer-stick back up. "Gabi and I are the only ones in range, here. Isabella is awaiting an air taxi, here. Zombies—they want us to call them Z-words now—from the clinic and the stack-and-pack apartments, are here. Robots being bussed in. Drones overhead. And the weather? It's going to rain."

Isabella reintegrated herself into the conversation, "On the bright side, The Machine is cleaning up the infected, but if a robot yeets mom out of the john, she's going to be flash frozen. Jamar, being 'SORS-adjacent,' will be a human popsicle, too."

"On a normal day, I'd challenge every word that just came out of your mouths as being high-on-something, insane babble."

"You've heard things in this timeline been normal, I presume?" replied Jamar.

"Yeah, zombie flash-freezing was not on my 2044 bingo card. But, I tried to convince Lucy to not go down rabbit holes and act normally. What have I done?"

"Your job, as you saw it. I blew this thing off, too, until I saw it myself."

Ryan ran his hand through his hair and pointed to the artificial landscape around them. "It's like an inversion. Who would ever think that things in here where I am look like normal, and things out there where you are look like crazyville? So, what's next?"

"As I see it, the mission is simple. We rescue Mrs. D., bring her back here, and we all lockdown until The Machine's robot armies get the world back under control. Assuming I can lockdown here in Eastglade."

"Well you're a welcome guest in my house anytime, Jamar."

"Yes, you can stay with us, of course." Isabella interjected, caught somewhat off guard by her mother's grief bot saying "'my' house" and dishing out invites. "And 'lockout' is the word mother uses, not 'lockdown.' Oh, there's something going on here at the office IRL. I think they're starting to move some people to the roof. Hang on a sec."

"That's great news, Izzy."

Isabella's avatar froze and she did not respond. Jamar took the opportunity to call out loudly for Gabi in real life.

"I'm trying to get back in," she shouted back. "But I'm, like, this transition warehouse I have to walk through is a mile long."

"Gabi will get used to me," Ryan informed Jamar. "For some people, it just takes time. Speaking of time, I'm only rented out for a short while longer. I need my wife to put coins in the meter, so to speak, or I'm headed back to dreamland."

"Maybe that's for the best," Gabi then said, her session finally loading. She approached along a little trail as the door to the edge disappeared behind her.

An unfrozen Isabella then gently admonished her, "There's no need to be rude. Grief bots feel emotions, too."

"Feel? Fine, whatevs. But no hugs, no 'I missed you' XOXO crap. He can stay, if he can help us plan in some way. If not, I want him gone. So, Jamar, what's next? What did you figure out?"

"On my way to the bathroom, I saw the smart thermostat display show it's going to rain, from 3 p.m. to 5:15."

"Great, so we all get wet?"

"No, remember, thunderstorms ground drones."

"Ruins satellite IoT tracking, too."

"Ah."

"Oh, good point."

Jamar used his branch pointer again. "So, we execute the mission with two bikes. My intent is to ride out there using all these Eastglade drainage lakes as stealthy avenues to approach, on the grass that runs along the lakes, staying off the streets. We wait until it starts to pour, and then make our final move on the bathroom. Ride back, next, with Mrs. D. on a slightly different route. Finally, we get back here, stay off the public Internet, apply to get our green TLA's back after it's over."

Ryan crossed his arms. "Go on."

"Everybody's got a task to do. Ms. Driscoll, I mean Isabella, that's easy; she just has to get home. I'll assume zombies can't fly, so she'll be safe. Now, Gabi. Gabi will be tasked with getting her mother from the actual bathroom. I'll pull any infected away from the clinic zone on my bike, like pied piper. Gabi will do that on the way back. Don't worry, they can be outrun on bicycles, I did it several times. Finally, I'll have the main task of putting Mrs. D. on my foot pegs and pedaling back."

Gabi and Izzy both challenged that part of the mission plan. "If the grass is wet, you're going to be exhausted riding all that way. I know you're strong, but be realistic."

"We can't ride in the green bike lanes?"

"We'll risk getting ID'd by the streetlight cameras."

"You'll have to keep your faces covered so the facial recognition can't work," said Ryan, rather familiar with the internal workings of The Machine's technology.

"Surgical masks and sunglasses?"

"For one guy, yeah, but if you have two, then three, people with their faces covered like that, no digital ID's being broadcast, the security protocols will flag it as you being on your way to an illegal gathering of some sort."

"Cover our faces a different way, then? With Izzy's pantyhose?"

"You are not touching my hose!"

"It would be the same issue, anyhow. Like a bank robbery, well, if they still had physical bank branches. For IoT edge computing, all of that face covering will look like some kind of crime is underway. If there's a free patrol drone in the police air-cap, it will definitely come after you."

"Pillowcases with the eyes cut out?"

"Like the Klan? Shady AF. And probably useless in the rain."

"Besides, we'd survive the Z-word Apocalypse only to have mom kill us for ruining her bedding."

"If too many people in one group are a problem, how about we split into two?"

"Another risk. Custer split his forces, and look what happened to him."

"So we have to gamble that all the patrol drones are busy? Or that it's raining too hard and they ground them?"

"Both? Neither?"

They all paused to think. It was unrealistic that Jamar would have come up with a bulletproof plan in the time it took to go to the bathroom.

It was Gabi who broke the silence. "It's Day of the Dead season, right? *Dia de los Muertos* is upon us. And, hey, National Trick-or-Treat Night is tomorrow."

"Yes, yes it is," responded Izzy in an "aha moment" voice. "It's normal for people to have their faces completely covered this time of year. The threshold that triggers a robot response will be temporarily modified. Stay below the cutoff, and you're fine. Imagine, you guys were at a Halloween, or pre-Halloween, party, got the lockdown order, and are making your way home. Nothing to see here, robots. Move along."

"I have the costume I just ordered for the school party," Gabi said. "All the good ones were sold out, don't get me started on what I had to buy. But it has a mask. Jamar, you have a hoodie, or we can improvise with something. A bandanna? Like a pirate?"

"And I can use my sunglasses to impede retinal scans. Plus use the hoodie to cover most of my face, like last night."

"You'll be trick-or-treating in a Unabomber pirate costume?" asked Ryan.

"No idea who that is, but yeah. And I can switch out the sunglasses for my goggles when I need them to zoom in on things. They're not connected, so they won't blow our cover."

"What about Mom?"

"Is that that old hockey mask still in the garage? She can be Jason, from Friday the 13th."

Jamar said, "Unless we think of something better, that will have to do. The next thing is how we communicate, which is better said as anti-communicate. Gabi and I will be offline and can't communicate electronically. Strict radio silence. Voice only. And we'll have to scrape the RFID tag off your bicycle like I did mine."

"There's a box of razor blades and a scraper underneath the gloves, in the box on the lower shelf by the water heater," Ryan contributed helpfully.

"How will I know you two are back, with our 'client'?" Isabella asked.

"You might be home before us, right? Who knows. If the cell network is back up, Gabi will text or call. If not, save the address and keep checking back here. Either we'll see you or I'll just write 'mission accomplished' in the virtual sand."

"Can we try to use your pocket drone as a scout of some kind? That thing is the size of a palmetto bug, right?" Gabi asked Jamar.

"That would be nice, but I doubt it," he replied. "The best thing is for you and I to go naked." Suddenly red-faced, he turned to address his girlfriend's father, fully clarifying his meaning, "Naked as in no-electronic signals, not, you know, her, me, nekkid, you know."

"I know."

"I mean, it's a plan," confessed a doubtful Isabella, feeling helpless. "I want to be there, but even if I were, I'd endanger the whole thing with this." She held out her RFID-chipped right hand.

"Well, you'll just have to pass the torch to the next generation, sis. Besides, none of this matters unless you get everyone green again."

"I'll handle the tantrums of the Machine Magisterium. You just keep mother's heart beating."

"Speaking of which, she will have a whole new heartbeat waveform and need a new digital ID? Right? If the mRNA has fully modified her, she could go right past a scanner and it couldn't confirm precisely who she is."

"Exactly."

Jamar then turned to Ryan. "You okay passing the torch to the next generation, Mr. Driscoll? How does this all sound?"

Ryan tightened his arm-crossing gesture, and scowled, "Let me see if I have this straight, okay? My wife is in mortal danger, in a bathroom. Probably the most scared she has ever been. She's got no access to autonomous transport, not that I am a fan of that anyway, obviously, so you plan to exploit holes in the bikeable city layout to bicycle to her, off-pavement, while hiding your identities in Halloween getups, no electronic comms, outrunning infected people by pedaling faster than they can run, even though Jamar here hasn't slept a wink, then have my wife ride on pegs like she's a dizzy teenager, counting on the rain to block surveillance drones? Oh, and then, hide from getting ID'd inside our house, filled with sensors, and, after it's over, have Izzy file for post-pandemic amnesty? That's the plan?"

"Yeah, basically."

"Pretty much. 'Driscoll's plan,' that's what you always said, remember?"

Ryan took a deep breath.

"That is the dumbest, most random, ridiculous, nuttiest, divergent idea I have ever heard of."

The three of them, dejected, stared wide-eyed at shaking-my-head Ryan as he pointed out the obvious. And there wasn't much time to come up with a fresh plan.

"Frankly, it's . . . retarded."

There was an air of total shock among the three listening to Ryan employ the nuclear R-slur. Anyone would have utterly trashed his or her social score so openly using it. People just didn't go there, even if they were safe in a mesh or away from a microphone. But Ryan was already canceled, and free. His whole existence was a first amendment-permitted activity zone.

Uncrossing his arms, he would speak as he pleased.

"Which is, exactly, why it will work."

CHAPTER 22

THE RESCUE

The faces of Jamar, Isabella, and Gabriela assumed an air of relief mixed with confusion at Ryan's R-word assessment.

"I know a thing or two about how The Machine thinks, or thinks it thinks."

"That would make sense."

"It scrapes up near-infinite data of human activity, makes more connections than there are stars in the sky, trillions and trillions instead of billions and billions, and models patterns it sees in graphs. The Machine looks imaginative, but it doesn't handle the divergent stuff well, despite all that singularity crap they tell you in press releases. So, something completely random, out of the blue, like kids on bikes, one dressed like the *Friday the 13th* serial killer, riding into, instead of away from, a Zombie Apocalypse is not part of its core data set, to say the least."

"Completely random," concurred Jamar.

"Random, and, you know, ahem, the other R-word," Ryan replied, avoiding a second dose of the slur.

"So, the same reason it can't ever get dad jokes quite right? They're too R-worded?"

"Yeah. Exactly. The only way to hide from the algorithms is to make a plan so, so R-worded, that The Machine won't see it coming."

"But won't it still try to send robots after us?" Gabi asked. She was having moments of doubt. Her anxiety issues struggled to return from just below the surface, as she fought to keep them down. Dad 2.0 would have to sub in for Dr. Silberman as her anxiety therapy-bot.

"I don't think so. Here's the thing. Near-infinite data. Near-infinite processing power. But, finite number of drones. Finite number of sensors. Finite number of bots on the ground. Even after the militaries of the world cranking them all out by the zillions. The Machine can run all the stochastic scenarios it can dream up in the ether, predict with digital twins what masses of people will do before they do it, but it can't put an armed centaur on every street corner out in the physical world. Digitally, infinite. Physically, limited."

"And the priority of the robots they do have out there has to be rounding up the visibly infected first, zombie-adjacent second," Jamar stated. "Alex's dad helped come up with that whole CONPLAN 8888 stuff. The milbots do a damn good job, too. I saw that myself last night."

"No doubt. So, like Isabella said, there will be a threshold, a trigger, that if your activities stay below it, you two should be able to operate freely. You'll be fine, Gabi," added Ryan in therapy-mode. "I have confidence in you."

"Thanks," Gabi began to reply, catching herself before saying "Dad." Still, the reassuring voice, the sound of which had not faded in her memory, seemed to banish the anxiety away.

"Now, you, young man, Jammer, just remember, you're not a soldier or a lieutenant or any of that in real life. No offense."

"None taken."

"When I was your age, I thought I was indestructible. But milbots can really zip cuff you. The infected can really bite you. Understood?"

"Understood."

"What will you do if things don't go as planned?"

"What soldiers always do, even if, yeah, I am not a real one. Improvise. I attended a speech with General Patton once. Synthetic Patton, of course. He said basically that 'no plan survives contact with the enemy.' Don't worry, I'll adapt to meet the contingency."

"He's good at that," Gabi said of Jamar, still conspicuously avoiding adding "Dad."

Jamar continued, Patton also said, "A good plan executed today is better than a perfect plan tomorrow."

"What you said, Jamar, reminds me of this time I met Mike Tyson. Synthetic Tyson, sure, but still." Ryan pointed to himself to say, "like me." "Iron Mike told me 'everyone has a plan till they get punched in the face'."

Isabella shook her head at all the toxicity on display.

"Roger that. Funny."

"Speaking of funny," said Ryan as he leaned in and whispered something into Isabella's ear, just loud enough for Jamar to hear as well. The two of them broke out laughing.

"What? What did he say?" asked Gabi.

"Nothing about you," replied Jamar.

"The perfect dad joke," added Isabella. "But only if you believe he's a dad." It had been the best dad joke Ryan had ever delivered.

"For real, Izzy?"

"I'll tell it to you later, Gabi."

"And, who's a Mike Tyson," she then queried, hesitating only slightly before adding "dad?"

"Well, this is awkward," Ryan said, not addressing Gabi's question. "They are telling me it's time to wrap things up."

"Who's 'they,' Mr. Driscoll?"

"Oh, that's right; you can't see them, can you?"

Gabi and Jamar looked around, but no one had joined them by the campfire.

"On a very practical, financial level, my session balance has zero crypto left and your mother's TLA is red. Think of it that way. The rent has come due, so to speak. I am out of time."

"That's ridiculous."

"I have to go back from where I came. Remember, we all do, at some point. That great null node in the sky. Sorry to leave you three like this." Ryan made a move to give Isabella, who was closest to him, a hug. Engrossed in their conversation, none of the other three had noticed that her avatar had frozen up with connectivity issues. A profound sadness washed over Ryan.

Gabi, seeing his emotion, unexpectedly gave him a hug in her stead.

Behind Ryan, a tunnel of light then began to appear. A bright light, as colorless as Lucy's store, shone from a focal point far off in the distance. "I missed you, pumpkin," he said to his youngest, using the pet affectation that was exclusive to her. He didn't need haptics to feel the squeeze of her hug tighten. "I missed you, too," and she finished her sentence with "*papá*," without a hint of hesitation. Even without haptics, in her mind, she thought she could feel his arms around her loosen. He vanished to the words "I'll be back." Tears streamed down her face as Ryan disappeared, perhaps joining the souls of the warriors in the campfires in the sky. The tunnel, life's ultimate liminal space, shrank back into its source.

"Wait, I never got to say goodbye."

Gabi was talking about the first time.

Not knowing really why, Jamar had come to stand at attention, like an attendant soldier at a funeral. Commenting on the scene he just witnessed, he stated pensively, "You know, uh, that didn't feel fake to me."

"No. Not at all, *papi*. Not at all."

* * *

"What did I miss?" inquired a frustrated Isabella as her avatar unfroze. "Where's *papá?*"

"Gone. That product really should be for sale instead of for rent," Gabi replied.

"Oh. That's a shame. Don't worry, he'll rise again. That's why they call them subi-bots. Like sooth-me bots. At least we got to meet him."

Jamar used his thumb to gently brush away the tears under Gabi's eyes. Gabi performed a mental chad-checklist, using her own criteria. *Sensitive. Check. Strong. Check. Smart. Check. I am loving the timeline with this new Jamar.*

"No tears," Isabella told her sister, comforting rather than taunting. She still planned to get justice for her father in court, once other matters were fully behind them.

Gabi felt she had to cover for her emotions. "It's my oak tree allergy," she said defensively.

"In a fake forest?"

The three of them smiled.

"Therapy bots are designed to bring out your emotions, sis. You know that. We have a more practical problem at the moment. Mom's headset has timed out from inactivity."

"No parents around?"

"But this ain't no party."

Isabella then randomly exclaimed, "Here, in here!" very loudly. In her office on Las Olas, she began using her butt to push the desk away from the door. "Yes, yes, I'm coming," she added, obviously talking to someone nearby in the physical world. Her hasty motions moving the desk resulted in her avatar making some contorted twerking motions in the meeting place.

"Izzy, you okay?"

"Guys, there's a short window of time for me to get to the roof. One of the senior partners is outside my door with a robodog escort. I have to go. Like right this second." The focus of her eyes changed. "Marv!"

Isabella's avatar broke up as something booted her off the network. The last thing Gabi and Jamar heard her say was "Hi, Shoshanna, thank God you're here, too," coupled with the background sound of Mindy shrieking "why does she get to go first?" loud enough for the practically the whole world to hear.

* * *

"Just the two of us, now," observed Jamar.

So many of the campfires had been extinguished that even the lonely meeting place felt extra lonely to the pair at this point. The otherworldly stars painted above became extra distant.

"Just the two of us," replied Gabriela. "So what now?"

"Finish working out our plan. Rehearse next. We always do a rehearsal before a mission," Jamar walked over to the far side of the makeshift sand map. "But I'm not sure we have a whole lot of time for that."

"Ok, so I say we depart the way we came, out our sliding glass door. No neighbor doorbell cameras to track where we came from."

"Actually, you plan backwards. We have to start at the objective, here. The timing of the whole mission is determined by that weather forecast on the smart thermostat. The 4:05 P.M. thunderstorm coming in from the

Everglades. We miss that, and the mission's more or less toast. That would mean we have to make it to this intersection here, what, by a quarter till, the latest." Using his pointer, and the milestones he worked out on the map, he and Gabi estimated the time it would take them from the house out to the park.

"Which means we have to leave here," Gabi pointed to the stone that represented the Driscoll house. "Basically, in 20 minutes." Gabi concluded. "No rehearsal?"

"Unfortunately, no. Like Patton said, a good plan today is better than a perfect plan tomo … you get the point. We have to get going."

"Let's get the stuff from the garage. My bike's there."

"Your costume?"

"After the garage."

The two rescuers each began to draw a door with their fingers, separately. With a smile, Jamar leaned over and finished Gabi's exit door together with her, carefully saving their spot so they could return precisely to this particular campfire if they needed to.

Fully back in the Driscoll house, Jamar and Gabi both stooped down low to avoid the camera viewing arc of the smart refrigerator. They made one last check of the weather forecast before heading past the smart washer and dryer. "When everything is smart, nothing is," repeated Gabi, taunting the camera-less appliances as she opened the door at the end of the laundry hallway into the garage.

"Check that bin over there; I think the hockey mask is in it." Gabi instructed Jamar as she went over to the box on the shelf by the water heater that her father's avatar told her had the razor blades. She lifted up the leather work gloves, and, just as he had said, was a box of the blades and a little yellow plastic scraper that they snapped into.

Gabi said her thoughts out loud.

"Weird. How could a chatbot of my father know that my real father had hid a box razor blades here? There's no way it's really him, right? Is he, like, a Ghost in The Machine?"

"What did you say, Gabs?"

"Nothing. Nothing."

"Do you think I could use this drop cloth as a makeshift cape?"

"I thought capes were bad?"

Jamar swept the drop cloth across his face in Dracula's fashion. A large spring clip, used to keep tarps down, affixed the cape around his neck.

"That works. Can you scrape the RFID tag off my bike while I go get changed? Oh, and maybe grab my Dad's hockey stick. We could use that as a weapon, maybe?"

"I'd rather bring that landscaping machete your dad left hanging from that hook in the corner."

"A weapon like that would be detected by every image processing program in the places were we have to cross camera arcs."

"It's not a 'weapon,' it's part of the Freddy the 13th costume."

"It's 'Jason' in *Friday the 13th*. I think."

"Whatevs. Let's just hope the centaurs are doing their job on the infected, and we don't have to use it to actually protect ourselves." He unsheathed the blade, still oiled, from its plastic scabbard and moved to scrape off the tracking device affixed to the rounded metal tubing of the bike frame.

"Here, this will do it cleaner," Gabi said as she handed him her father's razor blade scraper.

"Wish I had one of these for my bike yesterday. I damaged the paint. All right, get changed and we'll assemble by the glass sliding doors."

Jamar had a bit of a struggle bringing Gabriela's wide-handled bicycle through the spring-loaded door that separated the laundry room from the garage. The camera of the smart fridge would only see a hand reaching up to hold the handlebars as a bent-over Jamar pulled The Machine with its click-ety-clack gears across the tile floor. He looked down to check his smartwatch, but he had removed it the night before. The only time he could see was on Lucy's non-IoT coffee maker.

"How do I look?" a self-conscious Gabi inquired nervously as she emerged from her bedroom.

"Squat," replied Jamar quickly.

"Like, fat?" Gabi was taken aback by Jamar's answer.

"No, squat down. To avoid the smart frid . . . uh, too late."

"Oh, crap. I forgot. Well, if this mask obscures my identity, it should do it now, right?" She stood front-and-center in the smart fridge's viewing angle, hands defiantly on her hips.

"I kind of expected you to be dressed up as a nurse, how you always do in the 'Verse. This costume is a bit dark for you."

The self-conscious Gabi returned with a fury. "I told you all the good costumes were sold out along with the candy. The only nurse costume was a 'naughty nurse' getup that would make a fansaverse porn star blush. I had a choice between Freaky Frankenstein, Gordita the Ghost, not an option, and ..."

"... and black leather biker bish?"

"Domina of the Damned," Gabi deadpanned.

Jamar let out a hearty laugh. "Oh, God."

"I guess I should be glad that Marksohn will have to cancel the costume party on the 31st."

"Society going back to cute witches and harmless scarecrows might also be a good idea. You look great, though. Truly." Jamar was telling the truth. *Flakita* had matured to fill out the black faux leather costume nicely. The most important part, the shiny black plastic mask, was Mardi Gras–style. It covered her whole face, with just small slits for the eyes.

"Good thing your father did not see you in this getup. You might be the one getting the spanking instead of the other way around."

"Careful, or I'll use one of those red ball gag thingies on you. It'll keep you from biting me if you turn into a Z-person."

"Can you imagine the Health A.I. making those things the mask mandate?"

The two of them shared a laugh together. They were both nervous about the craziness they were about to embark on. A simple moment of laughter dispelled the jitters better than a therapy bot ever could.

"Oh, this is perfect!" exclaimed Gabi. "It's still here!"

"What?"

In a small cabinet, a leftover from a kitchen remodeling done over a decade ago before the house became a rental, Gabi's father had taken a large plastic jack-o'-lantern, filling it with extra bolts and screws and assorted man-garage bric-a-brac in the place of Halloween candy. In an age of on-demand, owning nothing, drone delivery in under an hour, the real world Ryan still had felt it was useful to keep some spare parts lying around, just in case.

Gabi dumped the noisy mixture onto the floor, and hung the orange container from her handlebars to show Jamar what she was thinking.

"It will complete the 'we're just poor, lost trick-or-treaters' disguise."

"That's good, because I was thinking the red-bandanna-makes-me-a-pirate look wasn't going to cut it."

"All right, Lieutenant Jammer, ready?"

"I think I'd rather be Jamar."

"You got it."

The sliding door opening hit them with a blast of humid afternoon air from the backyard. Gabriela wheeled her bicycle out of the open portal and down a small stoop onto the little patio, walking it past the family's illicit gas grill, hidden under black plastic to obscure it from prying eyes. They walked across the lawn on their way to the lake shore, holding their now-unregistered bicycles by the handlebars.

The sound of a robotic mower greeted them as they mounted their bikes aside the alligator-friendly waters.

"Wait, I have to go back!" declared Jamar.

"What? We just left! Don't tell me you have to go to the bathroom again?"

"No, just hold on." Jamar raced to the back door, reemerging with something in his hand. He pressed the power button of his handheld drone controller.

"I thought you said The Machine was tracking the radio signal from your unregistered drone," challenged Gabi, upon seeing what Jamar had gone to retrieve.

"Exactly!"

Jamar scurried quickly up behind the noisy robot, which flung shards of grass about it in a green mist. He lightly tossed the palm-sized drone controller atop it, as the plodding machine made its way in the opposite direction that Gabi and he were going to be traveling in. His illegal, flying-roach-like drone dutifully followed along, like a loyal electronic puppy dog.

THE ZOMBIE IN THE MACHINE

"All warfare is deception," Jamar then declared as he retrieved his bike off a new strip of freshly mowed grass, with the unmowed, straight grass on either side, forming a neat little path inviting them to ride upon it. He added, "If they send a hunter-drone out to intercept, that's one less that we have to deal with."

"Clever. Well, you did tell my dad you would improvise."

"Yes, but I will miss my favorite little scout, truly." He puckered his lips into a mock boo-boo face.

"You told me you were going to listen to my sister and ditch all those dingable things when you turned eighteen. So, you got an early start."

"I guess I'm ready to not be a kid anymore. When I was riding last night, I kept hearing this voice in my skull saying 'time to grow up, Jamar, time to grow up.' Over and over. The voice was as clear as you talking to me now. And the voice actually sounded like your dad's. Crazy, huh?"

"The least crazy thing, considering everything else."

"Wait, aren't there alligators in this lake?"

"There was one yesterday. A small one, though. You missed it because you were dealing with your grandmother going to the hospital."

"Today will be better. It's a good omen that a robomower just happened to passed by at the exact right moment," Jamar responded, as the two began their bikeable city adventure down the grass-trail, side by side.

* * *

Indeed it had been a good omen. Staying on the grass, Gabi and Jamar made it past their first-planned checkpoint—the entrance to the community—without incident. The gatehouse area was heavily monitored for vehicular traffic, recording in a never-truncated database every license plate in and out for over four decades. The sidewalks in and out were heavily monitored for pedestrians, bicycles, and micromobility like scooters. But the lakefront, barely at all. Counting on the canopy of tropical trees to provide concealment, they made their way out of the bridge-like entrance unrecorded.

They could hear the roar of a police vehicle's gas-powered engine on its way into the community behind them, and see the flashing lights. At least one human cop must still have been alive and unbitten. The police rarely used their sirens out here unless they were headed out to I-75. Carried by the smooth lake, a Halloween horror movie–worthy scream came from one of the houses they had rode behind, but there was no way to tell which one. There was also the sound of drones, more than one. Jamar imagined at least one of them was honing in on his flying friend.

"Let's keep moving," he said decisively.

"Yes, sir, L.T. Jammer. We keep moving, roger that," concurred Gabi. She gave him a cute little salute.

As they had drawn on the makeshift sand map, along their way, there were several places they had to leave the obscuration of the tree canopy and lakeside pathways to cross the street. They made a point of going outside of the designated crosswalks.

The Machine registered two dings in its database each time, but with the column labeled "digital_id" having to be left blank.

In two communities over from where they started, Jamar and Gabi passed by behind people's houses the way they had in the Driscoll's home community. Again, riding along the lakes, in the easements. The late afternoon sun began to yield to gathering clouds, but the trip, absent the nagging sense of disquiet over the circumstances, was otherwise pleasant. Gabi imagined doing this again someday. There was plenty of time for some light conversation. Gabi's main focus revolved around a "like, what took you so long?" theme. Jamar related some additional details of his night journey, which again explained his near-religious IRL transformation from introvert to extrovert without him having to explicitly say so.

"Don't lots of these people have cameras in their backyards?" Jamar asked Gabi at one point as they pedaled. His thighs were just beginning to burn from the exertion of pedaling on grass instead of pavement. Isabella may have had a point that bringing Mrs. Driscoll on pegs would push the limits of his athletic ability. His afterschool activity was golf, decidedly more upper than lower body. He hoped Gabi's legs were doing okay. The costume had these curious vertical fake leather straps that descended from the corset to connect with shiny rivets to other straps that wrapped mid-thigh, where the tops of pantyhose would go. It was hard for Jamar not to stare.

"I don't think we have to worry about the view from up there," Gabi responded. "As long as we keep ourselves way down here." The level of drainage lakes were all significantly lower than the grade of the homes they served. "At best any backyard cameras can see the tops of our heads, and our faces are covered." Gabi was wrong. The cameras in some other people's homes could see much more, but so long as the duo was just passing through and not approaching anyone's patio, no home security thresholds were crossed.

"The layout of Ranches West is completely different than this. Your mother is lucky Eastglade and Weston have these drainage lakes. Very lucky." The sound of thunder added an exclamation point after the word "lucky" on Jamar's behalf. A small V-formation of white ibises, sans AR-labels, skimmed the water's surface, moving in a direction away from the gathering storm.

"Right on schedule."

"The residential side of the park is just past the golf course. Almost there," observed Gabi.

"Do you think I should go and grab one of those drivers?" asked Jamar. There was an abandoned golf cart at the eighth hole, along with abandoned clubs. Roughly two-inch diameter footprints of a robot dog or cheetah pressed into the sand trap offered a clue as to what had transpired. Had Jamar approached the cart, he would have seen a spray of blood on the steering wheel and across the cart's white plastic hood. He envisioned himself bringing along one of the steel drivers, and, if an infected person dared approach them, using a *kino* swing to knock them into oblivion.

"I know what you're thinking, Jamar. But no. It's stealing."

"Law and order breaks down in a Zombie Apocalypse." He persisted in using the now-disfavored word.

"Not this time, I would say. In fact, every time one of these crisis happens, it's like we get even more 'law and order', so we'll prolly get a poly-punishment if we get caught stealing during a poly-crisis."

"For sure."

"So let's not find out. Besides, it's wrong. I wouldn't want someone nicking my stuff, so I won't do it to them." She could hear her father talking as she relayed the biblical morality. Another round of thunder added emphasis to the sentence.

A light drizzle began, and the approaching storm, sucking the heat out of the atmosphere, announced its approach with a blast of cold air across the tightly clipped artificial green hills of the golf course.

"Roger that," affirmed Jamar, sticking to the use-the-machete-as-a-last-resort plan instead. "You're right," he confessed.

"What did you say?"

"You're right. You're right. You like hearing that, don't you?"

"A girl could get used to it you know."

They kept riding right up until the near-rainforest level thickness of the plants that formed a living border for most of the residential-recreational-health isobenefit zone where Lucy, presumably, still was waiting patiently. Helpful walking paths breached the barriers in convenient spots on the zone's southeast side. Jamar, like a dismounted soldier, sneaked into the brush. It was a role he had played in plenty of simulations. Only in IRL it was dirtier and buggier. Muddier, too. Gabi followed him into the tangle of plants, declaring the situation "gross."

Trading out his sunglasses for the optics of his disabled headset stored in the plastic pumpkin. He zoomed in to the playground and bathroom, the objective. He felt a bit like Patton, the George C. Scott version, surveying the battlefield at *El Alamein*.

"Your mom is supposed to be waiting for us inside that family bathroom, right?"

"Right. Oh no, what do you see?"

"That Mrs. D. doesn't follow directions well. She just opened the door and jumped outside. She was waving her arms like a crazy woman."

"That's my mom for ya. Random. She's okay, right?" Gabi pushed away a large philodendron leaf that was blocking her view, but not in time to catch a glimpse of her mother.

"Well, she slammed the door shut again. I can't tell if she saw anything to make her do that. No zombies in the park, at least as far as I can see from here."

Their primary concealment while they scouted the park was a popular Florida landscaping plant called *philodendron selloum*, which might as well translate into "leaves the size of elephant ears with lots of jagged edges." The perfect plant to hide behind, and for insects to hide under, philodendron also beat like a drum when pelted with large drops of rain slamming onto its leaves' surfaces, obscuring their conversation from any microphones nearby.

An unexpectedly cold dollop of water hit Gabi right at the base of the neck, and traced its way down her spine. The uncomfortable part of the mission had begun.

* * *

"Like we traced on the map, I'll take one lap around the bike trail to draw out any infected. Drones, too, presumably. We need to be certain the coast is clear. For now at least I don't see any our flying friends. They are either grounded or must have moved on to another hotspot. You stay put until I circle back, and then we'll go to the bathroom together. Rescue your mother together. You know what I mean."

"Good luck."

Gabi planted a soft, good-luck kiss on Jamar's cheek. It was his turn to have the goose-bumpy feeling, except in this case his arm hair was being patted down with streaks of rain. He had kissed someone, once, and it hadn't turned out well. He let out a little shiver down his spine as he began to pedal counterclockwise around the walking and biking path that surrounded the zone. He rode standing up on the pedals, letting the raindrops find their way straight down his rigid back while the wheels flung a spray of water up his soaked cape in the other direction.

Alone in the brush, Gabi bounced up and down on her tippy toes in nervous anticipation. Jamar passed the church that had been converted to a clinic. No infected or robots outside. He could have just made a sharp right and zipped straight over to the playground at that point, but he stuck to their plan. The soccer fields were next. Nothing gave chase. Just rain. The last landmark was the stack-and-pack and the racks of rentable bikes.

"Oh, shoot."

Gabi could see someone staggering out from the small courtyard that connected the zone's two primary stack-and-pack buildings. She was too far away to see if Spider Rash covered the person's face or not, but, no matter, Jamar raced down one of the trails that took him away, not towards, their objective. Neither a fast-zombie or a slow-zombie, the medium-speed zombie gave chase.

What should I do now? We agreed I would wait until he came back here, but for how long? I could just bike to Mom in a straight line . . .

The rain started to lighten, diminishing the obscuring effect they were counting on. Like a quarterback changing the play at the line of scrimmage, Gabi decided to just go for it. Accelerate the plan. Streaks of water flew off her bicycle's back tire up onto her faux-leather costume as she beelined it to the bathroom.

Impatient Lucy peeked out from the bathroom door yet another time, this time looking to sneak a drink from the refrigerated water fountain rather than from the bathroom sink. The other times she had tried to gather information by opening the door, she slammed it shut at the second she saw the slightest motion anywhere in the surrounding area. This time was different. The bizarre image of a woman in a black mask, waving wildly at her from her cruiser handlebars, was too strange to peel her eyes away from. Lucy stood there watching, while pressing the bar on the fountain that let the untouched water run straight into the drain.

Gabi braked hard enough that her back tires wheeled around on the wet concrete to the right, nearly ending her race to the playground with a tumble. From Lucy's perspective the bike rider might be crazy, but clearly not infected. She could see quite enough skin, everywhere, to verify that.

Removing her hand from the fountain, Lucy crossed her arms.

"Aren't you a little short for a dominatrix?"

"Oh, the costume." Gabi lifted her black mask slightly, wanting to partially ID herself without fully exposing her face. Unlike Lucy, she was in a spot she knew was within a camera's viewing arc. "It's me, *mama*; I'm here to rescue you. It's me."

Gabi expected a huge, dramatic hug. A sigh of relief. An "oh, thank God you're here." A "you saved me from certain doom."

Not quite.

"*Mija*, you left the house looking like *that*?"

Lucy's mom's instinct was too strong for her not to criticize. The rainwater had made the clingy outfit extra clingy. This hardly seemed the time, but Gabi's instinct to push back was too strong for her to resist, in return.

"This is not as bad as what some of the other girls wear. I had to have something for Halloween dress-up day."

"I told you to order a better costume before they sold out."

"You're always judging me for what I wear."

"And what were you planning to do in that getup? If we get attacked by a zombie, you'll spank them over your knee? Whip them with a cat 'o nine tails?"

"No. And, how do you know what a cat 'o nine tails is?"

"Don't get fresh with me."

"Glad to see your feeling like yourself again. Anyway, if we run into the infected, Jamar has dad's machete from the garage, if it comes to the last resort having to fight them face-to-face, actually."

"Jamar? Why would you bring him?"

After a pause, Gabriela finally shot back with a sarcastic-but-friendly, "Let's start over. Soooo, nice to see you, too," which broke up the back-and-forth of a conversation that had gotten strangely off on the wrong foot. Or over the wrong knee.

Conscious that she was supposed to stay out of the cameras and not wanting to step out from the overhang into the rain, Lucy simply opened her arms to signal her desire for that huge hug.

"Oooooh, thank God you're here," she said as she embraced Gabi.

Unlike an embrace with Ryan, both parties could feel the tight squeezing of the other. Gabriela was treated to an endless stream of forehead kisses from her grateful mother. Against Gabi's rain-soaked skin, Lucy's lips felt warm. Her temperature was way up as the injected nanobots implanted their magical RNA into a lattice of repaired heart muscle. If she wasn't already red, she'd at least be yellow until the fever cleared. But she felt okay, all things considered.

"So, I don't see Jamar. Where is he? And has he still not acknowledged that he likes you, in public?"

"There was an infected person way over there by the smart racks. He's doing a pied-piper type maneuver and getting the infected person away from here. We planned it beforehand. Jamar's very brave. And yes, he did. In public."

"There's a fine line between bravery and stupidity. Those things can move fast when they want to. And, it was about damn time with him. I knew he'd come around eventually."

"They can't run faster than a certain brave someone on a decent bike. And, he held my hand in front of everyone, at the ride pool."

"Brave? I see. Look, here he comes."

Jamar was riding quickly across the soccer field, his tires spraying up plumes water like a jet-ski. The bicycle swayed side-to-side with the power he pumped into the pedals.

No infected person was chasing him, at least for now.

"That poor boy looks soaked from head to toe. Both of you kids need a hot shower when you get home. Different showers, obviously. I don't want you to get sick."

Gabi loved that, at what could conceivably be the end of the world, her mother's first thoughts were on being a mother.

"Why didn't you wait inside, like you were supposed to?"

"There was a flying palmetto bug the size of a small drone in there. If you had to pick between staying in a room with a huge Florida roach, or risking it out here with a zombie, you'd pick the zombie, believe me."

"True that," Gabi agreed.

Jamar stopped at the edge of the playground, roughly nine or ten meters away, breathing heavily. A hint of fog, no more than a centimeter of it, rolling off the heat of his heavily soaked cape. He just stared ahead, mouth agape, looking past the mother-daughter duo at the water fountain, focusing on something behind them.

Despite the ambient noise of the rain, he was close enough for Gabi to simply ask him why he had stopped, but she directed her next comment to her mother right next to her. "There's a Z-word right behind us, isn't there?"

"You mean a zombie?" Lucy gasped, as the two of them spun about.

The man who had lingered on his bicycle too long to watch the events at the clinic was no longer on his bicycle. He had come, on foot, through the tangled landscaping philodendrons on the east end of the zone and was running west in the direction of the stationary trio. The dense underbrush of the landscaping had done the seemingly impossible—partially tripping up the centaur chasing the infected man through it—and the former bicyclist, his ear bitten off Tyson-style between the triangle formed by his helmet's straps, would close the gap between himself and Lucy in two blinks of an eye. Jamar reached for the machete. The timing of the centaur's intercepting of the man, if it could pull it off, would be no more than a blink.

Lucy's sandal flew through the air faster than that.

The centaur tackled the infected man from behind the instant after the flying footwear smacked him under his helmet's brim, square between the eyes, with the precision of a SEAL Team Six sniper.

"That's *La Chancla*, retard!"

Nobody was going to mess with Lucy or her kids. But a little help right now from a military robot hadn't hurt.

"*Kino*," remarked Gabi both of her mother's accuracy and of her mother's outburst of the R-word to describe the Z-word.

"*Domo arigato*, Mr. Death-bot-Oh," then said Jamar patronizingly to the centaur, stealthily resheathing the half-drawn weapon while the centaur pulled a white zipcuff from the storage clip on its flank. The milbot must have been busy already that day; of the twenty "do what I say or else" nylon cuffs that were in its basic loadout, it employed the last two to hogtie the stricken cyclist.

"Citizens must leave all public spaces immediately," came the centaur's authoritative sounding voice, deliberately designed with a computerized twang to emphasize the machine's non-negotiable, non-humanity. The bot spoke as it turned away with its prey still gyrating and struggling while being carried in powerful metallic arms. Most significantly, the voice did not identify any of the trio by name when issuing its command. Lucy's face could easily be recognized by the centaur's multiple cameras, but, with a new waveform, it could not 100% confirm her heartbeat ID. And the kids looked just like they had gotten lost on their way to a Halloween party. Apparently, that part of the crazy plan had worked, albeit with a ziptied twist.

Only the sound of the rain remained. In Lucy's imagination, she could hear "Eye of the Tiger" coming from her playlist.

All at once, the trio exhaled with relief.

"Damn, Gabi, both your parents dropping the nuclear R."

"I know. Seventeen years of getting punished for it, and now twice in one day."

"This apocalypse really IS gonna be lit."

"'Both' parents?" inquired Lucy in response to Jamar.

"Long story."

Jamar pointed over in the direction of four fresh entrants to the residential-health-recreation zone, in the distance near the stack-and-packs. Had they not heard what was going on and were looking to rent some e-bikes from the smart bike rack? Or, were they already zombies looking to spread the virus? The trio just knew one robot, no matter how dexterous and strong, could not stop all four of the infected as they started their run towards fresh potential bite victims in the playground. And the zombie that Jamar had lured away on his bike was still out there somewhere beyond the bushes. It was past time to go.

"Here, Mrs. Driscoll, put this mask on."

"Oh, my husband's Panther's mask. I remember this. Good idea. And good thing I procrastinated in cleaning out the garage. So, where's my bike?"

"No bike."

"Scooter?"

"No, too electronic."

"What then?"

"You're riding with me."

"On your handlebars? Like the movie *E. T.*?"

"No idea who that is, but, no, like on these pegs."

Lucy looked confused.

"Put your feet up here, on these two things, and you'll be holding on to my shoulders." A wave of heavy rain drenched Lucy as she tried to balance on the metal tubes. Lucy slipped and fell in a lump onto the spongy playground mat, thankful that the soft surface protected older bones as much as younger ones.

"Helmet?" she asked as Jamar offered his hand.

"We left it in the garage. You're not a kid. Besides, they don't protect against zombie bites, clearly." Jamar resisted saying the sanitized "Z-word" for biting people.

"Don't you grown-ups love to brag about growing up without bike helmets?" Gabriela threw in.

"That was Gen-X. What if I fall again?"

"Try not to. If the stupid Gen-X'ers could survive without bike helmets, we sure can."

Lucy abandoned her other sandal, unconcerned about littering dings, deciding to try the pegs barefoot. Gabi, unaware that her companions had fallen behind, was well on her way to the treeline that they would escape through. Jamar's tired thighs instantly informed him that the journey back would be as arduous as they had imagined, but, with a joyful laugh at the novelty of the situation, Lucy finally got her balance. Jamar struggled to get up to speed, but began to close the gap with Gabi. None of the three looked back to see how close the infected at the bike rental racks had gotten to them.

"You might not want to use the word 'peg' around a woman dressed like that," remarked Lucy mischievously about her daughter's scandalous costume, counting on a blast of loud rain to obscure her voice. She was over-the-moon thrilled to be out of the stinky, flying roach bathroom. She had feared spending the night there. Even though dark blue sky was visible ahead at the end of the storm, the night would soon be upon them.

"What did you say about pegs, Mrs. Driscoll?"

"Never mind. Very innovative." Lucy spoke louder, "Good to see you, Jamar. We were all so worried about you."

"And us about you," Jamar said over his shoulders. Lucy gave him two squeezes with her fingers as a response.

"At least the rain is starting to lighten up."

Jamar had caught up with Gabi, who provided commentary on the rain. "The weather clearing was actually not a good thing, *mamá*. We were hoping the rain would keep drones grounded."

Had she been in on the planning session, Lucy no doubt could have poked numerous practical holes in the hasty rescue plan, but she was getting a live lesson in a good plan well executed being better than a perfect one later. Or what happens when a plan gets punched in the nose. She summed the situation up with three words.

"Works for me."

"Look, Jamar, someone must have been here. They made off with that golf cart we saw."

"Maybe they didn't get the memo about stealing not being cool in the Zombie Apocalypse."

"I kinda thought about suggesting using a golf cart instead of bikes."

"Wish you had mentioned it before, low-key," Jamar remarked, his thighs, and now his rear end, burning with the strain of riding on wet grass. The smell filled his nostrils as he huffed. He pushed on his heavily soaked cape's clip, releasing it to the grass. "I used to love this smell after the rain."

"Petrichor."

"Great SAT word! Though I doubt we'll be having any SAT's anytime soon."

Gabi's wet plastic costume was beginning to chafe her skin horribly. The two were at the limit of their physical ability.

"Are we there yet?" asked Lucy, in the manner of a kid in the back seat, pestering their parents on the way to Disney. She was not familiar with any of the drainage lakes other than the spot behind her house.

The two rescuers let the question go. Instead, Gabi and Jamar caught her up on most of the details of Izzy and Ryan.

"We make our way to the lake by the gatehouse from here," stated Jamar. "But there's a problem." He used the zoom on his lenses to scan ahead. Peeking at spots through the thick trees was the yellow of a school bus, stopped at the community entrance. Flying above the treeline, an escort drone monitored the situation. The rain had stopped long enough for flights to resume.

"Crap. Can't go that way."

"So, what, take the long way around to the other entrance? What if there's drones there, too?"

"We have to improvise. And gamble."

"It's ironic. Going the long way will take us right past our house, but on the wrong side of the water."

"Swim across?"

"In the lake with alligators?"

"We might have to."

"My mom can't swim that far on a good day."

The sky was darkening noticeably, despite the clouds making their way in the direction of the coast. None of them wanted to be out after the sun fully set. Who knew if the infected had glowing zombie eyes and could see them while they were in the dark like infrared drones.

"One piece of good news. At least with the storm gone, Izzy will have a smooth ride down to the aerodrome," remarked Gabi as they trudged along the wrong side of the lake.

"I have to take a break," declared an exhausted Jamar, as the back of the Driscoll house came into view. They were so close, yet so far. They might as well have been trying to reach a rich man's colony on Mars.

"I can take over," offered Gabi.

"Maybe you don't have to," interjected Lucy. "Look."

A lone canoeist was making his way down the long waterway. It was the same guy Lucy had labeled **"creep"** in Augmented Reality mode.

"Yoo-hoo. Hi, Sandeep!"

"You know that man, Gabi?" Lucy asked, adding under her breath, "Good heavens, does his name actually rhyme with 'creep?' What are the odds of that?"

"Yeah, he works part-time at the community coffee house. Very friendly."

Lucy felt terrible that she ever wished the 20 MPH-swimming gator had chased down and chomped the man's canoe. Sandeep had been the one to report the nuisance gator in the first place.

I'll have to make a point of relabeling him if I ever get Augmented Reality again.

"Hello, ladies, and, hello, young man," Sandeep said, using his paddle to slow the canoe down.

Gabriela lifted her mask enough to identify herself. "It's me, Sandeep. Gabi!"

"Gabriela Driscoll?" Sandeep then had a moment of his own inner monologue.

Your mother lets you out of the house dressed like that?

Out loud, Sandeep simply said, "Haven't you heard, young lady, you're not supposed to be out of the house at all. Curfew at 5 P.M., right?"

"We could say the same for you. Besides, we've been offline."

"I prefer to be offline, too, when I can. I don't even know what exactly what time it is. Oh, well. The lock on my front door went red, but I don't have a smart lock on my sliding glass doors in the back." Sandeep gave an over-exaggerated wink.

"Neither do we."

"They monitor the streets and sidewalks for vehicles and people, but they don't make you put those RFID tags on canoes. I thought I would get a last workout in before tomorrow, because who knows what will happen."

"We were doing things along the same lines. But now we realize we never should have left the house. We're stuck on the wrong side of the lake. And there's people with rabies around."

"Yeah, I heard something about that. But they can't swim, right?"

The trio was amazed at how clueless Sandeep seemed to be about the severity of the overall situation. Perhaps he needed to stop and listen to rumor Guides more often, but Sandeep was one of those rare birds who only traveled into the Metaverse if he absolutely had to.

Lucy lifted her hockey mask and asked Sandeep if he could be so kind as to ferry them across the lake.

"Is this your mother?" he asked of Gabi as he maneuvered the canoe closer to the shoreline.

"Yes, how rude of me. This is my mom, Lucinda Driscoll."

Lucy hastily removed her hockey mask and tried to restore a semblance of order to her soaking hair.

Sandeep padded the canoe right up to the grassy shore through patches of sawgrass and lily pads.

THE ZOMBIE IN THE MACHINE

Gabi continued the introductions, "And this is my, my boyfriend, Jamar Rice."

They all exchanged a round of friendly nice-to-meet-you's.

"I think we're gonna need a bigger boat," observed Jamar, worried about any nasty creatures hiding beneath the water's surface.

"Well, it will be a tight fit unless I make multiple trips. I suppose we can jam everyone in. It will be like Washington crossing the Delaware," said Sandeep in jest, "although Washington had to leave his army's bicycles behind as far as I remember."

"We'll come back for them later," Lucy clarified. "And thank you so much."

While Lucy told Sandeep "you're a real lifesaver, a hero," the children had a side-bar conversation.

"Who's 'Washington'?"

"George Washington, I think."

"The guy with the slaves?"

"*Acchē bhagavāna*, Good God, what are they teaching these kids in school these days?" asked Sandeep quietly of Lucinda as he gently took her hand and helped her into his canoe. She felt very self-conscious of her ragged appearance, soaking wet, barefoot and braless, again. But Sandeep was a perfect gentleman, sticking to the "my eyes are up here" rule faultlessly.

"I know, right?" Lucy responded sardonically to Sandeep's remark about education, bonding with her new friend. "And, can you believe it? I pay a fortune in crypto for human teachers instead of public school A.I."

"It's like paying a fortune for RaaS and then listening to people say, 'well you're living on stolen land, so what do you expect?'" Sharing his residence, Sandeep was struggling not just to keep up with expenses, but with paddling. "Like residency fees make up for that." Jammed with people like a refugee-filled boat, the canoe was low in the water, and it took a significant effort to paddle across the waterway.

"Exactly," continued Lucy, "you feel like the only stealing going on is from your crypto account." She felt even worse now that she had ever labeled the man a "creep" in AR. Sandeep appeared to be a kindred spirit. Like the help *abuela* Bianca had received when fleeing Cuba by boat from Mariel 1.0, Sandeep was truly a brother to the rescue.

The two bonded over their talk of modern life's follies as Sandeep rowed. Watching them interact, Gabi realized it had been a long time since she had witnessed the near-hermetic woman interact with live human beings. It was pleasant to see. Her mother should really get out more.

"You two should grab coffee together sometime at the cafe," she suggested as the shore approached, forcing the issue.

"When this is all over, I'd like that," said Lucy.

"Me, too, Lucinda." He grunted out her name as he gave one final push to bring the canoe onto the friendly side of the lake.

"Call me Lucy."

"Lucy."

Sandeep helped her out of the canoe with the same gentle handhold that he had used to help her in it.

"I'd love to stay and chat, but I was planning on being back indoors before it got too dark."

"We'll be in touch, Sandeep."

"See you," he replied over his shoulder as he hastily paddled away.

The trio treated him to a round of multiple "thank you's!"

Lucy twinkled her toes into the cool, wet grass in the way she would do her reality-check in the mornings on the carpet, grateful for every day on earth. Touching grass, indeed. Blocks of events had to have happened in a chain, every single event in sequence, in order for her to reach this precise outcome. Had any single one of them been missed, instead of practicing gratitude, Lucy would be yellow-busing her way to cryogenic popsicle-land by now.

I feel like the luckiest woman who ever lived.

"Did you leave the lights on?" she suddenly asked, in a "you're wasting electricity" accusatory fashion, immediately resuming her role as head of household as the three of them made their way up the unfenced slope separating the backyard from the lake.

"How? Smart lights only come on if someone's there," answered Gabi.

Someone was. Isabella could be seen at the sliding glass doors, cupping her hands against the dark glass to see outside as the lighting reversed.

The first thing Isabella noticed was what looked like a shooting star crossing the sky over in the direction of the airport. The next was a dark trio making their way up the lawn. She grabbed the handle and pushed the door open, screaming "Mom!" with unbridled joy, followed by "Gabi!" and "Jamar!" The smart light on the back patio came on, illuminating the scene.

The wet lawn under her heels was even softer than the ground in the man-cave had been, but Isabella managed to sprint out at full speed to greet them regardless, nearly knocking Lucinda over with a diving, grasping hug. The four of transitioned into a bouncy-spinny group hug without anyone having to actually say "group hug!" the way Ryan used to.

"We did it!" Gabi exclaimed.

"No, YOU did it," immediately replied Isabella. "You two. I never could have done that."

"Your father would be so proud," Lucy declared.

"I know," Gabi answered, for the trio.

"It's over. Thank God."

"I'd say it's all just getting started," Isabella clarified. "But at least we're together. Whatever comes next, we'll handle it together. Family. That's all that matters."

Less than 48 hours ago, Gabi and Isabella were fighting all the time. Lucinda now saw them acting as a team. And with a new team member, too. Family. Partners. Partners in crime, maybe, depending on what The Machine did next, but they would all be inseparable from here on out. Just the way Lucy had always wanted it.

Yeah, I'm the luckiest woman who ever lived.

EPILOGUE

The joyful quartet separated from their group hug, and resumed heading back inside.

"Is this where the alligator was?" Jamar asked. He would have liked to have been part the gathering the previous morning.

"Right here." Gabi stopped walking and pointed to the spot. "It was huuuuuge!" She exaggerated the danger in the way they all would when later retelling the story of the actions they took that day.

"I heard a drone tried to chase it away," Jamar replied, also stopping and pointing in the direction they had ridden their bikes.

"It came from that way," Gabi clarified. Up until Operation Liberate Lucy, the gator had been the most exciting Gray World thing she had experienced in a quite a while.

"Kids, you should come inside," chided Lucinda, standing in the open glass door. Isabella, having returned to the kitchen counter with her now-bloodstained crystal award resting atop it, was already lecturing her mother on staying away, until they sorted things out, from the smart fridge, the smart mirror, the smart speakers, and basically anything smart. "You'll sleep in my room, okay?" Jamar would later suggest simply changing the password on the Wi-Fi to force-disconnect all the monitoring devices and start again from scratch, but for now, he was pointing up at the sky.

"Did you see that shooting star?"

"Missed it. How romantic, though," Gabi semi-joked.

"No, seriously. And, look, another one. There!"

"Kids!" shouted Lucy, "It could be dangerous." She wanted to draw all the curtains, hold a much-needed family meeting, hunker down, and have the kids put up the steel hurricane shutters from the garage the moment the sun came up the next morning.

"In a second, *mamá*. We'll be right there!"

Jamar still held the plastic pumpkin bucket with the handle of the machete hanging out from inside it. Lucy was reminded that this was now a young man who could take care of himself, and protect her girl. She lightly slid the glass door just barely shut, to keep any bugs from flying in. The porch smartlight turned off.

"That's odd," Gabi said. "I doubt those are meteors. Drone fireworks, maybe?"

"Why? Like it's Juneteenth in October or something? Nah, I don't think so. And drones normally don't break up into fireballs, last I checked. Meteors, I suppose."

"Satellites?"

Streaks of fiery light, by the dozens now, put on a dazzling display overhead.

"You might be right. Satellites. There's zillions of them up there. Well, not anymore, from the looks of it."

"Gee whiz," said Gabi with a smile and a healthy dose of *schadenfreude*, another great SAT word, at the Internet of Things' apparent misfortune. "How is the whole Internet of Shit going to operate TLA's without all their satellites? Read our minds?"

"Who cares?" responded Jamar. He put the orange bucket down and reached out to hold her hand. She gladly gave it to him.

"It's like a show created just for us."

"Well, it looks like someone's sure got a shit-show going on up there. What's up above a polycrisis? A mega-polycrisis?"

"A poly-kiss?"

"Trying a dad joke, Gabs?" mused Jamar softly. Pulling her closer, he was not going to make the same mistake as the past and not shoot his shot.

Lucinda slid open the glass door again to admonish the two of them for the delay in coming inside. The porch lights came on. Observing the scene, she gently closed it again. Lights back off.

"Mega-ultra-super-duper-poly-kiss?" Gabi teased, returning Jamar's confident embrace while cocking her head and smiling broadly. "I'll bet A.I. can't do that."

Izzy joined her mother's side in cupping her hands against the glass to spy out over the dark lawn.

The descending hurricane bands of category 6–intensity celestial sparks provided the perfect backdrop for the perfect. first. kiss.

Once everyone was indoors and accounted for, Lucy gave one last look and listened out back. Ambulance or police sirens could be heard faintly in the distance. A large drone, one at least the size of the alligator-chaser that morning, buzzed somewhere beyond the trees. And the loud sound of someone screaming nearby in terror, from what direction Lucy could not say, carried itself along the smooth waters of the drainage lake.

She manually flicked the sliding dumb lock, controllable with flesh and bone instead of an app, and with a loud, satisfying click, she left the world behind.

"Now, that's how it's—" Lucinda breathed in. And out. "Done."

Sneak Peak – *Zombies in The Machine*

CHAPTER 1

Prisoner 43-000911 was leaving one year six months and three days before his sentence was up.

Prisoner 42-444222 was leaving four years early, precisely to the day.

Dressed in orange with a bleached white undershirt, the man assigned the curiously repeating pattern of fours and twos reached the front gate first. Riding along a smooth metal track, the chain link barrier of the main gate was closing, before being abruptly stopped by a motionless body sprawled out on a bed of white gravel that extended out from the prison's central courtyard. The gate halted automatically once it struck the stomach area of the stricken man wearing a mixed tan and brown guard uniform. It bounced backward like an elevator would after hitting someone pushing their luck past the closing door. Seizing the opportunity, the escaping prisoner used a small skip to get over the guard's right arm, while vigorously discarding his prison-issued Mixed Reality headset—special glasses that fed droll rehabilitation videos endlessly over the eyes—down onto the man's over-the-belt-buckle abdomen. The MR device bounced off the jiggly belly fat, like the gate had, and landed on blood-soaked gravel next to the guard's neck. A part of it had been torn away, leaving a jagged, oozing mess.

The escapee was fleeing a violent riot the likes of which no prison in history had ever seen. The older prisoners, many of them streaming out like angry hornets from the infirmary block, were biting everyone in sight. The ultra minimum security Blandingwood, operating using the "inescapable surveillance under the skin" model, had few internal barriers to stop their rampage. 444222 was not leaving this "prison of the future" by choice. Or lawfully.

"Think of it as an early release" were his last words as an inmate. The guard on the ground didn't respond to the quip. An agitated buzzer sound, obscured largely by the shrieks of prisoners behind him combined with the high-pitched din of overhead patrol drones, also acting themselves like angry hornets, heralded the his departure.

Leaving his numbers behind, the man would be "Vito" again. Vito Vitale DeMito.

He quickly rubbed the sweat forming over the top of his eyebrows all the way back over the top of his bald head as he glanced back-and-forth over his shoulder at the open gate behind him, and the open world in front.

"Hey, 911, get your ass over here! Hurry!" he shouted back to his cellmate, whom Vito had assumed was right behind him. He left off the rest of the 43-this-and-that, dehumanizing numbers when calling out to the man he had come to trust as a brother, who had been incarcerated in mid '43.

The time since then had flown, practically as fast as his cellmate running to the gate. It was now 2044. October the 28th.

Ahead of Vito, two bubble-shaped "Connected Autonomous Vehicles" were in the roadway in front of the prison. The first CAV was stopped. A near-obese prisoner had jumped atop its curved roof. The surreal agility required for a man of his heft to get up there was not as surprising to Vito as watching the much older man furiously punch his fist clean through the glass and reach for the occupants underneath. With a herky-jerky lurch that failed to dislodge the bloody, guard-mauling prisoner from his perch, the first CAV pulled away, terrified passengers still inside.

The door of the second CAV then opened, revealing a well-dressed woman within. The solo occupant, wearing designer MR glasses, was riding in the seats facing backwards and was utterly unaware of her surroundings until the humid Florida air flooded in. She put down the virtual manila folder that was being projected into her eyes in Mixed Reality by her digital lenses, and lifted the glasses off of her face to address Vito, eye-to-eye.

"What is this, some kind of breakout?" she asked with a practiced nonchalance concealing her utter surprise. The prison certainly didn't use its orange-suited residents as valets.

"Not a 'break-out.' Some kind of 'out-break.' No time to explain." Vito wasn't sure how to ask the woman for a lift, instead just blurting out, "You, us, we, we have to get out of—"

The woman cut him off with a shriek when she spotted the events at the main gate. Vito's cellmate leaped over the body of the prison guard as the gate bounced off his midsection and retreated yet another time. Leaving his numbers behind, the fleeing man was no longer "911." He was—

"Romeo Antonio Driscoll!" shouted the woman, in the manner of a mother scolding a child at the top of her lungs.

The lawyer, who went by "Yazzi," had come to the prison to inform her client, the Driscoll family's oldest child, that his conviction had been overturned. The deepfake video that had condemned him had been proved utterly false. Driscoll, innocent and vindicated, was poised to be released later today, after some routine outprocessing paperwork and such. Lawfully. Not in a desperate sprint for his life.

With the digital lenses off of her disbelieving eyes, Yasmin Bijan gave a nearsighted squint in the direction of the open gate. A horde of men in orange jumpsuits, some visibly stained with blood, were racing towards the portal. A tactical robot, one of the tireless, four-legged guards that had displaced the careers of most correctional officers, tripped and tackled the man in the lead. He tumbled to the ground at the same time Romeo practically flew into the seat bench facing opposite his "you sound just like my mother" lawyer. Technically uninvited, Vito slid in next to Yazzi, greeting her now with nothing more than the sweaty smell of having dodged violent, virus-infected inmates since the sun came up.

In the courtyard, the quadrupedal robot would have been wiser to have moved the body blocking the gate's tracks rather than tackling the lead prisoner in the mob. The Artificial Intelligence that governed its behavior, however, had not been trained on any empirical data showing what do when masses of prisoners begin biting the necks of other prisoners. Not recognizing a uniformed guard as a threat, it prioritized the first prisoner, leaving the rest of the unimpeded mob racing for the still jammed-open gate. The only obstacle, a mere speed bump, in a beeline to the open door of the CAV was the unmoving guard, seemingly in no position to do anything. But the presumptively dead man suddenly sat up, like a corpse's upper body popping out of the top of a half-open coffin. Slack-jawed, he was close enough for all to see that discolored veins, in ugly purple and red, had crawled up onto his cheeks from the bite on his tattered neck. His soulless blue eyes stared up into the sky.

In a blur of orange, white, tan and brown, the cohort of running prisoners tumbled over the reanimated guard, creating something akin to a line of scrimmage dog pile at an American football game.

The collision of twisted bodies bought the CAV's seated trio a few extra moments of life.

"What is this, some kind of . . . Zombie Apocalypse?" asked the stunned lawyer, with no trace of nonchalance remaining.

His head poking out from the scrum, the guard's dead stare then locked directly onto Yasmin. Vito pushed her deeper into the CAV behind him, instinctively moving to protect her.

"You're about to find out."